LIAR'S LANDSCAPE

ALSO BY MALCOLM BRADBURY

MALCOLM BRADBURY

LIAR'S LANDSCAPE

Collected Writing from a Storyteller's Life

Edited and with a Foreword by Dominic Bradbury

Afterword by David Lodge

PICADOR

First published 2006 by Picador
an imprint of Pan Macmillan Ltd
Pan Macmillan, 20 New Wharf Road, London N1 9RR
Basingstoke and Oxford
Associated companies throughout the world
www.panmacmillan.com

ISBN-13: 978-0-330-43532-1
ISBN-10: 0-330-43532-9

1 3 5 7 9 8 6 4 2

A CIP catalogue record for this book is available from
the British Library.

Typeset by SetSystems Ltd, Saffron Walden, Essex
Printed and bound in Great Britain by
Mackays of Chatham plc, Chatham, Kent

FOR MY GRANDCHILDREN

JASMINE, JESSICA, FLORENCE, CECILY & NOAH

Acknowledgements

Some of the material in this book draws on pieces published in a number of newspapers and magazines, including the *Daily Mail*, *Mail on Sunday*, *Daily Telegraph*, *Sunday Telegraph*, *Sunday Times*, *The Times*, *Financial Times*, *Irish Times*, *Independent*, *Scotsman*, *Spectator*. We are also grateful to Rod Gilchrist, Kensington Films and Associated Newspapers for permission to publish the screenplay of *Furling the Flag*.

The family of Malcolm Bradbury also wish to thank the following for their much valued help and support: Andrew Kidd & Sam Humphreys & all at Picador, Jonny Pegg & Mike Shaw of Curtis Brown, David & Mary Lodge, Peter Straus, Chris & Pam Bigsby, Howard & Kitty Temperley, Anthony & Anne Thwaite, Jeremy Hardie, Johnny Rich, Val Striker, Jon Cook, Alan Preece, Breon Mitchell, Joan Winterkorn, George & Alayne Fenner, Maurice & Jean Wealthall, Bruce & Sheila Adam, Ros Brown & Brian Smith, Geraldine & Richard Berry, Nicky & Keith Roberts, Mary Hubble, Shirley Brooks, Beryl Bradbury & family, Trevor Salt & family, Barrie Salt & family and the many generous contributors to The Malcolm Bradbury Memorial Trust.

Foreword

For a writer such as my father, death can be a great inconvenience. The inconsiderate rush of illness cut short not just his life, but also his work, leaving unfinished novels and stories, as well as tantalizing notes and ideas for other books. Until the end both he and we continued to hope for recovery and second chances, understandably avoiding darker possibilities and promoting optimism as far as any of us could. Even when recognition of my father's decline was difficult to ignore, in the last breaths of the autumn of 2000, the subject of death itself was never mentioned. And there was certainly no room, in those sad, awful, devastating days, for any thoughts about what might happen after – after the death of Malcolm Bradbury, husband, father and beloved friend, of Sir Malcolm Bradbury, the writer. My father often wrote and joked about the Death of the Author, but reserved judgement on how it might one day apply more directly to himself.

After the day that changed everything, and after a small funeral for family and close friends, and then a large public service that filled Norwich Cathedral, a number of ideas circulated about how my father's achievements and writing might be honoured. There were suggestions of anthologies and books of tribute, prizes in his name and other grand gestures. Still buried in grief and missing him desperately, none of these ideas seemed appropriate to us. Nor did there seem any need to rush into something that might come to seem, when our thoughts were clearer, inappropriate or out of keeping.

Only much later, some years in fact, could we really begin to think as a family about how my father might have wanted his life and work to be commemorated beyond a headstone and memorial day. To begin with, we supported the creation of a scholarship fund in his memory for students attending the creative-writing course at the University of East Anglia, the course my father and Angus Wilson famously co-founded in 1970, with Ian McEwan their first pupil. My father, as anyone who ever met him will know, had devoted an extraordinary amount of time and love not just to this course but to encouraging new writers more generally. No doubt this cost him a novel of his own, or more, but in its way it helped to feed a passion for storytelling that went far beyond his own work. With the valued and much appreciated efforts of Jeremy Hardie, Johnny Rich and others, as well as the support of many of my father's friends and contemporaries, the Malcolm Bradbury Memorial Trust is now able to continue to assist, in some small way, a younger generation of storytellers.

At the same time, I turned to the unfinished work and uncollected stories that lay in my father's study. Looking through his papers and archives, I began to find the notes and clues which led to this book. There were sad teases and lost temptations: an idea for a novel on Cold War spies in the genteel world of academia, *Bloodstains on the Bushes*; a handbook on creative writing; a compilation of short stories; a book on the fiction of the fifties, and so on.

There was also a fragment of the novel my father was working on at the time of his death. This story of Chateaubriand was a frustrating suggestion of what might have been, littered – in hindsight – with bitter ironies. *Liar's Landscape* was, after all, a letter from beyond the tomb ('What is written lives far longer than we do – or so we would like to think,' its narrator tells us. 'Words persist: revised, recycled, reprinted, rewritten, they go on forever.') Frustrating though it was to read, especially knowing the history of the months in which it was written, it was also fascinating, and clearly suggested the direction of my father's work following the success of its predecessor, *To the Hermitage*.

There were other plans and sketches – notes of intent. My

father had started work on another book, based on an unmade 'television novel', *Furling the Flag*, about the British handover of Hong Kong. This original script, written in the late nineties, had much in common with my father's other television novels of the late eighties and early nineties. His frustration at not seeing the script filmed had transformed, over time, into the desire to rewrite the tale as a comic novella. Again, all that existed was a fragment. The intention to publish was there but, to avoid further frustration, it seemed that publishing the script alongside offered a way to air the full story, a story that my father thought of fondly and one that is vintage Bradbury in its lightest form – a foil, perhaps, for the more earnest voyage begun in *Liar's Landscape*.

Added to that were a number of recent and uncollected short stories, again illustrating different sides of the writer's personality: the comic follies of *Convergence* and *The Recent Adventures of Robinson Crusoe* from recent years contrasting with the youthful seriousness of *The Waiting Game* and *A Week Or So In Rome* from the fifties. Alongside, there were brief notes for an autobiographical book called *Time-Pieces*, a loose collection of sketches and episodes from my father's life. Sadly – again – only a few pages existed. It then made sense to gather up the more intimate pieces of my father's more recent journalism, in which his newspaper style became relaxed and easy, the voice so recognizably his. A number of more personal compositions from his book *Unsent Letters*, now out of print, also sit well alongside them. These are pieces set apart from his essays and criticism (which I feel belong in another place) that reveal his personal landscape and concerns; brief pages in which I can hear my father's voice and see his face, as though sitting down again for a weekend lunch in one of his best-loved pubs – favourite times when as his family we had him to ourselves.

This book, then, evolved from clues from my father's desk. (And the knowledge that my father himself would never want his work wasted: perhaps because he spent so much time teaching, travelling and lecturing rather than at his typewriter or keyboard, his own writing was precious to him. An unpublished short story from the fifties might be rewritten thirty years later to appear in *Unsent Letters* or an anthology. This was not laziness – my father was, after all, a notorious workaholic – but a healthy respect and fondness for the stories themselves.) Assembled over time, with love and regret, I wish I could ask Malcolm Bradbury, father and writer, if this compilation feels right to him. As it is, any errors of judgement or omissions in the selection of the material are mine. We have, however, kept any editing of the text itself to a minimum and respected my father's own voice throughout. This is, after all, his book, one which slowly evolved into a collection which explores the art, craft and life of the writer and commemorates the work and passions of someone who lived a storyteller's existence to the full.

My father had too many ideas to realize, not enough time to get them from the endless pages of his writer's mind to the foolscap of reality. Thoughts and themes swirled in his imagination, I know, until the end. On his last day my father dreamt of walking through a small French village, streets once walked by Chateaubriand perhaps, and no doubt stopping at a café here or there. One day I hope to find him there and settle down for lunch with a very fine bottle of wine. I hope he will forgive my mistakes, made in love.

Dominic Bradbury

CONTENTS

CONTENTS

MACCLESFIELD, 1940

ON A HOT SUMMER DAY, very close to the beginning of the Second World War, my father ferried me right across London to Euston Station, where he handed me over to the care of the guard of a train going north to Macclesfield. My first dated memories are all of the War, which started four days before my seventh birthday. Everything that lies before that stays vague, or at any rate timeless and dateless: the thirties. The thirties, in the general record, are the Age of the Depression, but that is not really how I remember them. For me, or my family, they were the age of Metroland, the era of suburban London, the time of the clerks. My own father was a clerk, who worked for the London and North Eastern Railway, and had moved down from the North – Manchester, Sheffield – to take a job in London. He worked at Liverpool Street Station, then a steam-filled, glass-framed train shed with a striking clock tower over its portico, and to my mind the finest gentlemen's lavatories in the world. His office, high in a neo-Gothic block that has only just lately been demolished, looked out through smut-grimed windows at the array of platforms below. They showed a daily scene of extraordinary human movement. Bankers and stock-brokers and businessmen, with briefcases, pipes and umbrellas, came out of the Great Eastern Hotel to take their seats in the dining cars of the evening trains. Clerks with watch chains across their suits, typists in slim thin dresses, hurried into the cramped third-class compartments of the smoky commuter trains.

In summer, steaming excursion trains stood in platform after platform, headed for Clacton-on-Sea and Southend, Great

Yarmouth and the North Norfolk Coast. These were places romanticized on the billboards and on the elegant carriage panels that decorated every train compartment, which my father commissioned and had had designed. They crowded with summer holidaymakers, in pullovers and sandals, wool cardigans and floral dresses, carrying mock-leather brown suitcases and fishnets in their hands; the thirties was the age of the excursion and the claims of the great outdoors. 'Harwich– Hook of Holland,' said the exciting signs for the Continental services, the boat trains, surrounded by advertisements for the glowing bulbfields of Holland and the ancient pleasures of the city of Bruges, which, again, my father had had designed. Then, sometime in the thirties, in this booming railway age, he moved over to King's Cross, where he became 'Head of General Section', looking after advertising, design, the planning of stations on the East Coast lines, including many of the stations on the long, slow line out to Norwich – the place where I now happen to live.

Nowadays the clerks in the City lived not so much in Essex but out toward the West, where the great new suburban estates were going up, as the Metropolitan and the Piccadilly tube lines pushed ever further out, into Middlesex and toward the wooded countryside. They rode home in the evening on the red and white tube trains, through the dark underground tunnels, then out into the bright open air. Out past Harrow-on-the-Hill, where the large Edwardian villas stood in shrub-filled gardens beneath the church spire high up on the peak, everything suddenly grew newer and neater. The houses were smaller and squatter, the streets more schematic and easier to understand. The new brick and tile tube stations were designed in modernist style, with blue and white lettering by Edward Johnston. Around them the new conurbations grew, tract after tract of houses designed by the same builder, with stained-glass door panels, small tidy gardens, shops near to hand. In the year of my birth my father and mother bought their first house, new, 'labour-saving', builder-fresh, at Rayner's Lane. 'A Masterpiece of Efficiency, a Freehold Three-bed House for £595,' says the advertisement of the builders, Nash's, which I still have, 'Why pay the landlord?' Why, indeed, when you could have a brand new house in a neat row of four, a mortgage, a long garden of your own, still to be dug, a neat simple kitchen, an easy walk to the shops and a school for the children. The shops on the main street, just as new, were filled with mythological names: Dolcis and Saxone, Home and Colonial, Sainsbury's, and an elegant new Odeon in the art deco style. Rayner's Lane was neither city nor country, but something of neither and a little bit of both. Returning there today, you find it still keeps its unitary character, its Thirties wholeness, its houses all of a piece (then they were, and looked, modern; now, the modern having moved relentlessly on, they are simply 'Tudorbethan'), even though the clerks have long gone, and the houses, heavily remodelled in the DIY boom of the eighties, now house Asian families and craftsmen and workers from Heathrow Airport, not so far away and getting ever nearer. The men commuted each day to their jobs in the City, the wives stayed at home and shopped and reared their children; everything was clean and neat and new and safe, and very modern. There were weekly trips to the cinema, occasional visits to the London shows, and then in summer the holidays: at Broadstairs, Minehead, or Mr Billy Butlin's new chalet holiday camps at Clacton and Skegness-on-Sea, where the air was so bracing.

The thirties stopped short on 3 September 1939, the day, a Sunday, when the families all sat round their Bakelite radios, and the Prime Minister, Neville Chamberlain, announced that all negotiations with Mr Hitler had failed, and Britain was now at war with Germany. Soon afterwards, right across London, the air-raid sirens wailed in a test-sounding that marked the collapse of an age. This is my first date-fixed memory, and it is the memory of a feeling, of incomprehension and fear. The safe world was not safe any longer, and I realized, with all the terror of childhood, that the adults who ordered and controlled the world were no longer in control, and could do nothing at all to change or prevent whatever was now about to happen. To the houses in the long neat streets, corrugated iron air-raid shelters were delivered; my father, who had proudly planted his garden with standard roses, now planted this fragile defence in the rose bed. Ration books and gas masks were issued, and my father made a neat plywood box to carry his with him to work every day. We were all given identity cards, and numbers; mine was BIBR 41 3. At school, Roxbourne Infants' School, we practised doing lessons in the new brick and concrete shelters in the playground, looking piglike with our gas masks on, trying to listen in a stink of rubber and urine. Silver-grey barrage balloons rose up over the red-tiled rooftops; we were near to the military aerodrome at Northolt. Then there were dogfights low over the houses, and the night-time raids began. I would lie in bed in terror as the sirens sounded, and then my father would come and collect me, and, ignoring the inefficient tin shelter, huddle us together, myself, my mother and younger brother, under the stairs until the all-clear came. In the morning we went to school, through streets filled with shrapnel and new war damage; one of Mr Nash's houses now obliterated by a landmine, or a house roof still burning from an incendiary bomb.

When the school summer holidays came, the War was already looking worse, and London under threat. My parents decided to send me to Macclesfield, the town on the Cheshire edge of the Pennines where my father had grown up, and where my grandparents lived. I had been there before, briefly, with my parents, but now, for the summer, I would go there alone. My mother packed a case. My father, with his black homburg hat, his leather briefcase, his gas mask in its plywood box, took me on the tube into central London, a shattered, shaken London, many of its buildings already battered, sandbags stacked in front of all the windows and doorways. The windows on the shaking tube train had been covered in sticky paper, the light bulbs removed or replaced by small blue lamps. We came to a crowded Euston Station, where the troop-packed wartime trains, large white numbers on their smokeboxes, stood. My father tied a luggage label to my lapel, found a train guard and, one railwayman to another, tipped him and asked him to see me safe off the train at my destination. Then he found me a seat, shook my hand, and, in his homburg, with his gas mask, he hurried off to work. I sat in the crowded compartment, waiting for the train to move, and wondered what would happen to me now.

I DIDN'T WANT TO go to Macclesfield. I simply wanted to stay with my family, in the place I trusted, with the people I trusted; I didn't want to go north. And I didn't want to be with my grandparents; my grandparents, waiting at the other end, were not modern, and I was almost as afraid of them as I was of the War itself. They came, it seemed to me then, and still, out of a nineteenth century that had somehow never ended – or rather, since the idea of the turning of centuries and the shifting of values wasn't then clear to me, they came from an eternal and timeless past that was nothing like my present. I knew them a little – I had visited them briefly before, and they had come to stay with us in Rayner's Lane – and found them severe. They belonged to a world of rules and strict behaviour, a time when children had to be seen and not heard. They were my father's parents, and I now suspect that my mother, who had lived with them for a short time at the beginning of the marriage, had not got on with them at all. In our pleasant small family, such things were never said, but they could be sensed. Both of them were formidable, square, and somehow black. My grandfather was chapel, a builder's foreman and, as I later learned, a very fine craftsman; he was a Methodist lay preacher and a man of strict and clear principles. He wore – always, it seemed – a thick black suit, a white shirt with a loose high collar, a black silk cravat held with a tiepin, and a large grey-white moustache that matched his shock of grey-white hair. A silver wind-up hunter watch hung, audibly ticking, in his waistcoat pocket, with a stone on the fob that hung on the other side of his chest. He was also a great handyman, always at work on something: a writing desk, a bookcase, a chair. My grandmother was small and squat, with grey hair in a tight bun; she wore high-necked floral blouses and a black skirt that reached from high above her waist to her ankles, sweeping along the ground. Over this she generally wore a black coatjacket, and, even in the house, a vast domed black straw hat, with a big buckle decoration on the front. She suffered from ailments, used smelling salts, took a great deal of patent medicine, and rested frequently, when she was not to be disturbed, even by the noise of play. Indeed the Victorian horsehair sofa seemed to have been invented exactly for her needs.

At this time, and predictably enough, I was not interested in the past. In fact I was disturbed by it; it seemed to me oppressive, threatening – perhaps, I now think, because my father was so obviously in escape from it, leaving his own past behind for new opportunities, a career, modern times. It was not a good feeling to be going northwards, backwards, and I blamed this on Hitler and the Germans, just as I blamed all pain and evil on them too. The train moved on toward them, stopping frequently, at stations where, to confuse the Germans when they landed, most of the signs had been removed – bleak, urban, shuttered, shattered places, all bathed in the uneasy half-silence of wartime, when so many were away at the fronts. Even in the general gloom of wartime, the greater gloom of the North – with its unrolling trackside factories, camouflaged in dun and grey against the bombing, the long unbroken terraced streets of workers' houses, the little yards with their outside lavatories – was plain. There were the vast dirty marshalling yards and train sheds of Crewe, the bottle-shaped potbanks of Stoke-on-Trent and the Potteries. The long journey confused me, made me anxious; I sat in the crowded compartment, with soldiers and wartime travellers, and had no idea where I was or when it would end. At some unmarked station the train stopped, started, then stopped again. A railway-man from off the platform came along the corridor; the guard had forgotten me, but some station foreman who knew my father (he had worked at this station once) was waiting, and he found me and collected me off the train. I got out on to the platform and into a Macclesfield smell – the smell of coke from the steaming, stinking gasworks, near to the line.

An aunt, Auntie Laura, in steel-framed glasses, was waiting for me, in the station waiting room. She took me by the hand and led me through the town. There, across the market square, was the blackened stone parish church, and leading up to it the 108 Steps, which someone my father knew had driven up in the first car to arrive in Macclesfield, before the previous war. We went through the great arches of the railway bridges, and walked past the great glass-windowed emporium of Arighi Bianci's, the Macclesfield furniture store, which provided the contents for most of the houses in the town. Everywhere there was the sound of clacking looms; Macclesfield, a town of silk mills, was busy in the War, making parachutes for the air force, and the mills were busier than they had been for a long time. There were the stained brown waters of the River Bollin, smelling of industrial waste. We walked through cobbled streets, past millworkers' cottages in long rows. Many were three-storeyed, with a long row of upstairs windows, meaning that home weaving went on there. My aunt, whom I liked, was elderly; she lived in a backstreet near my grandparents, with another aunt, Auntie Louie; neither was really my aunt. We turned up Hurdsfield Road, a steep cobbled climb up past Brocklehurst's Mill, one of the biggest in Macclesfield, a great industrial monument from the Victorian age. Horse-drawn drays came out of its yards, and girls in snoods sat or stood on the steps. Hurdsfield Road went up to the Pennines; halfway up it was the tower of Hurdsfield church. Just below it, opposite the little general shop with the Hovis sign and the Rising Sun pub, in a terrace with raised steps and railings, was No. 191, the small, stone-fronted house in which my grandparents lived.

ROYAL TRAIN

MY FATHER really loved trains. Railways, for him, were the iron bonds of civilization, tying the whole world together, creating wonders of mechanical engineering, raising up cathedral-like monuments called stations.

Each winter he sat down ritually in his armchair and read the obscure, long-columned pages of *Cook's Continental Railway Timetable*: an orange-coloured paperback, as I remember, entirely filled with numbers. He was devising remarkable rail journeys through the wonders of Europe, a continent he only knew by its railbeds. Thus if – let's say – you took the railway ferry to the Hook of Holland, picked up the sleeper express from Zeebrugge to Milan and then, just after midnight, with a clear ten minutes to spare, changed trains in Zurich (Hauptbahnhof of course), you could board the schnellzug from Barcelona to Vienna. By disembarking at Salzburg, you could be among the bierkellers of Munich by the middle of next morning – which left plenty of time to pick up the slow train to Nice.

There were some serious problems in turning this from winter dream to summer actuality. One was the unsupportive attitude of my mother. Another, rather more serious, was the outbreak of the Second World War. He could divert the first, but not the second. With hostilities declared, battlelines drawn, frontiers closed, stations bombed flat, marshalling yards torched, tracks used to move troops, tanks and material, his winter planning grew more difficult, rather more idealized, as it were. Yet he was never deterred. There was, after all, the British railway system itself: the first, the best, and – before the horrific advent of axeman Dr Beeching – probably the most rambling in the world.

As a result, my own growing up was illuminated by a series of zigzag railway journeys, perfectly educational in intent, totally surreal in character. The unlit and window-netted passenger trains we travelled in were regularly shunted into sidings for the sinister duration of an air raid, or to allow troop-trains and wagonloads of tanks or jeeps to trundle by. We must have made a strange little quartet – my father with timetables and railway privilege tickets in hand, my unwilling mother, my squally younger brother, my schoolcapped self, all carrying our gas masks – as we circulated mysteriously around wartime Britain.

But, despite Hitler, circulate we did. Up the East Coast line to Edinburgh, over the Forth Bridge (several times), over to Glasgow, on to the camouflaged Clyde steamers, which belonged to the railways, up to Loch Lomond, which was partly netted against, I believe, flying boats. Down the West Coast line, perhaps popping over to Rhyl and Holyhead on the way. East to the mined beaches of Skegness and Mable-thorpe; they simply had to be seen. South through the old kingdom of King Brunel, to Exeter, Penzance, and Land's End, where the next train beyond here ran from Boston to New York. Everywhere he talked to stationmasters, signalmen, engine drivers, booking clerks, guards, in the great brotherhood of the rails.

Yes, my father did love trains. He loved, of course, the great ones: the Orient Express, the Mozart Express, the Blue Train. And we did travel on them finally, after hostilities ended and Continental timetables resumed, despite bombed stations, closed frontiers, visa problems, travel restrictions and ration books. But he no less loved the little ones: the unsung plodding stoppers on the most obscure of branch lines. He loved the great locomotives: *Mallard*, *Sir Nigel Gresley*, the long-pistoned French monsters you found fuming at the Gare de Lyon. But he cared just as much for the saddle tanks, the grimy pit engines that nobody bothered about at all.

He loved the great luxury coaches, the pink-lamped Pullmans and the grand wagons-lits. But he took equal pleasure in non-corridor third-class coaches with moquette seats and gas mantles. Though he could never afford to stay there, he also loved the great station hotels: the Great Eastern at Liverpool Street (where he worked), the North British, Gleneagles. He equally loved those little B & Bs kept by some signalman's wife three streets back from the seafront, where, with our cardboard suitcases and gas masks, we usually ended up. And he would surely have loved the *Royal Scotsman*. Or that is what I told myself, when I decided – in grateful and nostalgic memory of those ancient journeys which I now know he devised to provoke our childhood wonder – to take a tour on board it in his homage.

NOW THE *Royal Scotsman*, in case you don't know it, is a dream of a train. In fact it is just the sort of dream my father might well have dreamt when, changing at Crewe at two in the morning, he found the Holyhead train unaccountably delayed, the waiting and refreshment rooms surprisingly closed, and we slept on a station bench till the dawn rose and the signals on the platform began clanging again. The *Royal Scotsman* is a classic of nostalgia, a museum of the iron-horse age, a loving restoration, in fact a kind of royal train for the unroyal. Its chief journeys are in the Scottish Highlands – which in my father's imagination was ideal railway land. And it begins and ends its five-day tours at Edinburgh Waverley, the railway station he most loved.

Our homage started, appropriately enough, at the Balmoral Hotel on Princes Street. In our day of political uncorrectness, fifty years ago, it was called the North British, and was one of the great railway hotels. Then you could enter it by a subtle entrance from the station itself: go up in the lift and into its grand public rooms, where the grouse-shooters gathered and the kilts swung. We could not afford to stay there, of course, but we did run to an indulgent tea and scones in the lounge. Its noble rooms look out over Princes Street, where in the drizzle the clowns are already gathering for the Festival, and across to the rock and castle. You can also glance down to the glass-roofed train shed of Waverley, its raison d'être – though the subtle entrance from the platforms is now blocked.

And the lounge of those tea and scones is where, next day, the new aficionados gather: us dedicated takers of the train. It seems we're mostly well-dressed Americans, though there's a definite Scandinavian or German or two, and a number of British nostalgists like myself. The departure of the *Royal Scotsman* is evidently an Edinburgh occasion, like Burns Night or the one o'clock gun. Down in the station, bagpipers wait to groan us aboard the long row of maroon-liveried, fresh-painted, gleaming carriages, while the kilted train crew is resplendently out, holding silver platters of champagne. And then we are away, into the dark gullet of the Waverley Tunnel, and out into the light.

The *Royal Scotsman* is, we find, a mobile grand hotel. It has a solid nine-carriage rake, its cars richly converted from various classic rolling stock. It boasts an observation car, complete with a back iron balcony for any presidential speeches you might be called on to make. There are two soft-cushioned dining and recreation cars, named *Raven* and *Victory*, one of them being formerly the Chief Manager's coach for my father's company, the LNER. Most of the remainder are dedicated sleeping cars – for every cabin is a fully-fledged hotel room, with real beds, desk lamps, grand mahogany walls. Only one tiny but niggling thing disappoints me. At one time this grand apparition was pulled by steam. Now problems of power generation and railway management mean it is pulled by a grosser diesel.

Otherwise, everything is indulgence. The comforts and meals would have astounded and bewildered my father. From the couches of its observation car, Lothian looks oddly different already. There is small sign of Irvine Welsh, and none at all of James Kelman, as a spectral Glasgow disappears off to the south. Even the persistent drizzle looks like a special effect. Soon we are off up the Clyde, and heading for the great, folkloric West Highland line.

Up by Garloch, up by Loch Long. I can remember this
ascent. My father brought us along this route in darker times,
when the lochs were filled with warships and gathering con-
voys, and Clydebank clanged to the sound of wartime production. Now everything seems austerely quiet and peaceful, clean
and conifered, like so much of modern non-urban Scotland.
Up past Arrochar and Ardlui, with a long, glinting and now
unnetted Loch Lomond coming up through the conifers on
the right before we reach the tops.

There, at Crianlarich, we shunt off the West Highland
line, that classic route that goes onward to Fort William and
Mallaig. For we're heading toward Oban, by an even quieter
line. At Dalmally station we halt, and the second arm of our
tour appears: this is the supporting *Royal Scotsman* charabanc,
which is taking us to Inverawe Smokehouse, on Loch Etive.
We descend to see salmon being cured and smoked; a glass of
wine is put into our hands. There's another of the same waiting
for us on the platform as we rejoin the maroon composition in
the yard at Taynuilt station, just short of Oban, where the long
train is quietly stabling for the night.

NEXT MORNING, even while we eat a kippery Scots breakfast,
the train has already started to retrace its route. For each day of
the tour is dedicated to a different segment of the railway
system. This time we're heading for the Central Highlands, via
Stirling and Perth (another bus tour here, for us to hear, from
an excellent guide, a little of that mixture of strange fact,
romantic fiction and cultural resentment that in Scotland is
called history). By Birnam Wood, on by Blair Atholl, we ride
on quiet lines to the Cairngorms, and so to Speyside.

Here our train is to stable at Boat of Garten, which has its
own private railway: the Strathspey Railway, running between
here and Aviemore, and soon beyond to Grantown, for more
track is being laid. Our splendid maroon confection sits in
the depot, among restored or still neglected locomotives and
coaches that would have filled my father with painful delight.
Goods engines and saddle tanks. A carriage from the *Flying*

Scotsman, even a perky Thomas the Tank Engine. A railway museum, a ripe wonderful smell of steam.

By now, the distinctive culture that is Walter Scott's Romantic Revival Scotland has begun to make its claims. Today we've been to Ballidalloch Castle, at the join of the Spey and the Avon, one of those splendid, towered castles where John Brown romanticism has been wisely rescued by sensible commercial rationality. The estate can claim to be the source of the Aberdeen Angus, but has other claims to attention. Like most Scots families, the Macpherson-Grants have striking forebears. One governed Florida at an ill time, the era of the American Revolution; another, when secretary of legation in Lisbon, acquired a mysterious collection of Spanish Masters. Neglected as inauthentic for many years, they have now been found genuine, but still surprisingly adorn the castle walls.

AFTERNOON, and we're heading north again, across the Great Glen, via the Firth of Inverness, to take another very important leg in the great Scottish railway tour. For, through the Northwest Highlands, runs another treasure of a line – from Dingwall, via Garve, beneath Ben Wyvis and the Luib Summit, through Achnasheen to Kyle of Lochalsh. Strategic during the War, it is idling rather now. It has not quite had the fame or attention of the Fort William–Mallaig route, but has been under a similar threat of closure. And that would be a tragedy, since it runs through some of the most impressive of Highland landscapes – ancient mountains, clearance lands (meaning shortage of passengers), rough-managed great shooting estates, open wooded slopes and moors, finger lochs.

At last it descends, by way of Loch Carron and picturesque Plockton, with their warmed-up microclimates, to Kyle of Lochalsh, the fine little port to Skye. I have been here before – fifty years back – and I would not say it has changed very much, except for that exorbitant if elegant toll bridge that now soars over the sea to Skye. It has dulled the port, quietened the water traffic, broken a frontier, and opened the island to coaches (possibly those high tolls are some pathetic attempt at control). At any rate, our train takes its place on the ferry pier, next to a moored tall ship. Skye lies moody over the water; our festive dinner this night is wreathed in drizzled Scots mist.

Skye is always moody, and the mood was on it next day too: low mist, hiding the Cuillin peaks and skylines, keeping the light and the shade flickering over the moors and the waters below. We charabanc there too, round the watery island, and so touch the furthest point of our tour. For now our journey begins somewhat to retrace itself – back up Loch Carron, over the Northwest Highlands, where the sun's now beginning to come back over the heathered moorlands and bring out the singing birds.

WE STABLE this last night at Keith, inland from the Moray Firth. There's a final dinner in penguin suits, a rapid exchange of addresses. For next morning we're rattling south down the route everyone knows: through Aberdeen, over the Tay Bridge at Dundee, past the tragic stumps of the old bridge McGonegal made so famous. They're still trying to restore the rusted iron tubes that hold up the Forth Bridge, so mysteriously neglected during the final days of British Rail rule, before they finally pulled down their little lion flag.

For my father this was the greatest of all the railway engineering triumphs. That's why as kids we crossed it so often, for he would take endless excursion tickets over to Burntisland to experience and re-experience the strange ironwork thrill. From the back of an open observation car, it's magnificent, its rusting stanchions soaring, its one-track railbed rattling danger-ously, the waters of the Forth greyly washing below.

And then . . . we're back into Edinburgh Waverley. Black Great Northern 125s with BLT menus, flashy red and white Virgins, cheeky little Sprinters everywhere. Backpackers pour-ing in for the Festival. Our train buffs descend, say their farewells and disappear among the backpackers, carrying their flight coupons to Florida or their tickets for the Festival fringe.

The homage is over. At home there's a full answerphone to see to, and rewrites for the next *Inspector Morse*. That's all it was, indulgence, but I've loved it. And in all honesty I think my father just might have loved it too.

DRACULA COUNTRY

FOR ME THERE'S something moving in the story of Fred Offiler, the Nottingham greengrocer who went on holiday seventy-five years ago to the Lincolnshire resort of Mablethorpe, and has returned two or three times a year ever since. Now ninety-five and a widower, he still goes. The local council have made him a presentation in recognition.

Fred's loyalty seems almost foreign to our age of mass international tourism. Now the options are massive, the packages many, the general idea to go each year to a fresh, more exotic destination. Yet, for several generations, a holiday in the same English resort was for most ordinary people the familiar rule.

Each city had its destinations. Nottingham went to Skegness or Mablethorpe ('Nottingham by the sea'). Leicester went to Great Yarmouth, Rochdale and the Lancashire mill towns to Blackpool. Sheffield, Leeds and Bradford went to the Yorkshire coast: Scarborough if you could afford it, Filey or Bridlington if not.

When I was a child, I went to them all. My father organized the excursion trains that, through the summer, brought the visitors in. You could go by charabanc, car if you had one. But the railways made the resorts function, and the visitor's first memory was generally of the seagulls screaming over the station forecourt as you looked around for the sea.

Today the historical posters ('Skegness Is So Bracing') and the seafront boarding houses, many filled with benefit claimants, mark what's left of a once dense, very English holiday culture. It bred summer colds, friendships, holiday love affairs, and many loyal visitors who came back to the same boarding house in the same week, year after year.

The Beeching cuts did these places terrible harm, and the temptations of modern tourism and amazing travel offers mean it makes sense for the British to flee the country in summer, when the rain is likely to pour and a Siberian wind blows in down the east coast. The result is that the resorts that were founded in the nineteenth century and boomed with the growth of mass holidays have suffered a long slow decline.

Now Hotels de Paris sit half-empty over the harbours. Piers never see any of the steamers they were built for. Bandstands covered in graffiti lack their musicians. Skateboarders occupy the concrete promenades that were built – of course – for promenading, taking a stroll, looking at the girls or boys. Day trippers rather than regular boarders crowd the streets.

Yet the reasons for the existence of these resorts – the sweeping bays and rock pools, the fishing sheds and fish-and-chip shops, the dancehalls, the amusement arcades and cliff funiculars – are still to be found. And I confess to a special fondness for the many English resorts that are a bit off the beaten track and a bit out of favour.

Around the start of the 1960s, I visited many of the resorts along the Yorkshire–Lincolnshire coast. I went in the middle of winter, teaching adult evening classes. I worked in the evening in the local library, stayed in a boarding house. Resorts in winter reveal their secrets: bedrooms that stay eternally unheated, wardrobes with doors that can never shut, drained swimming pools revealing a serious need of re-tiling.

We kept our cottage in the Yorkshire Wolds, and I returned each summer to write there. But the attractions were greater. I have always loved to go back to the coastal resorts, from Hornsea and Withernsea, down by the disintegrating Spurn Head, to the tiny fishing villages of Staithes and Runswick in the north.

Scarborough, which can boast Alan Ayckbourn and a massive conference trade, needs no recommendation. But to appreciate many of the other places along this coast, it helps to have a touch of nostalgia. They are redolent with old holidays, past ways of doing things. It's not difficult to recall the spirit of the boarding houses that took in vast extended families, and turned them out between breakfast and supper rain and shine; or the large cavernous hostels that did group weekends for mechanics' institutes and cycling clubs.

I love these places: Hornsea with its dark mere, Bridlington with its Georgian square round the fine parish church, Filey with its brig and the best fish and chips in the universe. Midweek in early summer, before the school holidays start, is the best time: water, wind, fish, chips, antiques, bygones, curios, fishing nets, sand in the shoes, crying children, nothing smart, celebrity-obsessed or designer-led at all.

But the finest places lie further north, toward Dracula Country, where the great North Yorkshire moors cut off the coast from the inland world. Here are strange places: Ravenscar, where the remains of some once ambitious holiday resort scheme survive like an old monastery on the lonely clifftops, and Robin Hood's Bay, where, sensibly avoiding the windswept tops, the cottages huddle dangerously under the cliff on the sea's edge.

A little further is Whitby, where, according to Bram Stoker's novel, Count Dracula of Transylvania came ashore as a dog during a remarkable storm. Writing in the 1890s, Stoker picked his location perfectly. Whitby is the heartland of Victorian Gothic. The box pews still rattle in the clifftop parish church during every storm. The graveyard is filled with those lost at sea, some no doubt with a stake through the heart.

Down by the harbour you can buy Whitby jet, Victorian mourning jewellery. Old photographs of the ancient whaling and fishing port show grim seafarers, and whale tusks still form a portico on the very top of the cliff, where Captain Cook looked out before he sailed.

I have returned to Whitby year after year. In the days when I taught my evening classes here, I was from time to time snowed in for several days when winter blizzards blocked off the twisting dangerous road over Fylingthorpe Moor, and the sea-storms washed across the road down the coast.

It took the Victorians to develop the wonders of places like Whitby. The Brontë sisters came here, and their friend Mrs Gaskell wrote a novel about the area, *Sylvia's Lovers*. Even as late as Stoker's book, Whitby was a major European harbour, and all the way up and down the east coast the steamers went back and forth, bringing tourists from Teesside and coals from Newcastle.

Whitby still heaves in the summer, though mostly with bikers from Teesside and caravans from everywhere. The Dracula experience is available down by the harbour, and you can still take fishing trips off the coast. The spectacular railway line that ran down the coastline has disappeared, and so have parts of the cliff.

But the reasons why once upon a time Whitby was as romantic and important as Geneva or Florence are still apparent. I love to go back, as often as I can, and take every excuse to do so. Which is why I think I understand Fred Offiler – and wish him all the luck in the world.

SONS AND MOTHERS

MY MOTHER lived a long life, and saw nearly all this troubled century. When she was born in 1898, Queen Victoria still had three more years of her reign to come. By the time she died, in 1993, in her mid-nineties, there had been a moon landing, and the Berlin Wall had come down. The inventions and quandaries of the twenty-first century were already in sight. The nature of marriage, the family and gender itself had all deeply changed.

Over her lifetime, my mother had seen two World Wars, as well as the long Cold one. She had seen Britain go from the proud imperial confidence of the Victorian age to the gradual drain of power after the Second World War. She'd started her life in an age of long skirts, widows' weeds, houses packed with servants, churchgoing each Sunday. She'd seen votes for women, easy contraception, a total change in female opportunities, and the wild fashion styles of the modern catwalk.

Like all children, I only knew a portion of my mother's life – from her mid-thirties on. She married in her late twenties, and I was born in 1932. Just at this time my father was appointed to an office job with the London and North Eastern Railway, at Liverpool Street Station. He bought a fine new semi in Metroland, out in Rayner's Lane, still close to the countryside, and commuted to work each day on the new red trains of the Central Line.

I think these years were the happiest of my mother's life. She'd moved down from the North into her first married home. This was a good time for family life in Britain. Modern domestic appliances – Hoovers and gas cookers and modern fireplaces – were taking many of the old chores out of domestic existence. In new communities like this, there were friendly modern neighbours, a Home and Colonial store, a brand new Odeon to watch romantic Hollywood movies, a smart hair salon where you could have a permanent wave.

My mother was light-hearted and very spirited; she was also quite reserved and shy. She was tall, dark-haired, willowy – a kind of look I find I have always admired in women. She wore very little make-up, and bought all her clothes with care, looking for things that would outlast the season's fashions. She liked going to the cinema once a week 'for a treat', but she also read a great deal, borrowing books from the local public library and Boot's. She had not had the chance of anything more than a board-school education, but she was highly intelligent.

As her first child, I was probably something of a trouble to her. I had been born with a heart defect, and was supposed not to run or play games. From time to time she took me round the London specialists in the great hospitals of Edgware or Great Ormond Street, and she looked after me with enormous care. My younger brother was born in 1935, and throughout the thirties she devoted herself to the problems of raising a young family on a just about sufficient income.

For various reasons she almost never talked about her own earlier days. It was partly reticence; partly, I think, her pleasure in getting away from home into a new life of her own; and partly a kind of embarrassment – very common in the thirties – among people who had already done better than their parents, but were doing all they could to make sure their children would do better still.

So it was not really until after her death, when a small suitcase of papers filled with those things that families always keep – certificates of birth and marriage and death, old photographs that get pushed away in the backs of drawers – came my way amongst her possessions, that I began to have much sense of her earlier years, and how her life had started out. She had been born in Darnall, a working-class district of

Sheffield, which until quite recently still clanked with the noise of the nearby steelworks and the railway carriage and wagon works. Her father was an engine-driver, her mother – remembered by me only as an elderly grannie with grey pinned-back hair, wearing a long black dress and a flowered pinafore, sitting all day in a chair tended by three unmarried daughters – a linen power-loom weaver. One generation back of that, her grandmother, on her marriage, had signed her name with a cross.

She grew up in a family of seven children by two different fathers; five of them were girls. In the twenties, her father had been killed in a street accident, run down by a 'car-owner' named Garside, who was prosecuted but acquitted. The two sons had already married, leaving together a household of women, who fended in various ways: nursing, hairdressing, shorthand typing. Only two of the daughters ever married. This was the generation whose marriage prospects were blighted by the wholesale male slaughter of the Great War.

My mother must have had a short but quite good education, which included learning to play the piano. Then she trained to become a skilled shorthand typist, and worked as a railway clerk for the Great Northern Railway, and afterwards the LNER, at Sheffield Victoria Station. Here she met and married my father, an ambitious young booking clerk from Cheshire who sang with the Sheffield Orpheus choir. When he got the promotion to London he wanted, she remained with her family in Darnall to have her first child.

I was born at Nether Edge Maternity Hospital. According to the family papers, I cost £5 4s 3d, only a pound or so more than the fine maroon pram she pushed me in when she rejoined my father in London. She and my father were close, but with very different temperaments. He was strong-minded, firm in opinion, talkative, gregarious, fond of travel. And, as he worked for the railway, he got free or cheap travel round Britain and in Europe – even in the difficult postwar years when foreign travel was restricted.

So we went – my father, mother, younger brother and myself – to the Butlin's and Pontin's holiday camps at Skegness and Portcawl, the classic family holidays of the thirties. In wartime, when the trains were filled with troops, he took us off to bed-and-breakfast in Scotland and Ireland. After the War, when much of Europe was still in ruins, we went by train to Spain, Italy, France and Austria. My father had no foreign language, but a great ability to start conversations. My mother was uncomfortable – it got much worse after they began taking holidays by plane – and longed for the place she liked best: home.

When war came in 1939, our life of the thirties came to an end. The railways were strategic, and my father was moved all round the country, organizing troop train movements. When the Blitz began to shatter London, my mother moved to stay with her married sister in Sheffield. It wasn't perhaps an ideal move. Sheffield was blitzed heavily, and we spent much of the War huddled in a garden shelter, as the German bombers smashed the city.

It was a grimly unpleasant time, but we survived it as a family. Finally my father was able to move us to the greater safety of Nottingham, and there, in the last years of the War and the postwar austerity, I grew up. The new educational opportunities of the welfare state gave children like myself a fresh layer of opportunity. I won a free place at grammar school, then went on to university. Slowly my life began to move away from that of my parents, intellectually and geographically.

But we stayed very close. I returned home as frequently as I could, and I remained particularly close to my mother. I was never very sure what she made of what I did. When I started to write articles and then books, she was plainly proud I had written them, but I was never sure she read them, and she never commented on anything I produced. Until she died, so recently, I worried that in some way they might upset or offend her, though I don't know they ever did.

And when I became a university teacher, she was just as unfamiliar with that world. Universities were strange distant places, places she hardly ever visited – though she did go to see my brother graduate, and I would sometimes drive her through the campus to look at the buildings, without her ever wanting to go inside. She was not fond of restaurants; she rarely went to the theatre, except once in a while for the pantomime when we were young. She preferred reading and home entertainment – though by the time I started writing for television she was convinced the programmes were already 'going off'.

Once my father retired, my parents moved to a bungalow on the south coast. Then came the great tragedy in her life; another car accident first paralysed, and then killed, my younger brother, who was also a university teacher. The accident deeply upset her. Always reserved, she became withdrawn and almost agoraphobic, not wanting to leave the house. When my father died, my wife, to whom she was wonderfully close, brought her to Norwich, to a flat nearby. Though she rarely left it, she remained interested in everything, following the world in newspapers and magazines.

I greatly miss my mother, and feel every day that I have inherited, like some gene, a considerable part of her character. Like her, I have a taste for home and family life. Like her, I seek privacy and my own independence. I distrust crowds, and I don't much like big cities. I feel very suspicious of fads and fashions. I distrust extremes and wild enthusiasms. I respect ordinary common sense, and want people to behave with moral responsibility.

All these feelings are hers, ingrained in me, I suppose, when she spent so much time with me as a child needing considerable attention, before and during the War. Today I suppose her life would be seen by modern women as narrow, self-sacrificing, too much devoted to others. I don't think that was how she saw it, and I don't think that was how it was. It was a private, unspectacular life of great value. And I still look for qualities like hers, considerate, thoughtful and restrained, in the women, and the men, I meet.

A WEEK OR SO IN ROME

AFTER THEY HAD LEFT the Fergusons at their hotel, the Boyles walked back through the streets of Rome to the smaller hotel at which they were staying. 'It's good of the Fergusons to take us around so much,' said Jenny Boyle.

'Well,' said Boyle, 'I suppose he feels he rather owes it to us.'

'He doesn't owe us anything,' said Jenny.

'Oh, I don't know,' said Boyle comfortably. His attitude annoyed Jenny. 'Don't be ridiculous, Robin,' she said. 'You see debts where there are none. The Fergusons owe you nothing.'

'Perhaps he feels he does,' answered Boyle. It was true that a strange relationship had sprung up between Boyle and Ferguson. The two couples had met one day while on a conventional bout of sightseeing. Robin Boyle was a lecturer at Oxford, a citizen, as he liked to put it, of no mean university; David Ferguson described himself, wryly, as 'a creative man' in an advertising agency; but they found that they had much the same interests in Rome. Boyle insisted on condescending to 'poor old Ferguson'; he would, he said, have made a damn good classicist, but of course there was nothing under the present dispensation to do with a classics degree except do what 'poor old Ferguson' had done. And, on the other side, what the relationship had brought out in David Ferguson was deference. He saw in Boyle, perhaps, what he had wanted to be; rather perhaps he felt the need to give homage to what he counted as integrity.

The Fergusons had a car, while the Boyles had not ('A

university lecturer with a car?' cried Boyle, when Lena Ferguson had asked them where they parked it. 'NOC, dear lady; not our class. We can't live like *you*, you know.'), and they had taken the Boyles about a good deal, inside Rome and even up to Siena. It may have been that she came from a good family, it may have been an unbecoming pride, but Jenny Boyle liked to think that she was 'independent'; she was disturbed by this tacit agreement that Ferguson, with his agency background, had somehow sold out his cultural interests, and that his superior possession of commodities had to be made up to Boyle, who had stayed so honest and so poor. For one thing, she couldn't see the situation in that light; Boyle surely had indulged himself in his way by doing what he wanted to. Then she was disturbed by her husband's open willingness to accept this humble patronage – the trips in the Fergusons' car, meals and drinks at the Fergusons' much better hotel, evenings at the opera on the Fergusons. Nothing was ever refused, invitations were angled for, no return offers were made. 'If he gave you his last pair of trousers you would take them,' she said.

Of course, Robin Boyle had come from a bad home, had been a scholarship boy, had fought his way up the academic ladder. But nowadays that was really rather easy, and she found it hard to see why Robin should still feel angry about his background, and the energy he had had to put into his efforts. They disagreed about politics, of course; Boyle still felt imposed upon, wanted to destroy things. It was illiberal no doubt to think it, but perhaps the implicit doctrines of her own family did make sense – perhaps bad blood showed. He was not, to use her family's most painful condemnation – a condemnation none the less painful for being made so gently – a gentleman, for Oxford cannot make gentlemen, but merely improve them. For instance, he did rather leech onto people; she had noticed it before. Not that he was humble; humility would have got him nowhere, and he had got somewhere. He took because he thought he deserved; and that, my lass, thought Jenny, is how he married you. He made even that seem a favour, though to see our families together at the wedding, you could see where the breeding was. But (as he had often told her) this *was* the twentieth century, and you can't live on breeding forever.

She knew that Lena Ferguson agreed with her, knew it from the first moment. Boyle disliked Lena, and of course he would. She was a woman of strong features and equally strong character, and Boyle disliked assurance when it was founded upon nothing, or upon something undeserved, like pride of class; the fact was simply that Boyle was made uncomfortable by people who approved of themselves. Lena's assurance was based upon something – it was based upon the fact that she was a woman. And Boyle disliked her surely because of the evident feeling she had, a feeling commoner in women than most men suppose, that anything, for a woman, is all right – that because the female lot is hard and difficult, a woman has the right to forget abstract morality, human feeling, human responsibility, in her efforts to get for herself and hers the things she wants. Lena *was* naturally acquisitive; life was a stocking up of goods; the making over of things into her realm was the function of life. This, Boyle insisted, was what was destroying Ferguson. Jenny saw his point, and yet admired Lena's single-mindedness; it had the air of a virtue.

After all, Lena was pregnant – 'Just barely pregnant,' she had told Jenny – and one could understand how she felt, one did surely want to carve out a safe and secure and *rich* plot in the world for one's children. To Boyle, the pregnancy made her seem all the more unpleasant. And he was uneasy about the influence that she might have on Jenny, on *his* Jenny, in whom, Boyle liked to think, this protective acquisition, and this material stockpiling, were not real motives. 'We'll miss them when they go to Positano,' said Jenny. Boyle agreed, but he could not help wondering just what it was that Jenny would miss.

UNCERTAIN OF each other, still tasting the expensive and therefore excellent wine that the Fergusons had given them, they walked on in silence through the hot streets. Somewhere behind baked houses, dogs barked. The sky was a hard blue.

A violent heatwave had possessed the city, making the very air they breathed dry and dusty. After the air-conditioned hotel, which they had just left, the heat was an offence.

'I admire his choice in wines,' said Boyle suddenly. Boyle had a palate; he had worked hard for it. 'Yes,' said Jenny, who had a palate too, but had not worked for it at all, 'and such splendid food . . .'

'I suppose,' said Boyle, 'I should apologize to you that we're not staying *there.*'

'Oh, Robin, for *goodness'* sake . . .'

Suddenly, in a narrow street, they found their way blocked. Standing in front of them was a youth in a cotton suit, light blue with faint white stripes, a dandyish, vain, cocksure suit; he wanted to sell them a Parker fountain pen. The city was full of these shifty street vendors, who clustered on corners, preying on visitors who looked American or English or German. 'Come on, you buy,' said the youth. Boyle, who resented – and was intimidated by – these intrusions, said surlily: 'It's a fake, an imitation.' He tried to walk on but the youth stepped in his way. Looking, surprised, into his face for the first time, Boyle saw that he was extremely ugly – his eyes were badly crossed and his features ill-shaped. There was a scar. All this, combined with the dandyishness of his appearance, which so plainly suggested that he did not withdraw from making sexual claims – indeed the way he looked at Jenny showed that he made them all the more, that he felt his ugliness to be of sexual interest, something special – put Boyle into an impotent rage. 'No,' he said. 'Go away.'

The youth laughed. 'No, these the real thing. Stolen. Look inside,' he said, talking to Boyle, looking at Jenny.

'No,' said Boyle. He took Jenny's arm and rushed past. 'Where are you staying?' said the man suddenly to Jenny. He named some hotels, among them the one where they were. They walked on quickly; and still the man was behind them. 'Pen like this very cheap for such a lady. Special offer for the lady.' He continued to pursue them for the length of the street; 'No, wait, mister, take a look at this watch; turn round, lady,' and the joke was that while it was Boyle he was shouting to, it was Jenny that he was pursuing. The chase continued down several streets, narrow, baked, and Boyle hurried on, with his arm under Jenny's, regardless of where they were going. Then finally: 'Hey girl, don't leave me,' shouted the youth, and he dropped away. 'I find you again.'

They came out, suddenly, from between the houses into a large open square. The burning sun filled it; there was a parched tree or two; a dry fountain, composed of cherubs gasping for water from the mouth of a fish, which now refused to oblige, stood in the centre; saddened dogs hung about it with their tongues panting. 'Well, after *that*,' demanded Jenny, 'where have you brought us?'

Boyle looked at her in rage, as if the whole misadventure were her fault; and indeed in a way it was, for had it not been for Jenny's attractiveness, the foolish pursuit would never have taken place. Jenny's eyes dropped at his look. 'The randy little beast,' said Robin wildly. 'All right,' said Jenny, 'don't be indulgent. He didn't hurt you.'

But he had: Boyle's incompetence welled over straight away into self-pity. Why had he let the little bastard frighten him? And why, he asked himself, looking at Jenny – in whom no consolation was promised – why did he always offend simply by being self-chastising? Why did his misery in his own performance have to disgust her?

Jenny looked around; she saw, under the parched trees, some little carts where they were selling slices of chilled melon; the bright scraps of fruit were packed in ice, which was melting and dropping to the pavement, to dry with a hiss. 'Buy me some melon,' said Jenny. Boyle felt that the words sounded like a challenge; and he was in no mood for a challenge. For Jenny did not like to be left to do all the purchasing, to ask the way always, to work up, always, her *Italian*. He caught the note; he knew she thought he lacked stamina, consideration for her, responsibility for her. But he was sorry for himself; he was damned if he would; he had no space to deal with more situations, even little ones like asking prices. He didn't like situations which rested squarely upon him, and if she didn't like the way he handled the tout she knew what she could do. He'd always considered that he was somehow constituted so that his spirit broke when outside its range. It was broken now, but the range, he believed, was right and sound. Rome was at fault; he had no place in Rome.

Jenny looked at him a moment, shrugged, and went over alone to the little carts. A hot wind blew toward them both, bringing up the dust. Birds hopped in the sandy gutters. 'Oh, this infernal city,' said Boyle, as Jenny came back with a slice of melon which she silently shared between them.

IN THE YEARS after the last war, Rome presented to the visitor the aspect of a defeated city. It was not that there were bombed buildings, or that army occupation forces toured the streets in jeeps (a condition which still prevailed elsewhere, in Vienna, for instance); the sense of defeat lay rather in a mood of moral anarchy, for which the War had simply provided the physical forms. Wars only tired what was there to be tired. By the early fifties this mood seemed established as a way of life, though poverty and hardship and suffering were no longer quite the issue; they were an old issue on which the new manners had been built. Even the rich lived as though they were poor. Small cars and motor scooters filled the streets, braying their mechanical noise among the buildings, where it seemed to hang in a kind of permanent resonance. The noise continued all night and it was difficult to sleep. Indeed in Rome there was, really, no sleep; at any rate that was how it seemed to the Boyles. Combined with the noise – as if each was an attribute of the other – was the stifling heat. August in Rome is always stifling, but this year was an exceptional one; a curdling heat lay all over Europe, spiralling off its pavements and ricocheting between its buildings. In Rome it was a heat that reached into the throat and dried it, a sour, savage density in the air that seemed to desiccate the brain, to provoke lust, to irritate the temper. The effect of this on the Boyles, whose marriage was already under strain, had been at once to stimulate their passion for one another and yet to exaggerate the characteristics in the other that each found irritating.

Boyle, for instance, found himself infuriated by Jenny's choice of clothes; like any decent Englishwoman, she had always been an uninspired dresser, more interested in the material itself than in the way the dress was made up. Now, as Boyle kept telling her, they weren't in England and she might at least try to develop a competitive flair in the company of the chic young things of Rome. He made invidious comparisons; he pointed out girls who raised his sexual desire at once, by their appearance; and he found he could scarcely control the wish to satisfy the appetites that the Roman girls had raised. If only Jenny were not there, if only she were more liberal-minded. But even she, under the influence of Rome, was granting more than she usually did; at the same time she found him merely vulgar.

On the edge then both of passion and irritation, they spent their days wandering around the city, in a consciousness that, having extended their feelings in all directions beyond their proper, their normal, their appointed limits, all the conventions of their marriage had been challenged; they couldn't go back. Nor was that all; they had questioned not only the accommodation that they had achieved, in time, in their relations, but also the accommodation with what they conceived to be the moral life, with the proper rate at which the moral pulse should beat for honest living.

IT WOULD BE hard to go back now, Boyle perceived. It was night; they sat in their hotel room reading; still the dogs barked outside. Lying on the bed, unable to summon concentration, Boyle looked across at Jenny, who sat in a chair, fitted with difficulty between the door and an old-fashioned washstand. Jenny, in spite of the sly young men (like the youth of today) who waited outside the hotel or followed her in the street, subsisted on an image of the Italians as loveable and properly emotional, living *real* lives from the blood and the instincts. She had brought with her D. H. Lawrence's *Letters*, in the fat brown Aldous Huxley edition; she would look up – 'Listen to this; we must go there!' – and read a passage from Lawrence's warmest accounts of places and people. 'But this is all so very romantic, darling,' he said, 'you know what Lawrence is like.'

'I suppose you would find that,' said Jenny, looking across at him, 'since the furthest your own feelings go is to the occasional little pang of lechery.'

'I'm a damn sight closer to Lawrence than you are, anyway,' said Boyle; 'He was *my* class, not yours. You're hardly a Lawrence heroine yourself, you know; every time you get into bed you feel you're selling your soul to the devil. Like spitting on the family heirlooms. Four generations of the upper middle class and sex is something for horses and dogs.'

'You can hardly say I've failed you that way.'

'Come to bed, then.'

'All right, then,' said Jenny, 'show me how good you are. But you weren't very good with that boy, this afternoon, were you? I could have laughed. You were so jealous.'

'What was there to be jealous of?'

'Nothing, darling,' said Jenny, 'but that didn't stop you, did it?' She started to undress, and then halted for a moment. 'You don't think I'm turning into a nymphomaniac, do you?'

'I like you like this,' said Boyle.

'I quite like you, too,' said Jenny.

LATER THAT NIGHT, as he slept, fitfully, in the hot and noisy room, and looked at her face, beaded in sweat, in his waking moments, Boyle seemed to see the image of another face. It was a male, mean, olive-skinned face, at once lecherous and treacherous and cocksure, that was the collective Face of all the youths who hung about the Roman streets pursuing girls, foreign women and homosexual rich Americans, the Face of the sly street vendors who sold fake pens and watches, the black-marketeers in cigarettes, the youths who sold themselves on the Via Veneto. It was a face one saw a thousand times all over Italy, North Africa, France, at home in England even, the face of the people to whom cheating someone was life and sexual adventure a triumph – they were all marks scored against the world. So sure of itself, so unassailable, so arrogant, it seemed to spread its horrifying triviality all over the new world. One claimed to be a teacher; but there was nothing one could teach the Face. Boyle tossed and turned. He ran with sweat. He determined to leave Rome the next day for a clearer and more honest air. But in the morning he woke to find that the sweat seemed somehow to have eaten into him; he was feverish and the room did not seem to clear, the night-time fantasies to abate in the light of day. Jenny was up and washing at the basin. She looked at him curiously.

'I don't thing I can stand it here any longer,' said Boyle.

'Are you all right?'

'Yes, I'm all right. We've got to get out of this awful city.' He tried to get out of bed; he felt wildly dizzy. 'I can't bear to look at another picture or another church.'

'You don't look very well,' said Jenny.

'What *use* is all this culture and civilization we talk so much about if it doesn't play any part in the lives of people who live with it? What good is it?'

'Perhaps you'd better stop in bed.'

'It's a bloody losing battle, for people like me. You talk about truth and they think about watches and fountain pens. Truth, how much can you sell truth for? You talk about the honesty of the liberal and behind your backs there's all this degrading corruption. They pass these churches every day, these pictures, these buildings, and they're just so much nothing. They're just a means of fetching in the tourists so that you can empty their pockets.'

'Well, it's all very fine for people to be civilized, isn't it, if they have their share of worldly goods and a nice little wife who'll speak Italian for them and friends who'll buy them a good dinner. But you're protected against the germs of the world. You have messengers and intermediaries. These people don't.'

'Hell, I feel awful,' said Boyle. 'I feel as though the sun's boring into my head. We must get out of here.'

'Nobody's going anywhere today,' said Jenny, 'you get back into bed. I'm going to get a doctor to look at you.'

'I don't want a doctor,' said Boyle. 'I just want to leave this place. It horrifies me.' He remembered again the face in his dream, and remembered too that what shocked him was the sense of its newness, as if it were a fresh force in the world that he had to reckon with. The beggars outside the catacombs, the stray cats wailing in the ruins of the Forum, the small boys searching the ashtrays of the cafés used by American tourists, because Americans only smoked their cigarettes halfway down – all this became an image of a new dereliction. It was as if a way of life had collapsed and men were living in the ruins of a once organized society, among the scraps of all old religion. But the ruins and the defeat were not tangible ones, not those of war; all the physical ruins were of wars too far gone to be of interest to anyone except scholars and tourists.

Boyle felt all this with the hypersensitivity of illness. And he was ill. Jenny, after feeling his brow, looked a little grave. She walked away from him across the room and put on a summer dress. Tied to his bed, he felt his impotence, the nonsense of his arguments, which could affect her not at all. 'Doesn't this worry you?' he said. 'Doesn't it worry you that people are immoral and disgusting?' He said this to provoke her; this was something she would never admit; she never could believe in evil. To her the world seemed sweet – and because she thought it was, the world often obliged. She said: 'What about the people who painted the pictures we've seen. They were special people. There are always special people.'

'Really, Jenny, the world simply isn't as lovely as you like to think it is.' Jenny was two years older than Boyle, and sometimes she felt she paid hard for it; she carried all their practical burdens, and being a mother as well as a wife to Boyle was a sturdy task, for his helplessness was phenomenal – not without its charm; but she was not a strong-minded woman, and she wanted to feel that he would look after her. Yet though Boyle left most of their commerce with the world to her, he always affected to be more experienced in it than she.

He *was*, she granted, more experienced, in his capacity for valuation; yet she would have liked him to observe that it was not always *she* who was naive. His lack of stamina – which had once seemed to her a charming intellectual fecklessness, a proper concern for the things that *really* mattered – now seemed a weakness, an evasion. 'You mean us to go, don't you?' she said. 'Just because a man was rude to you on the street. But what about me? I don't want to leave. I haven't seen anything yet.'

'You like it, then?'

'Why not? What has it done to me? I find it a beautiful city. In any case, you know we've no more money to go on somewhere else.'

'We could ask the Fergusons to take us down to Positano with them. It's different there. They have room for four.'

'They wouldn't want us.'

'Ferguson would be only too pleased—'

'I just don't understand how you're able to blackmail—'

'Really, Jenny, that's absurd. It isn't blackmail.'

'You make him feel ashamed of what he is, and then take advantage of it to make him feel in your debt.'

'Ferguson doesn't think so.'

'Lena does.'

'No doubt,' said Boyle, 'because it exposes her. It shows that she's made him what he is. She's afraid he'll turn back into a civilized human being instead of a money-making machine.'

'A civilized human being, of course, being what you are.'

'Well, that's unfair, isn't it? All I can say is that I try to be; it's my job and my function. I happen to think that it's worth all the loss of status and rank and money to do that.'

'For me too?'

'Would you want it differently?'

'But you don't mind sacrificing for us both?'

'No,' said Boyle, 'because I happen to think that you're the better person for it. You're the better for not being Lena Ferguson.'

'But perhaps I'm tempted to be Lena Ferguson, and have a baby, and a future, and plans.'

'Then I'm sorry for you.'

Boyle saw that he was on dangerous ground; he felt frightened. Yet he could not believe he was selfish. He had to make this commitment, this sacrifice – that was the word he cared for most – because he was too strict to compromise. There could be no mistake about the fervour of his dedication to . . . what was it? Culture? Liberal humanism? It was something too complex for expression, but honesty was the issue, honesty and standards. It was by its nature a losing battle. The role he maintained was perhaps an effete one, since he was maintaining a one-sided dialogue. And the trouble was that there were satisfactions in it which he had – and which Jenny did not.

His vision of the world was one in which violent forces were actively at work destroying the things in which he believed. He had looked at the outbreaks of violence in Europe and shuddered; but it was the nature of the kind of liberalizing force he stood for to look on, helplessly. And now the corruption of Rome – all through the War he had talked happily of the time when one would be able to get back to Rome, that civilizing city, again – was so concretely the aftermath of this disaster, so permanently there, so untouchable. Jenny did not share this; she had that strange feminine optimism that was tantamount to an act of faith, the belief that the world was worth bringing children into. It gave her a stamina that he did not have; it was always he who was ill, and not she.

'You see,' he said, 'I believed you were with me.'

'I suppose I am,' said Jenny, 'but you need an awful lot of being with.'

'Aren't I supposed to ask even that?'

'Oh, you need someone,' said Jenny, 'look what a mess you'd have been in if you were ill like this and alone. Or even if I were ill. What would you have done? Look, I'm going out, and I'm going to get some medicine and see the Fergusons; we were meeting them this morning.'

'Ask them about Positano.'

'No,' said Jenny. 'What are you going to do while I'm gone? You're not to get up. I mean that.'

'I'll lie here and think.'

'Don't think,' said Jenny, 'go to sleep.'

Boyle lay there and began to wonder about himself. He thought back on the long history of travellers and expatriates who had come to Rome. He recollected all the artists and writers and scholars for whom the city had been a spiritual home, and he began to consider, from his so hardily worked out cultural stance, what had changed. Was it Rome? Or was it the capacity to deal with what Rome was – was it, in short, himself? For his Rome was not the one he had expected to find, had been taught, by his forebears, to find. Whose tradition had lapsed? Could it then be his?

He fell asleep. When he woke, the room was dark, yet full of heat and of the noise of traffic outside. He sensed rather than saw that someone was in the room, that Jenny was back. It worried him that he could not see her; he wanted to find her with his eyes. The shades had been closed, and his head was whirling. He was aware of an urgent need of her. Finally he picked out her vague image in the half-dark; and he had a sense of unrest about her, a suspicion of diminished possession. 'Jenny,' he murmured. She stirred but said nothing.

'Have you been out?' he asked.

'Yes,' said Jenny, 'don't you want to sleep?'

'No,' he said, sitting up. Jenny got up and put back the windows, and a white glare filled the room.

'Robin, an awful thing happened when I was out. Two awful things really. I agree to what you said; we'll leave. I asked the Fergusons and they'll take us if we can go the day after tomorrow. They have an hotel reservation for that night.'

'But why, Jenny?'

'That's only if you're well,' said Jenny.

'But, Jenny darling, what awful things?'

'Well, one's just silly. It's just all these cats in the Forum . . .'

'Cats?' said Boyle.

'Yes, there are a lot of cats, all down in the bottom among the ruins. They can't get out, and people throw them down there to get rid of them. They starve to death. So I took some bread and stuff and threw it down.'

'That's horrible,' said Boyle.

'The other thing was something that happened to me at the bank. I went to change some traveller's cheques. I was at the counter and behind me there was a youth, in a yellow sweater. I put the passport down on the counter and I was talking to the clerk, and then when I looked again the passport wasn't there any more. I told the clerk and he just didn't care! He said I ought to be careful. He didn't want to do anything about it at all. So I ran to the door and there was this yellow sweater just hurrying off. So I shouted and he stopped, and didn't know whether to run off or not, and suddenly I knew it was him. I was just going to ask him, you see, if he'd *seen* anybody. But he stopped, and I ran across to him, and I asked if he'd seen where the passport went. So he looked angry, and said, in a bit of English, "You accuse I steal your passport?" There was a crowd all round, and I could see they were angry at me, not him. So I said I just wanted him to come back to the bank and tell them whether he'd seen anything. He got so angry, and waved his arms, and I didn't know what to do. Suppose it wasn't him?'

'What happened to the passport?' demanded Boyle. 'We've got to have a passport.'

'Yes, I know; that's what was so awful. It's like stealing a bit of *you*. And I wondered whether we could get home, even, without it. I was so upset; I was crying, and all these people around, looking at me, but not really caring at all. And then suddenly he just put his hand in his back pocket and took out the passport and gave it to me. And then he ran off.'

'You've got it?'

'Yes, it's here. But it's such a thing to *happen*. Why take a passport? It's yours and mine. It's no use to anyone else. It's all so strange; I could hardly believe it. I stood there with my mouth open and watched him run away. And the crowd just disappeared. I didn't even go back into the bank, I just came here and you were asleep and I didn't feel right until you woke up.'

'They smuggle people into England with them,' said Boyle. 'An English passport fetches a high price here. But everything's all right now.'

'You weren't there,' said Jenny, 'it happened to me and it *isn't* all right now. I never want to go out alone again here.'

'Never mind,' said Boyle firmly, 'we'll soon be gone.' He knew that tomorrow Jenny would probably change her mind, so artless was she; it was a good thing that the incident had happened.

BUT TWO DAYS LATER, when the Fergusons came to collect them for the drive down to Positano, Boyle was worse. It was a simple stomach disorder, and he shouldn't have been; yet he was. Moreover, he felt himself beginning to enjoy his illness. He couldn't have said in what his contentment lay, nor how it was that he could attain such peace in such a state of acute personal discomfort, and in a city he detested. He was cut off; but he was coddled. Jenny waited on him. She thought first of him. The room was theirs; they were closed up in it, and though the city turmoiled around them, it was adequate enough as a background, its mood, like his own state, sweaty and soured and warm.

Ferguson had been very good, visiting daily, going to the chemist, having Jenny back to dinner. Of course Jenny had been thrown with Lena, especially as she hated to go into the city alone; but he was sure that he was always in Jenny's mind. And even now, when it was time to go and he could not go, he couldn't seem to care very much. He had Jenny back, at least. The Fergusons had come now, and Jenny had let them in; Ferguson stood awkwardly at the foot of the bed. He said how sorry he was that the Boyles would not be coming. Lena sat in a chair, looking arrogantly about her, and Boyle realized that she was annoyed. The Boyles' plans had become involved with her plans, and she did not brook interference in them. Now her irritation broke through; she said to Boyle: 'I don't know why you don't let Jenny come down with us, and then follow when you're ready.'

'Oh, I can't,' said Jenny, 'who'd look after him?'

'The people in the hotel, if you paid them to.'

'He'd be so miserable.'

'Well, so would you, cooped up here with him all the time.' She stood up, tall and strong-featured, and came over to the foot of the bed. Boyle had to admire her assurance, even though he found it contemptible. 'How ill are you?' she asked.

'I don't know,' said Boyle.

'Oh, really,' said Lena impatiently, 'you must know. You're the one who's ill, aren't you?'

'It seems to be some sort of dysentery,' said Jenny.

'But he's nearly better, isn't he? It's Continental tummy. I've had it before. It's nothing very much. He just has to keep going to the lavatory.'

'You know I have to stay,' said Jenny.

'Well, he's not going to die, is he?' asked Lena. 'I mean, he'll survive if you leave him, won't he?'

'He needs looking after,' said Jenny.

'Oh, *go*,' said Boyle, 'yes, go, go.'

Jenny looked at him as if she understood the impatience and the self-spite that lay behind his cry. He knew she would not go; he trusted in it. Perhaps then she saw this assurance too. She looked oddly at him; she had seen something else in his remark; she looked, and turned, and then to Lena, quite casually, she said: 'All right, then, I'll go. I'll arrange with the hotel about doctoring him and feeding him. They can send me a telegram if he's not all right. He'll come down by train in a day or two.'

HE KNEW, of course, that she would come back. She would realize that he spoke out of illness, and that he was not well enough to be left alone. He lay in bed and waited. The sun filled the room, though the shutters were closed; it seemed to enter his throat, and he coughed. She couldn't leave him. He had nothing. He couldn't even speak Italian. He couldn't get to the station. He couldn't live without her; she had always been an essential functionary in his life. He felt hideously unguarded. The whole illness, which at first had seemed to him one face of his sensitivity, now seemed a weakness. The human body was a self-destructive organism which committed gradual suicide, now collapsing at one point, now another. It could not bear the weight of being Boyle. Yet perhaps he had betrayed it himself, had let it fade, had kept it too highly sensitized to live in the world. The very sensitivity on which he had prided himself now seemed a hideous curse. How should he escape from here? The journey from the room to the station would be fraught with pitfalls, encounters with cheating taxi drivers, with luggage-stealing porters, with youths like the one on the street the other day. Jenny had once told him that he was simply not strong enough to be as sensitive as he was; the remark, which had formerly appeared amusing, now appeared simply true. She had judged him, before he was ready to be judged, before he had achieved anything. He had not yet justified his way of life. He had lived as if isolation itself were a merit, but he had yet to show why. In doing that he had depended on her for ceaseless acts of generosity, and she had to be shown why. The strange thing was that she was not by nature generous-spirited; she was tense and withdrawn and gave nothing easily. Yet giving had been her role; she had fallen in with this until now, perhaps, it had been too much to bear.

'Come back,' he begged into the air, 'come back.' But she did not come. At noon a waiter came in with a meal. He brought it on a tray, quite silently, and departed without a word being spoken. He knew she had really gone and, as he lay there, and as he thought about her somewhere away on the road, sitting in the car, laughing with the Fergusons, her hair blown back in the draught of the open windows, he began to cry.

He had not thought of her as a resolute woman, not since

their courtship. Then she had been resolute in the irresolution; he had begged her to marry him, advanced all kinds of convincing arguments, and she had said: 'I have to know first.' It was her parents who had broken her, by their dislike of him. She always had a special kind of self-possession, of disdain, of hauteur, the assurance of a much-sought lovely young woman. She administered all kinds of unexpected checks and coldnesses, of a kind that the less well-favoured woman does not have; so much beauty can be a restriction to a fullness of life. Jenny would sit on trains or buses without letting her glance move one way or another, carefully diminishing her faculties, never for a moment unguarded or relaxed. Yet this callousness seemed to fade after their marriage. At that time it had seemed a challenge; if one could break down this permanent resistance, what a hero one would be. It had faded very simply . . . so he believed, or perhaps he had grown used to it, and their relationship had never been any more fulfilled than in those hopeless-seeming days before the wedding.

She was not coming back. It was afternoon; the sun had moved round. He was trapped here, locked in by illness. He would die without her. He could not stir. He was getting worse. If he got out of bed and tried to leave the hotel he would surely collapse; he would die in the streets. Yet how could he stay here? The city was hostile to him. He was alone.

A little later the doctor came in. Once more his business was conducted in silence. Then once more he was alone. The whole business of illness − the constant noise grinding in the head, the heat in the throat, the sweat on the body, the flies in the air, the hideous business of being cut off from one's homeland, the suppositories with which the doctor had taken his temperature − was all terrible to him. To be the sort of man Boyle believed himself to be one required an extraordinary strength. And he was not. He could not live alone; he could find nothing in the foreign air to sustain him. Like the Roman culture, living on in a void, Boyle's own culture seemed now useless to him. Like Jenny it had proved fleeting when the test came. For a while you can hang on, splendidly uncorrupted, while the others sell out around you; their selling out gives you the strength to carry on. There is a pleasure in feeling oneself to be out of the mainstream. For a time the things one wants and respects are nearer, then the capacity for enjoyment fades. The saddening process begins; stamina can fail inside one's independence as well as outside it. So . . . who had betrayed whom?

IT MUST, by now, be late afternoon. Boyle got unsteadily out of bed and reached the window. He threw open the shutters. The agonizing heat struck him with an unexpected violence. The white walls of the room shone, and the flies buzzed in the air. He could see across roofs and trees to a bronzed cupola, somewhere in Rome. The heat struck him harder; he got back into bed and lay there in a hot sweat. The sun beat directly down on his head and face and on his curdled body. There was a white wall and a little crucifix facing him. He saw it hazily as the sun's glow corrupted the clarity of his vision.

And then, outside in the corridor, he heard footsteps. They were the steps of a light, female foot. It was, he felt sure, Jenny. She had come back as he had known, all along, that she would. After all, she did owe it to him. But the footsteps went by and faded away. He fell into fitful sleep; and every time he woke, he seemed to hear them again.

IN PRAISE OF GRAMMAR SCHOOLS

In 1944, I was a short-trousered pupil at a depressed bomb-threatened elementary school in Nottingham. That year, the Butler Education Act – a piece of social planning that looked forward to the brave new world after the War – came onstream. A new examination suddenly appeared in front of us, the 11-plus. I sat it, and passed. While a portion of my fellow pupils went hopefully off to the secondary modern, I was one of the select band who was awarded a new free place at the local grammar school.

It was an amazing piece of fortune, which shaped and changed my whole life. I'd become a 'scholarship boy' – a postwar social type famously depicted in 1957 in Richard Hoggart's influential book *The Uses of Literacy*. Hoggart gives a vivid portrait of a new generation of young people plucked by their brains and their new educational opportunities from the warm soil of their working-class roots.

His scholarship boy is a pretty sad figure. He 'probably pushes himself harder than he should,' Hoggart says gloomily, 'He begins to see life as a series of hurdle-jumps . . . He loses something of the gamin's resilience and carelessness.' These sudden beneficiaries of Butler no longer knew where they fitted in society, and you could recognize them anywhere 'by their lack of poise, by their uncertainty'.

Maybe. It didn't feel like that. The grammar schools were undoubtedly part of a large social revolution that changed the postwar world, and social and family relations too. Today, now grammar schools are back on the educational agenda, they are generally seen as ancient and historic (in other words very old-fashioned) institutions. Certainly they've been part of British education for a very long time, and Shakespeare, we know, went to one.

But their heyday came in the twenty years after World War Two, when the Butler Act deliberately changed the whole landscape of opportunity, making these once fee-charging institutions into places for academic pupils of any background, as long as they passed the exams. Old grammar schools were changed and expanded, new ones built. My own school, for instance, was no long-established institution with tall elms over the cricket pitch and a proud academic history. It was a modest, modern suburban school erected just before the outbreak of war.

The grammar schools were unashamedly 'selective': schools for academic pupils. Their great achievement was to bring ideas, books, intellectual concerns, wider human horizons to a socially wide-ranging group of young people who in previous generations would not have had access to them. I was typical enough. My own parents, of working-class background, both left school at fourteen, my father to be an office clerk, my mother a typist. By the War's end, according to the class rankings that obsessed the period, they would have been called 'lower middle class'.

My family were not at all educated or bookish. But they did firmly respect education – most of all, I suppose, because it helped in life's greatest problem, which was 'getting on'. They were in no position to support me through a fee-paid education, and could never have thought of it. The free places in the Butler Act came for me just at the right time.

From the moment I appeared, in second-hand uniform, at the grammar school, I knew I'd been transferred into a world I liked. Unlike most of my very physical unacademic friends from elementary school, I'd already developed a love of books, and that now prospered into a love of art, of history, of ideas in general. I spent long hours in the school library during games periods, digesting everything I could find.

In the late forties there were no teenagers, no adolescent

peer groups, no youth culture. I liked teachers, liked being taught. Like many others in my generation, I got my life's horizons from my time at school. There was, by luck, a fine English teacher, another for Latin. I happily acquired a classical education in grammar and languages, a commitment to the literary tradition and to humanist ideas and to the word – which is, I suppose, what grammar schools have traditionally been about.

By around the age of twelve, I'd already picked my role in life. I would be a writer. This meant less than nothing to my family, who thought of writing as some obscure and privileged profession for an idle elite. It was a totally non-registered job, unpaid and pensionless. It built no roads or bridges, and didn't help put the Sunday roast on the table. It was the dangerous product of far too much reading and not enough exercise, and the school was to blame.

To make matters worse, it seemed that once grammar school education started, it never stopped. There were, of course, more exams. At fifteen I took School Certificate, the precursor of O-level, raising my parents' hopes that I would now leave school and start doing something useful and wage-earning instead. But after the results appeared, the headmaster summoned my father and told him that three more years in the sixth form now looked like a good idea.

My father, a suspicious man, understood everything perfectly. It was clear to him that, while he was expected to keep me in idleness, the headmaster was well rewarded by the government for each pupil he managed to detain in his hands. After long negotiations, a bargain was struck. I could have two years in the sixth form, not three – meaning I would not enter the scholarship sixth, which took the entrance examinations for Oxford and Cambridge.

Two years on the headmaster summoned my father again. I had now passed Higher School Certificate, the A-level of the day. There was the weird prospect of even more education ahead: the university. With the headmaster's aid, a local-authority grant was secured for me, and I went: not to the dreaming spires of Oxford and Cambridge, but to one of the redbricks which, now expanded, were waiting to pluck their fruit from the grammar-school tree.

Starting as a scholarship boy, I now turned into another basic fifties type: the first-generation student thrown amazed into the world of learning, the redbrick 'meritocrat'. University – this even included the small Midlands university college I went to – proved even more of a wonderland. I duly became a model young intellectual, read Jean-Paul Sartre and Beckett, started a novel, and wrote for newspapers and magazines. I have been a writer ever since, and also spent most of my days in academic life.

Not that I expected to. Like those at the small grammar schools, redbrick students (we were not even called undergraduates) were not really expected to nurture great ambitions. We didn't think ahead to jobs in the civil service, diplomacy, banking or the upper slopes of business. We knew who would get those. We expected to be teachers, minor executives, journalists or workers in the world of the media.

But the meritocrats too had their heyday. They found their voice, in the Angry Young Man literature of the fifties. With education expanding, they won employment in schools, adult education, the new universities. The media too were expanding, and they found their place in that too, not least in the new socially conscious theatre of the sixties and seventies.

Their influence had a strong effect on the character of postwar British culture. The high-mindedness of postwar British institutions – schools, universities, the BBC, the theatre – owes much to them. In the age of market-led mass culture, they had been nurtured in ideas of quality and standards, of the humanizing function of the arts. The 'social responsibility' aspect of British broadcasting and media, now much challenged but not totally gone, was largely shaped in those years, often by the ex-pupils of the grammar schools.

By the sixties, the complaint against these schools was growing. They were thought divisive and elitist. In a sense they were, though it had not seemed like that at the time. It was simply that, as in most countries, academic pupils went in one direction, the non-academic and practical in another. Grammar-school pupils generally regarded their friends who went to secondary modern school with a kind of envy. They didn't do hours of homework, stood on the street corners, got the girls, went more quickly into real life. Those who proved 'academic' were generally upped later into the grammar schools.

The sixties solution was, of course, 'comprehensive' education, another new revolution. Comprehensive schools were designed for the equalization of opportunity and a common social mix, and, as a matter of justice, this had obvious appeal. But the stated aim of bringing the advantages of grammar-school education to an entire age group, rather than a selected twenty or so per cent, soon proved to mean fundamental change in the nature of the education itself.

So did the fact that the move to mass secondary schooling coincided with the emergence of the teenager and the dominance of the peer group. School culture transformed. Schools grew pupil-centred, and all selection was distrusted as 'elitist'. New educational theory emphasized equalization of opportunities for all – often irrespective of the needs, and the social and cultural contribution, of the top twenty per cent. Above all, the awe and respect for education and ideas so important to grammar-school culture began to dissolve.

Today the 'selection' debate has resumed, in the wake of the growing discovery that a totally permissive egalitarian notion of secondary education doesn't always produce the talent, energy, intellectual achievement or cultural ambitiousness a society needs. There will always be better and worse pupils, those who are 'academic' and those not, those exhilarated by ideas and pulled by artistic or scientific aspiration and those who, for whatever reason or disadvantage, will have nothing to do with such things.

Education is always a sensitive issue – but at the heart of it there has to be, as a priority, a love of ideas, a value for abstract thinking, a care for words. There will always be pupils who 'selectively' want and deserve that, just as there will always be parents who desire it for their children; they should be able to find the schools to serve them. Giving our children a good education is one of the greatest services we can do them, not simply to improve their social chances, but to enrich their minds and lives.

The grammar schools of the world after 1945 were a great educational ideal that, for honourable reasons, was let go. They can never come back as they were. Our society has changed profoundly, not least in its attitudes toward culture, education, ideas, the nature of teenage experience. But their commitment to standards, ideas, education for its own sake, is a heritage we can't afford to lose.

DEARING UP THE CAMPUS

As THE FIFTIES STARTED, I set off for university: a modest provincial redbrick university college, awarding an external London degree. No one in my family had ever been near such a place before, and I had little idea of what it might be. I was one of a brand-new generation of postwar meritocrats, scholarship boys and girls for whom the doors of higher education had suddenly opened. It was a mysterious, wonderful experience, and led on to a lifetime that's been mostly spent inside those suddenly opening doors.

The shock, social and intellectual, was enough to stir me into writing fiction. The academic novel – which was so in vogue from the fifties to the seventies, and to which I've contributed my own share – partly made its mark by social comedy and satire. But in truth it was an exploration and celebration of what was publicly seen as a major cultural change – a quiet welfare state revolution that transformed the class mix, career prospects, intellectual horizons and world view of an admittedly select cadre of the young in postwar Britain.

The key fact of this revolution was that, for a good many of us with less than wealthy parents, it was free. In exchange for my hard-won exam results, a generous state – the local authority in alliance with government funding – paid for my tuition, and topped it up with a grant for my termly survival. Since my parents could not afford to contribute, the funds I received – my precious grant – were quite remarkably modest. I couldn't afford to drink, smoke or date. I managed the cinema a couple of times a term; theatre or a trip to London were annual events. The number of books I bought each term had to be rationed severely.

It didn't matter. These were the austerity fifties. Teenage spending hadn't begun. Nor had teenage itself. The important fact was access to learning. Universities in those days were perceived as high-minded, independent, critical institutions, as were the libraries and the BBC. To be admitted as a student was to become a prospective intellectual, the product of a selective university system that was at the time considered probably the best in the world. It taught mostly by tutorial, standards of entrance and exit were high; a three-year degree in Britain was worth a four- or five- one anywhere else.

The British system – elite institutions plus free tuition – was distinctive, as I discovered when, in the mid-fifties, I won a (free) postgraduate scholarship to the USA, the great destination of the day. The American system was not free. On American campuses students paid their tuition, often by working their way through college (virtually unheard of then in Britain). Fees themselves varied greatly: from the expensive, prestigious Ivy League colleges to the huge, ever-expanding state universities, which had lowered fees and scholarships for in-state students.

This was a very different system. It was in fact mass higher education, which America had pioneered in the nineteenth century and was now massively expanding in a time of post-war affluence and global power. College fees had to be paid, but higher education was highly accessible: walk-in-the-door entrance standards, constant expansion of places and subjects, flexible user-friendly ways of accumulating credits toward degrees. The degrees themselves were flexible too. A BA in law or comparative literature from Harvard was – as any American knows to this day – just not the same thing as a BA in skin-diving or driver education from Florida State.

In 1960s Britain the Robbins Report was published, recommending a fresh expansion of higher education. Six new universities were built, the teaching of new subjects encouraged, and grants even improved. At the time all this was seen as yet another fundamental revolution, probably a dangerous step towards mass higher education of the American type. More means worse, pronounced Kingsley Amis; more students and universities will produce lower academic standards.

In fact the new universities brought in much academic innovation, a variety of new subjects, syllabuses and teaching methods; but they still maintained the elite, selective, highly personal nature of British higher education. They also became smart and trendy places to be, competing with Oxbridge in the academic stakes. Around 1968 they also became rather radical places. The student revolutions that swept America and Europe found a special home in those pristine, architect-designed citadels, which today are beginning to show the signs of age and even a certain grey-haired traditionalism on their various fine greenfield sites.

The biggest changes to the British system came a little later. They started with the development, in 1969, of the Open University, with its flexible credits, distanced learning, wide age-mix of students, use of media technologies. What seemed a useful supplement to the 'real' university system, comparable to the development of adult-education departments in older universities, became in reality a new type of further education, with powerful implications for the existing institutions. If a university didn't need residential places, regular tutorials, long vacations for study and research, colleges, gowns, senior common rooms and such rituals, what else might it become?

The bitter answer came with the famous Thatcherite 'cuts' of the 1980s. They struck not just at the basic funding of universities, but their very sense of function. For nearly half a century, universities had managed to sustain the illusion that they could be dependent on government funding, yet be critically independent of government policies and planning. When Oxford University refused Mrs Thatcher her traditional honorary degree, that sense of lost independence was, very largely, what the Revolt of the Dons was about.

Over the remainder of the eighties, the transformation in British universities was to grow fast. The quiet political consensus that the campuses of Britain could be state-funded but left alone to run their own enlightened, disinterested affairs was increasingly challenged and broken. Funding was no longer guaranteed for five-year periods. Established institutional reputations were no longer honoured. Universities were no longer perceived as cultural citadels but state institutions like hospitals or prisons, and just as troublingly expensive to the national purse.

Universities were pressured to teach more cheaply, accept more students this year, cut them back the next. They were asked to find commercial sponsorship, develop practical, 'relevant' subjects, sell their courses, subject themselves to business practice and management review. Modular systems appeared, allowing courses to be examined internally and completed for credit. There was talk of the accelerated two-year degree, with teaching in the summer (most countries still have four-year degrees).

Professors – once appointed to profess their subjects – became processors. They managed forms, research reviews, staff appraisals, teaching-quality assessments. Tutorials faded into huge lectures. Lecturers faded into onscreen videos, as their duties were demanded elsewhere. Subjects that were once the material of ironic academic jokes became part of the syllabus. If courses were not being judged for commercial applicability, they were tested for ideological topicality.

The largest change has come in the nineties. With the mass upgrading of polytechnics and a variety of other institutions of higher or further education into universities, the number of degree-awarding institutions has been doubled at a stroke. Britain has now entered the age of mass higher (or further) education. The proportion of the age group now in institutions called universities is comparable to that in most other countries of the world. And Britain is now going through some of the same campus crises of standards and academic confidence we've seen over recent years in Italy, France, Germany and elsewhere.

The change has passed without public fuss, almost unnoticed in popular folklore: unlike the emergence of the meritocrats in the postwar years. The seismic upheavals that follow – problems of maintaining the level of academic standards, the value of the BA, of sufficient funding for research and teaching, of the fast-emerging distinction between the better, research-oriented universities and the degree mills – are a major part of the problems Dearing is now seeking to address.

The fact is British universities are in considerable trouble. They have been pushed into undertaking a major academic revolution – the largest of the century – without any release of massive funds to pay for it. University vice-chancellors, university teachers, do not want to see their students paying for tuition. But the cost of the vast increase of those in university education has to be paid for. And the obligation on universities remains to sustain quality and standards as best they can.

Meanwhile the role of student has changed too. When I went to college, I was, without quite knowing it, the beneficiary of a generous welfare state. I saw it differently. The university represented the nation's high valuation of disinterested intellectual and cultural activity, its belief in standards and in abstract ideas. The modern student will become the consumer. Investing in education, he or she will demand the reward: a degree, a valid relevant training, the acquisition of professional skills, courses to order. And universities will have to compete with each other for intellectual and scholarly survival, striving to maintain standards in the world of ever more open access, and constantly declining cash.

UNDER THE DOME

IT WAS IN 1953 THAT, after a great taking-up of references and a rigorous examination from the superintendents, I first acquired one of the most precious badges to which a young writer and would-be academic could aspire. I was granted a reader's ticket to the Round Reading Room of the British Museum. For several years after, I became a daily habitué of what, for me and many others, was the most literary and scholarly spot in the world.

It lay, of course, in the heart of Bloomsbury, a postal district that still, in the Angry Fifties, kept much of its old aura. 'I ask nothing better than all reviewers, for ever, and everywhere, should call me a highbrow,' Virginia Woolf once wrote in a letter, 'If they like to add Bloomsbury, WC1, that is the correct postal address . . . But if your reviewer . . . dares hint that I live in South Kensington, I will sue him for libel.'

By the 1950s, Woolf had gone. So had some of the associations. Houses she had had in nearby Georgian squares were shattered by bombing; some were being monstrously rebuilt as hotels or flats. Still, the area round the Museum and the Senate House hung mistily on to its strong literary associations. T. S. Eliot, whose magazine the *Criterion* had carried much of British literary modernism, still worked as a publisher in Faber and Faber, over on the corner of Russell Square.

Great Russell Street remained packed with small publishers, odd bookshops and printshops, and the wet, dingy pubs and teashops were crowded with writers and would-bes who casually survived on casual reviewing, or were about to start up some new, hideously underfunded magazine or poetry imprint. Postwar Bloomsbury still remained a literary district; the Round Reading Room, with its great spoked desks, still remained its hub.

The regular users were the freelance writers and academics, casual researchers and makers of arguments, for whom it was the dry spot in a wet London, the sanctum of sanctums, the heartland of books. Though solemnly guarded and protected from careless intrusion, the great book-lined room was somehow always open to bohemia. It was filled with random eccentrics with theories about the key to all knowledge, to theosophists and Gurdjieffians, Talmudic scholars and decoders of the meanings of Nostradamus.

It was the sum of literariness, the condition to which I aspired. As Britain's great library of deposit it (or its outlying colonies and dependencies, like the newspaper library at Colindale) held the stock of everything. Or not quite: the bombing had depleted it too. The great catalogue, painfully stuck together with paste by human hand, showed the wartime depredations, which the keepers were now trying to restore.

I was, as it happened, working on a history of the modern British literary periodicals. Many of them had been born in Bloomsbury, some created by editors – like Eliot himself, or John Lehmann or Cyril Connolly – one could still meet about the premises. Literary periodicals are writing's living edge; they are where the interesting new writers and the powerful new movements generally show up first. Imagism and Vorticism had begun here, just round the corner. The Rebel Art Centre and the Poetry Bookshop had been just a stone's throw away.

Writing, as everyone knows, had long flourished under the 140-foot dome. That meant not just Karl Marx writing *Das Kapital*, or Virginia Woolf researching her reviews. Poems and short stories were still habitually worked out during the long morning wait for books. With a peculiar appropriateness, the Deputy Superintendent who surveyed the doings of the gathered scholars and eccentrics from his glass cage was Angus

Wilson – whose high-pitched administrative voice resounded round the silent room, and who was writing there himself.

I wrote poetry and fiction there, and even fell in love. It was with Jean Rook, who records her own thesis-writing experience in her autobiography *The Cowardly Lioness*. 'Eight hours a day in the British Museum is a killer, unless you're a mummy,' she notes, adding that the chief relief was to escape to the music room with the present writer, who was (as she reminds me) writing his first novel down at desk D4.

For my fifties generation, the BM was home to many novels, and some of them did explicit homage to the hallowed room. Margaret Drabble wrote vividly of working there. So did David Lodge in *The British Museum Is Falling Down*, a novel richly filled with epigraphs from the many previous writers who had written in what has rightly been called 'the favourite working space in the world'.

Given the multiplication of publishing, it was inevitable that one day the Reading Room would outgrow itself, and a new, dedicated British Library be built. It has not been an edifying tale; and the departure of books, scholars and writers from Great Russell Street to St Pancras has been about as emotionless and unpassionate as the new, unromantic building itself.

Worse still, though, is the planned future of the Round Reading Room. I am unhappy to say it, since the architect is Norman Foster, whose work I profoundly admire. Yet the world's most bookish space is to be robbed of its bookishness. It will be re-incorporated into the British Museum itself. Some of the great iron stacks which are essential to its atmosphere will be removed; the great open space will be divided by a glass screen.

Looked at abstractly, we can say that what's happening to the Round Reading Room is a metaphor for a kind of bookishness we have come to dispense with. It will be appropriately deconstructed into a new room of glass walls and computers. As one of the Trustees puts it, its main function as 'a centre of information will be unchanged, although it will use the latest technology.'

The reading room was never a 'centre of information'; it was a great place of writing and scholarship. What we are deconstructing is an entire history of literariness. Taking one of the greatest human spaces ever devised for imagination and enquiry, we are robbing it of its meaning.

TIME CALLED WHILE
YOU WERE OUT

THESE DAYS, I SUPPOSE, I am one of the more high-minded
sorts of writer – ever ready to advise a close friend on experimental paragraphing, or lecture any passing journalist on the
meaning of art, the confusion of life, the promise of literature,
the future of the novel, the nature of the liberal dilemma
on the horns of which we now, rather uncomfortably, sit, and
other matters of like weight and moment. I write more or less
what I like. What I write I believe in. And give or take an
editor's intervention, or two, or three, the way I wrote it and
meant it is the way you get it. But I have done my share on
the downside of writing, sweated on the hard rock face where
most writers have been tested at one time or another. The
youngsters don't realize it now, but in my early days writing
was tough, really tough. We had to rise at four, wash in cold
water, stoke the furnace and then work on hard, heavy manual
typewriters that brought the blisters out on your hands, for
all hours God sent. Lunch was bread and dripping, and the
reviewers used to come and lash us every single day, one thing
that has somehow not changed since.

I am reminded of all this by a letter I got the other day
from some young writer who was in a considerable lather
because someone had approached him and asked him to, well,
'collaborate'. The idea of co-authorship appalled him, he said,
though his publisher was all in favour, pointing out how well
such things had gone in the past: Beaumont and Fletcher,
Gilbert and Sullivan, Masters and Johnson, Morecambe and

Wise. Would I guide him through the morass? Naturally I understood his nervousness, and tried to think of a way of dissipating his worries. Would it be enough to remind him that in my young day, when writing was 'ard, really 'ard, we had to collaborate all the time? But then so had some of the French during the war. No, better to tell him a little tale – the tale of the time when, once, I was Nathalie Pelham Barker.

Dear Young Writer,

Thank you for your letter, asking whether I would ever consider collaborating on a work of literature. The truth is not only that I would, but I have. From the experience I learned a number of lessons, about how to do it, where to do it, why to do it, and when to stop. Whether the story will be helpful to you I am not sure, but I can assure you that apart from an odd graduate course on *The Last Duchess* or two, the process taught me a good part of what I think I know about life and literature. The tale takes us some way back in time, back to my early literary youth. For like many young people I was determined from an early age to be a writer. I didn't know what it would be like, I didn't know what I would write about, and nothing much had happened to me. But the dedication was there, and somehow it led me into academic life, where I duly became a research student, desperately trying to reconcile art and scholarship. It was not surprising that this quest led me onto the campuses of American universities, where this kind of double life is more common and more readily accepted. As you know, British universities do accept and study writers, but with one stern proviso I was not prepared to accept: they must be dead first. American universities seem to have the opposite attitude, filling their campuses with errant poets and wandering novelists, who write their work in one room and teach it in the next, so short-circuiting many of the problems of reaching an audience.

So, for much of the Fifties, if you wanted me you were likely to find me on some American campus or other, where the double business of my life seemed to fit in best. It was not just that

American universities were very tolerant of writers, but that among the friends I had there – most of them brilliant fellow-graduate students, fresh from doing PhD at Columbia – literary ambitions ran rife. All of them seemed to be planning Great American Novels that were even Greater than the Great American Novels they were teaching in class, or if they were not doing that they were planning the Great American Screenplay, which meant lowering your standards slightly, but paid a lot better. There were, as I say, many of us, far more, to tell the truth, than the world of letters could bear. But with one of these writers, a young man from Philadelphia called Barry Spacks, I struck up a particular friendship, forged through working together in editing the campus literary quarterly, a journal called *Folio*, where articles on Christian imagery in *The Red Badge of Courage* jostled for recognition side by side with the literary outpourings of our friends.

Both of us had the highest literary ambitions. I was determined to compete with Saul Bellow on his own terms, while Spacks was resolved to dominate the world of poetry and pick up the mantle so carelessly cast down by Ezra Pound. We shared that in common, but also something else, called penury. The problem is common among the literary fraternity, though we couldn't afford the fees to join even that. Nonetheless, Spacks was a man of great resource, and was determined to finance his talent through engaging in various avant-garde commercial enterprises. It was Spacks, for example, who with characteristic Tom Swift cunning invented the first gramophone record that could be used as the lid of spaghetti cans in supermarkets, so providing pasta and the Pastoral Symphony at one go. Due to lack of venture capital, it got nowhere, and as far as I know the idea, even more suited to the compact disc, has yet to be tried. It was Spacks, I recall, who first thought of the Dial-A-Poem service, where you called Bell Telephone and got a breathless voice on the line reciting *The Waste Land* at you, a fine and worthy idea, though not necessarily what you want when you are actually trying to get a taxi.

Spacks was also a great literary innovator, determined to gather great writers around him and transform the literary scene once and for all. He was constantly planning new literary magazines, which had titles like *Transmogrifications* and *The Better Mousetrap*, and then, picking up the telephone, he would begin hunting out gullible patrons to finance them – though these, alas, proved curiously difficult to find in the cornfields of Indiana, where we happened to be at the time. Nonetheless, we were not dismayed. Our literary friendship prospered, our ventures multiplied, we wrote articles of high critical moment together, and there was a feeling of promise in the air – a bit like that in Paris just before the coming of cubism. And it was with a feeling of tragedy and creative loss that, at the end of the year, we separated, Spacks to make his way to some new American campus, and I to return to Britain, my grant exhausted, to spend the next year overhauling my thesis and making a very indigent living teaching the odd evening class on Montherlant to anyone who was interested, and few, it proved, were.

It was one day the following summer when my telephone, or rather my landlady's, rang. I picked up the machine and a voice vibrant with American enthusiasm greeted me at the other end. It was, of course, Spacks. For a year he had put his literary invention to the best of uses, writing applications for travelling fellowships to be held at British universities. Now he had won one, and was on his way to Cambridge, no less, to write, of course, a thesis. He bade me come to London at once, and show him the literary scene, and we spent a happy few days looking for it, not realizing then that the British literary scene usually lives in the south of France or Tuscany. Spacks had not lost his zest, and made it his custom to accost strangers in pubs and ask them to finance a new literary magazine. I think we raised three-and-fourpence that way, a large sum in those days, though the magazine itself never transpired, largely because other matters attracted our attention.

It happened, I recall, on the fustian seating of the British Railways train to Cambridge – for term now beckoned, and it was time for Spacks to be on his way. He asked me to go along with him, to carry his box files, packed with manuscripts, his two portable typewriters and a few suitcases full of British sports jackets, for which he had a particular taste. Determined to come to terms, once and for all, with the British literary scene, Spacks

Thus at once he invented both the principle of bathroom tissue and the basis of modern computing; if, today, there is a hi-tech marvel known as the 'Cambridge phenomenon' which has made that fenland city into the British Silicon Valley, you now know just who to thank for that. More awesome still was the distribution system he devised to deal with our product. For, at the end of the first week, we halted to reflect on our progress, and discovered that there on a table in a corner sat fifty completed stories, ready for submission. Suddenly we were stuck with the dismaying revelation that, if we maintained production at this place, and there seemed little reason why we should not, we would have, by the end of the academic year, something like 2,500 stories, a formidable prospect even for a Charles Dickens. It was true that the supply of magazines appeared plentiful, if not endless, but the thought that they would fill their pages with all the products of our joint byline seemed improbable.

Then there was another worry, as it occurred to both of us that, if our thesis-advisers chanced into the popular corners of the media and found them filled with stories of the type of our very early 'The Stain of Guilt' ('Sergeant Philpott was a sanguine man, but today he was worried. The case seemed an open-and-shut one. Except for one worrying thing. The stain, the small red stain, on Joe Harrison's horny hand'), they might wonder about our academic competence. Indeed it might damage altogether the credibility of the work on 'Chistian Imagery in the Koran' with which Spacks hoped to become the toast of the Cambridge colleges. Nonetheless academic life itself suggested the solution, Many a great don has written stories under a nom de plume, and there was no reason why two young research students should be any different. So, retiring to the newest hostelry we had discovered, we devoted the evening to devising, not plots, but a gallery of pseudonyms, various enough to prevent editors from feeling that they were overwhelmed from one single gushing creative source, well-flavoured enough to be associated with very different types of work – for the fact is that we were devotees of all the genres, from the most rugged of detective stories to the most sensitive kinds of romance.

So, that night in a pub by the river, there was born our stable of authors, and a varied and fascinating group of talents they were. There was, for instance, Norman Blood, whom we came to imagine, as time went by, as a rather sweat-stained fellow, in late middle age, and definitely running to seed, though his rather sleazy detective stories about the mean streets of London and Los Angeles suggested a decidely feisty past. He was evidently quite unlike the open-air, sports-loving Millingham Harshly, whose name came, in fact, from the conclusion of one of Blood's own earliest and finest creations, 'The Gorilla That Cried', which ended with the notable last line: ' "He was merciless. Well, the law, too, can be merciless in its own way," said Inspector Millingham, harshly.' Millingham Harshly, evidently widely travelled, stocky and a little grizzled about the ears, wrote powerful tales of distant, exotic, Bessarabian adventure that thrilled even us as we thought his stuff up over crisps in the Baron of Beef ('There are parts of the desert that few men have known. Towards one of them, as the terrible desert wind called the muezzin dashed sand into their faces, there steadfastedly marched a small, brave band of foot-weary legionnaires . . .'). But even Harshly lacked the suave, knowing charm of Peter Eton, the famed clubland dilettante, with his thin, hairline moustache, his red-silk lined cloak and his talent for tales of upmarket romance in an ambiance of adventure, gambling and espionage ('He was walking through the cocktail bar at the Morocco Club, a silk scarf knotted carelessly into the neck of his expensive Pierre Cardin shirt, when Corinne looked up from the roulette table and caught his eye for the first time').

It was not hard to imagine Peter as the darling of the women who also shared our literary stabling. Certainly he would appeal to the sweet, romantic heart of Faith Simple, matronly and sympathetic, with greying hair, a large bosom and tea-cosies over her teapots, who wrote tales of romantic life among typists ('It took me a year to get over John'). Possibly he got on somewhat less well with Barbara Bingley, whose sad and seamy life came authentically out of the narratives she told of rise from northern poverty to blue-rinsed success ('There was nothing to eat that Christmas when I discovered I was adopted and an orphan'), and who probably rather preferred Millingham Harshly. It was hard to imagine any of them getting on well with Norman Blood, and there were moments when we ourselves found we were liking some of our authors more than others. Happily there was one of them that no one could fail to take to. Indeed it seemed unlikely that our little creative family would have survived at all had it not been for Nathalie Barker – or Nathalie Pelham Barker, as she would later become when her, and our, circumstances changed.

What can we say about Nathalie? A petite brunette with brown eyes and an excellent taste in clothes, she was author of such touching tales of female romance as 'A Kiss in Time!', 'Just for You!' and 'Don't Let Him Get Away!' – tales filled with girls running across heaths with hair blowing in the wind, handsome architects of thirty-five left widower with a small child of five and a droptop Mercedes and an unusually vast number of loose exclamation marks. Yet she was the one who was the hub of our rather large household – a household that began to worry our postman, as his sack grew heavier by the week. 'I don't understand how you fit all these people into this little flat,' he would say suspiciously as he handed over a great pile of self-addressed envelopes that bore the names of Norm and Jack and Mill, Peter and Faith, Barbie and Nattie, as we came to call them. But there was no doubt it was Nathalie who held us together – Nathalie with her winsome ways, Nathalie who never lost faith, even in the dark days when the return manuscripts rolled back in and the outlay on paper and typewriter ribbons was greatly in excess of the profits accruing to the enterprise.

For it was not always easy, being a writing factory. Spacks had devised a system of submission as efficiently organized as the one we had for creating the goods in the first place, though in the early days it was decidedly less productive. Up on the wall, above the little mailboxes labelled Norm and Nattie, Peter and Barbie, was a large flow-chart which listed all the many magazines that might be a market for their various wares. Each day each author sent out a story to one of the magazines, and we all of us sat back to wait. To this day I sometimes wonder whether the editors of Britain, who serve us so selflessly with reading matter, ever understood the reason for the spectacular increase in their work-load that year. For, no sooner did a story come back, and all too often it did, than it was in the mail again, on its way to another magazine, while a fresh story was sent to the previous one. Our system indeed ensured that no desk in, to recall one crucial address, Bream Buildings was ever without something from one of our family, and possibly all of them. In fact it was a busy year for the British postal system indeed, and I'm told that in retirement resorts round the country old sorters still talk about it.

In the early days it must be admitted that we did not do well, our stories returning to us with the same regularity that we maintained in submitting them. The sheer mechanics slowly began to overwhelm us, as we spent much of the day stuffing stories into envelopes and writing the self-addressed envelopes required by the magazines for their all-too-frequent return. Our production began to drop alarmingly, especially as we grew overcome with a disease familiar to all writers, known as the 'mail-fraps'. The mail-fraps is that disabling state of mind that comes to authors when they find they cannot begin a day's work until the mail has arrived; the symptoms include making the breakfast coffee last all morning, smoking heavily and standing in lacklustre posture in the window, awaiting the sight of the postman coming round the corner. As if he sensed this, our own postman reacted accordingly, reshaping his round so that he always came to us last, just to ensure that our hysteria had peaked. We would snatch the letters from him with a cry, rip the packages open, drop the rejected stories to the floor and scrabble through the litter, hunting for some sign that there had been just one acceptance.

It came now and again, but I fear, all too rarely – far too rarely for us to feel that Norm and Mill and Peter, Faith and Barbie and Nattie were becoming the household names that we desired for them and they, plainly, desired for themselves. We felt not just for us but for them; they felt not just for them but for us. Now and again there was joy in the household, as Jack had a lucky week, and then it was Faith's turn. Millingham earned eighty pounds in a week once, with three stories; Barbie once earned almost as much with just one weepie cry from the old Northern orphanage. Peter broke the London papers, and was asked for more, though when he sent it the editor had changed and he had to start all over again. Most of them got some acceptances, though never enough. Most of them did, but not Nathalie. Poor Nathalie! Perhaps her style was too exotic for British readers, perhaps her exclamation marks did not strike the popular chord. Whatever it was, she seemed to get nowhere at all, with never a credit to her name.

I think probably had it not been for Nathalie we might well have given up our writing stable altogether. After all, Spacks and I both had other ambitions. There were our theses to consider, and the great novels that each one of us was writing. Then, one night in the yard of the Eagle, Spacks came up with a new project – a musical of *King Lear*, to be called *Crack Your Cheeks!* – that excited us both enormously. But there were other people to consider; we were not just writing for ourselves. We worried and fretted about the writers we had nurtured. Perhaps Norman was drinking too much, and Faith getting tired and depressed. How was Barbara, with her sad orphanage history, taking yet another experience of rejection? And wasn't it getting time for Peter, now well past his great days of hunting the whale and harpooning the rhino, to think of settling down a bit – possibly, indeed, with Nathalie, who was admittedly a good deal younger, but a delightful homemaker and friend.

Thus, as often happens with writers, the greater the rebuffs, the more frenziedly we wrote. And, as the atmosphere grew more frantic, the more frantic, too, became the kinds of tale we devised. Our plots began to display greater and greater extravagance, in a mute appeal for recognition. Then came an unhappy moment when we had Peter Eton resolve some complex narrative crux by having one of his exotic French heroines raped by a Russian spy suspended on wires from an Ilyushin aeroplane. It bore all the marks of desperation, and we realized that it was time to take stock. As usual it was Spacks, who had spent a gloomy day studying a pile of writers' magazines sent from America by his cousin in Chicago, who spotted the nub of our problem. Here we were, two authors who had had our share of successes, with a score or so of our tales in print. Yet the fees of twenty-five pounds a throw still did no more than pay off the bar bill and the supplies of Tippex required for their invention and creation. Being a commercial writer in Britain, he explained, was simply not economic.

On the other hand, according to the magazines he held out to me, commercial writing in the United States was a very different affair. There were magazines by the score that would pay thousands of dollars for just one short story. American contributors were reporting tales of riches galore, and endless holidays in Bimini from their creative earnings. We were, after all, a transatlantic collaboration, if not a multinational corporation, and nothing but inertia bound our product to the British market. No, the answer was clear, and we must transmit it forthwith to our writers. All that was necessary was for the settings, rather than the plot-lines of our stories, to change, for the length to extend a little and the style become a little more vernacular. Of course our postal bills would increase, but happily a new instalment of Spacks's research grant had arrived, and that might well give the necessary capital injection. So we reprogrammed our authors, and our tales now began to wing across the Atlantic, to the great American El Dorado.

And it was now that fortune began to smile more sunnily on us. It was Peter Eton who scored the first successes. A certain aggressive machismo had always been apparent in his work, but now he put it to good use; various American journals with titles like *Knave* or *Playmate* began to take to him, and several of his tales appeared amid photographs of strange bodily contortions. Norman Blood shifted his locals to the American deserts, and began to attract a little editorial interest here and there, and even Faith Simple sold a recipe or two. But the sun that now shone happily shone brightest on Nathalie Barker – or Nathalie Pelham Barker as, for the purposes of the American market, she had now become. It was as if she had found a world she had always been made for. In the magazine for romantic housewives that flourished in those days – *Redbook* and *Good Housekeeping*, for example – but which have changed or gone today, she found those who were ready to relish her talents and her winsome way with prose.

Perhaps our greatest moment occurred one evening when we returned from a story session at the mill which had gone on rather later than usual, possibly because we had been celebrating some good American sale on behalf of Nathalie, who could not of course be there herself. The landlady met us at the door, in quite a lather of excitement. 'Time called when you were out,' she said. 'What did?' asked Spacks. 'Time did,' said the landlady. 'It wanted to do a feature story about being a writer.' 'Time,' cried Spacks, 'You mean *Time* magazine?' 'That's what I said,' said the landlady, 'Time called, but you were out.' 'Great,' said Spacks, 'Which one of us did they want to write about? Him? Me?' 'It wasn't either of you,' said the landlady. 'It was a writer called Nathalie Pel someone they thought lived at this address. But I told Time nobody round here had ever heard of her.' 'You told *Time* that?' asked Spacks. 'That's what I told Time,' said the landlady.

Time never called again. Or perhaps it did, but in a rather different way. For, a few weeks later, the academic year ran out, our theses were due in, and the tickets arrived for Spacks to transship himself back to his familiar haunts in the United States. High on Benzedrine he finished off his thesis by night and day, and we retired to the Baron of Beef for our last drink. Staring into the beer, we stared into vacancy. The partnership was over, and it was time for the stable of writers to be dissolved. But could Faith and Barbie survive, out there in the lonely world on their own? Would Norman drink himself to death, Peter retire to some old authors' home or other? And had Nathalie really written her last – dear, successful, Peck-and-Peck-dressed Nathalie, with her cashmere sweaters and her sorority pin and her brave, brave ways? As Spacks said, there was only one answer. And when, that summer, he took ship for Philadelphia, on some shoebox-sized freighter, I was with him, typewriter in hand, file-boxes of stories under my arm. And a good summer we had of it, a real Nathalie summer, as Spacks and I sat by some swimming pool in trunks and helped Nathalie gush out more and more and more of her lovely stories. Late in the afternoon we went down to the drugstore and wandered among the magazines, seeing our – no, her – byline flashing from the covers.

For Nathalie was a success. Time never called again, but there was fan mail, such fan mail as you never saw. Then came the day when a letter arrived which I have, to my shame, since destroyed, but it went something rather like this:

Hi, Nathalie!!! Remember me? Sure as hell you do!! This is Chet, and darn it I do believe you're Pel, right? – Nathalie Pelham who was sweetheart of Sigma Chi that sunlit year when we were in the same great old class of '48 together at dear old Wholesome State!!!! yes, I'd know those exclamation points anywhere!! Remember how we practised them all that summer when we decided fate and our grade average had really chosen us for each other!!! Oh boy, weren't those great times, kid? I still ask myself why we never stuck together!! But I always had these big dreams about really making it in the Big Apple!! Okay, there've been good times, and bad!! I tried the marriage stakes, and I guess from the Barker bit you must have tried them too!! Okay, I made my big dream come true, and today I'm one of the biggest architects in town!!! If you look at the building next to the Pam Am you might see a little name on the cornerstone that will really bring back memories!!! But, Pel, I learned one other thing in life – never turn your back on romance!!! My wife left me last year, leaving me with a dreamy daughter of five and a host of bad dreams!! Right, I've got fame, and the kind of salary check that keeps me in nearly new Mercs, but there's something missing. 'Pel', could it be you?? Listen, I don't like to write like this, but I've been reading your stories, and I think there's something in there that sounds like a message to me!!! Why don't we give it a whirl, sweetheart!!! I mean, let's just meet, how about under the clock at Grand Central!! I'll be wearing a yellow rose (remember how you loved them???) and carrying a copy of *Redbook* . . .

I'm wiser now, and I know we should never have answered that letter. And certainly we should not have gone to Grand Central that fatal day to watch all the lovers meet under the clock. For Chet looked a very pleasant fellow as he stood there, for two hours or more, under the clock in his horn-rimmed spectacles, holding up his copy of *Redbook* and flipping his yellow rose from time to time. He was just the kind of guy Nathalie would have loved, and it was with pain in our hearts that, leaving him there, we stole softly away. It was, as Nathalie would say, strange after that. For just as fiction has a way of destroying reality, so reality has a way of destroying fiction. The next day we could not even lift the covers from our typewriters, and, like ghosts, not just Nathalie but all of our writers somehow just began to slip away into the shadows. Perhaps it was as Nathalie always said: you can't play around with romance and get away with it.

Of course it could well have been all for the best. Soon we were back in the deep waters of serious creation again. Spacks reconceived his novel about the Korean War, and I went back to my magnum opus on the Fifties in the British provinces. In due time I became a wellish-known British novelist, and Spacks became a very distinguished American poet. And indeed I more or less forgot about the whole youthful episode until, just a few days ago, a large envelope dropped through my letter box. It came from some British magazine and it was returning a short story; I looked and saw it was one of Nathalie's. On the usual brutal rejection slip the editor had scribbled a few words of regret, saying the story somehow seemed a little old-fashioned for them. They apologized for being a little slow in coming to a decision, but apparently the story had been lying under the cat in the office. I did parcel it up and sent it on to Nathalie, at the last address I had for her, a very nice-sounding property somewhere in Bel Air, California. It probably never even reached her. But if it did, I doubt it made any difference, one way or another. That was how it was with Nathalie. Like any good writer, she was the kind of girl who could always take a rejection. As for the lesson of the story, that is probably very simple. There is a lot to be said for collaboration; I still occasionally do it. But don't, on any account, assume it will make life any easier.

Yours, etc.

READING PARTIES

PERHAPS THE MOST FAMOUS reading party in literary history occurred in 1816, at a villa on Lake Geneva. It was the Swiss summer, and so was raining hard. Those shut in began to read and discuss German ghost stories. 'These tales excited in us a playful desire of imitation,' said one participant, Mary Shelley. Others there were Shelley, Lord Byron, and their physician Dr Polidori. From that reading party several famous tales emerged. One was Polidori's *The Vampyr*, the source of *Dracula*. Another, of course, was Mary Shelley's *Frankenstein*.

Not all reading parties are so productive. But reading groups are multiplying, as a distinct late twentieth-century phenomenon. In one form or another, they have long existed. Chaucer's pilgrim ride to Canterbury was a sort of reading party. Boccaccio's *Decameron* depends on the idea that a group of people would flee plague in Florence to recount a hundred tales to each other – chiefly, by his account, as a way of avoiding sex in contagious times.

The contemporary phenomenon has different motives, is more universal, and grows ever better organized. 'You may have read the books,' says current publicity, 'but you haven't experienced them until you have discussed them with other readers.' A pleasant social custom that once existed chiefly among social reformers, rained-off intellectuals, WEA classes and university wives' clubs is taking off like Tupperware parties, with the warmest support from publishers and booksellers.

In the USA, where the current boom began, there are thought to be up to a million such groups – in bookstores, libraries, schools, colleges, private homes. Some are specialist, dedicated to anything from crime fiction to experimental poetry, feminist politics to the many universes of Terry Pratchett. Most are more general, often dedicated to current bestseller lists, and meant as a way of cultural keeping up.

Oprah Winfrey has concocted her own TV book club, generating instant bestsellers. The book clubs and reading groups, often predominantly but not exclusively female, have added to book sales and helped highlight popular titles, like the current bestseller *Cold Mountain*, by Charles Frazier, or *Captain Corelli's Mandolin*, by Louis de Bernières. Some groups are energetic enough to invite their writers along too. But essentially they are about reading a book, then sharing the experience.

I have my own reasons for being grateful to the organized reading party. As a child in the 1940s, growing up in a provincial suburb, I attended a little group for children run weekly by the local sub-branch librarian. This not only helped me with the actual skills of reading. It bred love of books, and led me to the wonders of the adult library. To that group, I owe my first encounters with H. G. Wells and John Masefield, Robert Louis Stevenson and Charles Dickens.

A decade later, I had my first teaching experience tutoring adult classes in literature in Nottingham, another kind of reading party. In those days, a WEA class had nothing to do with paper qualifications; it was devoted to self-education, book knowledge, exchange of ideas. A studious group of us worked our way through French existentialism, and so helped give Nottingham its first outsiders.

Reading is always helped by talking about it. Books become real and memorable when shared and discussed with like-minded others. In the last decade or so, books, authorship and reading have alike grown far less private, helped by the friendly new ambience of high-street bookstores, the extensive republication of classics in attractive editions (World's Classics, Everyman), the growth of writers' promotional tours, and the expanding number of lively literary festivals.

Bookshops have grown alert to the promise of the reading

groups, which encourage both sales and an active climate of book talk. In America bookstores have been in the forefront, encouraging the formation of groups, suggesting titles, providing information about books and writers.

Now, in Britain, Waterstone's have issued an excellent brief guide for the use of such groups, with good advice on how to go about it. They recommend regular monthly meetings, and the practice either of moving from home to home, or taking a room in a college, library or local pub. They wisely propose the group share some common interests, and advise that groups of around ten function best in homes, with fifteen in bigger locations. Each member needs to participate, one each time researching the writer's life and work, or giving a talk on the chosen title.

They give cautious advice on how to choose titles for discussion: from, say, the various listings or book guides issued by various bookshops, or the shortlists of the well-known prizes. Waterstone's have also backed a scheme for community reading groups (Joined Up Reading) and distribute a list of Vintage Reading Guides, which so far have mainly American content. Not surprisingly, publishers have spotted reading groups as a way of promoting their titles and heating up a bestseller, so these lists and aids are bound to multiply.

There is no doubt more objective listings are needed; there is more to reading than keeping up with current bestsellers. Listings are despised by some, but they can be an invaluable aid. The speedy rise of book clubs has become visible on the websites, where reading groups report on their activities or solicit information about books and authors, where there are even 'virtual' book clubs.

It would be good to think the clubs encourage extensive and quality reading, reaching beyond currently fashionable titles into the great works and the historical classics. The fact remains that reading itself is always good. What is more, while reading, like writing itself, was once seen as a solitary activity, it is widening in its public nature and social aspect.

The modern writer is increasingly confronted by the real

presence of the reader. In a famous essay, the French critic Roland Barthes spoke of 'the Death of the Author', adding that 'the death of the author marks the birth of the reader'. Barthes meant that books are not monumental texts with a firm, certain meaning. They are, as we say now, interactive. The book is one side of a relationship, the reader is the other.

Readers multiply the meanings of books, redefine their use. A reader is not the same person as a critic, who reads for professional judgement and analysis. The reader seeks pleasure, enlightenment, self-identification, a certain kind of seduction. And the reading group enlarges the literary circuit, creating fresh space for debate, interpretation and understanding.

If I were thinking of beginning a reading club (I'm not), I should begin with a remarkable, playful novel about writing and reading, Italo Calvino's *If on a winter's night a traveller*. It starts off many different stories, in many different styles, but does not finish them. It portrays the wonder of writing; it also portrays the reader. Or rather two readers, male and female, who are trying to disentangle the mystery of the unfinished books – and end up in love with each other.

Several years back Marshall McLuhan warned that, in the global village, with its increased leisure and visual technologies, the book would disappear. He was wrong, and I think he will remain so. Books have changed, but if anything have widened their appeal. They fill our increasing leisure, gratify our growing appetite for story and history. They appear in their plenty, and the spirit of reading has been restimulated by what's on offer. And, if the experience on Lake Geneva is a guide, stimulating more good readers could well stimulate more good writers.

THE WAITING GAME

ESTELLE HAS JUST GONE, has just walked out into the hot London street, and is looking now for a taxi, or taking a bus at the corner; it was not the evening it promised to be. That I sensed, perhaps, even before she came. All day, as I walked down those heated streets, jostled to the murmur of incidental politenesses, I had been conceiving in my mind the exact passage of the events of the evening, invoking the very movements, the precise exchanges of words. But even as I foresaw these pleasures, and considered how I would take her hands in mine, what we should say, by what stages we would come to our vital moment, I knew at the same time that in invoking these things I was destroying them, and that because of my premeditation they could not and did not deserve to happen.

And when the lift came up and I hurried over and opened the door, and she stood there, heels neatly together, her skirt tight across her hips and thighs, her hair newly cut, her face sweetly powdered and her lips unsmiling, I knew that in this moment of realizing our contact once more, an experience on so much more wearing a level of sensation than foreseeing it or recreating it afterwards, nothing could happen; by all this I had prepared for what must now come about, the end of our relationship; we can hold everything except actual events, which escape us easily. She stood in the doorway, very pretty: I sensed her coldness, which made her prettier for me. Desire plays fullest over things nearest to the impossible, and I never felt more strongly about her than this evening.

Previously the things of our relationship had moved under some outside impetus or excitement, nothing I could supply myself. Now, as she crossed over to the window, looking out over the street lights and the dirty rooftops of London, I planned already my concessions. 'How pretty you look,' I said. Outside, the dogs barked.

This was the summer of 1955, a very hot summer for Europe; spirals of heat rose from the pavements, the grass of parks and gardens dried, an official drought was declared. What was it like to be alive in this day and age, believing nothing, feeling little gusts of love or anger or contempt, plotting no future, scheming no good fortune? It was an empty time. The heat had begun some three months ago, ricocheting among the dirty London buildings, sweating our underarms, souring our milk. It was just after it had begun that I had met Estelle, at a birthday party in a Bayswater flat. No one knew her at all, it seemed; Marianne Veckner, twenty-one today, had invited in charming exuberance everyone she knew and many she didn't; one woman, elderly and dressed in black and looking most embarrassed, as though she had mistaken this for a religious meeting, whispered to me that she had passed a bottle of ketchup to Marianne in a café and Marianne had told her that if she didn't come to the party the evening would die on the stem. There were about a hundred people trapped in one small flat, the living room of which was so full that if you were sitting down you had to stay that way for the rest of the evening. Marianne asked most of the taxi drivers who brought the guests and presently the street below became so packed with discarded vehicles – taxis, motor scooters, a hansom cab brought for affectation – that the police arrived; Marianne invited them too. Someone dropped a bottle of gin in the hall, and tramps came in to smell the fumes; the toilet was flushed so often that it went wrong and people began to wander about the building asking other tenants for the use of theirs; at midnight, when the first guests were leaving, new ones were still arriving. The landlord, who had come in early to complain about the noise, was still there at two, a shade from a standard lamp on his head, being helped back to his flat by five strong men; 'What nice people,' he kept shouting, 'what nice people.'

And somewhere in the crowd was a bishop, incognito, for a pair of ecclesiastical gaiters stood unattended just inside the doorway.

When I arrived, Marianne Veckner greeted me dewily at the door: 'Did you bring a bottle, lamb?' she demanded. I produced a bottle from my coat pocket. '*Vin rouge*,' she read disappointedly from the label. 'The man at the shop told me it was an aphrodisiac; that's why I got it,' I said. 'Oh, that's wonderful, then,' said Marianne.

Then she made me take my coat off, warning me that I'd never find it again, and asked me how I got there. 'I came on the bus,' I said. 'Oh, you didn't?' she cried. 'With all those people? Sheer affectation.' 'It was rather interesting, actually,' I said.

That was the sort of party it was; a crowd of wild people in a flat looking out over Battersea Park and Battersea Power Station and the river, all gilt by a warm evening sun, waiting for the hydrogen bomb to drop. The flat was horribly dirty; no one cleaned it; the sink gurgled all the time; in a corner the gas meter ticked away at a steady measure, noting the passage of meals and baths and cold evenings warmed. Laughter trilled here and there in the room; 'But you can't make value judgements about value judgements, can you?' demanded a brittle incisive voice above the noise; one's eyes tired as one looked into the room. Marianne said: 'There's a girl here who wants to meet you; she read something you wrote and disliked it.' This was Estelle; she came over, brown and richly shaped, set sharply in focus, somehow, by a dress of pink candy-stripe, cut low in front; we were introduced and she stole us a chair and sat in my lap. She was warming and expansive, like one's imaginings of an Italian mistress. She looked in my mouth, found that our gum charts matched exactly, declared we were twin souls; 'Isn't that a wonderful coincidence?' she said. 'Do you believe in predestination?' She made me look in her mouth; I peered cautiously in; nothing blew up and, warming to this intimacy, I inspected the contents closely. 'Very good,' I said.

Soon we retired into the kitchen, which was empty and dark, with a touch of sun falling across and shining the metal of the gas cooker. Estelle asked me why I looked so sad. 'I don't know,' I said, 'I didn't even know I looked sad.' She got out her powder compact and made me look into the mirror of it; 'See?' she said. 'And I know why. You understand about things. You see into things. You know all this isn't real!' I demurred modestly; 'Isn't it real? It's as real as anything else, surely.' 'You don't have to say that to me. I'm the same,' said Estelle, 'I see it too.' She then began to speak very rapidly, telling me that parties made her cry because they were so sad, little bright oases in the desert of the world. Her eyes were wet; her head rested on my shoulder and I placed my arm about her waist, while she said that we were the victims of a vast economic process that whirled us about and about. In the flat people were laughing and shouting. Estelle said that they were nobodies; they led their lives cheaply, going from sensation to sensation. She explained that she, on the other hand, lived everybody's life: 'We all have to live other people's lives, though our time is small and before us and after us life keeps on,' said Estelle. Then the door opened and Marianne Veckner came in, putting on the light. She laughed and said we'd picked the best place; the bedroom was crowded out. 'Who was it I came with?' demanded Estelle vaguely. Marianne said she didn't remember because her mind had stopped working at nine and all the repair shops were shut. 'Never mind,' said Estelle, 'tell whoever it is I've been called out to a fire.' I must have been looking somewhat embarrassed, because I had never meant to do this in the first place. I said I'd never do it again; I said I wouldn't go to any more of these parties. I asked quickly where I could get a haircut; I said my head was too heavy to carry around any more with all that hair on it. Estelle said that it was a lovely party and a lovely kitchen; she told Marianne that she had on a lovely dress. 'Someone wants lemon in their *vermout*,' said Marianne, opening the refrigerator door and slicing a lemon. 'Sheer affectation,' said Estelle. 'Shall I put the light out?' said Marianne. 'Yes, please,' said Estelle, 'and don't tell anyone where we are.' When she had gone we found greater sadness than ever, for nothing is sadder than the fuller moments of love. Here we were, at our point in time, right there where someone could easily break in, switch on the light, disclose us. I say, again, I hadn't come for this; I didn't deserve it; it was no reward I aspired to.

WE WENT OUT down the fire escape and took a taxi to a restaurant which Estelle chose because she was in love with one of the waiters, a handsome Italian who came over, ignoring me completely, smiling brightly, saying, 'Good evening, miss, is nice to have you here again. You have done your hair differently, I like it.' 'Good evening, Roberto,' said Estelle, brightly. 'Do you really?' 'Very nice,' said Roberto. 'How brown you are.' 'We're going to have something exotic to drink,' said Estelle, and then, dropping him with one of her strange shifts of attention, which I was to learn were so common, so annoying and yet intriguing – where did her motives come from? – she turned to me and said, 'There, that's him. I'm hopelessly in love with him, and he just knows it. He's rather horrible, isn't he?' 'That is one of my assets, I think,' said Roberto. Estelle ordered drinks for both of us and he went off for them. I could see this was all going to be very expensive and felt subtly into my wallet to see how much money I had; fortunately I had had a cheque for a newspaper article, and cashed it, that day. The article was on 'Our Future Prosperity'.

'Where do you live?' I asked; she refused to tell me. I was being conversational; I dropped to banalities, not being rich in social expertise; 'Do you come here often?' 'Quite often,' said Estelle. 'Do you go out a lot?' 'Yes,' said Estelle, 'I'm always going out somewhere or other.'

I was growing to doubt my capacity to handle her; if the waiter had annoyed me, this fact invoked a deeper perturbation, for I was by contrast a provincial recluse, a visitor only of picture galleries, museums, libraries, a detester of London life, with its society constantly in flux, its lack of roots, its failure to offer close and intense relationships; events were everything. 'I'd be bored if I did what you do,' said Estelle, 'I need lots of people, lots of places, lots of activity, lots of friends.' 'Do you have a lot of friends, then?' I asked. 'I know a lot of men,' said Estelle, 'I'm quite promiscuous, you understand.'

We watched the meal, cooked beside us on a wagon, and then began to eat, almost in silence. I thought that she must find me boring. 'Do you like me?' she suddenly asked. 'Yes, of course,' I said, 'I like you very much.' 'Why?' demanded Estelle. 'I find you interesting and unusual.' She thought about this for a moment, obviously not liking it, and then said, 'I don't think you can have been around very much.' 'I don't know,' I said, 'does it matter?' 'Well,' said Estelle, 'maybe it does.' I pondered conversation, darings, timidities, foolishnesses. 'I'm not very hungry,' said Estelle after a moment. 'Let's go.'

She went off to the ladies' room while I paid the bill, and I sat uncomfortably awaiting her. Of course, she wouldn't like me; why should she? Her perfume was still in the air. Her fingerprints stood out on the wine glass. Her gloves lay on the table. There remained closely with me the sensation of her bright clothes, her light hair, her refulgent smile, her white teeth, and against this sensation I tested my warm feeling. I was aware of a daring which was, for me, excessive, in my desire to embark on a relationship whose exact shape, the nature of whose crescendo, whose emotional texture, was not within my grasp. As I considered my reactions, at the same time sipping the last of the carafe of wine, Estelle returned and, as she sat down, I examined scrupulously the physical fact of her presence, her wide hips, the folds of her dress, the skin texture of her bare arms, her brown shoulders and neck. The fact differed from the dream. 'There, is that better?' she asked brightly. 'Yes,' I said, though I saw no difference save for a slight thickening of powder and lipstick, 'wonderful.' 'I'm so late it just isn't true,' she said in her bridge chorus girl's way; I brought her coat and slipped it over her shoulders. 'Just a minute,' she said, 'write down your address.' While I was

doing this she said, 'Lend me a pound for the taxi, will you?'
She took it graciously. 'How shall I let you have this back –
shall I post it to you, or shall we meet again?' 'We'll meet
again,' I said, 'but please forget about it.' 'You're a white man,'
said Estelle. 'Now come and get me a taxi.'

As the taxi I had signalled gyrated in the busy road, as the
heavy traffic flowed, people pushed by, and as I recollected
the strangenesses of the evening, I tried to kiss her. 'Get away,'
she said. 'Why?' I asked. 'You weren't like this before.' 'But
I see you differently now,' said Estelle. 'You aren't my sort of
person. You mustn't be offended,' she added, seeing that I was,
'you're better than my sort of person, I suppose. But I don't
think of you in that way now. I meant it when I said I was
promiscuous; I didn't just say it for effect. That is, perhaps in a
way I said it for effect, but it's true. So you mustn't fall in love
with me, you see.' 'Yes,' I said. 'And you would have done,
wouldn't you?' 'I don't know,' I said. 'You were nice,' said
Estelle, 'you were a comfort.' 'Do you need comfort?' 'Oh, I
do, I do really,' she said, and dropped her head onto my chest;
I think she was crying. Gently I held her; pity flowed out from
me, at least I have pity, that gentle superior emotion. How full
the pains of the human lot, how the city weighs on me, how I
grieved for Estelle. She began to speak rapidly to me, saying, 'I
am sad, you know. People pass, of course, and one gives them
a little and they give you something. But sometimes one thinks
there's more than that. I was going to marry; perhaps I
shouldn't have liked it. But I wish I hadn't lost him. Can those
feelings ever come again, have we grown past them into
something worse? Can one be simple any more? You hope
that it will come, you hope life is kind further on. But when,
and how? And in the meantime, what can you do? You play
with things, go to lots of places, see lots of people. You try
things out, you just play a long silly futile waiting game. That's
all it is, a waiting game.' 'I know, honey, I know,' I said. 'Even
if one hadn't loved once it would be the same, don't you
think? One wants a peaceful centre; you know. All this noise,
all these people.' I kissed her lightly on the brow and she clung

to me, suddenly, as she had at the party; I helped her into the taxi. 'Shall I come?' I asked. 'No,' she said, 'you'll hear from me, really.' The taxi meter had been ticking all this long time; 'You'd better give me another pound,' she said. The taxi drove off and she did not look back at all.

AT LUNCHTIME the next day she telephoned me; she was at a rehearsal for a new ballet; she missed me; she wanted to come to my apartment that night. Why was I delighted? This was a world, the 1956 world, that I lived on the fringe of, half despising, half admiring, but in no way committed to. It was, to begin with, a world out of my grasp, offensive to my honesties, pretentious, inharmonious, grasping at less than it claimed to. 'How can you? How do you?' I thought. 'What a fool you are.' I was selling out, and yet there it was, the warmth and acceptance of love. One couldn't hold oneself apart, insist on one's distinction, for ever; one was of the race of men, and these were their ways.

She arrived, that evening, late; she said that Bayswater, like her father's house, had many mansions and she couldn't find the one in which I lived. Her manner was extremely bright, fresh from the parties she belonged at. She brought me a present, a large statuette of a coy whistling shepherd boy which she had seen in a second-hand shop that afternoon. 'As soon as I saw it I thought of you,' she said. 'That's not entirely a compliment,' I remarked. 'Oh, yes, it shows I thought of you,' she said, 'and I thought you'd like it.' 'But look how ugly he is,' I said, 'look at his big ears.' 'You know that poem about come live with me and be my love and we will all the pleasures prove?' said Estelle. 'Don't you think of that?'

That good evening, when peace was offered and accepted, and the traffic outside roared past to invoke the contrast of disquiet, and below a radio played jazz, I can still hold on to; perhaps it seems now finer than it was. Here, when we played over the range of all the light lovers' passions, a new stream of emotions and scheme of sensations came into my life; tasted, relished, some discarded, at least they happened. It was our best time; even the shame, the touch of disgust and disappointment, were themselves pleasant. The sun went down outside and the heat of the unbroken drought held on in the shadows, the walls of the old building. Then the moon would come up and drop light into the room, where, in contrast to the world, life went on.

We met, after this, quite often; I would wait for her to finish her rehearsal amid the garish neon, the bright ugly shop windows of Piccadilly Circus, me arriving early and trying to sort her face from the panting, chasing crowds with their blank and hostile stares, moving amid the wild traffic. At last she would come, her bright eyes shining, easy in the crowds, carrying her little vanity case packed with sandwich wrappers and her ballet shoes, which I would take from her, and we would go to a restaurant in Greek Street, or we would buy steak in Old Compton Street and go home to my flat to cook Wiener schnitzel. And then a theatre, ending the evening in the half intimacy of some saloon bar, talking quietly amid the press of people, the bright lights and shining mirrors, while Estelle drank gin and tonic water and I brandy, or beer, according to my financial state. We moved amid the Edwardian plush that London still has, in its theatres and pubs, or more often, perhaps, amid the contemporary, the espresso bars which tempted you to think that it was not Oxford Street outside, but the Via Veneto or St-Germain-des-Prés. Young men with duffel coats and beards appeared and disappeared, sailing yachts around the world, working for the *Daily Mirror*, getting girls newly up from the provinces pregnant. Or to a foreign film in Tottenham Court Road, or a Prom, or to the Institute of Contemporary Arts, or to a lesbian bar north of Oxford Street. But wherever we went it was of her choosing; it was her London; they were her friends, the French or Austrian or post-Oxfordian Englishmen who lived in Hampstead and were members of string quartets, owners of espresso bars, programme planners at the BBC. I lived her life completely, coming to no judgements, just living it. She had, too, a passion for going slumming or ritzing, which we were constantly gratifying; we would pass a dismal East End apartment house, or the Dorchester; she would say, 'Ooo, let's go in.' We would be robbed or spend all our money and she would telephone for a trombonist in the London Symphony to take us home in his MG. And then, when we arrived at the flat, tired, quarrelsome, the gas meter would tick as we sped through the splendid resolution that in spite of all we gained of each other.

The china shepherd boy stood on top of the bookcase, her memento, and when she had gone it offered some confirmation of the fact which then seemed so uncertain, that we had been here, done this and that, that at some time she had been in this room, we had felt so, and so. And I was this kind of person now, I was now these things that had happened to me; here was my place in the world. All I had to do was to apprehend it completely. For every event that happens means something to the soul. We meet events halfway; they are part of us and we are part of them. And every event is taken up again; nothing is that accidental. Things do not simply follow; they follow from. We make all beauty, all love, all goodness, from inside ourselves, if we can, and are ourselves made of them. What one is now happened to one then.

I did not even wonder whether I loved her; love is an old word and does not fit us any more. What more can I say except that I am oppressed by an awareness of change, a knowledge of human insecurity, a consciousness of infinite time; and that, out of loneliness, I seek company, an answer to this dreadful infinity. Why then was I not satisfied; why did I rebuke it?

We decided that in the summer we would hire a car and drive down through France, along the Riviera and into Italy, perhaps Yugoslavia. This, too, was her idea; I accepted it. We drove down from Paris along wet roads; we took a night at Avignon, filled the back of the car with food and wine and set off. We picnicked by the roadside and afterward I let her drive. She was not a good driver, lacking concentration, and when we skidded on the wet road she lost control and we smashed into the side of a small French car. A little girl was hurt.

There was no guilt and I tried to make none. 'It could happen to anyone, it's always happening, it's the price we pay for being in this modern world and using its things,' said Estelle, annoyed by my grief and anguish; and this was true. Yet here was what I had committed myself to. I had come down to concessions. And when we reached the coast, and found a hotel that Estelle liked, and we stayed, I found myself possessed by something close to terror. I wanted to go home; I felt apart from the security of my fate and at a loss among these events. I was not free and maintained nothing of myself all the time that I was with Estelle. At times I wanted to escape from her; I would go down to the beach alone and lie there and within moments would feel alone, remote from my roots, completely lost, so that I had to go and look for her and get away from the great universal movement of sea and sky that was all there was.

And, therewith, she was coming to know me, to observe the character of my doubts and disorders. She saw my weaknesses, my lack of authority with waiters, with the hoteliers who tried to cheat us, the porters who asked for larger tips, my slowness at coming to decisions about which restaurant to eat at, where to go each day, my inability to invent a good time, to make conversation, my poor social performance with people she wanted to meet. When she saw in the bathroom my array of pills, throat washes, haircreams, suntan lotions, mosquito creams, she could not at first believe that they were mine. She came over to me on the balcony, well-lotioned, protected with sunglasses, looking out across the rich sweating vegetation and the sharp rocks to the peace of the sea, and said, 'What do you want all those things in the bathroom for?' I told her they were all necessary.

She pondered this all day and that evening, as we sat in a café in Villefranche, with the harbour waters before us pearly grey and the lights coming on, she demanded, 'You're not going to die, are you?' 'Why?' I asked, surprised. 'Perhaps you shouldn't do so much,' she said. 'You mustn't die on me.' 'It would certainly be embarrassing.' 'You're older than I am, after all,' she said. 'Would you be sorry if I did?' I asked, doubting suddenly if she more than conventionally would and knowing that she could never be sorry enough; what we all want is someone to feel a sorrow deeper than love when we die. And even this question seemed to betray to her an inordinate weakness; 'That shouldn't matter to you,' she said, 'you try to tie me up too tightly with you.'

Yet if to her I seemed to tire and grow less heroic, and if I myself grew increasingly aware of the encroachments that she was making on me and felt a terrifying disintegration of all I had thought myself to be – yet still, because of her excitements, insights, all that she was, she seemed to have more and more to offer. That lovers' process whereby, as the face of beauty declines as one comes to know the underlying constituents – the myopia, the concealed blemishes visible close to, the sweating in the heat, the unflattering poses usually avoided but not always – there comes a delight in, and a sense of contact through, the weaknesses. Love is partly disgust, I would swear. So – we were both human, and small; she was seasick on the cross-Channel ferry, she wore a sundress that didn't suit her, she was frightened of swimming too far out, her hair looked terrible when it was wet.

Love was giving up both parts; both wanted more. The accident still hung round our necks. She still had a certain glitter. I always took great delight in her. When we went to the cinema, though she did not understand French, she would cry copiously at the sad moments and cling to me while I patted her behind and murmured, 'It's all right, it's all right.' When it was funny she would laugh with natural extravagance, wriggling in her seat, clutching me with excitement, looking to see whether I was enjoying it *this* much. Often as we lay on the beach, or drove along the corniche, her warm soft hand would insinuate itself into mine and I would glance down and examine this tender construct of bone and sinew, for what it gave me. I thought of the tenuousness of life, imagining her dead, lying drowned on the sea-edge or smashed in a car, and would touch her quickly. Sometimes I would put my hand

about her waist as we walked in that dry heat, resting it lightly
on her hip, feeling the movement of the lively padded flesh
beneath, her powerful body, that rich architecture of bones and
cartilages, pores and arteries, throbbing with the beat of life,
imbued with soft feelings. I was conscious of her participation
in the animal vital world of love and feeling, the bright plants,
the glowing sun, burning and engendering, the brown figures
on the beach, the burnt edges of the leaves. She liked to be
smiled at and importuned on the streets, talked to in cafés,
approached as she was swimming; she admired herself in shop
windows, had me take her photograph often, wore the smallest
swimsuits.

And meanwhile she perplexed herself with questions, feeling as I was that human peace was not full enough, but not
feeling in the same way. She simply doubted if I gave enough.
'Do you like me?' she would ask as we lay in bed, the window
open, the music from the casino resounding. 'Yes,' I would
say, running my hands over her. 'No, do you like *me*? Would
you like me if I didn't let you come near me?' 'Yes,' I said,
doubting the truth of the answer. 'No,' she said. 'No. You
don't like *me*, you just like being with me.'

But if I was delighted with her untrained openness of
manner, her bad taste, her vulgarity even, and found this a new
world full of insights, offering new extravagances of feeling,
honesties and lies, new manners and events, I did not accept
it for myself. When she wanted me to go to the casino I
demurred, not wishing to disclose to myself the precariousness
of chances, the weight of fate against me. 'You can't enjoy
yourself,' she cried angrily, 'you're as cold as bloody ice; you
never enjoy a damn thing, not even me. What do you think
when you're with me? What sacrifice do you suppose you're
damn well making?' And sometimes she would say, 'Let's talk
about you'; there was nothing to be said. 'What? There's
nothing about me?' 'What were you thinking about?' she
would ask in the sad moments after passion or as we stood
silently under the evening lanterns on the promenade. What
could I say? That the good things – taste, integrity, honest

emotions, deep feeling – were failing around us as we loved, and in our love? That love, instead of being an escape from human evil, loneliness, mortality, made these things more pressing; that time did not stop in these moments but beat out loud and clear in our heart beats? So, 'Nothing,' I would say, 'I wasn't thinking.' 'Yes, you were, and you'll have to stop it. For goodness' sake, forget about other things. Or at least tell me; don't keep everything from me.'

On my own side I was content to enjoy what she was without getting to know her. I took pains not to come close to her past; I didn't ask her about her life as a child, or what she did when I was not there. Perhaps I did not want to think about her as a person, but rather as a series of sensations; rather, I think I wished to avoid both the jealousy and the obviousness of her character, that I would have been faced with. She was disappointed; what she wanted was not love but interest in herself, perhaps for a woman the same thing, for to her love was interest, a concentration on the person and the personality to the exclusion of all else. While to me it was the concentration of many wider concerns, out of which my love and ways of loving came; the world was in our bedroom for me, and far off outside for her.

Thus as we lay on the beach after swimming smoking cigarettes she would talk about the things that excited her, how her father had been in India, what horrible men she had known, what lovely holidays she had spent, how she had been in two car smashes and a fire. I hardly recognized these things as having happened to her, nor did I sympathize with the way in which she sought my attention or her pain at not having it. One day she would not talk to me. 'What's wrong, tell me what's wrong.' I begged all day. 'Don't be silly; of course there's nothing wrong,' she said angrily. In the bedroom as we undressed we chased a mosquito and she became so angry over my incompetence that at last it came out, 'You didn't ask me what I wanted to drink.' 'But you always have gin and tonic,' I protested. 'I know,' she said, 'but you should have asked me.'

And when at last I told her that I was lost here and didn't

want to go on to Italy, but to go home, she tried to find wherein our lack lay. 'Why? Why?' she said. 'Is it me?' 'No, you know it isn't; it's just that we can't get away, and there isn't any peace here, and I don't belong here, and ought to go home.' 'What *is* it?' she demanded. 'Why do you treat me like this? Why do you keep yourself apart? Why don't you tell me things? What do you feel all the time?' 'I don't know. Leave me alone. I only know I have to stay free. I don't belong to you, or anyone. I don't belong to anything. I haven't any causes to push; I just want to do what's right for me. I have to decide. I'm sorry. It's selfish, of course. But I must get away; if I don't something bad will happen. I just know there's something wrong.'

She got off the bed and came over to me, and we looked together out at the wedding-cake decoration of the town, still holding the heat of the day, and she said, 'Are your feelings so much rarer and richer than everyone else's? I feel too, you know; we all feel; we aren't so hard.' 'I'm sorry,' I said, and looking at her I wanted to be possessed by her again. 'It isn't you, don't think that.' 'But what happened?' she demanded. 'I don't know; we've been open and honest, and we needn't reproach ourselves. But I'm just not safe in this country. The fates don't reach this far. I'm off my course; I'm not doing what I want to do.' 'The flattery's worn off,' said Estelle in a metallic tone of voice, 'I must have been rather flattering for you.' 'It isn't like that. And this isn't a conclusion.' 'You know,' said Estelle, 'you stifle me, you really do. For one thing, you never damn well say anything. You always look as though you pretend you're not here. You never look at me. You never *do* anything. You've never properly planned one event for us. You never have anything laid on. I did all that. You had to be pushed and planned for; you had to have everything suggested to you. A woman wants more than that. And do you realize that you never once have called me by my Christian name. I might be anyone to you. I know I expect too much . . .' 'No, you don't,' I said. 'But you didn't enjoy being with me one little bit, did you? You just live off the things I

do, not because you want to do them, because you damn well
don't, but just because you think you're missing something.'
'That's not true.' 'It damn well is, near enough. You think
I'm nothing; you don't even need or like me.' 'But I do need
you, very much. I need your affection.' 'Why mine? Why not
anybody's?' 'Well, I do need anybody's. But I admire you,
your excitement.' 'Listen, honey, you don't really need me.
Really. It isn't an easy conclusion to come to, believe me . . .'
'I do need you. It's just that I have this dreadful sort of feeling
that I'm . . . well, selling out . . .' 'Hell,' said Estelle, 'For
goodness' sake.'

We left the next morning. We drove out along the corniche
road; below us the vegetation sprouted ferociously through the
rocks. We had lain in bed all night, furious with each other;
but a double bed is a great healer, for the moment, and we had
made love again. It was despairing and yet peculiarly good.
'Let's stay; let's not go,' I said afterwards. 'We go,' said Estelle.
What am I to have done this? I wondered. And what salvage
was there? At least we shared a need. When, on the bed in the
afternoon or on the beach after an evening swim with a wind
blowing in off the sea, cooling the heat, we came together,
there had been, not pleasurable ecstasies, but rather a softer
glow, almost depressed, even dissatisfied. But it had happened;
for a moment there had been possession, a little possession in a
world of no possession.

When we reached London the drought was still present; the
grass was fading and the dry air was bringing sore throats. The
town seemed, nonetheless, less shoddy, less worn, or rather it
was worn as Rome, with its summer sun, is worn. And now
that past of shared prolix events has seemed to fall apart, and
tonight when she came her eyes were quite untendered. She
does not quite understand what she is doing, but like us all she
has the ruthlessness to accomplish it; people are easily passed
over once other consolations come in sight. She would take no
kiss and the conclusion is inexorable. She is looking, of course,
for someone better.

'Have you eaten?' she said. 'Shall I cook you something?' I

refused, and she went on, 'What you need is a nice wife, a home bird. I'm not that, you know. Why should you eat out all the time? You can live better than that.' 'I don't feel like marrying,' I said. 'It's one way of keeping people. You know how wide life is, how many people there are. And people get lonely, spread themselves around, take up with others. They come to want more. You can't possess. Time passes and they go.'

We have said our goodbyes and now she is gone; I have heard the lift go down, the gates banging, and she is looking for a taxi, or meeting someone else. I am too old for that, the waiting game. My feelings can go unpurged, hang depressively in a sensation like excessive tiredness, a misery not only in my mind but in my muscles and intestines. There is nothing left but to go into the rooms where she has been, and plan a future with no choice, where my veins will swell, my ears fill with wax, my heat abate. Like a sick man whose wants diminish beyond the personal into the general, whose entity is not more than that of himself sleeping, I may still live on, witnessing the world souring in the heat, thinking that there is nothing in this world more important than the affection of one person for another, and not having it, not even having a cave in her into which I can retire from the world, the others. At least there were feelings to have, now that there are no causes to believe in, no public patterns of integrity to maintain.

It will be too hot tonight even to sleep, which will not help; but at least the radio forecasts that the drought may end soon.

THE AGE OF ANXIETY: THE 1950s

'THE AGE OF ANXIETY' was the name W. H. Auden, in a long poem of 1947, gave the postwar world. For the fifties the shadows of very recent history lay blackly over that newly 'postwar world', which in the event would go on for another forty years or so. If this was a time of peace following one of the worst, globally most extended wars in history, it was a peace that was tense, tainted, uneasy, restless. The European order that had been in increasing disorder ever since August 1914 seemed shattered. It was now a world of Iron Curtains, occupied zones, divided cities, military build-up, eyeball confrontations, toppled regimes, puppet dictators.

Hot war had created not peace but 'Cold War', a military and ideological division which not only split Europe from top to bottom but divided East from West and sectioned the politics of the globe. With European regimes unstable, frontiers and nationhoods obscure, cities flattened and economies fragile or non-existent, the Second World War handed history over to two new superpowers, Russia and the USA. Their actions, conflicts, fears and crises would not simply shape the future of the world; they would decide if it had a future at all.

War left a huge legacy of horrors the fifties had to reckon with. The dropping of the first atomic bomb on Hiroshima in August 1945 initiated the age of nuclear anxiety. But it was in 1949, when Russia tested an atomic bomb of its own through espionage in the West (and China went communist), that the age of mutually assured destruction began. Meantime the discovery of the massive scale of Nazi genocide – the slowly dawning realization that beside all the bloodshed and ruin five or more million had perished in the 'Final Solution' – pointed to a crime beyond imagining.

And yet imagining what had happened over the wartime years was the great initiation for many as the second half of the century started. The imaginings of the fifties were mostly disturbed and often desperate. Two of the decade's marker novels were George Orwell's *Nineteen Eighty-Four*, which appeared in 1949, just before Orwell's death, and Günter Grass' *The Tin Drum*, which came out ten years later (and whose author has just been honoured with a belated Nobel Prize for Literature). Both are books about an age of militarism and total disorder – where the clocks strike thirteen, or the young do not grow older or bigger, politics unfold to the sounds of despair and mockery, the familiar and orderly are there only for history to destroy.

The age felt terrifying, conspiratorial, dangerous, phobic. It was a time of intricate and corrupt infiltrations, cunning deceptions, strange alliances of opposites (old Marxists and new conservatives, spooks in Washington and spooks in Moscow). Unsurprisingly, the spy-thriller became the most popular form of literature. Graham Greene and Carol Reed made the great 'noir' film *The Third Man*, set in occupied and battered Vienna, in 1949. The genre flourished, and by the sixties the age of John Le Carré, Len Deighton and the Cold War spying game was here to stay, certainly till October 1989. Nor is it surprising that, using another popular genre, the boys' book, William Golding wrote *Lord of the Flies* (1954), which is a meditation not only on survival after the nuclear holocaust but on the infinite corruptions in 'innocent' or boyish human nature.

The philosopher for the fifties was Jean-Paul Sartre; the philosophy in question was existentialism, with its portrait of existence without essence, its vision of eternal anxiety and the absurd. It too was a noir philosophy, which reached maximum intensity when Sartre's *Being and Nothingness*, written in wartime, was translated into English in 1957. As Iris Murdoch said in her 1953 book on Sartre, he has 'the style of the age'. If the movement had a literary laureate, it was Beckett, whose fictional trilogy artistically dominated the early fifties, whose *Waiting for Godot*, staged in London in 1956, was (far more than *Look Back in Anger*) the play of the age.

A recent book by Frances Stonor Saunders, *Who Paid the Piper?*, does a fine job of capturing the remarkable cultural politics of the age, when the great ideological divide touched, illuminated, sometimes seriously tainted those who tried to understand the prospects of history and the divide between liberal democracy and collectivist and totalitarian communism that split the minds of the European intelligentsia. Many had been left wing in the thirties, and cut their teeth on the Marxist dialectic – only to find far deeper ambiguities when the great God of History failed, or wore Stalin's moustache, and the Iron Curtain started to descend.

Saunders shows these postwar years as a *Kulturkampf* – an extended conflict over cultural values and ideologies between the 'West' and Russia in which the postwar literary community and the intelligentsia were deeply involved, whether conspiratorially or otherwise. America's decision to accept its new historical status – the land that in the thirties had been associated as much with Depression as Hollywood movies was now the War's outright victor and a land of plenty – was as much an internal as a global question. But once the political decision had been made to reject isolationism, revive flattened Europe and develop, through massive injections of aid, troops and commercial influence, the re-emergence or emergence of democratic institutions, the game was on.

In the ruins of flattened Berlin in 1945 American personnel devised a cultural as well as political strategy to win artistic, intellectual and literary hearts and minds against the no less determined campaigns of communism. In 1947 the CIA was founded, using wartime alliances to secure a cultural campaign of influence. This coincided with a widespread intellectual defection from communism, the God that failed. In the years that followed, the land across the Atlantic that seemed to have produced only chewing gum and Mickey Mouse became a cultural dream. Saunders' book looks at the massive input of

CIA funding – to congresses and foundations, publishing houses and magazines – that encouraged this process, and its impact on the fifties cultural climate.

America had been plunged into world history as never before: a landscape of international crisis and political upheaval, as old empires dissolved (the British, the French, the Dutch, the Portuguese), new independence movements and wars started, fresh alliances were forged. In 1946 Churchill had seen the Iron Curtain descending; by 1947 the 'Cold War' had begun. In 1949 a whole new concern over espionage issues rose, and the Alger Hiss case opened. As the fifties started American troops were again in action, in Korea.

American – and many European – intellectuals now often found their old allegiances an embarrassment. As Lionel Trilling put it in the preface of *The Liberal Imagination* (1950), the connection between literature and politics was 'an immediate one' – but 'it is no longer possible to think of politics except as the politics of culture.' For 'the literature of the modern period . . . has been characteristically political', meaning it had to do with the moral value of life and the search for the self. Politics was a human necessity, but ideology was the curse: hence the liberal imagination.

The question of hearts and minds dominated the fifties. According to Joseph McCarthy, Republican senator from Wisconsin, the 'enemies from within' were to be found among the 'eggheads', 'the bright young men who are born with silver spoons in their mouths' who were sapping the nation's strength in a new kind of war that could not end 'except in victory or death for this civilization.' McCarthyism displayed much about fifties America: the popular anxiety over intellectuals, national engagement in foreign aid, the role of global superpower. Arthur Miller's play *The Crucible* (1953), about the Salem witch trials, captured the atmosphere of 'witch-hunt' that enveloped the hearings of Congress and Senate committees as the concept of 'Un-American activities' came to embrace all left-wing allegiance, past or present.

Yet for all the anxiety things were getting better – as the

American book titles showed. In *White Collar* (1951), C. Wright Mills charted the rise of a new service class – who by 1956 were forming the ranks of William H. Whyte's *The Organization Man*. These were, as David Potter put it in his book of 1954, *People of Plenty*, who lived, as J. K. Galbraith observed in 1958, in *The Affluent Society*, a land of private wealth and public squalor. On the other hand, said David Riesman, Americans now felt robbed of traditional values and were *The Lonely Crowd*. And, as C. Wright Mills observed in a later book, *The Power Elite* (1956), the price of new affluence and speedy innovation might be living in a society run by the 'military-industrial complex', on which the entire 'Eisenhower equilibrium' was based.

Annihilation was the terror, affluence the dream of the fifties. It was the reward that came after the grim pattern of the century's first half: war–boom–crash–war again. Even in Europe affluence slowly came. In Britain a decade that started with rationing and austerity, only partly alleviated by the public celebrations of the Festival of Britain, advanced through the Suez Crisis, which sharply divided nation and generation, through to the spirit of You've Never Had It So Good. Even the wave of Anger that so closely coincided with Suez had most to do with the transformed meritocratic opportunities of an expanding, a far less classbound, welfare state.

Europeans divided in their allegiances, but, CIA funding or not, the great court of appeal was going to be America. Twenty years ahead of any other nation in terms of innovation, technological resource, lifestyles and fashions, personal possessions, individual opportunities, it was the land of iceboxes, finned cars, Elvis Presley, rebels without a cause, teenagers and the smartest international corporations. It had good claim to being seen as the artistic and intellectual capital of the world as well.

Its older writers (Faulkner, Hemingway, Steinbeck) were dutifully awarded Nobel Prizes. Its younger writers (Mailer, Bellow, Salinger, Welty, McCullers, Baldwin, Ellison, Robert Lowell) captured the tone of the times. The issues they explored – the experience of war in Europe and the Pacific, the Jewish and the African-American experience; the strains of racial discrimination and urban alienation that came from the lonely-crowd cities – touched home everywhere.

The American fifties was a period of great cultural energy. The New York art scene dominated through the movement of abstract expressionism, the great new playwrights (Arthur Miller, Tennessee Williams) were American too. American movies caught the flavour of the age; the very look of the American skyline showed the Bauhaus spirit of European architectural modernism had fulfilled itself in a postwar merger of European theory and American technology and investment; American jazz was world music. The irony is that the great Americanization of European culture the CIA so busily financed would surely have happened anyway through classic laws of cultural influence.

By the end of the fifties it was possible to claim the Western world had reached an 'Eisenhower equilibrium', or in other words an age of American-led capitalist affluence and 'The End of Ideology'. It was not quite so. The notion that the fifties was straight and conformist and the sixties radical is far from true. Much that was considered as part of the radicalism of the sixties, including much passionate anti-Americanism, developed in the fifties. The Beat Movement came to its peak with *Howl* in 1956 and *On the Road* in 1957. And as some declared the Eisenhower equilibrium as the decade ended, the people were (only just) electing a new generation youth president, John F. Kennedy.

The fifties began feeling like an austerely postwar time; but as it developed it soon contained the sixties in embryo. It was the bridge between the hard ideologies of the Thirties, and the counterculture. War and Cold War brought other changes: rapid technological innovation, the growth of modern media and communications, international travel, prospects in space. Futurologists began to scout the year 2000, mostly getting it severely wrong (we are not living on the moon). And for a young writer like myself, trying to write a novel that caught as much of it as possible, it was a tense, contradictory, anxious, existential and a rather wonderful world.

THE DAYS OF THE HISTORY MEN

KARL MARX UNIVERSITY Leipzig is one of the world's ugliest academic buildings: a postwar Marxist monstrosity of a sky-scraper where the roof ventilation, by a fragile deceit, is fanned to give the appearance of a half-open book. It dominates the city of Bach and book fairs, strange compacts and odd philoso-phies, once called the Paris of the East. In Goethe's magnificent *Faust*, it's the place where daring Doctor Faustus is shown the student inns and offered all knowledge and pleasure in exchange for a small contract. His handler is Mephistopheles; the contract is for his soul.

As the latest spy scandal shows, Leipzig keeps its reputation. Deep in the DDR, before 1989 it was no city of open books. It was the ideal place for an international course on German history, set up by the Stasi's foreign-intelligence unit. It was perfect recruiting ground for visiting foreign students, includ-ing, allegedly, Dr Robin Pearson, Hull University senior lec-turer and the latest spy to be fished from the cold.

To this day Karl Marx University, totally restaffed, and dominating a city now rebuilding, feels a grim monument to the recent era when universities and spying felt intimately intertwined. We know many British spies emerged from the stone quads of Cambridge, where no sooner was an atom split than it was exported east to the Dark Other. Redbrick seems a less common scene for the secret keypad and the dark debrief-ing. Experts in the history of fire insurance hardly seem the most useful spies.

Yet the truth is that for an entire intellectual generation over the Cold War (forget the 'low dishonest decade', the Marxizing thirties) every campus, course, conference, intellectual trend and tendency had a heady flavour of conflict and conspiracy. For forty years from the descent of the Iron Curtain, every major argument, issue, interpretation fell within the frame of ideology. Or rather the two ideologies, for in each mind there were two: liberal Western individualism (a.k.a. capitalism) and the Marxist dialectics of history (a.k.a. communism).

Minds divided, brains split, between the great interpretations, which were to the late twentieth century as Protestant–Catholic wars were to the Reformation. Anyone who went to a university from the fifties to the late seventies will know Marxism's intellectual appeal – or, as its proponents would say, 'necessity'. Jack Straw knew it, and many a Blair government minister. On every campus, British or American, there was 'Marxist interpretation': history made urgent, the withering of the state, the defeat of the military-industrial complex, the completion of the dialectic, the triumph of the proletariat.

No matter many of the most influential Marxists were well endowed, and Western Marxism a largely bourgeois phenomenon. The Marxist version runs through nearly all the powerful intellectual movements of the age – existentialism, structuralism, post-structuralism, deconstruction – and was part of the joy and urgency of modern intellectual life.

It had its high moment at the end of the sixties. As student revolution surged, this was the triumph of the History Men – the radicals who knew that to redeem the world and raise the passions all you needed was a little Marx, a little Freud, a little history. Ideology was what gave every campus its spice. It gave every student union an air of heady conspiracy, loud secrecy, excited sexuality that went back to the days of the Enigma codes and Bletchley Park.

For the campus was hardly pastoral space. It had nuclear physics labs, did research for the army and great corporations, was a site of power and false consciousness. It was also the perfect place for winning hearts and minds. Here were the politicians, bureaucrats, scientists, writers and intellectuals of the future, most still in a condition of near innocence.

No wonder a Cold War campus was a scene of plots, conspiracies, suspicions. No wonder there were persuaders, strange gurus, odd societies, mysterious foreign conferences and courses (it might be Moscow or Leipzig, might be Rome or Santa Barbara) from which no one returned quite the same. It might be temptation – the offer of the travel grant, the scholarship, the fellowship, the lectureship. It might be the call of pure ideas: in this book or lecture the truth told at last.

The History Men prospered as minds swung between capitalism and utopia, America and Russia. The Hull lecturer was not the only lecturer to be solicited, and, if he fell, to fall. He will not be the only one who trawled through the papers or wrote a report on his academic fellows. In the great game of ideas and ideologies, the campus was battleground, the opposing argument the enemy, a spirit of conspiracy, seduction and blackmail (well perfected by the Stasi, the most intellectual and academic of the Marxist spooks) the true smell of academe.

As *Who Paid the Piper?* shows, duplicity bred its double. The battle for young hearts and minds was played by security forces on *both* sides of the Curtain. The truly amazing thing is how in the last ten years, since Marxism collapsed and the Berlin Wall came down, the ideological divide by which a whole generation found intellectual seriousness has quite disappeared.

How distant it seems. Now there is only one ideology; if you believe in dialectics, that means none. We live in postmodern times. Ideas aren't beliefs but commodities. History's a theme park. Thought is irony. Liberal individualism turns out not to be a great humanist belief but pure capitalism, crass commerce, after all.

The strange smell of the Cold War – spying, conspiracy, recruitment, betrayal – comes from an age when ideas really were important. But perhaps the great and dangerous game – which ruined careers, cost lives, raised global terrors, corrupted intellectual honesties, smelled of betrayal – is not over completely. The spy in the City of Trawlers was 'exposed', it seems, by a trawling reporter who had a camera in his tie.

CONVERGENCE: A STORY

1

ALOHA! This word means welcome in our islands. Perhaps you have already experienced some of our traditional warm hospitality. People who come here always seem to enjoy to be greeted with the lei, our necklace of tropical flowers. This is one of many customs from our old days that still survive. Especially here at the airport.

Maybe you know our islands have a very varied history. They were discovered by Captain James Cook, a very famous Britisher who made a tour of the Pacific in the eighteenth century and discovered many things. Of course he didn't really discover the islands. They were here a long time before that, as everyone who lived here knew already. Captain Cook was a very famous navigator and he was received here with the lei, and other great demonstrations of astonishment and delight. It is very sad he was killed here a little while after, simply because of a misunderstanding over a canoe. But our chiefs made an idol of his bones, and they worshipped him, until all our idols and tattoos were abolished by the Christian missionaries. Cook gave these islands a name, the Sandwich Islands. Don't think this is because of what we eat here. They were named after a British earl who liked fast food. In history these islands used to have their own kings, who have been depicted on the postage stamps. For a long time we were part of the famous British Empire, and in those days the islands had two names. Then we became a territory of the United States, and now we are a very proud state of the union. Of course we like being American very much better. By the way, the name Sandwich Islands is no longer used.

(When I first learned to stand on my head, says the girl, I got so excited I wanted to do it wherever I went.)

Many great writers have authored books about these islands. Persons as famous as Captain Cook, of course, who wrote about them before he died, and Isabella Bird, and Mark Twain the humorist, who came to the islands after a volcanic eruption and wrote some letters about his experiences which helped to make him very famous. Of course I don't need to mention the famous name of James A. Michener, who wrote the biggest and most famous book of all, which I expect all of you have read. If anybody likes history, you might like to look at a book called *A Portrait of a Sandwich Islander*, which is all about the old days. By the way, the map in it is no longer used.

Because they are located right here in the middle of the Pacific Ocean, these islands may seem very remote to some of you. That does not mean they have not played an important part in history. For example without these islands we might never have had World War Two. Who remembers the date of December 7, 1941? That was the day the Japanese air force took off from their carriers and bombed the American fleet over at Pearl Harbor. That made President Roosevelt declare war on them and that was the start of World War Two. You can visit the site today and see a floating museum and memorial to this effect, with some of the real wrecked ships and a video presentation.

(Do you jog at all? asks the girl. I jog twenty minutes at least every day. If I miss more than three days I know my muscles are going to fall to pieces.)

But here on the islands we like to think all these things are way in the past. We like to think here all persons of all races can get along with one another just fine. We like to think maybe we're the real hub of the whole Pacific Rim. Most peoples from everywhere come through here these days, because we're a great stopover, and so our population has every kind of ethnic source. Successive waves have placed many nationalities here, including Chinese, Taiwanese, Japanese, Filipino, Indonesian, Portuguese, Hawaiian and of course mainland American, all living in happiness together. Many languages are spoken in the islands, including pidgin. One of the great attractions of the islands is that you can eat here in all sorts of ways, and dress any way you like.

Someone once called these islands paradise, and we think those guys really knew a thing or two. Except did you know there are no snakes in the islands, so that makes it even better than paradise, right? At least, there are two snakes, but those are in the zoo, and they're both male. This is required by federal legislation. One important fact about the islands is they have very little wildlife, and that's because they're isolated and volcanic in origin. A marvel of nature, they rose from the deep bottom of the sea in a number of massive explosions. There are many mountains, their lower slopes all enrobed in dark forest. Altogether there are forty volcanic peaks, but don't worry, most of them are inactive. On the eastward islands eruptions can occur quite often, even as often as last year. By the way, we don't expect anything of this kind during your visit, and if we hear anything unusual we'll let you know.

(Are you interested in Rudolph Steiner at all? asks the girl.)

As I said, many people have come to call these islands paradise, and you only have to look round you or stick around a little on vacation to find out why. The vegetation is lush, the air is temperate, and the sea is blue. Average daytime and night-time temperatures are available in your travel and vacation packs, complete with beach and interisland travel information, and advice on the best hotels and rentals. I guess I don't need to tell you we got beaches and surf. Have we got surf! I'd also like to remind you about our show, because we have a really nice little show here on the island. It's called *Invitation to Paradise*, and it's performed on selected days. A cast of 175 real islanders perform authentic folk dances, from Tahiti, Tonga, Samoa, Fiji, Maori and the old Hawaii. As the show unfolds, a fiery volcanic effect will command your attention. By the way, you'll find plenty more information about all that in your travel packs.

So again we say aloha!, and will you now make your way to the car park, where you'll find transport provided to take you to your next destination.

(It seems so weird, says the girl, being here without John. He's had to stay on in New York City. He teaches a course on the enjoyment of death.)

2

Aloha. Welcome to the Hale Kokua Center. In order to make your stay more comfortable, we have designed this handy information pack, to fully acquaint you with our various services, rules and procedures.

State law forbids gaming, firearms and solicitation on state property. There are no special quiet hours, but we request you to keep noise to a minimum in the evenings out of consideration for others. The orange arrows identify your floor. The elevators take only ten adult persons. Request a key if you stay out late. The desk provides the following services: loan of sports equipment, typewriters, hairdryers; light-bulb exchange; lost keys; messages; checkout; information. Bare feet are at your own risk.

Remember, this is an experiment in international living among different races and creeds. Be tolerant of others. Avoid embarrassment in the corridors. In an experiment in international living, most tension occurs in the bathrooms. Attached is a list which indicates the items you're supposed to receive in your room during your stay. They've already been checked by your staff, so they should be properly provided. Please sign the bottom of the sheet to show you have received them.

Table lamp (1)
Soap dish (1)

Toshiba fan (1)
Digital radio-clock (1)
Tumblers (2)
Pitcher (1)
Towels (2)
Washcloth (1)
Personal soaps (2)

Have a good stay with us. Lock your room and your valuables at all times. The Center is not responsible for personal loss or damage to resident possessions. Theft or suspicious person: notify the staff on duty.

Thank you!!! Wallace Yamashita, Your Staff Assistant.

(Why don't we take a walk in the gardens? says the girl. It helps you get over the jet lag.)

3

Japanese garden. Visitors welcome. Garden is maintained for your viewing pleasure. Please restrict traffic to front grassy area. No private or commercial use. No food or animals. These are sacred Japanese carp (koi), symbols of longevity and order. They cost a hundred dollars or more. Please don't feed me, I'm on a fish diet. A garden is a place of peace, and always there is running water.

(The carp are big and solemn. They navigate seriously under the flow. Then they jump, take flies from the air, plop bug-eyed back into their own element again. Their eyes seem highly attentive to the upper world. Their mouths are large, noisy, sucking orifices. Around us underground water jets burst into stuttering life and spray their rainbow jet streams over the artificial lawns.)

(I think those Japanese fish are really lewd, says the girl, tucking her long skirt under her thighs on the watered and highly green grass. Well, don't you think sucking is sexy?)

4

Aloha! Hi! Welcome to the conference restaurant. Attention! People with pacemakers: microwave oven in building. This restaurant operates a serve yourself system. Please choose only one: Thousand Islands OR Roquefort. Try the local tropical fruit. Low-calorie. High-protein. Salt-free. Use heat-resistant cups for hot drinks only. Wait until machine totalizes before putting in new coin. Vending guaranteed, do not kick. Express lane: five food items or less. This fountain is for human use only. Smokers: please respect the rights of others.

(I guess I'm really a vegetarian, says the girl, but I'd like some of that.)

This table can accommodate you. In our culture no part of food is wasted. Even the webbed feet of duck are dried and used. The food is allowed to have its own nature. It is fibre and semen and fat, eggy and uncooked, the raw fish, the poo poo . . .

(Hey, you must be hungry, says the girl. Wouldn't you like me to give you a proper calorie count on all of that?)

5

Aloha, everybody! The ones on the right are juices and soft drinks, these on the left are manhattan, martini and gin and tonic . . . Oh, Kim, Kim, my old Korean friend, you are so far from us in Asia. So what are you doing these days, why don't you send us zen any more? . . . It is my privilege on behalf of the foundation to bid you all welcome to what we all expect will be a major conference and talkfest . . . Ah, but let the Westerner always remember that for instance *Mansfield Park* is not always perfectly comprehended by our students in Japan . . . So many people, from so many countries, ensuring a meaningful dialogue . . . To take a single example, baths do not mean the same thing in every culture . . . Where better

than here in these islands, the meeting place of East and West?
. . . I think man–woman relationships are changing now in all
the places . . . That is why so many people, writers and scholars,
have been invited to come here. Where better, with such
distinguished guests, to understand the multicultural universe
of the new millennium? . . .

(Between my divorce and the AA I've had so much to do,
says the girl.)

6

Great! I think this has been a really excellent session. I'm sure
we all of us want to thank both of you, for presenting us with
that very beautiful poem and that very beautiful story. I wonder
if you could explain them to us just a little?

In my poem, we have the pear blossom passing across the
face of a fixed star. Then, in despair, the girl spreads the hairs
in her armpit, and the wind carries her away. You must
understand it does not translate very well. In our language we
have a phonetic syllabary and ideogrammic symbols, and we
can also add the phonetics of the Chinese characters at the
side. Also in my culture there is no word for 'I'. Therefore we
have to manufacture a way to say. In the poem I use a foreign
character that means a private person. Now we have a rebellion
against the classical, a return to the collective and moral culture.
Oh, by the way, women in my culture have a different form
of literature to write in. At the end of the poem the woman is
speaking, and we are no longer looking at each other.

(It's a necklace I bought at the stopover in Pago Pago, says
the girl.)

That's great! I suggest we all discuss that.

Excuse me, in Sanskrit there is no word for conscience.
You are moral and mental people, but we are metaphysical . . .
Perhaps we should ask this question: why so many Japanese
novelists in recent times have committed suicide? Maybe it is
because they tried to grow an unnatural foreign ego in their

native souls . . . Yes, but the role of the narrative self has also been subsumed in contemporary Western, that is to say, postmodern writing. The lore of Marxism and deconstruction has been increasingly applied. In the French *nouveau roman*, as you remember Roland Barthes has once noted, language acts lexically, foregrounding the elements of text and certain tropic states of mind, to the point where perceptions of objects exceed their apparent function, and conventional literary space is redefined. Of course, we all see ourselves as part of Asia in his new global age . . . Excuse me, sir, I should like to point to a falsie in your argument . . .

In the story you heard, the boy flees into the bush, pursued by the ghost of his grandfather. This is a bitter indictment of a modern world which has distorted progress. In expressing the story, the writer senses the postwar world is over at last. He makes a free stream of consciousness, using the simile of sex surrounding a person's soul like a rainbow . . .

(Have you ever tried taking a shower with a Korean? asks the girl.)

7

Aloha! Welcome to the Ala Moana Shopping Center, which for a long time was the biggest shopping centre in the world. Maybe it still is. That's because the islands have always been a meeting place for international trade, a crossover place for style. Take my word, there's hardly a country in the world that isn't represented here by a store. I think you'll find there isn't a thing you need you ain't going to be able to get. You'll find Polynesian things, Japanese things, German things, Iranian things, Chinese and Taiwanese things. I'm sure our French representative will be glad to know there's a boutique française, and for our British representative an authentic British pub with Guinness. I think you'll want to take a long time looking round, so why don't we all meet again by Ben and Jerry's, right across from the McDonald's. Don't forget we have another official reception at five. And if there are any special souvenirs of our island culture you want to take back to your homes, I'll be only to glad to guide you . . .

Trees. Musak. Umbrellas, fire-eaters. Mickey Mouse, twice. Escalators up, escalators down. Screeching macaws, screeching stereos. Japanese teahouse. Hawaiian mummu store. Belgian chocolate shop. Finnish textiles. Thai ties. Xian antiques. Style booths, food booths: Korean, Polynesian, Jewish, Turkish, Polish, Armenian, Szechuan, Mandarin, Cantonese, Russian, Filipino, junk. Yuppie, guppie. Hippie, faddie. Essential oils and aromas. Ginseng, couscous. Edible panties. Condom of the Month club. Store after store, orifice after orifice. Level after level, flavour after flavour. Convergence.

(What kind of lifestyle are you shopping for today? asks the girl. I think I see you maybe in French silk underwear with Nike shoes and something Japanese on top.)

8

Aloha. As maybe you've already discovered by now, this is the traditional native word for welcome in our islands. This is papaya juice and that is rum. I am sure now that you've seen a little of our glorious sea and our beaches you would like to know a little more about the history of our islands. Ours is an ancient Pacific civilization with its own famous kings and queens. Most of our indigenous people were of moderate stature, with reddish-brown skin. But the chieftains and the women of their families were remarkable for their height, and four hundred pounds wasn't an unusual weight. This superiority in physique amongst the nobles is said to be due to a system of massage called the *lomi-lomi* . . .

(Oh, don't you love massage? says the girl.)

As you'll have found out, there are few animals here, and there are no snakes on the island. The only reptiles are skinks and geckos. We have plenty of insects, and cockroaches and green locusts are serious pests. Owing to the nature of our origins, the proportion of endemic plants is greater here than anywhere else. The chelo berry is famous in song and story, and formerly served as a propitiatory offering to Pelé. In old times, birds were protected by the native belief that messages from the gods came to us in the form of bird cries, and also by a royal edict that forbade the killing of the species used for making feather cloaks. There are several old languages, but these are no longer used.

(I'm really starting to get kind of hungry, aren't you? says the girl.)

9

Well, good evening, hi there, and how are you tonight! Welcome to Top Floor. Customers tell us we're the best restaurant west of San Francisco, and we want to show you they're right. So I'm Steve, and tonight I'll be helped in serving you by Suzie and Ya-Ya, who are at your full service. Cash is your wine waiter, and he'll come by to greet you in a minute. We want you to feel really wonderful here, and I'm ready to answer any questions you might have about our menu. The soup of the day is asparagus, and that comes with pitta croutons. Chef's choices tonight include pan-fried sturgeon, Cape Cod clams, French escargots, trout from the Maine rivers, venison and several varieties of Alaska salmon. Our produce is fresh, we have flights every day from Boston and San Francisco to make sure you get the cream of the crop. If you wish to take a little longer, I'll gladly leave you for a few minutes to study our hand-printed menu and make your personal selection. Meantime duck pâté is served at our pleasure. So welcome, you guys, sit back, enjoy, and have a real nice evening.

(I just don't know which me is me any more, says the girl, the person who was back there with John or the person who's here. I just have this feeling that somewhere everything should just come together. Converge, you know what I mean?)

(I too have this feeling: everywhere people meeting, orifices opening, the mouths of carp snapping, the garden streaming, the water jets juddering.)

(Oh, and that question you never made up your mind to ask me, says the girl, I guess the answer is yes.)

10

Manoa! We hope you enjoyed your stay in our experiment in international living. If we've succeeded with you, please let us know. If not, just tell us on this form where we went wrong.

1. Your room was as clean and orderly as your own home, right?
   Right: ___
   Wrong: ___

2. Everything in your room worked, right?
   Right: ___
   Wrong: ___

3. Your kitchen was properly provisioned at all times, right?
   Right: ___
   Wrong: ___

4. Maybe it wasn't the most fantastic experience of your whole life, but it came close, right?
   Right: ___
   Wrong: ___

   THANKS FOR YOUR HELP. AND COME BACK,
   YOU ALL.

(I don't think it's such a great idea if I give you my home address, says the girl. I don't really have a fixed location, and I don't think I know who I am anyway.)

11

Manoa, everybody. I hope you had a very fruitful conference in our lovely international islands here in the middle of our beautiful Pacific ocean, and that our really fine weather helped you get together in a useful way. I hope you're all going back to your countries feeling refreshed.

In these islands we have a pleasant custom on departure. It is the lei, a necklace of flowers. It means welcome, of course, but also farewell. What it really means is we wish you will come back to see us because after what you have experienced you will never want to stay apart from us again. These leis are presented to you by the society for Eastern and Western friendship, bringing together all races and creeds. Please check with your airline to make sure your countries will accept them.

(Sometimes I'd like just to spread the hairs in my armpit, and let the wind just carry me away, says the girl. And, flowers round her neck, she goes to the New York check-in, while I head for the London flight.)

LOVING NORFOLK

IN WHAT I CONSIDER to be the most wonderful act of literary generosity, John Fowles, author of *The French Lieutenant's Woman* and *The Magus*, and one of our finest novelists, has had the notion of bequeathing his house, Belmont, in Lyme Regis, Dorset, to a new generation of writers. The gesture seems so fine because it is surely true that writing is nourished by environment and atmosphere, community and place.

I have spent some of the most productive as well as the happiest times of my writing life in the colonies: that's to say, in writers' and artists' retreats. America specializes in them – Yaddo in New York State, the MacDowell colony in New England – knowing that time, space and facilities can make the difference. So they have; American literature has been the better for them, and the list of resulting publications (Bellow, Roth) proves the point.

In Britain they are a rarity, and Fowles' gift – though interrupted at the moment by problems of planning, funding and lottery support – is inspired. All the more so because Belmont is one of the best of writers' houses, Lyme Regis one of the finest writerly locations. Fowles, who has lived for thirty years in the house, celebrates its perfect setting in the opening scene of his most famous novel, *The French Lieutenant's Woman*. He starts the story on the Cobb, used by Jane Austen in her last complete novel, *Persuasion*. He also employs the Undercliff, part of the great fossil trail of the Victorian and Darwinian age. And Lyme sits nicely on the edge of Hardy's Wessex, one of the greatest literary regions 'invented' by a British writer.

It so happens that among the writers John Fowles wishes to

encourage and support are those from my own university, the University of East Anglia, where twenty-seven years ago I started what proved to be a very productive MA course in creative writing. Asked by the press about why writers might wish to move from Norfolk to Dorset, Fowles offers the obvious answer: 'Because Dorset is so much more beautiful than Norfolk.'

It's a view for which I have much sympathy. If I didn't live and write in Norfolk I should love to live and write in Dorset. But I do live in Norfolk; I moved here over thirty years ago and fell in love with the place. I love it even more when, as happens now and then, Norfolk comes in for one of those periodical bouts of Norfolk media-bashing that seem to start in the Groucho Club or from the wit and wisdom of Jeremy Clarkson.

I'm never quite sure why this is. True, probably the most famous literary association the county enjoys is that single clipped line of Noël Coward ('Very flat, Norfolk'). Many people assume it sums up not simply the flatness of the landscape, but a total state of mind. And if you only come up weekending, go wandering off in the waterlands of the Fens, always a place on its own, or listen to Alan Partridge, it may very well seem that way.

In truth Norfolk isn't all that flat (the Cromer Ridge, etc), and isn't all that dull. What it is, like Dorset, is a clear and rural region: a part of Britain that feels absolutely like nowhere else. It's a place defined by its geography (cut off on three sides by the sea and the fourth by British Rail, is what they always used to say when we still had a British Rail), and shaped by its very distinctive history. Before the fens were drained, and routes to the Midlands opened (still only to a point), it felt truly islanded: open by land only to the south, but by water everywhere.

Norfolk was rich. It lived off its wool trade, its great acres, its fine coasts, its big ports, its fishing, its Continental links, at least till the industrial revolution. Lowestoft was one of the world's greatest fishing harbours, King's Lynn a major port (there were others, which drowned beneath the waves). As for the east coast sea traffic, a great shuttling trade of coasters, wherries and ferries went up and down by Norfolk along North Sea routes that were once the equivalent of Virgin Rail plus the Great North Road.

To the eighteenth century, Norwich was the second city of England, and a busy cultural capital. But above all this was a Continental region, heavily settled by those who came here over the North Sea: Vikings, Scandinavians, the Dutch, the Huguenots. They created its trades, its arts, its printing and painting traditions. The Dutch-gabled architecture you see everywhere shows the depth of the influence. Many people here still think the nearest capital city isn't London but Amsterdam.

With its great houses and parks, rolling acres and marshy broadlands, its ship-like great churches, which have often lain stranded villageless amid fields ever since the plague, its isolated rectories (and rectors), Dutch-gabled ports, bracing beaches, dunes and precarious cliffs for tough summer holidays, the region has always produced its own writing: very distinct in nature, very strong on the sense of place.

This is a land of writing parsons (John Skelton and Parson Woodforde) and farmer-writers (Rider Haggard, R. H. Mottram, Henry Williamson, John Middleton Murry). It's a region that's always been rich in poets, from William Cowper to George Macbeth, Anthony Thwaite, George Szirtes. It's a wonderful scene for the remote and unusual crime and for so the classic detective story: see Dorothy Sayers, Ruth Rendell, P. D. James, Sherlock Holmes himself.

As the hub at the centre of Norfolk's great wheel, Norwich sponsored painting, writing, culture. It was the city of Julian of Norwich and Sir Thomas Browne. Its Nonconformist tradition bred a range of Victorian talents: George Borrow, Anna Sewell, Harriet Martineau. When in the early 1960s a new university started (and one had been intended for at least as far back as Cambridge), another literary and artistic generation began. Angus Wilson became professor, and many other writers gathered round him, including Rose Tremain and Clive Sinclair.

I was one of them, and so it has gone on. In 1970 a creative-writing course started, with Ian McEwan as first student. Kazuo Ishiguro soon followed, and since then there has been crop after crop. Norwich stays a place of many writers, one reason that brings other writers to it. For the fact is that for all the metropolitan, cosmopolitan, and multicultural times we live in, literature is still very much born of place. And we all need the places that host it and let it happen and flourish.

Place does not often work on writers directly, and its importance is often not as subject matter. Writers have always been both rooted and placeless, natives and émigrés at once. Many books very clearly rooted in one place – James Joyce's *Ulysses*, for example, the great novel of modern Dublin – are written in another, over a long critical distance of time and space. Most writers wander widely and freely. Yet they still want some place that truly feels like home.

And in my own case this is now Norfolk: a place I have written about very little, but have chosen to write *in*. I'm shaped by its present landscape, its scenes and associations, its pleasant literary and artistic communities. I like its peace, its strangeness, perhaps most its sense of being almost at the edge of things – a feeling many have had about Norfolk.

In truth it's a region not just of one landscape but many, distinct but interlocking. Thanks to Arthur Ransome, the most familiar is the Norfolk Broads, old peat-diggings that, developed for inland sailing, have become a major area of recreation. At times the Broads can become a gridlocked waterfilled M25 of summer-holiday cruisers. Most of the time, and as soon as you leave the most-used rivers, they are deeply relaxed and quiet.

And beyond the Broads lie the two east coast ports, Yarmouth and Lowestoft, which still retain a Dickensian strangeness. The great herring fleets have mostly disappeared; the North Sea oil and gas industries only partly took their place. But, lacking good inland communications, still tied tight to the sea, they have retained their distant character.

Then to the north, around and beyond the Burnhams, is

the world of the great country houses (Blickling and Houghton, Felbrigg, Gunton and Holkham) and the north Norfolk coast that lies beyond. In Edwardian times its resorts like Cromer and Hunstanton were 'bracing'; this was where brisk sea-bathes in what felt like Baltic waters fitted young men and women for a hard life in the colonies. Now it has lapsed, much of it handed back to nature and wildlife, its vast bird and seal sanctuaries giving this whole region an air of Siberian peace and remoteness.

Round the wheel a little further, and there's King's Lynn. The home of Fanny Burney and Margery Kempe, it sits inland on the deep Wash estuary, an ancient port with a massive past. Now it hosts a fine literary festival which, amongst other things, brings a great many of the local writers together. It also leads on to Norfolk's second waterland: the Fen Country, shared with Cambridgeshire and Lincolnshire.

Captured in print in the novels of Dorothy Sayers and in Graham Swift's marvellous *Waterland*, it remains an amazing landscape. To me, no part of England feels stranger. Huge sluices built by the Dutch in the eighteenth century control the river-flow that runs out of the Midlands. The villages here were often once little islands amid the marshes and sea-waters of a great archipelago. The big churches brood amid the dykes in their own isolation.

Like everywhere else, Norfolk is changing these days. In Norwich big science parks are emerging, new technologies are developing around its industries of printing, insurance, and biotech, and it's part of Silicon Fen. It's busy with artistic activities, having a National Film theatre, a great painting culture, and a proud base in its regional arts.

Yet the region feels different still – and somehow faintly elegiac. This is partly because of the long wide landscapes, the reedy marsh and waterbeds, the lost lonely churches, the misty coasts with their drowned or disappearing histories, the many layers of visitors and 'strangers', and the odd relics left by the last touch of wanton devastation to be visited on the region, when the mad Dr Beeching axed its railway veins and arteries.

All this explains why it seems so right that the best book I know about Norfolk is by the most unexpected of writers. His name is W. G. Sebald, and he's a colleague of mine at the University of East Anglia. German-born, he writes in his native language, and has won much fame as one of Germany's leading contemporary novelists.

Yet he constantly writes of Norfolk. Now translated into English, his book *The Rings of Saturn* appeared last year [1998] in Britain to great acclaim. It's a novel, a journey-book, a meditation. It's also a troubled wandering round the coasts, the quiet and lost places of the region, connecting everything to the past, the Continent, the many strange histories that criss-cross through these landscapes and spaces. His book is indeed an elegy: for the ghosts of shattered worlds, lost villages, lost histories, lost meanings.

It's a book about the *strangeness* of place, and about what place means to a writer, which is not exactly what it means to the rest of us. For books emerge mysteriously out of places, and out of the exiles and extremities writers feel. 'The truth is, fiction depends for its life on place,' said the American writer Eudora Welty. 'Location is the proving ground . . . that is the heart's field.' I agree; writers need their place, whether it's Dorset or Norfolk. This is where I've found mine.

The best book on writers' Norfolk is Julian Earwaker and Kathleen Becker, *Literary Norfolk: An Illustrated Companion* (Chapter 6 Publishing, Ipswich, £14.99 [2006: Aurum Press, £16.99]). On the region's artistic scene, see Ian Collins, *A Broad Canvas: Art in East Anglia Since 1880* (Parke Sutton Publishing, Norwich, £19.95 [2006: Black Dog Books, £25.00]). W. G. Sebald's *The Rings of Saturn* is published by Harvill Press, London, at £12.00 [2006: Vintage, £7.99].

THE RECENT ADVENTURES OF
ROBINSON CRUSOE

MY NAME IS Robinson Crusoe. I am a common mariner from the fine city of York. As a young man I ran off to sea, entirely against my wise father's advice. Then, as you perhaps know already, it was my fate – quite a long time ago – to find myself stranded alone off the coast of South America on an uninhabited island, the single survivor of a most terrible shipwreck.

On that inhospitable and distant island I remained for twenty-eight years, sustained only by my remarkable diligence and fortitude, and by the benevolence of the Great Creator. Using every art of survival, applying every skill I possessed, displaying the enterprise of which only true Britons are capable, I raised fire, built a dwelling. I tamed the local wildlife, I cultivated unusual crops. Threatened by many enemies, I fought off pirates and marauders, disposed of cannibals and savages. I acquired an excellent native servant, Man Friday. I also, incidentally, invented the folding umbrella.

After many tribulations and struggles with everything that Providence could throw at me, I returned to England quite a wealthy man, with a whole rich colony in my possession. There I happened to meet a writing hack, Mr Daniel Defoe, who persuaded me against my best judgement to publish an account of my remarkable adventures.

The tale was remarkably successful, and won the Booker Prize of 1719, as not only the best, but the only, British novel so far. Soon, as is the way with literary success, it was being imitated everywhere. Desert islands became a popular location.

British schoolboys were constantly getting stranded on them, to the point where they became severely overcrowded. The Swiss (a people without even a navy) pretended they had an entire family of desert-island Robinsons. Pantomimes were made of my life. The umbrella became a popular item of apparel.

So it went on – until one day lately I was approached by a certain Miss Lawley, a much-respected London lady. She told me the passion for sending celebrated people to desert islands had become a popular fashion, and she liked to interview famous people about such experiences. She therefore invited me to relate my own island history to her, illustrating my account with eight pieces of music which would be selected entirely by myself.

I let myself be persuaded. It was, I fear, one of the more foolish decisions of my long – and thus far productive and diligent – life. I promptly set off for London. In my youth, the quickest way was by sailing ship from Hull. It was a perilous journey, prone to storm and shipwreck, as I found out once to my cost when I was cast up at Yarmouth. Now there is a convenient Awayday, changing only at Doncaster and Peter-borough, with a buffet-car service serving BLTs.

As soon as I arrive in Britain's capital – noticing that the folding umbrella has now become an enormous success in these parts – I manage to hire myself a conveyance. Strangely, the coachman seems to recognize me – possibly by my goatskin suit and hat, though my garb seems to me no stranger than what the bulk of modern Londoners choose to wear these days. 'You'll never guess who I had in the back of the cab the other day, squire,' he says. 'I am not a squire, merely a successful merchant of the middle station,' I explain to him, 'but who?' 'That Joanna Lumley. Gorgeous. Wasn't she stranded on a desert island too?' 'Not on mine,' I tell him, 'I looked.'

My conversation with Mistress Lawley occurs in a basement of advanced machinery. I recount my tale of courage and infinite hardship once again, illustrating the matter to a musical accompaniment of eight pious hymns, strangely and celestially beamed in from afar. Asked to select a book for my return to the island (not something I had ever meant to do again), of course I choose Mr Bunyan's *Pilgrim's Progress* for its impeccable piety.

I am then invited to select a 'luxury'. There is, of course, no need for luxuries on desert islands. I prefer to choose the one thing without which one cannot survive, never mind luxuriate. 'A bag of salt,' I say. I then discover that, through some miracle of modern invention, many people have over-heard our little encounter.

And ever since that unfortunate occasion I have not had a single moment's peace.

NEXT DAY to 'Wood Lane'. I have been suddenly summoned there to describe my island adventures further. 'One of those travel shows, is it?' asks the coachman. 'Guess who I had in the back of the cab once?' 'I'm a stranger from afar, I have no idea.' 'That Michael Palin. He's a laugh, he is.' 'Ah, but I come from Yorkshire,' I explain. 'There we never laugh.'

'Wood Lane' proves to be a vast madhouse of ill-dressed people, coming and going this way and that without any discernible purpose. Here I am quite suddenly placed in front of an audience of howling modern savages. The public conversation, with a Mr Anderson, does not go at all well. He asks a series of crude questions about my extended state of celibacy ('I thought only of work and the Lord,' I explain), and then he coarsely suggests I might have cared to share my desert island with his fellow 'guest', a Mr Eddie Izzard. I take one look. 'Under no circumstances would I permit the man even within sight of the shore,' I say.

Later I am guided over to another part of the same building. Here I engage in a strange confrontation with a very insistent, petulent young man called Paxman. He asks me if I would deny I am a colonialist. 'No, I would affirm it,' I say. 'You'd affirm it?' 'I would gladly affirm it.' 'So you wouldn't even deny it?' 'No, because I would affirm it.' 'You'd affirm you're a colonialist?' 'I hope you would too, Mr Paxman, for your entire life and that of your nation is based on the benefit of it. Would you deny it?' 'Not exactly deny it.' 'But you would not affirm it?' 'Not exactly affirm it.' 'Then it seems to me, Mr Paxman, you do not know your own mind, or understand the benefits of your providential situation,' I say. Now seeming confused, Paxman turns away from me, and then he suddenly begins reading aloud the vulgar gossip printed on the fronts of the daily journals.

Still, it seems my views and experiences are beginning to win some public attention. As I am about to depart the building, I am accosted by a certain Mr Clifford, a man of strange looks and very considerable gall. He looks a little like Mr Daniel Defoe, and is evidently of the same persuasion. He explains to me that he is a 'publicist', and asserts I have a very promising future as a 'celebrity'. 'I have been one already,' I say, 'it has been quite enough.'

The problem is, Mr Clifford insists, my 'angle'. I could do with a 'makeover' to make me 'more audience-friendly'. He then suggests we had better get rid of my fur-skin. At first, quite mistaking his meaning, I am highly affronted. He then makes me understand he thinks my clothes might give offence to a dangerous tribe of animal-liberators who are presently roaming the land.

Then he remarks it might 'put a better spin on it' if I wear the 'designer creations' of some itinerant Italian tailor he admires, a Mr Armani. I tell him true clothes are not 'designed'. My clothes are natural. They are made from our fellow creatures, but out of necessity, since we must cover our uncleanliness. 'Like Body Shop,' says Mr Clifford enthusiastically. Then he gives me his 'card', and says he will call again if he has any further 'hot' ideas.

LO, THE VERY next day, as I am about to return to Yorkshire, I am called from my lodgings to Whitehall. It seems that none other than a senior minister of the Queen at the Foreign Office is urgently seeking to meet me. A small and gnome-like man, this nabob of the state sits grandly in a vast and luxurious office, decorated with the finest treasures of India. He has a big tie, a short red beard and, he tells me, an 'ethical foreign policy'.

He asks me to tell him the history of my island, at the same time looking for it with his officials on quite the wrong map. I explain to him that it is not off Scotland but at the mouth of the Orinoco, another pestilential region peopled with cannibals and savages. 'We don't call them that any more,' he says. 'It is ours, is it?' 'Of course it is ours. Though the Spaniards and all the other savages attempted to seize it, I claimed it for Britain in the name of the King.' 'Oh, dear,' says the red-bearded gnome. 'I then introduced all the blessings of the Christian religion. I began plantations, I encouraged slavery, and I made the place completely defensible against the savages round about.' 'It seems they want it back,' he says. 'Who do?' 'The Spaniards, the Brazilians, the Guyanans and the Argentinians. And, for some reason, the Irish and the Chinese.' 'It is not theirs to have,' I say, 'it is a product of British industry, British enterprise, British courage, Divine Providence, and my own fortitude.' 'In that case we'll have to give it back,' says the gnome. 'What was the name again?' 'Thatcher Island.' 'Right. I doubt if we can defend it, either militarily or above all ethically. I'll see if Chris Patten's available, and then we'll send him down there to furl up the flag.' 'I object most fiercely, sir,' I say, 'and I shall gladly defend it myself, if necessary, as I have before.'

When I return to my lodgings in Southwark, a huge crowd of shouting and highly assertive strangers with short ladders has for some reason gathered to greet me. 'Look this way, Mr Crusoe' they shout, and 'Over here, Robbo'. It appears that my support for the little, sandy, uninhabited island off the coast of South America has not gone unnoticed. My fur-clad image, as man of nature, covers the journals next day. 'BRAVE CRUSOE DEFENDS THE LAST BRITISH ISLAND' says the headline in quite the pleasantest of these papers, the *Daily Mail*.

THEN, NO SOONER have I taken breakfast, of goat's cheese and some ill-toasted grains and seeds from a ridiculous packet, than

I am summoned back to Whitehall again. Now it is to 'Number 10', and it is the Queen's own first minister who wishes to see me. He proves to be no more than a boy; yet one of those cheerful, willing, very Christian young men who have always represented the best spirit of the nation and the backbone of the Empire. 'Hi there,' he says with a great grin, seemingly delighted to see me.

He invites me to share what he calls a 'photo-opportunity' with him. I stand furrily on one side of him, with a man dressed as Mickey Mouse on the other, while the image-takers call out 'Big grin, Tony' and 'Robbo, this way'. Then he takes me within, introduces me to several spectral and strangely sinister aides-de-camp, and describes me as a 'classic British culture icon'. Offering me coffee from which the coffee has been removed, he then asks if I do foreign tours and promotional appearances.

'I have lived out of my beloved land of England for far too long,' I confess. 'All I would ask is I be allowed to put my skills – my diligence, my ingenuity, my commercial enterprise, my gift of invention – at the service of my people.' 'You sound just like our kind of guy,' he says. I repeat to him the wise words spoken to me once by my own father, when he warned me against excessive ambitions and dangerous foreign adventures: 'The state of life all people envy is the middle state, between the mean and the great, where we pray to have neither poverty nor riches.' 'I love it, go on,' says the grinning boy. 'Then let me quote him to you in full, your most noble excellency,' I say, ' "The middle station in life" – said my father – "is calculated for all kinds of virtues and all kinds of enjoyments. Peace and plenty are the handmaids of a middle fortune, and this way men go silently and smoothly through the world – not embarrassed with labours of the hand or the head, not sold to the life of slavery, nor enraged with the passion of envy, or the burning lust of ambition, sliding silently through the world . . ." ' 'That's some quote,' says the grinning youth. 'You know what it is – the middle way! I knew it, you're one of us!'

Since that day it has all been trouble. At one minute I am asked to give advice to the 'Desert Island Project', zone seven of the Millennium Dome. The next I am asked to advise some maker of perfumery on their Desert Island scent, promo-ed by Naomi Campbell. Our Desert Island theme park in Shropshire opens shortly, and the Desert Island Café in Leicester Square is being provisioned by Marco-Pierre White and premiered by Arnold Schwarzenegger. The Desert Island CD-ROM is in the shops now. The Crusoe designer fashion range in synthetic goatskin is being developed by that same itinerant tailor, Mr Armani. Crusoe Self-Sufficiency Awareness Week is in February.

Which is why you find me now waiting here at Stansted Airport, with my bag of salt, *Pilgrim's Progress*, and an old folding umbrella. Flights today are delayed due to the usual celestial overcrowding. But as soon as I can manage I'm going back to the island. It's lonely, it's hard, it's dusty, it's pestilential, it's sexless. It has neither cable nor digital. The goats will have gone and I shall have to start again from scratch.

But at least I shall be alone – and this time I mean really alone. No Lumleys, no Izzards, no Andersons, no Cliffords, will be allowed to come there. I don't even want to see a Man Friday. I'm sorry, but that's how I feel now. I've had it with all the people I can eat.

DO WE HAVE GREAT NOVELS
ANY MORE?

THIRTY YEARS AGO an international food company with a bookish name planned to found a new literary prize, 'rather like the French Goncourt'. The Booker Prize for Fiction started in 1969, in obscure circumstances. This year it has celebrated its big anniversary with fanfare and governmental receptions. The Booker is a national institution.

In that same year, 1969, some colleagues and I at the University of East Anglia decided to start a course in the writing of fiction. The reasons were similar; literary fiction in Britain was in the doldrums. There was no similar course in Britain, so we borrowed an American name for it, and called it an MA in 'Creative Writing'.

The university was suspicious, but allowed us one trial year (1970–71), with one single student. By enormous fortune he was a young man called Ian McEwan. He wrote twenty stories, which became his first two books. The course flourished, the author flourished. This year, for a fine satirical novel called *Amsterdam*, McEwan has won the Booker Prize for Fiction.

The Booker Prize is a prize for 'literary fiction', and in this age of Blairite populism and a supposedly vibrant popular culture there are many people around who dismiss it as an 'elitist' irrelevance. It recommends difficult books nobody wants to read. It fails to reward the trendiest and most popular writers. It just doesn't speak for the culture.

There is another argument, almost the opposite. Nobody can write the great novel any more. Our writers are too narrow, our social experiences too dull, our Britishness too damning, to let the grand themes spill. We have plenty of slick and trendy writers, no shortage of Nick Hornbys, no absence of Bridget Joneses. But do we have great books?

The truth is that, from its beginnings in the eighteenth century, the novel has always been a ragbag. Some of its greatest works have been popular books with absolutely no literary pretensions. *Robinson Crusoe*, one of our first novels, was disguised as the true record of a castaway, and not called a novel at all. *Gulliver's Travels* was an angry political satire, not a great fictional work for children. Only slowly did Dickens take himself seriously as a novelist, as opposed to an entertainer.

It took a couple of centuries for the novel to be taken seriously as a literary form. By then it had become our most important genre – displacing poetry from its long-lived eminence, driving drama into a corner.

It had become the instrument for some of the world's greatest storytellers: Jane Austen, Balzac, Dickens, Melville, Dostoevsky, Tolstoy, George Eliot, Henry James, Thomas Hardy, Mark Twain. It had told the grand story of the growth of modern bourgeois society, charted the growth of great cities. It had invented some of the world's great characters: Jane Eyre, Mr Micawber, Anna Karenina, Huckleberry Finn.

It had also invented an enormous number of genres – romance and gothic, science fiction and detective fiction, horror, fantasy and so on. In the twentieth century it added new ideas of modern psychology, fresh notions of time and space, a changed view of the nature of consciousness and the universe. It also became serious. With writers like Joyce, Proust, Kafka and Virginia Woolf, the idea of the 'literary novel' was born.

The novel was also under challenge. It was no longer the great genre, the leading technology. When film was invented, it turned into a great storytelling medium, and became a challenge to the book. When TV became the main medium of social record and interaction, the informational function of the novel – it used to be the great means of exploring and recording society – was challenged.

By 1969, when the Booker began and my own course was planned, things looked gloomy for the novel, and for the book as well. In the global village, said Marshall McLuhan, the screen would replace the printed page. To make matters worse, British fiction seemed to have grown hideously provincial, preoccupied with working-class life in Northern cities or dull questions of class. Readers were disappearing, and publishers showing signs of despair.

Thirty years on, and everything looks different. The book is back with a vengeance. Admittedly it has adapted, and become enfolded in the age of movies, digital television, screen adaptations, Internet and the World Wide Web. But book sales rise, vast new bookstores with coffee shops appear on all the high streets, and Waterstone's is just about to open Britain's biggest and grandest bookshop, on Piccadilly.

The novel does well too. Publishers are hungry for new writers of fiction, especially if they are young and trendy. Writers have turned into *Hello!*-style celebrities. Writing festivals prosper; so do reading clubs. Everyone writes novels: catwalk models and stand-up comedians, politicians and sports celebrities.

Creative writing, too, is everywhere. Over twenty universities now have courses like the one we started. There are week-long programmes like those run by the Arvon Foundation, created by the late lamented Ted Hughes. Hotels mount creative-writing weekends with literary celebrities; so do holiday firms on the Greek islands. Everyone, but everyone, seems to be writing a work of fiction.

But if the book is prospering does that mean we live in a serious age of the novel? Do we have writers who are exploring society, reflecting on history, rendering the excitements, the novelties, the absurdities, the crises of our age? For the novel is still many things. It's a trivial pursuit, but it can also be great art. It can be a commercial niche product, or a world-shaking event. It can follow the crudest rules of writing, or reach the greatest heights of style.

We are certainly not short of novels. More are published than ever before, of every kind, in every genre. We have regional novels and world novels, teenage novels and adult novels. We have gay novels and feminist novels, ethnic novels and multicultural novels, novels out of every layer and every niche in the culture. We have expert performers in every genre, and to top it off we have more cheap editions of the classics than were ever available.

Yet the grand novel, the novel that seems to distil human experience and capture the times, seems as elusive to us as ever. Much of what is called 'literary fiction' is mannered writing, indulgent prose capturing small intimate sensations or elusive corners of experience. The huge inclusiveness of the novel, its power to capture everything, seems as elusive as ever. It's something, it seems, we leave to the Americans, or Indian or South American writers.

Perhaps there are just too many novels, too many people who now have the storytelling skill but have little to write about, too many people who have a corner of life to explore for us but who cannot reach beyond it. Perhaps the idea of the writer has diminished, so that our idea of the author has merged with the idea of the popular celebrity, as famous for existing as for anything actually achieved.

I think myself our dismays and suspicions are overstated. In our own times, we do have our own share of great novelists, comparable with the finest figures of the past. There is no one as inclusive as Dickens, no one as philosophically grand as Tolstoy. There is no James Joyce to capture the precise and intimate detail of modernity, no writer of metropolitan society as complete as Proust.

Yet writers like McEwan himself, Julian Barnes, Angela Carter, Martin Amis, Beryl Bainbridge, A. S. Byatt, Peter Ackroyd, Kazuo Ishiguro, Salman Rushdie have shown us that the novel is still a major exploring form. Most of them emerged in the early 1980s, a remarkable time of revival in the British novel. They form a crucial generation, and it is always good to see them acknowledged and rewarded.

The death of Ted Hughes this week reminds us that in a writer's lifetime it can be hard to see the scale of what he or she has achieved. Death reminds us that big careers have shapes. Hughes was seen first as an important young poet, one of the best of his time, but then as a fading middle-aged one, driven to reclusiveness over the sad fate of Sylvia Plath. Only with his last writings and now his death can we see that this was a career as complete and important as that of Byron or Browning, that we had among us a great poet.

The same is true in fiction. Novels appear, hundreds of them, far more than ever, in each autumn season, all looking pretty much the same. We notice their themes, their subject matter. We look for new talents, and hunt for new subjects and themes. We note the regular return of the famous and familiar faces: another Martin Amis, one more Julian Barnes.

It is harder for us to see that some of these writers, some of these books, are exceptional. It does not help that the Booker shortlist is inevitably made up of many things: writers of enormous talent with an accumulating lifetime of achievement jostle with a new writer of promise deserving encouragement, a work by a writer of fashionable but fragile reputation competes with a work from some fashionable cultural source.

And, in our age of populism, the judging of books is itself more difficult. Judges themselves have agendas — a cause to promote, or a personal viewpoint on what the novel ought to be. Fashion, presentation, hype and cultural niche are more important than ever, so that a fragile topicality can often make a far greater impression than a deeply serious book. We all know now that important writers get neglected, or that the best books or writers fail to win.

What is a good, a great novel? It can be simple, or it can be difficult. But, first and foremost, it is not an imitation. We feel there is an originality of talent, a personal passion to the writing. It is a work that has been considered, studied, examined, not written according to a handy prototype. It is a book that has its own inner voice – a voice we want to listen to, because it is a clue to knowing more about life and the world.

It is a work of ambition. Perhaps it is social ambition, a great and Dickens-like reaching out to the way we live now. Or perhaps it is intellectual ambition, a splendour of ideas. It is also the work of a writer who believes in writing, and uses the novel as a discovering form.

I sometimes guiltily wonder whether 'creative writing' has become responsible for the illusion that everyone can write – and that all books, if they follow certain rules and show certain skills, are equally good. The truth is that we can teach many of the skills of writing: how to structure, how to pace, how to explore human character and social existence, how to begin and how to end.

What we can never teach is the originality that is at the heart of good writing. It comes from a love of language, a depth of experience, perhaps above all a crucial and lifetime theme which we can feel the writer developing. Ian McEwan may have all the skills of writing, as he does. But it is that originality, that inner seriousness and purpose, that, I think, won him the Booker Prize.

WELCOME BACK TO THE
HISTORY MAN

JUST OVER thirty years ago, I invented, for fictional purposes, a character who quite wonderfully turned into a long-lasting literary figure. His name was Howard Kirk, he was a radical university lecturer and he appeared in a satirical novel called *The History Man* (1975). Howard, the 'history man', then took on a splendid new lease of life when, after Mrs Thatcher had come to power, he was played by a magnetic and Zapata-moustached Anthony Sher in the BBC-TV dramatization of the story.

I say I invented Howard Kirk, and yet no character ever came my way more naturally. He was an entirely familiar figure on every modern campus – if, like me, you happened to teach in one of those bright concrete-and-glass new universities that sprang up over the sixties in Britain, and right across Europe and the USA.

Most people then on campus knew a Howard Kirk. He was the easy-going left-wing lecturer from the Swinging Sixties who had seen it happen, seen it fail, and had to live through what came next: the Sagging Seventies. Always radical, always seductive, always seducing, he was eternally on the side of the students against the fascistic institution that paid his salary, and always against those who were over thirty, even if he was himself thirty-five.

Howard believed in history, progressive history, and where it was inevitably leading us. As he said, if you wanted to understand, you needed to know a little Marx, a little Freud and a little history. Yet the subject he taught wasn't history at all, but something vastly more 'trendy' (as everyone said then). Howard taught sociology. And sociology was the most fashionable, radical and popular of all subjects in the academic canon of the day.

In new universities like mine it acquired a special place, as one of those interlocking, interdisciplinary subjects that allowed us to widen and reintegrate the great map of learning. It united philosophy, political science, anthropology, economics, history, cultural and popular studies, literature and art in a spirit of quasi-scientific objectivity.

It was high theory, the most conceptual of subjects – and yet it was data-based, empirical, very hands on. It was a master subject, offering an overarching account of all social phenomena, entire historical epochs or ideologies – yet it was fascinated by the topical and the ephemeral. It was a 'value-free' approach to the world – yet it was also political. It stood beyond ideology, yet was a super-ideology.

Sociology had a glorious heyday in the sixties and then began to fragment and die – not as a discipline among others, but as *the* great discipline, the key to all knowledge. In this process it seems I played a part. In an interesting article in the January issue of *Prospect*, 'Return of Sociology', Ian Christie, deputy director of the think tank Demos, says the turning point was clear.

It was the appearance of *The History Man* in 1975 that led to the backlash against sociology, when 'Bradbury's demolition of his anti-hero's hypocrisies and pretensions was hailed as though he headed up an army relieving a city besieged by Marxist academics.' In fact I had no armies, and even I don't believe novels make that kind of difference. But out went the baby with the bathwater, says Christie, and sociology has not really recovered its authority since.

I WOULD naturally be sorry to feel I alone had done such irremediable damage to a subject I respect and consider a major component of learning. Sociology, I would be among the first to say, is a distinguished, historical and very European form of study, whose origins go back to the Enlightenment – like much else that is good. It was shaped by great thinkers – Rousseau, Hegel, Comte, Mill, Durkheim, Weber – and, for good or ill, has much to do with human progress and social understanding.

Over the last two centuries, sociology sought to provide a comprehensive account of society, show models of how institutions work, compare our and other societies. It studied class, race, gender and ideology. It considered how and under what determining influences people thought (sociology of knowledge) and how they believed (sociology of religion). It explored suicide, alienation, anomie, sport and advertising.

Yet something distinctive did happen to sociology between the 1950s and 1970s. The subject reached its heyday, particularly in Britain and the USA, and then quickly ran off into its decline. What must have become obvious to all parties was this was a sociological phenomenon in itself. Why, then, did sociology achieve such a central role in Britain and the USA in the postwar years, and why did its pretensions collapse later?

One explanation of the rise of sociology to its queen-bee role in the postwar map of learning was given by the left-wing American sociologist C. Wright Mills, author of influential books on the power elite and the military-industrial complex. In his 1959 book *The Sociological Imagination*, Mills claimed the sociological viewpoint was itself the product of the radical alienation that was one of the consequences of modernity.

'Nowadays men often feel that their private lives are a series of traps,' the book begins. The modern individual came to see the world as 'an outsider, a permanent stranger'. Individuals cease in the modern mass to feel like individuals; they feel themselves as part of a process, a mob. They struggle to understand the history in which they're trapped, but it is beyond comprehension: 'The history that now affects every man is world history.'

Mills proposes the 'sociological imagination' as a form of what we would call, in another hideous word culled from the wreckage, 'empowerment'. He was offering, in a sense, a form of Marxism without a manifesto, a social critique in the form of a science, a view of history where history already is powered with a well-guided sense of where it's supposed to go.

Mills was right: his age had turned to the sociological viewpoint. It was the time of the embracing cultural analysis, the handy social textbook. Postwar society was different from prewar, and required new reporting. In Britain, at this time, Richard Hoggart was publishing *The Uses of Literacy*, Raymond Williams' *The Long Revolution*, the New Left analysing such forces of social change as youth culture, sport, pop music.

In the USA popular sociology flourished, as if the New World was being discovered anew. In the early fifties David Riesman had published his remarkable study *The Lonely Crowd*, identifying a quite changed American identity in the age of urban mass society. Other key studies – such as Vance Packard's *The Hidden Persuaders* – portrayed Americans as docile, in the hands of commercial manipulators, deceived by their own leaders, driven to conformity and social consent.

The 'sociological' reading of postwar society came after the massive crisis of world war and the growth of a new era of ideological conflict, the Cold War. The mid-century crisis left earlier political thought discredited: Fascism disgraced, Marxist theory in a state of Stalinist stupefaction. Ideology itself was challenged, yet the intellectual apparatus of ideology – the study of society, class and politics – was in demand.

All over Europe, old societies were being reconstructed with new political orders. Old balances of power and borders of empire had collapsed. Newly emergent post-colonial societies were multiplying, some fledgling democracies, some various forms of peoples' republic. Above all, a new social order based on commodified mass capitalism was evolving in conflict with an opposite order, and the world was being rapidly transformed by economic and ideological forces that were constantly in conflict.

The Sixties Revolution was itself a confused radical paradox: Marxist utopian dreams were somehow to be financed by endless bourgeois wealth. It was never consistent, and both succeeded and failed. The great sociological syntheses of the fifties and sixties lost their inclusiveness and certainty. Society ceased to be the great wonderland and became, simply, the mess we're in.

Popular radical sociology was an episode. It gave us much, not least the enquiring, relativistic spirit in which we now perceive our 'membership' in society. Despite the many claims it made, it did little to deepen or enrich the sense of society or social existence. The atomized, random, value-free, self-creating, hedonistic self of the nineties is just as much the product of all that radical sociology as it is of some Thatcherite distrust of the very idea of society.

Like most Enlightenment projects, the great enterprise became lost in its own ironies. The idea that our cultural understanding needed to spread democratically from elite to popular culture has turned, in the hands of the media makers and programme controllers, into the great nineties dumbing down. The ideological scepticism of the sixties about the institution of the bourgeois family has given us the aimless modern household and the erosion of the ethical and self-responsible individual. In short, the radical, Marxizing, countercultural sociology of the sixties has largely provided much of the ideological and moral framework of postmodern consumer capitalism.

Ian Christie suggests the time is ripe for a return to sociology, and proposes that the 'defeat' of the seventies is being reversed. I hope he's right. It is one of the paradoxes of our time that a society that is heavy with social self-description and self-documentation is so bad at defining the larger level of its moral, familial and community dilemmas.

In a number of recent books – he mentions *Conversations with Anthony Giddens* – Christie sees a return to serious debate about the nature and the workings of society. Yet he also notes we do not yet have the equivalent among contemporary sociologists to a Richard Dawkins or a Stephen Jay Gould, the large thinking figures who construct a significant relationship with theory and practice for an entire discipline.

As Christie sees, if sociology is to make its return, it will have to swim outside the think tanks, and recover some of that grand intellectual energy that delighted us thirty years ago – when the likes of David Riesman, Talcott Parsons, Richard Titmuss and Jürgen Habermas could make us understand the power and wonder of the idea of society, the mysteriousness of history.

Howard Kirk was a rogue of rogues, but at least he believed that. No doubt in 1979 he would have voted for Thatcher, and in 1997 for Blair. He would be enjoying his vice-chancellorship at Batley Canalside University, and the life peerage would be a source of the greatest pleasure. But at least Howard believed – even if it was chiefly for his own advantage – in all the things that still do matter. He believed in history, society, philosophy, ideas, human progress, mental discovery, all that's left of the Enlightenment Project.

As for his recent books, *The Prospects for the ECU, Or How Europe Got Rich* has done well this Christmas, and so has his *Brief History of Football*. The history men are not often sociologists these days. As for me, the ones I read are the Linda Colleys, the Norman Davieses or the new theorists in genetics or earth science. The fact remains that, if Ian Christie can find the published evidence that can persuade me, I shall be as delighted to hail the revival of sociology as I was sad to attend its fall.

THE WISSENCHAFT FILE

ONE OF THE LETTERS I regularly receive in my large daily post is something I have come to call the Wissenschaft letter. It comes with a foreign stamp, and can be from Germany, France, Italy, Spain, Denmark or Greece – certainly one of the European countries where they study contemporary literature in a decidedly energetic and theoretical sort of way. The impressively headed stationery declares it comes from an academic institution. The often spidery handwriting suggests it comes from a student. There are a lot of letters in my Wissenschaft file, but most of them, excusing a pardonable exaggeration or two, tend to run something like this:

Seminar für Englische Sprache und Kultur,
Liebfraumilch Universität,
Gewurztraminerstrasse,
Rheingau 13,
West Germany.

Dear Herr Doktor Professor Bradburg,
    Excuse please that I address you so, but I think in your country you do not mind such informality. My name is Hans-Joachim Wissenschaft, and I am advanced student in Anglisten-Studien at Liebfraumilch University, with nice manners, rimless glasses and a small moustache. I have already passed the examens for my Arbeitsnachtrichen, my Fernspreche and my Hinauslehnen mit Prädikat, and I also have good competences in Philologik, Linguistik, Pedagogik, Psycho-Analytik and Aerobik. Now I must

write my thesis for my Habitat. Always I love very much your English litteraturs, ever since as a boy I made holiday in Grimsby, and came to relish the distinct flavours of your country. My favourite authors are E. Waugh, A. Huxley and M. Python, and always I hoped to make a thesis of their works. Unfortunately, this is not possible, because my famous professor, Frau Doktor Professor Burnehilde Zwischenprüfung (who tells you know her very well), likes it better that I write rather on the 'campus-novel', called also the 'university-novel', which is much studied in my country. I do not find this so easy because the subject does not interest me very much. But of course I take her advices, because as you know she is a very big lady and one day she likes to write a very big book on this subject. Also there are not so many jobs now, even in Germany, and I like to take a little care for my future. So now I am very pleased to make my thesis on this 'campus-novel', and I write for your helps. I think you will please to know I intend to make a special concentrate of your works!

What I like is to take your 'campus-novels' *Forbidden to Eat People*, *Step to the West* and *Der Geschichtsmensch*, and compare them with the works of your better competitors – as, Thom. Hardy, Max Beerbohm, J. I. M. Stewart, Thom. Sharpe, King. Amis, Howard Jacobson and David Lodge. Perhaps you know a lot more authors whose works compare very well with yours. If so, please quickly send their names, as I am an efficient person and like to write a very complete thesis. In fact I like your helps with my work as much as possible. I write to you with the urgence of Professor Zwischenprüfung, who tells that once you met together in Hamburg in a very exciting congress, which was greatly enjoyed by all present. Now she sends you her very best greeting, likes to remind you what a small world it is, and also that she lended you a small black folded umbrella that she now likes very much to have back, as it is raining here. She tells also that you are a good critic, but even so a very nice person who likes much to answer big questions. This is good because I have very many.

Please give all the helps you can, for certain things of your writings cause here a confusion. Perhaps you do not know it yet, but this type 'the campus-novel' does not really exist in Germany, I think because all our professors are very great scholars who write only very serious books, and have no need of such strange publications. For us 'campus-novel' is a very peculiar praxis, found only in Britain and small bits of the United States. Explain me this please. I know your professors are not so well paid – I have met some once and seen their very worn clothes – and must find other ways to survive. Yet this does not explain the representations of universities in these novels, which seem always wicked and dishonest. Does perhaps your government pay you to write these books to stop students attending your universities now with economic crisis you have no more places for them? I have also been told that many of these novels are in the tradition of humoristic satire, but I do not think it is so. I do not understand how it is possible to make humour about a university.

Please give me a very full answer to these questions so I can write an excellent thesis. I would like an explanation of the history, ontology and aesthetik of the 'campus-novel', also full bibliography. I like you to interpret the representation of university life in these novels from the standpoint of *Landeskunde*, and explain me, from the standpoint of *Reception-theorie*, who likes to read them, and why so. If your books are funny, please tell me where, and send me your ontology of the comedic and your theoretiks of the humoristic, and how you like to compare yourself with Aristotle, Nietzsche, Bergson and Freud. Only one more question now! My professor hints me that you and David Lodge are the same person. Perhaps you are also T. Hardy, M. Beerbohm, T. Sharpe and H. Jacobson. If so please tell me in your letter, and give me a full bibliography of your writings, under all your names. Also please send a cassette of Supertramp, *Breakfast in America*, which is not so easy here to obtain. I hope you reply to this letter very quickly, as in my country we like an efficience in our correspondences. I thank you in expectation of your good helps, yours fidelistically,

Hans-Joachim Wissenschaft

Naturally, since I get so many letters of that kind, I have worked out a reply which is rather of this kind:

My dear Wissenschaft

Thank you so much for your letter. What a pleasure it is to hear again of Professor Z., all of whom I remember with vivid clarity. Please give her my warmest and most affectionate good wishes. It does not surprise me that, as her student, you are such a diligent asker of questions. I recall she herself was famous for her proficiency in the extended theoretical question, and indeed in Hamburg I urged her to collect hers together and publish them as a book. This doubtless explains why she thinks I enjoy extended interrogation, and why she has been so kind as to point you at me. Naturally I am delighted to help, to the best of my abilities – though I well know my answers can never reach anything like the standard of your teacher's questions. However, you will be happy to learn that, owing to the sudden cancellation of a ten-part television series I was writing, I do suddenly have several weeks to spare. So, out of my great attachment to your excellent mentor, I shall try to confront the many cogent points raised in your missive, or missile, as best I can. After all, even though I have supervised many theses myself and know the consequences, I am naturally delighted to hear that someone – indeed, anyone – is writing yet another dissertation on my work. I feel even more privileged to be invited to write the bulk of it for you. I fancy between the two of us we shall, for once, be able to get it more or less right.

Nonetheless I fear I could prove a dreadful disappointment to you. You ask me about the ontology, paleontology, teleology and neurology of this mysterious and unusual literary genre some of us practise in my benighted country, and has been called the 'university' or 'campus novel'. I do not want to seem discouraging to someone as evidently diligent as yourself, but I have to tell you the phrase causes me some anxiety, and has even brought me out in large red blemishes. It is said, I think, that Thomas Mann had similar problems when people described his *Der Zauberberg*, or

The Magic Flute, as we call it here, as a 'hospital novel' – and that Franz Kafka turned into something totally different from his so-called normal self when he was asked to compare his work in the field on the 'castle novel' with that of P. G. Wodehouse. Of course no one is more in favour of theories of genre than myself, so I will explain my antipathy with a personal anecdote. I know that answering a philosophical question with an anecdotal answer bears all the shameful marks of British empiricism, but I suggest you pour yourself a health-giving draught of the local product and hear my reasons.

My difficulties with the term 'university novel' began in early life, when I published my first book, which I like to call *Eating People Is Wrong*, though this clearly is up for argument. It so happened I published the book, took my first academic job and married my first and only wife, all in the same week; but we all have difficult weeks from time to time. No sooner was the book out than my publisher, Frederick Warburg, summoned me to London to discuss my future, and, drunk with expectations of literary fame, I and my new wife hastened to satisfy him. We lived in the North, and my wife had never been knowingly south of the River Trent in her life. Nonetheless she made a week's supply of sandwiches, in case they did not have food in London, and we took the train to the great metropolis. We arrived at St Pancras Station, where my wife, mistaking it for St Paul's Cathedral, knelt in the left-luggage office and gave prayers for our safe return. There was another small fracas when I tried to lead her down into the underground, and she refused, calling me a lunatic for supposing that trains could run underneath cities in small round holes. She made me hire the most expensive taxi I could find, and has persisted with the practice ever since – though she has now been to London frequently, and can find her way blindfolded from amy part of it straight to Harrods' food hall.

Warburg's office was at the very top of one of those charming Georgian houses in Bloomsbury without which the British publishing industry could not exist. And he made an impressive figure as he stood, infinitely tall and in a white suit, at the top of the stairs and ushered us into the lavatory, perhaps thinking this was what we had come to London for. 'This is your *author*, come to see you,' said my wife. Warburg bent graciously, kissed her hand, and led us into a vast white room with a great white desk. It had one chair opposite, and in this he seated my wife, gesturing me to a stool in a far distant corner. For an hour or so, my wife and publisher had an extended, warm conversation, she blushing prettily when he rose now and then to kiss her hand again or make her more comfortable in her chair. From time to time they waved at me. Then Warburg rose suddenly, and we were out in the street again. 'What did he want to say to me?' I asked my wife anxiously. 'Oh, well,' she said, stopping a passing Rolls-Royce and telling it to take us to the station, 'he just wanted to make absolutely sure you didn't write any more university novels.'

Frankly it was only now that I learned by book *was* a university novel – and that getting a place to write one was even harder than getting a place in university itself. Admittedly my book was set in the academic groves, but since I had spent my entire life in educational institutions, from kindergarten to graduate school (I fancy you will know the feeling, Herr Wissenschaft), I naturally assumed that trotting off to class or the library every day was normality itself. Everyone gave lectures to everyone else; life was books, and books were life. To me the true passports to being were reader's tickets for the world's great libraries – the London Library, the Senate House Library, the Sterling Memorial and the Widener, the Borg and the British Museum (about whose falling down I wrote my famous novel). I imagined the whole of life was the same – that my plumbers spent their pipeless hours writing PhDs on joints, that the friendly local barmaid took postgraduate courses in pumping, that everyone everywhere kept large shoe-boxes filled with file cards and footnotes. I had not written a university novel; I had written a universal novel.

So Warburg's warning came to me as a terrible shock. What was worse, I was already on the last lap of another novel – set on the, well, campus of an American, well, university. Back home again, I picked up the unfortunate manuscript and assaulted it desperately, trying all I could to alter the location – to a factory, a prison, the forecourt of a garage, anywhere but where it was. But despite all the grime, hard labour and street brutality I tried to smear over my characters, I simply could not prevent them from discussing things like epistemology and the liberal dilemma. I laboured for years to hide my crime, until one day the manuscript suddenly disappeared, along with my wife. For days I wondered where it had gone, and sometimes I missed her too. Happily it, or rather she, returned some days later, to say that she had delivered the very first draft to Warburg, who had been delighted to see her, and for that matter the book. In fact, if she was to be believed, it was just what he had always wanted. Apparently I had now acquired some reputation for that sort of thing, and he now wanted me to write yet *another* university novel. 'I knew you'd be pleased,' said my wife, taking out her chequebook and riffling through all the torn-off stubs.

I was not. Taking my publisher's warnings to heart, I had already set my next book entirely at the bottom of a mineshaft – which, incidentally is quite different from a *Gemeinschaft*. Indeed, if you have a course in colliery fiction I might be able to dredge it up from the lake where I threw it when I had this news. But, always one to follow the whims of a wise publisher's advice, I now sat down and invented a fiction partly set in a new university during the student revolts of the 1960s (you may remember you had them too, Herr Wissenschaft, though I doubt if you took part), the book called, as you rightly said, *Der Geschichtsmensch*. One day, when I suddenly looked up and discovered it had somehow become 1975, my wife, once more exhausted by my interminable revisions of this remarkable and metriculous manuscript, grabbed it from my feeble hands, rushed for the train and went to London. She was gone this time for two weeks, and naturally I began to worry. However, her explanation, when she came back, glowing, was quite convincing. Apparently my publisher had changed. Warburg had left, and been replaced by a man in a grey suit called Tom Rosenthal. The whole difficult relation between the author's wife and the author's publisher had had to be reconstructed from scratch. 'How does he feel about university novels?' I asked. But apparently the expensive London restaurants in which they had been forced to chat had proved so noisy that my wife had not really been able to find out.

Naturally I was on tenterhooks for days, until Rosenthal rang up, thanked me warmly for the wife I had submitted to him and said he quite liked the book too. It was published, and indeed became quite a success. However, by this time I had grown in cunning and deviousness. I set my next novel, *Wechsel*, in an imaginary Eastern European country called Slaka. That, too, appeared to generally warm reviews. However, several of them suggested that my imaginary country was not utterly like Eastern Europe, but remarkably like a university. I suffer through these harrowing experiences again because from them I learned a few lessons. One is that publishers, and the publics they speak for, like genres or sub-genres even more than we critics do, so they know what they are marketing or buying. Another is that, therefore, once a writer is known for one thing, it is almost impossible to do anything else, even if you do. It is with genres as with sports cars; once inside one, you will never get out of it again – except perhaps by death or the taking of a pseudonym, whichever is easier. Another is that, however fictional you say your books are (and all sensible authors say that), people insist that they describe some reality or other – even though reality was abolished in the 1890s, and if an imaginary country is the same as a university or vice versa we do have a problem of, as we academics say, separating our signifiers from our signifieds. Another is that it may not be such a good idea to let your wife keep going off to London, especially since the advent of the credit card; but perhaps you do not have that particular problem, Herr Wissenschaft.

I hope all this will explain why, as a writer, I am not always enthusiastic about being called a 'university' or 'campus' novelist. At the same time, as a literary critic, I do have to admit there is some truth in it here and there. I must also acknowledge that the 'university novel' does show some signs of being a commonplace form, especially in Britain – perhaps because the British novel has always been about places that are rather difficult to get into. We can even trace back a history of sorts, back to the sentimental Oxbridge romances of the nineteenth century, which you can, and doubtless will, compare with *Wilhelm Meister* and the *Bildungsroman*. These are tales about young men's education in pastoral surroundings, part of an Oxbridge myth that grows a mite more ironic in the twentieth-century novels of Forster, Waugh and Aldous Huxley. Perhaps what made the story more interesting was when it crossed over with the diction of the academically excluded, like Hardy's *Jude the Obscure* and the novels of D. H. Lawrence. Certainly it was after the Butler Education Act of 1944, which admitted cartloads of pimply social refugees to various academic destinations, that the whole affair took on pace. Many of the new books were set not in glowing Oxbridge but in 'redbrick' universities, which are frequently converted lunatic asylums or extended public lavoratories, and in time the 'new' universities, 1960s architectural wonders built in green fields by Finnish architects driven mad by the remarkable plastic properties of concrete. You may possibly find some trace of all this in my own works.

Since then, the university novel, like universities themselves, appeared to undergo a period of expansion. In fact the books began to acquire what you and I would call 'intertextuality', which of course is quite different from plagiarism. For example, a newish book by this young man Howard Jacobson, whose cognomen somehow seems to have come your way, refers I suppose very comically to an institution called 'Bradbury Lodge' – where, he implies, most British novels that are not about India are set. And I suppose that in theory one would have to say that where there is intertextuality, there is very probably a genre – or so my old professor told me, before he discarded Structuralism entirely, and took up hang-gliding instead.

But, as you rightly ask, why *should* this very peculiar practice have grown to such proporations? In the many boxes of scholarly apparatus I am shipping to you by separate sea-container, you will find various scholarly attempts to answer just this question. Study, for example, the article by P. R. Elkin, a fine scholar who sees the university novel as a kind of campus epidemic, rather like glandular fever or genital herpes. Throughout the Anglo-Saxon world 'Every kind of person connected with universities appears to have tried his hand at writing them', be they college don or campus porter. The main reason, he seems to suspect, is that people in academic life have an excess of leisure time, and no doubt get paper at discount prices as well. Alas, this creative spectacle does not exactly make him excited. Indeed he complains that all these books 'have much the same caste [sic, as we say] of characters, and much the same preoccupations – which is no doubt another way of saying that universities these days, wherever they may be, are in significant respects strikingly similar' – and also, I suppose, another way of saying he doesn't like them. If only at the time of writing Professor Elkin had, like ourselves, access to the word 'intertextuality' – that might have changed his attitude completely.

But perhaps not. For I notice everywhere throughout the many articles on the subject – when you collect the sea-container from Hamburg docks, which I take it are convenient to the Rheingau, you will see what I mean – a rather grudging note. Professor Elkin, for example, speaks of my own *Der Geschichts-mensch* as 'a step forward in the genre', thus showing himself a man of fine critical acumen. But then he complains: 'Like Zola, Malcolm Bradbury seems unable to leave a room without describing everything in it'. I will not try to speak for Zola, who has his own lawyer, but I should point out that in fact I am famous for not being able to leave a room at all, or certainly not until they have removed the drink and furniture, whether I have described it or not. I would also add that, just as Anthony Powell once observed that good books do furnish a room, so I believe that good rooms do furnish a book, or even a good room a good book.

What does seem clear is that critics who, when confronted with other kinds of fiction – books about Japan, for instance – will insist on their 'purely lexical existence', critics who will indeed passionately assault the entire concept of realism, and prove that it is dead, will become oddly different when they encounter the university novel. Thus I commend you, when you unpack the truck, to look up the two fine articles on the matter by George Watson and Professor J. P. Kenyon – whose recent study

of historians was, I note with the interest of a dedicated intertex-
tualist, called *The History Men*. Mr Watson's piece will provide you
with an excellent short history of our genre, good, I'd say, for at
least ten footnotes. But he then comments that 'he has several
reasons, all partly selfish, for hoping that Anglo-American campus
fiction will fade away and die', not a view he takes, I believe, of
epic poetry, for example. However, he does explain, a little surprisingly, that he thinks it hard for universities to have to do their
excellent work in what he calls 'the blaze of glamorizing publicity'.
Professor Kenyon's is also a thoughtful piece, offering many useful
social observations on the matter. He is generous in acknowledging
that the university novel 'fills a remarkable gap', though in what
he does not quite say. Yet he, too, concludes that 'we have had
too much of a good thing', and suggests that it is time for British
novelists to start looking elsewhere, to social problems and business
life – or, presumably, anywhere else but a university.

I will leave it to you, Herr Wissenschaft, to judge just why it
is that university critics do not always like university novels,
and even sometimes upset their entire critical theories when they
discuss them. Actually I suspect I know the answer, which may
have something to do with another word you use in your
capacious enquiry, the word 'satire'. And now I fear I am going
to disappoint you severely, Herr Wissenschaft. Yes, of course, my
novels are complex textual monads, philosophical reflections, tales
of human tragedy, novels of pain. But to be frank they are quite
heavily infested with satirical intentions, humoristic practices, and
the like. In fact, to be entirely open with you – not something
I do often when there are critics about – they *are* comic novels,
and certain pages here and there are intended to produce a physio-
logical comic reflex, which in Britain we call laughter. I fully
understand entirely why this should produce anxiety, not least
among my academic colleagues. For it is true that if universities –
communities of largely good, decent, brilliant, enlightened people,
committed to the best of ends, such as the survival of humanism
and the differentiation between B+ and B++ – can be subjected
to satire, then what cannot be done to all the rest of life, which is
so very much worse?

So it is proper of you to ask me about my ontology of the comic and my theoretic of the humanistic, and I wish I could answer you. Unfortunately this is a matter I usually leave others to discuss, while I sit in the bar with a few close friends. My relationship with Aristotle, Nietzsche, Freud and Bergson has been for some time a vexed question, and my lawyer advises me it could well be subject to litigation. So I will comment only briefly. As I understand it, Aristotle never completed his work on comedy, being overcome with a paroxysm of something. He did, however, argue that comedy is an inverted tragedy, or a tragedy written upside down, and this is exactly the way I have always tried to write my books. On the matter of Nietzsche, I have, to be frank, tried to avoid him as much as possible, and I believe he has taken the same attitude towards me. As I understand it, Nietzsche's theory, while admirable, applies effectively only to Wagner's *Ring* cycle, which only King Ludwig of Bavaria seems to have found a load of laughs. I have learned a good deal from Freud on many matters, but perhaps least in the realm of wit and the comic, which he sees as a manifestation of the unconscious, something we do not have in my country. Bergson on comedy is something enlightening, proposing that the comic occurs when the human is turned to the mechanical. As you know, he gives the example that we all laugh when a man slips on a banana skin, and no doubt in France they do; in Britain we always try to help such people. But I am most inclined to set my own work in the tradition of the modern British comic novel, which as we all know started with James Joyce's *Ulysses*, but has improved since. In my experience the best thing is just to mention the comedy briefly, and then get on to something more substantial as quickly as possible.

I hope all this puts you straight about university and campus fiction. Happily there are some writers who transcend or transform the genre in which they write, and I congratulate you on having chosen one. I trust all I have said will prove useful material for your thesis. I advise you to incorporate as much of it as possible, if only for what George Watson calls 'several reasons, all partly selfish'. For that would give me the chance to acquire yet another pseudonym, not something I reject lightly, as you – or more probably Professor Z. herself, never one to halt at the obvious in matters of literary study – have so cunningly surmised. It was clever of you both to work out that in fact I am several if not all of the authors you mention. To be frank, it is something I have been trying to conceal for many years, not wanting to overcrowd the market. But – strictly on the condition that this information is divulged to no one whatsoever, but is safely buried in your thesis, which will, I take it, shortly be locked up in an obscure university library and be securely protected by the unbreakable code of academic language – I am prepared to acknowledge to you, and you alone, the versatility and complexity of my literary achievement, as well as the fact that, although my wife and family believe me to be quite young, I have indeed been writing steadfastly and productively ever since the mid-nineteenth century. Over that period, as I have indicated, things with the university and campus novel have changed very greatly, as I am told they have in life itself, which for obvious reasons I never have the time to check. It is this that explains the inordinate variety of my styles, my rather swerving approach to my theme, and the fact that I look very tired these days, with so many books to write. In all honesty, it has been a difficult business, especially the episode of being married to Mrs Thomas Hardy. But now theses like your own are being written and all the pieces being put together it has all been worth it.

Just one of these matters is rather complicated, and that is the question of whether David Lodge and myself are the same person – the vexed issue of the well-known writer 'Bodge'. A great many people ask each of us if we are the other, and this had grown extremely confusing to the one or both of us. In fact there are distinctive differences, but also close similarities. He is small and I am tall, but he is dark and I am dark. He professes to be a rather sceptical sort of Catholic while I profess to be a rather sceptical sort of humanist, but he is a university professor of literature, and so as it happens am I. He professes his literature at the so-called Birmingham University, while I profess mine at the far better-known University of East Anglia, but both of us write critical works on the practice of fiction which deal with many of the same subjects. Hence quite often we find ourselves together at conferences, lecturing side by side or in consecutive spots, often he on my topic and I on his. His wife is said to be called Mary, and mine Elizabeth, but they are constantly confused, though more often by other people than the two of us. Some people claim that we both fell in love with a Polish girl in a shower in Warsaw, but this is vehemently denied by all three, or possibly two, parties concerned. He gets my telephone calls, and I get his telephone bills. Thus it goes on, leaving each of us with the conviction that one or both of us is the other, and if you were able to settle this matter definitively in your thesis it would solve a lot of problems, and the whole thing would have been very worthwhile. Again, please give your excellent professor my good wishes, and tell her it was not I but David Lodge that went off with her umbrella. Also say that either or both of us remember our solemn undertaking never to include her in any work of fiction; we will continue to respect it. And very good luck with the Habitat.

Yours sincerely,

Max Beerbohm

FURLING THE FLAG

In the mid-1990s Malcolm Bradbury began working on an original television series for Kensington Films, a story set amid the British handover of Hong Kong to China. It featured Michael Spearpoint, a career diplomat who was last seen in Bradbury's Channel 4 series *The Gravy Train* and *The Gravy Train Goes East*. The screenplay was, for a variety of reasons, never made but it remained close to Bradbury's heart. In the last years of his life, he decided to convert the screenplay into a novel – 'a short comic novella rather in the manner of *Cuts*', as he put it – and began working on the project periodically, while also working on another new novel, *Liar's Landscape*. The beginning of the novella is reproduced here, along with the remaining story in script form, to offer a complete version of *Furling the Flag*.

DB

Furling the Flag: A Tall Story

ONE

As most of the travelling sort of people would agree, the view you can get over Hong Kong and its famous Fragrant Harbour is one of the finest in the world. The British Royal Navy is not often to be singled out for its sense of the picturesque. But it did something for aesthetics as well as the promise of the opium trade when it took Hong Kong Island and the harbour from the resentful Chinese in 1841. There was an angry emperor on the Peacock Throne, there were pirates on the Kowloon waterfront and the Happy Valley was filled with notorious, endemic, life-threatening fevers. But once the Treaty was signed in 1843, something happened to the little island. It became a very special jewel in the red-blotched crown of Empire. Soon British judges sat in British courts, a British governor ruled the roost from Government House. British doctors eased the fevers, so that Happy Valley could turn from a graveyard to a racetrack. British statues squatted in the parks, British trams graced the crowded and noisy thoroughfares, British traders served British travellers in the British way.

An excellent way to see the modern Hong Kong view is from the deck of the busy Star Ferry, which chugs the busy and not quite so Fragrant Harbour from the Island to the commercial waterfront of Kowloon. Huge container ships, like longitudinal buildings, thrust between the junks and sampans, fishing boats and fast motor launches engaged in every suspect kind of trade, to head out for the fogs of the South China Sea. The fat jumbo jets of Cathay Pacific and South China Air cruise in over the water and the buildings to land at the airport of Kai Tak. Summer mists come up from the network of islands, some of them steaming and industrial, some of them ancient and peaceful, and morning sunlight picks out the tops of their pointy peaks.

It's the end of May, and coming up to typhoon season, but the harbour waters are still, sluggish and dirty. Modernity is not usually considered a friend to landscape, but with Hong Kong you could perhaps even think it has added and not subtracted. Tall apartments, witness to a tiny land mass and a great prosperity, rise up on every piece of green, landslippy Kowloon hillside, making the Emerald City. On the waterfront, the high commercial towers rise up in tall columns, just like ever improving statistics. Which is precisely what they represent. Hong Kong is now the world's eighth largest commercial city, the most international city in the world. Its banks rise and prosper, and their money spreads across the world.

Some of the world's best new architects have built these gilded high-rise columns. Sir Norman Foster, fresh from his long low hangar of a Sainsbury Centre in Norwich, raised the idea upwards to create the Hong Kong and Shanghai Bank building, one of the greatest and most avant-garde towers of the waterfront. Behind it, overlooking, is the Bank of China Tower – created by I. M. Pei, who had the idea of putting a Plexiglas pyramid in the classic courtyard of the Paris Louvre. It's not perhaps the most avant-garde of the buildings, but it is the tallest. This is just what it was meant to be, since the client, the People's Government of China, has always had every intention of overlooking everything, when the Fragrant Harbour returns from imperial rule in just over a month's time.

But of all the great towers, one – at least according to its taipan, silver-haired old Sir Dexter Chen – is a little bit more perfect than the others: the Marco Polo Bank. It's not the tallest, perhaps not the most avant-garde, though Philippe Starck designed it, doing his brave and original best. He put a technological pineapple on the top of it, and clad the walls in a distinctive eco-green. It's a teasing postmodern building for a teasing postmodern time. The chi is quite perfect; Sir Dexter consulted the best of geomancers before a hole was dug, a steel beam raised, a glassy, glossy window frame erected. He adjusted the alignment, checked all the energies, to make quite sure the tower will outlive all other towers, when as always in history what has now risen will have fallen, so that wealth will cascade to Sir Dexter's honoured descendants down the generations, just as long as he propitiates all the warring forces.

Sir Dexter is finely skilled at propitiating the warring forces. When, to escape Mao's revolution in 1949, he came from Shanghai to Hong Kong, he had no money, few friends and the wrong language. But, as you did in those days, he traded in this and smuggled that, across the water and over the guarded border that kept the tiny colony apart from the massive mainland. He made good friends, and he silenced his enemies. He laundered money, and he bought a little land, since too many people on too little territory spells profit. When, in the course of time, Hong Kong got wonderfully rich, he got wonderfully richer. He traded in goods and property, in margins and futures. Soon he was in banks. He assumed excellent manners, and acquired an excellent tailor: not a difficult thing to do in a busy colony where the tailors are amongst the best and the most expensive in the world.

In those days, and despite the Japanese Occupation, Hong Kong remained very British, with its Royal this and its Victorian that. So did Sir Dexter Chen. He had a coach for his voice and a librarian for his library. He had a house in Kensington, and was civilly admitted to most of the best clubs in Hong Kong. He had a stable at Happy Valley and a house on the Peak, where once the Chinese were not even allowed to live. When the British politicians came to solicit his advice and ask him for money, he gave generously: first to the Conservative Party and then to the Labour Party, for the warring parties do indeed need to be propitiated. When Oxford University solicited his educational donations, he gave it the famous Chen Chair of Equine Competition, and when Cambridge came shortly after, he gave it a small but comfortable college.

When the Queen came out to Hong Kong to review its progress, she generously knighted him. And when Hong Kong ceased to be quite so British, and became American and Australian and Indian and Japanese, he always helped where he could. When Deng Xiaoping reminded overseas Chinese of their loyalties, and invited their donations and their investment back into the mainland, Sir Dexter knew where his duties lay. He remembered his relatives in Shanghai, and built a banking tower there. Now, here in Hong Kong, the Marco Polo Bank has seventy storeys. It has forty more in Shanghai, another thirty-five in Bishopsgate, right in the heart of London's Square Mile, where it has merged with several British banks. There are thirty more in downtown Manhattan, twenty in Tokyo, nineteen more in Kuala Lumpur. All over the Pacific Rim, bankers are building towers now, higher and higher: my tower is taller than yours. But the Marco Polo Bank is the seventh biggest bank in the world; and the financial press, who write so often about the bank and its taipan, call it the Bank of Tall Storeys, which is just how Sir Dexter meant it to be.

Each morning Sir Dexter stands on the deck of the Star Ferry to survey the ever more excellent view. His house is high on the Victoria Peak, from which you can see the harbour only through the clouds. He sends his chauffeur to go ahead through the under-harbour tunnel, so the green Rolls can await him on the other side. Two well-trained, and well-built, bodyguards stand on the deck beside him, to keep his sacred space amid the busy crowds of morning commuters, carrying their laptops and talking at speed into their mobile phones. He stands there still until the ferry docks at the Star Pier, and the crowds and commuters push down the gangplank, into the hot bustle of commercial Kowloon. There is honking and hooting, shouting and shoving. Food sellers yell, antique stores spill their doubtful goods onto the pavements, old men do t'ai chi on the pierhead.

Sir Dexter waits till the rush is done. Then he goes down the gangplank, a bodyguard on either side. The green Rolls is waiting, the chauffeur holds open the door. Once he is seated in the leather, phone-filled cabin, the chauffeur silently hands him the morning paper, the *South China Tribune*. The headline reads: COUNTDOWN NEWS: 32 DAYS TO GO: SHARP RISE IN BUSINESS CLOSURES AS MANY LEAVE. Fainthearts who have made sure of foreign passports are already departing the colony, to go to Manila or Vancouver or Sydney or Seattle. Sir Dexter has no intention of leaving; he believes he has already propitiated all the warring gods. He crumples the paper in irritation, and says something to the chauffeur. Honking and hooting, the green Rolls drives through the outdoor bustle, and heads for the tall storeys of Kowloon.

'LET'S JUST look it over one more time, shall we?' says Athelstan Penhurst, bluff old Foreign Office hand, as he stands at the door of his FCO office, which looks down from the splendid balcony into the even more splendid Durbar Court. Across Parliament Square, Big Ben is gonging ten. You can just hear the clopping of the Horse Guards on their parade ground up Whitehall. Secretaries bustle, and they are hoovering busily somewhere down there among the flags and trophies in Sir Giles Gilbert Scott's fine old building – which used to be perhaps the most powerful building on the face of the globe.

They all come in, with their files and their diplomatic briefcases, the brightest and best of the breed. There are a couple of Old China Hands and a new Post-Colonialist. There's a young man in Armani from the British Council, which gets everywhere, and, from the office of the new PM, dry cynical young Kennett, who has worked for both sides. There's bright Ms Highsmith, power-dressed, with wash-and-go hair. Ms Highsmith is a definite high-flyer, and is already being groomed for the greatest things.

In Penhurst's vast and dusty office, not a great deal has changed over the years – those many difficult, power-losing years in which he has worked in diplomacy and defended British interests against everyone, not least the British government. Portraits of the old adventurers – Livingstone and Stanley and Shackleton – still hang on the dark panelled walls. Over his mahogany desk is an old map of Empire (Bartholomew, 1889, 'the globe open to, and available for, commercial enterprise'), which innumerable secretaries have attempted to put into storage, but which Penhurst has steadfastly refused to remove. Not until he retires or they privatize the building (and privatization is far more probable) does he mean to let it come down.

The brightest and best sit round the big baize-covered conference table, the coffee ladies take up their trolley and leave. 'Right then, Ms Highsmith, will you take us through it?' says Penhurst, taking the head of the table. 'Since you seem to know what it is.' 'Yes, sir,' says Ms Highsmith. 'As you know, the flag gets furled in Hong Kong at the end of next month. Joint Liaison Committee have reported, I hope for the last time. I'm passing these papers around now. I'm afraid negotiations with the other side have been unusually difficult and prolonged.' 'They've taken seventeen bloody years, to be precise,' says Kennett. 'But the Chinese did invent the word mandarin in the first place,' says one of the Old China Hands. 'Anyway, it all seems quite satisfactory,' says Ms Highsmith, 'There are a few loose ends to settle, but it's mostly minor detail. So a huge sigh of relief all round, say I.'

'Just how loose are these ends?' asks Penhurst, looking up curiously. 'Oh, the usual things,' says Ms Highsmith, 'mostly to do with the actual events of the Handover. We want this, so naturally they want that. We wanted to have one final Handover Banquet, so they want two.' 'Two?' asks Penhurst. 'Yes, a big one for them, and a small one for us,' says Ms Highsmith, 'We wanted to hold events in Government House, so they wanted them at Bank of China Tower. We suggested a concert by the band of the Gurkhas. They insisted on David Copperfield and the Three Tenors.' 'David Copperfield?' asks Penhurst. 'He's magic,' says Ms Highsmith, 'the Chinese like magic. And they don't want anything political.'

'Let's just check who'll be attending,' says Penhurst. 'Their side are fielding the entire National People's Congress, so lots of chairs needed there,' says Ms Highsmith. 'They'll be led by

Chairman Deng Xiaoping, always assuming he's still alive by then, otherwise they won't. Then it will be his successor, of course, assuming they can agree on one, but it will probably be Mr Li Peng.' 'And our side?' asks Penhurst. 'Happily our side's far less problematical,' says Ms Highsmith, 'we'll be sending the new PM and the new Foreign Secretary, to give them their blessing of fire. And of course we shall field the usual token Royal.'

'Mrs Thatcher, you mean?' says Kennett. 'No,' says Ms Highsmith. 'She's going, of course, in fact she's taken the whole top-floor suite at the Mandarin Oriental. With Dennis at the Hyatt. The other side didn't seem too keen on the Queen, since they no longer have one, so we're sending the Princess Royal. Rather a good choice, I think. Dignified, uncontroversial, used to handing things over. And her husband's Royal Navy, so that's another plus.' 'Especially since the Royal Navy grabbed Hong Kong from the Chinese in the first place,' remarks one of the Old China Hands.

'What's the form, then?' asks Penhurst. 'We shall ask Her Royal Highness to make the speech at the final banquet on June 30th,' explains Ms Highsmith, 'then she'll furl the flag, and the main party will sail home almost immediately aboard the Royal Yacht *Britannia*, so the Chinese can take everything over the next morning. Then when she arrives home, we decommission her. The Royal Yacht, that is, not Her Royal Highness.' 'So End of Century, End of Empire, probably the end of some of us too,' says Penhurst. 'Still, there it is. What has to be has to be. We have been leaving colonies for the last fifty years, so I dare say we're getting rather good at it. Is that acceptable all round?'

'Just one thing,' says Kennett suddenly, waving a document. 'I'm looking through the list of those at the final banquet. One rather important name seems to be missing.' 'Is there really?' asks Penhurst. 'Who's that?' 'The Governor,' says Kennett. 'His name doesn't appear on the list.' 'Oh, you mean Fat Peng,' says Ms Highsmith, 'Sorry, but that's what the Chinese call him. And Tango Dancer. Please don't ask why. They're a very poetic people. I'm afraid the other side refuse to have him there. They say if he attends the banquet, their side will withdraw.' 'But that's a deliberate snub,' says Kennett. 'I know, but apparently he said a rude word in front of Mr Li Peng,' says Ms Highsmith. 'Rude word?' asks Penhurst. 'Yes,' says Ms Highsmith, 'it was democracy, actually. Not the sort of thing one's supposed to say to the Chinese.' 'Tactless to say the least,' says one of the Old China Hands.

'I thought we supported democracy,' says Kennett. 'To a point, but not necessarily for everyone,' says one of the Old China Hands. 'Remember, they were a great civilization when we were running around hitting each other with clubs.' 'In my part of London they still do,' says the other Old China Hand. 'It's a deliberate humiliation, Penhurst,' says Kennett, 'it will be shown on TV and be seen as a betrayal of democracy by people right across the world.' 'Yes, I see that,' says Penhurst thoughtfully. 'Perhaps we should go back to them, Ms Highsmith.'

Across the table, the Old China Hands put their wise old heads together. 'Our view is that we should just get the Handover handed over and put the whole thing behind us,' says one of them. 'China is the world's biggest undeveloped market, and the main player in the twenty-first century. Once Hong Kong's reserves and China's potential are put together, they'll be a powerhouse. And our longstanding commercial interests out there give us a unique opportunity.' 'We have been back to them, sir, many times, at the highest level,' says Ms Highsmith, 'three prime ministers, five foreign secretaries, six ambassadors.' 'It's not something on which we can budge,' says Kennett. 'Well, of course, the Chinese never budge,' says the older of the Old China Hands.

'So what do we do?' asks Penhurst, looking round the table. 'What do you think, Ms Highsmith?' 'Well, sir, we could do what we usually do when we don't know what to do,' says Ms Highsmith, 'send out a special envoy with top diplomatic skills and try and get things smoothed over. The Chinese see themselves as clever diplomats.' 'But we're clever diplomats,' says Penhurst. 'Yes, sir, but their clever diplomats tend to run rings round our clever diplomats,' says Ms Highsmith. 'I think that's an excellent suggestion,' says Penhurst, 'do we all agree? Excellent.' Heads nod all round the table. 'Thank you, gentlemen, and Ms Highsmith,' says Penhurst. 'Now the other big question. Who?'

IN THE GLASS LIFT of the Marco Polo Tower, Sir Dexter Chen rises higher and higher, up through the tall storeys. The view over the glittering harbour grows better and ever better. Over there is the dusty scar of the new airport; an entire island has been flattened, and a huge suspension bridge raised, for a great project in the making. Over here is the new Container Terminal, which when finished should ensure Hong Kong retains the title of the great entrepôt to the whole Pacific Rim. In both of these ventures the Marco Polo Bank has committed heavily, and brought Western and Chinese investors together under one roof. Both are behind schedule, but both should be ready soon after the Handover: which of course is just when the Chinese want them to be ready anyway.

Inside the bank, in glass-walled open offices, bank workers with security passes sit at desks and terminals to keep the turmoil of business churning. The lift bell pings, the doors open, and a crowd of them move to get into the lift. Seeing the taipan, they stop suddenly; it is understood that Sir Dexter's space is not to be intruded on. A bodyguard presses the button, and the lift begins rising again; Sir Dexter ascends to the top of his domain. Here is the Taipan Suite, large but quiet and discreet; few people come here. Even the bodyguards descend again after Sir Dexter gets out of the lift.

'Happy morning, Sir Dexter,' says Jasmine Tan, his personal secretary, standing by her desk as he walks through the reception office toward the inner suite, glancing up at the screens that show Hang Seng trading, high on the wall. 'Happy morning, Sir Dexter,' murmur the other secretaries. 'Miss Jang is here to see you,' says Jasmine Tan. Sir Dexter stops. 'I don't know a Miss Jang,' he says. A Eurasian girl rises from one of the leather sofas, holding a pocket tape recorder in her hand. 'I rang you yesterday,' she says, 'Diana Jang, *South China Tribune*. You promised me an interview.' 'I'm busy,' says Sir Dexter. 'Of course,' says Miss Jang, 'but you did say you'd give me half an hour.'

Sir Dexter looks at the newspaper he's still holding. 'This is yours?' he says, holding it out. 'Take it. And tell your owner if he prints any more stories like today, he will soon not have a newspaper.' 'You didn't like our story?' asks Miss Jang. 'No,' says Sir Dexter, 'it does not create confidence in the future.' 'And you think we should have confidence in the future?' 'I know we should have confidence in the future,' says Sir Dexter, 'that is how we make sure there is a future. You are very fortunate to live in such a lucky place. You're Eurasian, aren't you? If you don't like it, better go, while there is still time.' 'You don't think there could be a debate about its future?' persists Miss Jang. 'Not with you,' says Sir Dexter. 'Now put that microphone away. There is no interview.'

'That's a pity,' says Miss Jang, 'because I wanted to ask you about family values.' 'I am for them,' says Sir Dexter. 'And also some questions about the future of the bank. Is it true it's about to be investigated?' 'Of course it isn't true,' says Sir Dexter, looking at her grimly. 'Who told you that? Why should it be investigated?' 'There were rumours in yesterday's London financial papers,' says Miss Jang, 'Can I report they're quite unfounded?' 'You can't report anything,' says Sir Dexter. 'Now get out of here, Miss Jang. And do mind what you write, because I have great influence with the Chinese authorities.'

'Oh, I know,' says Miss Jang, 'I realize you advise Beijing.' 'Better go, Miss Jang,' says Jasmine Tan. 'I'm sorry you won't talk to us,' says Miss Jang, 'but may I call you again if anything develops?' 'No,' says Sir Dexter, 'this is my bank and I told you to leave it.' 'Very well,' says Miss Jang, and goes out to the lift. Sir Dexter stares after her, then turns to Jasmine Tan. 'Get me my son Martin in London,' he says. 'Time difference, Sir Dexter,' says Miss Tan, looking up at the bank of clocks on the wall. 'He is my son, wake him,' says Sir Dexter, and walks into his inner suite.

'YOU DON'T MIND chopsticks, do you?' asks Athelstan Penhurst, as they walk across a blossom-filled, duck-noisy, fume-laden St James' Park, toward the Mall and the Duke of York Steps. 'Not at all, Athelstan,' says Michael Spearpoint, grizzled old diplomatic hand, a man with a charm only life at the sharp end can really provide, 'but do I take it this lunch has a purpose?' 'Have you ever known a diplomat do anything without a purpose?' asks Penhurst, steering Spearpoint across the Mall. 'Tell me, how old are we?' Spearpoint looks at him: 'Do you mean you or me?' 'Oh, you, old boy, I go on forever,' says Penhurst. 'I'm sixty-three, Athelstan, but I don't see—' 'Makes you one of the old reliables, doesn't it?' says Penhurst. 'You've flown the flag for us in half the trouble spots of the world.'

'I have done the state some service, though they often seem not to know it,' says Spearpoint, bitterly. And so he has. Spearpoint has fought on the beaches, representing British interests to the Belgian Empire in Brussels over the matter of seaborne sewage emissions. He has fought in the fields, defending the right of British cattle to madness or worse in the same courts of the European Commission. He has fought on the seas, speaking for the interests of British fish-and-chip shops in the long dark night of the Icelandic Cod War. Spearpoint remembers the Iron and Steel Commission, the old scheme of Monnet and Schuman which somehow turned into a non-existent country known as Europe. He remembers the Iron Curtain, when he did his turn in various embassies on either side of it. He remembers the Iron Lady, and not without affection, though she really should have given him that knighthood.

They go past the Athenaeum and up Haymarket, past the summer tourists queueing miserably for their tickets for *Les Misérables*. 'Should have made ambassador, shouldn't you?' asks

Penhurst. 'Hilda certainly thinks so,' says Spearpoint, 'I couldn't possibly comment.' 'How is Hilda, enjoying Tunbridge Wells?' asks Penhurst. 'Oh, absolutely loving Tunbridge Wells,' says Spearpoint. 'Not missing Brussels at all?' 'What, all those mad cows and pissing mannekins?' says Spearpoint. 'Not a bit of it. In fact I can see us settling down into a premature retirement.'

'Shouldn't count on it,' says Penhurst, heading over to Leicester Square, where the tossers and dossers of nineties London are out drinking tinned stuff in the sun. 'By the way, know Hong Kong at all?' 'I'm a Europe man myself,' says Spearpoint, 'I do know we're about to hand it back to its rightful owners.' 'You do realize it's the last one?' says Penhurst. 'The last one of what?' 'The last pearl of the empire you and I were created to serve,' says Penhurst. 'Best trade association the world ever had. Beats Europe into a cocked hat any time.' 'But that wouldn't be difficult, would it, Athelstan?' 'Shouldn't have lost the War, should we?' says Penhurst. 'My memory is we won it,' says Spearpoint. 'Only at the time, not later,' says Penhurst. 'In here.'

It's a big Chinese restaurant in Chinatown, one of those places where the pots of tea are already out on the table and actual Chinese are, reassuringly, eating lunch. A polite young waiter takes Penhurst's hat and his diplomatic briefcase; another steers them to a corner table and hands them a tasselled menu. 'I gather diplomacy's rather difficult out there,' says Spearpoint. 'No, same as everywhere else, only ruder,' says Penhurst. 'The only trouble is they've never forgiven us for the Treaty of Nanjing, the Treaty they had to sign in the Opium Wars. The Unequal Treaty, they call it. So they want to extract the revenge of history. Otherwise known as the piss.'

'Yes, sir?' says the waiter. 'Oh, I'll have a 17, a 49 and a small portion of that delicious-looking 121,' says Spearpoint. 'And the usual fish and chips for me,' says Penhurst. 'Thing is, after that we're on our own. A little offshore island with no friends anywhere that will have to live off its wits. If it has any.' 'A bit like Hong Kong itself, then,' says Spearpoint. 'Not a bit of it,' says Penhurst, 'they have wits. And the world's eighth biggest economy. And a better racetrack. And trams.' 'I assume we've secured our vital interests in the region,' asks Spearpoint. 'No, we haven't,' says Penhurst, 'that's the bugger of it. The Chinese just can't wait to see the backs of us. Anyway, we started discussing democracy with them. Always a bad mistake.' 'But we do have plenty of allies in the region?' 'What, the Yanks, the Ozzies and the Japanese?' says Penhurst. 'They're all born-again Pacific Rimmers. They can't wait for us to get out, so they can get in.'

'We have been doing this for half a century,' says Spearpoint, 'we should be getting used to it by now.' 'Getting out as fast as we can, you mean?' says Penhurst. 'Yes, but before this we've always done it in style. Mountbatten on an elephant with all the bands playing, that kind of thing. Different this time. The whole thing's turned into a bloody cock-up. Protocol nightmare. Worse than the Royal Wedding. Never mind the Royal Divorce. There's a Joint Liaison Committee that couldn't join Marks to Spencer. Time to knock heads together. Otherwise we'll be lucky to get out with egg foo yong on our faces. Don't want to close down the empire on a dying fall, do we? Shut up shop with a boot right up the Britannic arse?'

'I can see that could be a big political embarrassment,' says Spearpoint, 'no way for Britain to celebrate the millennium.' 'End of things, end of things,' says Penhurst. 'You see what I need is a special envoy to go out there and sort things out.' Spearpoint looks up. 'It would have to be someone rather special,' he says cautiously. 'Old diplomatic hand,' says Penhurst, 'a man of civility and charm. A master of pomp and protocol. Chap with a hand of silk but a fist of steel. Someone who can flatter the Mandarins, but still put the knife in where it hurts. Someone who'll stop it turning into an undignified rout. Someone who'll get Fat Peng . . . who'll get the Governor out in one piece. He could be the next prime minister, you know.'

'Oh yes, which country?' asks Spearpoint. 'This one, Spearpoint, ours,' says Penhurst. 'You realize there could be a knighthood in it.' 'I thought this new lot were abolishing traditional honours,' says Spearpoint. 'Do it right and they'd have to come up with something,' says Penhurst, 'maybe Comrade National Treasure. Be the last triumph, eh? Peak of a great career. Arise, Sir Michael. Hilda would love it.' 'Oh, I see,' says Spearpoint, 'you were actually thinking of me.' 'You knew damned well I was,' says Penhurst. The attentive waiter puts dishes onto the table, and then goes over to the cash desk, and picks up the telephone.

'DEFINITELY NOT,' says Lady Hilda, pruning the roses in Tunbridge Wells, 'I am not going to Hong Kong. It's all gambling dens and nightclubs.' 'I thought you liked being a diplomatic wife,' says Michael Spearpoint, clipping the hedge. 'Michael, I did not like being a diplomatic wife,' says Hilda, 'all I ever did was stand there serving drinks and canapés in the world's worst capitals, while you and a lot of big-bummed ambassadors stood about and talked for hours about how to eradicate the African warble fly. Or else you went off romping with those Eurosecretaries. I wasted my life, Michael. You fiddled and I cooked. Then just when I've been bored out of my socks for long enough, you bring me back to Britain and plonk me down in Tunbridge Wells. The home of the living dead. The end of the line.'

'It isn't the end of the line,' says Spearpoint, 'you can go on to Hastings.' 'The end of the line for me,' says Hilda, 'I am the daughter of an earl.' 'I know you're the daughter of an earl,' says Spearpoint, 'everyone knows you're the daughter of an earl.' 'Anyway, you know why they want to send you there, don't you?' says Hilda. 'British policy there's been a disaster and they want some idiot to go out and take the blame.' 'They want someone with diplomatic skills to bring them out with a bit of honour,' says Spearpoint, 'satisfy both sides, rescue the Governor, look after the royal party, and bring everyone safely back home into the sunset on the Royal Yacht *Britannia*.' Hilda stops pruning and looks at him. 'Did you say the Royal Yacht *Britannia*?' Spearpoint smiles faintly. After all, he isn't a diplomat for nothing.

'HONG KONG, Club class,' says Spearpoint, standing at the check-in desk for South China Air and handing over his Foreign Office tickets, 'And yes, I did pack everything myself.' 'No, he didn't, I did,' says Lady Hilda. 'You do have a lot of luggage, madam,' says the desk girl, inspecting the two large luggage carts that Hilda has pushed up against the desk. 'Yes, darling, well, we are coming back on the Royal Yacht *Britannia*,' says Hilda, 'my husband happens to be a very important British diplomat. Surely you have some room for us in first.' 'In Lotus Blossom class?' says the desk girl. 'I'd bump you up if I could, but I'm afraid it's impossible. All the flights are fully booked just now. Everybody's going out to Hong Kong to celebrate the Handover.'

Hilda looks over at the First-class line. 'Who are those people?' she asks. For a curious gathering stands waiting. There are lithe big girls of the kind that are always called Tara, and big young men in blazers that generally turn out to be junior aristocrats called Justin. There are stout middle-aged men in panamas with red neckerchieves, and women in hot pants. There is a person in clown costume, wearing a red plastic nose, and someone else with Dracula teeth. Others are in furs and kilts and tassels. Their luggage is Vuitton and Gucci and their clothes are Armani and Gautier. There are bottles of champagne out, creating an atmosphere of fragile hilarity, and one notes a certain amount of suspicious-looking sniffing. 'It's a party from the Hasta La Vista Carnival Club,' says the desk girl, 'they're holding a Handover Ball in Hong Kong. High arts and low bacchanalia. It sounds rather fun.' 'No, it doesn't,' says Hilda. 'Just tell them without my husband there won't even be a Handover.' 'Please, darling,' says Spearpoint.

'One moment, I think it just might be possible, Mr Spearpoint,' says a young man in the line behind them. He's Chinese, in a blazer, and he steps up to the counter. 'These people are very good friends of my father,' he says to the desk girl, 'I know my father would want you to help.' 'Oh, good evening, Mr Chen,' says the desk girl, smiling, 'we'd have to bump somebody.' 'What about the big party,' says the young man, 'can't you move some of these tango dancers over to Cathay Pacific?' 'I'll try, Mr Chen,' says the girl, attacking her computer.

'This is extremely kind of you,' says Hilda, being charming. 'Well, my father part-owns the airline,' says the young man. 'My name is Martin Chen. I run the London branch of the Marco Polo Bank. Perhaps you have heard of it?' 'I may have,' says Hilda, 'but one hears of so many things.' 'Maybe the seventh biggest in the world,' says Martin Chen. 'My father is the taipan. When you get to Hong Kong you must meet him. In Hong Kong you always need powerful friends. Chinese people always have many friends. That is because they also have many enemies. Which is why we try only to have the very best friends. I think you will like my father, Lady Hilda. He is a great collector of Chinese art.'

'There, I fixed it, Mr Chen,' says the desk girl. 'Thank you so much, Mr Chen,' says Hilda. 'Yes, have a happy travel to Hong Kong, and I expect I will see you there, Mr Spearpoint.' 'You seem to know who we are,' says Spearpoint. 'Yes, of course,' says Martin Chen, 'in China we have a little saying. When fiery dragons travel, the whole world knows. But we are a very poetic people.' 'Here are your tickets, Mr Spearpoint,' says the desk girl, 'and this is the card that admits you to the Lotus Blossom Lounge. Please enjoy the golden experience of South China Air.' 'Oh, we will,' says Hilda, 'thank you, darling Mr Chen.' And she swans off past the glitzy, bubbling, well-scented carnival crowd, waving the tickets at them.

THE AFTERNOON sun is gilding the slopes and towers of Hong Kong. In his executive office in the Bonaleck Building, Aleck Bonaleck, Australian media tycoon, and likely owner of the future world, is on the telephone in his shirtsleeves engaged in the intricate points of multimillion-dollar international trading. 'Just tell the Sultan of Brunei he's ten sheep short of a frigging paddock,' he's saying, 'remind him he may think he rules the soil of his country, but I hold the airwaves on top of it. Ask him to put away his numbers, and take another look at our numbers.' Diana Jang, looking through agency reports in the press room, can see him through the blinds of his office.

'Sorry about that long lunch,' says Will Huskisson, coming into the room and sitting down at his terminal. 'Better be careful, Will,' says Diana, nodding at the blinds, 'the chief pirate's back in town.' 'Oh God, Handover Fever,' says Huskisson. 'Is he doing secret deals with the Chinese?' 'I expect he's doing secret deals with everybody,' says Diana. 'He must be bored with NY.' 'And LA and London and Manila and Sydney,' says Huskisson. 'Why can't I be bored like that?'

Huskisson sits down at the blank screen in front of him. 'What's happened to our front-page story?' he asks. 'Sir Dexter Chen refused to give me an interview,' says Diana. 'I expect his astrologer warned him the day was inauspicious,' says Huskisson. 'I expect his lawyer warned him to button his lip,' says Diana. 'He threatened to shut down the paper if we went on writing about the bank.' 'That should be interesting,' says Huskisson, 'what does Smart Aleck say?' 'He said lay off the story too,' says Diana. 'Interesting,' says Huskisson, 'but that means we don't have a lead story for tomorrow.' Diana throws an agency report on to his desk. Its headline reads BRITISH SEND OUT SPECIAL ENVOY TO SOLVE HANDOVER PROBLEMS. 'Oh yes we do,' she says.

TWO

'CHAMPAGNE GLASSES, please,' says the Chinese stewardess, as the overnight jumbo begins its long descent into Hong Kong. Below is a sight of the Emerald City and the Fragrant Harbour, which experienced travellers agree is one of the finest views in the world. Red Chinese sun gilds the peaks, touches the wavetops, and lights up the great silver container ships that cut foaming white swathes through the water. Red Chinese sun gilds the television aerials and the white clothes on the washing lines. 'Oh my God,' says Hilda, peering through the window, 'we're not flying over these apartments, we're flying between them.' 'Don't worry, my dear,' says Spearpoint, 'the pilots are specially trained.' 'But there's a woman cooking soup just there,' says Hilda, 'chicken soup.' 'Enjoying your flight?' asks Martin Chen, passing in the aisle. 'Oh, it's lovely,' says Hilda, gushing, 'thank you so much, darling Mr Chen.' 'Have happy time in Hong Kong, and then you must meet my father,' says Martin. 'And don't you like the view?'

Down below, Leo Chesters – Number Four at Government House, and the Governor's left-hand man – is not having a good morning at all. The truth is that Hong Kong is no longer the sort of place he came out to, seventeen years ago, a young man with the sun in his eyes and bright skies in his heart. The Happy Hour is nearly over, and things are closing down. The signs saying Royal are coming down off the clubs and the buildings; the splendid old statues will probably not last very long. The gweilos who come here are mostly not British, but American and Australian and German and Dutch. Young Brits these days don't seem British at all. They drink lager in the streets, use the glottal stop with a promiscuous freedom and call themselves traders. But they're not the old traders who founded the colony and drank their sundowners at the Peninsula Hotel. They engage in strange commerce, consume strange substances and don't seem to make any real money at all.

His own time is closing too: he's wrong race, wrong colour, wrong training, wrong age, wrong sympathies, and the Chinese certainly won't want to keep him on. Government House is closing too; they're taking down the pictures and packing up the silver, and half the staff have gone. The Governor, Fat Peng, is growing sulky these days, and far more concerned about getting his claret home and putting his Yorkshire terriers into quarantine than saying all those dutiful farewells. The previous governors were all game to the last, wearing their peaked hats and uniforms and strutting the streets like gentlemen; the present Governor is a dresser-down of an oddly intellectual disposition, and very hard to predict.

Now, on a Saturday when the weather is lovely, the harbour water still, and the snorkelling is at its best, he has to get up early and go to the airport, to meet the visiting firepersons. The freeway out to the airport proves to be, as usual, gridlocked, since Hong Kong is a city with the many cars of prosperity and nowhere at all for them to go. Except that this morning quite a few people seem to be leaving already, and the cars are laden with luggage and possessions; the predicted exodus has already begun. Road tempers are poor, as the morning heat begins moving toward the tropical, and urban smog begins to form. And out at Kai Tak, the visitor parking area is already full, packed with long executive Mercedes and hotel-owned Rolls-Royces. Finally Chesters has to park his beloved pink beach buggy illegally on the sidewalk, hoping that the Government House sign he places on the windscreen can still perform its old imperial magic.

It does. As he gets out of the car, an angry Chinese demonstration suddenly surrounds him, its supporters waving banners that say British Remember Tiananmen and More Democracy Now. Two airport policemen hurry over, but by the time they have settled matters Chesters has a bruise on his cheek, a dent in his panama, and a tear in the sleeve of his linen jacket. Late, he hurries into the Arrivals hall, packed as it usually is these days, since the Chinese authorities have deliberately delayed opening the grand new airport on the island until the British have gone. Up by the barrier, the meeters and greeters, the chauffeurs and the hotel servants, are holding up signs (Mitsubishi and Citicorp, McDonald's and Toshiba, Womex and Daiwoo, Peninsula and Mandarin) to the passengers from the London flight, who have plainly landed already, and are coming from Baggage and Immigration in a steady horde.

A strangely carnival mood prevails this morning. Many of the passengers carry bottles of champagne, and others have evidently imbibed well during the flight. There are people with paper hats and plastic noses. They head for a desk saying Hasta

La Vista Carnival Club, where a bevy of organizing beauties directs them to minibuses and long low stretch limos outside.

'SEE IF YOU CAN spot anyone who looks at all British,' says Spearpoint, pushing his cart out into the Arrivals hall. 'There must be an official reception committee,' says Hilda, fanning herself with her hat, 'presumably the Governor himself.' But it's a fat, perspiring middle-aged man, wearing a dented panama and a torn coat, who finally emerges from the crowd. 'You wouldn't be Mr and Mrs Spearpoint?' he asks. 'Yes, of course we would,' says Hilda. 'Who are you?' 'Leo Chesters, Government House,' says the fat man. 'Let me push this. You have brought a lot of luggage. You're not thinking of staying on?' 'No, we're not thinking of staying on,' says Hilda, 'we're thinking about the Royal Yacht *Britannia*. One does have to look one's best.'

'You know, Chesters, I had thought we'd be met by the Governor,' says Spearpoint, 'I am a special envoy, after all.' 'Oh, yes, the Governor sent his apologies,' says Chesters, sweatingly pushing the cart toward the exit. 'He's at his summer house at Fanling, writing his speeches. He does have a lot of speeches.' 'And the Deputy Governor?' asks Spearpoint. 'She sent her apologies too,' says Chesters, 'she's in Shenzen.' 'Writing her speeches?' asks Hilda. 'I expect so,' says Chesters, 'she has even more speeches. She's been asked to attend the Handover ceremonies. The Governor hasn't.' 'Which is exactly why I'm here,' says Spearpoint.

'SIT, CHESTERS,' says Spearpoint. 'Sit?' 'Yes, sit.' Chesters sits plumply down on the leather sofa. 'Now, Chesters, I know the Orient is a very tempting place.' 'It is very nice,' agrees Chesters. 'And I do realize it can have strange effects on a man. You've probably been serving out here for many years and forgotten the way we do things.' 'I do hope not,' says Chesters. 'Well, for one thing it isn't customary to meet a special envoy in your beach buggy,' says Spearpoint, 'so I propose we start as we mean to go on.' 'Why don't I go and look at some of those little boutiques over there?' says Hilda. 'So you two diplomats can enjoy yourselves.'

'How do we mean to go on?' asks Chesters, wiping his brow. 'Number one, you will be here, in the hotel lobby, each morning at nine o'clock in order to brief me,' says Spearpoint. 'Really?' asks Chesters. 'As early as that?' 'Yes, Chesters, as early as that,' says Spearpoint. 'Number two, I have no intention of running my mission from a hotel bedroom, however well stocked the minibar may be. I need the use of an office with diplomatic facilities in Government House.' 'But there's only mine,' says Chesters. 'Very well, yours then,' says Spearpoint. 'Number three, I want you to arrange a meeting for me soonest with the top Chinese official.'

Chesters looks at him doubtfully: 'You don't mean Mr Li Han?' 'If he's the top Chinese official, I do mean Mr Li Han.' 'But Mr Li Han isn't very well,' says Chesters. 'I'm sorry to hear that,' says Spearpoint, 'What's the matter with him?' 'Well, we're not really sure,' says Chesters, 'he's perfectly well for the Americans. And the French and the Japanese. It's just the British he's not very well for.' Spearpoint stares at him. 'And when do you expect him to be better?' 'Not sure, sir, but probably after the Handover.'

'I see,' says Spearpoint, 'I've been sent out here to facilitate the Handover, and you are quite incapable of arranging a meeting between me and the Chinese.' Chesters looks pained. 'I wouldn't say that,' he says, 'in fact we've arranged a lunchtime drinks reception for you at Government House tomorrow.' 'And I can expect to meet some leading Chinese then?' 'Yes,' says Chesters, 'if they choose to come, of course.' 'Why would they not choose to come?' asks Spearpoint. 'They're not very keen at coming to Government House at the moment. You see, the ones who are pro-Chinese, that's most of the business community, think we're siding with the pro-democracy people.' 'And what about the pro-democracy people?' 'Well, they think we're letting them down.' 'And who is right?' asks Spearpoint. 'I suppose they both are,' says Chesters, 'We have been siding with the pro-democracy people. And we are letting them down.'

'So in other words you've arranged a reception for me at Government House tomorrow to which no one at all will come?' 'Oh, people will come,' says Chesters, 'a lot of the expat community. Some of them wouldn't miss a G and T at Government House for anything in the world.' 'The Governor will be there?' says Spearpoint. 'No, he'll still be in Fanling, writing his speeches,' says Chesters. 'And the Deputy Governor?' 'She'll still be in Shenzen, visiting her ancestors. They both asked me to give you their deepest apologies.' 'Oh, did they?' 'Frankly,' says Chesters, 'they both thought it was better if they didn't attend.' 'Just to ensure that nobody at all was there?' 'Oh, no,' says Chesters, 'so the people who don't come can't use as an excuse for not coming the fact that they wouldn't come because the Governor was there. A lot of people won't speak to him. Of course, he won't speak to a lot of people.'

Spearpoint stares at Chesters. 'So if I've understood the situation correctly – and do tell me if I'm wrong – the situation here has deteriorated so badly that Chinese no longer speak to the Governor, and the Governor no longer speaks to the Chinese.' 'Yes,' says Chesters. 'And I can't speak to either of them. And despite all that I'm supposed to achieve a Happy Handover at the end of the month.' 'I'd say that pretty well sums it up, sir,' says Chesters. 'It's bloody hopeless, isn't it, Chesters?' 'You could say that,' admits Chesters, 'but you do have to see things from the Chinese point of view.' 'Chesters, we were sent out here by the British government, all of us,' says Spearpoint. 'The one thing we are not expected to do is see things from the Chinese point of view. What is the Chinese point of view?'

'Well, their point of view is we took the islands from them by force, at a time when we were strong and they were weak,' says Chesters, 'in fact they call it the National Humiliation. For nearly two centuries they've had to kowtow to us. Now they think it's time we kowtowed to them.' 'Believe me, I don't kowtow to anyone,' says Spearpoint. 'Absolutely right, sir,' says Chesters, 'the only problem is, if you won't kowtow to them, they won't see you. Anyway, they just don't trust the gweilos any longer.'

'Gweilos, what's that?' asks Hilda, returning from her inspection of the glass cases of cashmere sweaters and chamois leathers. 'Oh, what the Chinese call us,' says Chesters. 'It means white ghosts.' 'I think that's rather lovely,' says Hilda. 'Yes, we came to haunt their land for a while,' says Chesters, 'now we're about to be driven out. Do have a good night tonight and recover from your jet lag, and I'll get back to my snorkelling. Oh, incidentally, the staff here do expect rather large tips. And the British taxpayers are paying, aren't they?' 'What a common little man,' says Hilda. 'What a bloody mess,' says Spearpoint.

IN A HIGH apartment in a high white apartment block looking down over the harbour, Jasmine Tan and Martin Chen are in bed together. 'How long you stay?' asks Jasmine, leaning over him. 'Until the Handover,' says Martin lazily. 'Then you take me to London?' she asks. 'If you're sure that's what you really want,' says Martin. 'You know I want,' says Jasmine. 'Tell me, how was London?' 'Oh, London was just London,' says Martin. 'It was grey, always grey. The sun wasn't real sun. The rain wasn't real rain.' 'Come on, tell me properly, Martin,' says Jasmine, 'I don't see you for so long. Are the buildings very old? Are the gweilos very stuffy?'

'It isn't the way you think,' says Martin, 'the buildings are new. The people dress like clowns. You know what we like about them. The Queen, those funny voices, always roast beef. Now they aren't that way any more. They don't know how to talk, not as well as us. The cows are poisoned. They don't like the Queen any more.' 'Of course they like the Queen.' 'Not any more,' says Martin, 'they don't want to be British any more, they want to be something else. The Scots and the Irish and the Welsh all insult them, and they like it very much. Sometimes they think it is nice to be European, but the Europeans hate them, because they are not European at all. Sometimes they like to be American, but they are far too dull. No, really they like best to be lager louts.'

'What?' asks Jasmine. 'You know, lager louts, Gazzas,' says Martin, 'You see them all the time in Lan Kwai Fok.' Jasmine laughs, then looks at him. 'I think you don't want me to come with you any more,' she says. 'Of course I want it, if you want it,' says Martin. 'Anyway, I am not permitted,' says Jasmine, 'I don't have passport.' 'If you want one, it's easy,' says Martin, 'in Hong Kong everything's easy.' 'Oh, yes?' she says. 'Every-one would like a British passport. And I am only secretary. I have no relatives there. But maybe your father . . .?'

'Now listen to me,' says Martin, raising himself up, 'you never say anything to my father. He wouldn't accept you, he wants me to make a good marriage for the hong.' 'I am not a good marriage?' 'You're not a film star, you're not a British aristocrat, not even a Fergie,' says Martin. 'Just leave it to me. I make it OK. I'm used to Hong Kong, I know all the right people.' 'And you are a Chen,' says Jasmine, smiling, 'they always help a Chen.'

Furling the Flag

EPISODE ONE

1/1. Titles.

Could be backed with shots of the countdown clock, erected in Tiananmen Square, Beijing, and showing the months, days, minutes and seconds to the Hong Kong Handover on 30 June 1997. And we could bring in that old big band jazz song that tells us about the guy who comes from 'old Hong Kong' – as we cut to:

1/2. EXT. Hong Kong. Morning.

A helicopter shot over the modern megacity of Hong Kong today. The Harbour and the islands. The high business towers and the white apartment blocks. The Chinese quarter and the British Peak. And the two seats of power: the Bank of China Tower and Government House.

Our shot swoops to take us out over the water, with the container ships, the rising bridge to the new airport, the old-style junks and sampans. Finally it picks up on one of Hong Kong's most traditional pieces of water traffic, the Star Ferry, as it chugs across from Hong Kong island to Kowloon.

1/3. EXT. Deck, Star Ferry. Morning.

On the deck stands *Sir Dexter Chen*, a silver-haired and distinguished Chinese. He's a taipan and a man of destiny. He's Europeanized and finely suited: after all, he comes from the city where there are some of the best tailors in the world. He looks out over the Harbour to the high commercial towers on the waterfront. The Hong Kong and Shanghai Bank. The great Bank of China Tower. And one of those towers is his.

We pick it out: **Chen Tower, the Marco Polo Bank**.

Sir Dexter gazes at his domain and destiny. The Ferry is moving toward the Pier. Chinese commuters rushing to work crowd round him. And *two bodyguards* appear to move the great taipan to safety . . .

1/4. EXT. Star Ferry Pier. Day.

The crowds pour off the ferry into the noise and bustle of Hong Kong. Shouting and pushing. Hooting and honking. Sir Dexter comes off the Ferry, protected by his bulky bodyguards.

A Rolls-Royce waits, the *chauffeur* holding open the door. Sir Dexter and the bodyguards get in. The Rolls moves off through the crowds.

1/5. INT. Sir Dexter's Rolls, Hong Kong. Day.

The chauffeur, driving on through the crowds, silently hands Sir Dexter the morning paper. It's the *South China Tribune*. The headline: COUNTDOWN NEWS, 32 DAYS TO GO. LEADING BUSINESSMEN SAY: TIME TO LEAVE HONG KONG.

Sir Dexter crumples up the paper in anger.

Crowds press round the car – he's recognized. Someone presses a banner to the car window saying 'More Democracy Now'. The bodyguards react. But Sir Dexter, the grand taipan, waves through the window . . . Sampans in the Harbour.

1/6. EXT. Whitehall, London. Day.

Red buses. We pick up on Big Ben, striking twelve. Our shot moves along Whitehall, to pick up Gilbert Scott's great imperial building, the Foreign and Commonwealth Office. As Big Ben continues to chime, we move under the arch to see our central character, *Michael Spearpoint*, walking into the building with his briefcase.

Spearpoint is an old FCO hand who has served in less than splendid offices in various difficult parts of the world. He's smooth, silver-haired and silver-tongued. Elegantly suited, he has a charmed air of grizzled wisdom only life at the sharp end can provide. So why has he never quite made it? Maybe his wife . . . ?

1/7. INT. Durbar Court, FCO, London. Day.

The famous Inner Court with its great imperial associations and pictures. British diplomats and civil servants scurry about their work. Pick up Spearpoint, waiting with his briefcase, glancing with interest at passing female diplomats and secretaries. *Ms Highsmith*, a power-dressed civil servant, comes up.

Ms HIGHSMITH Mr Spearpoint? Morning, sir. Mr Penhurst is ready to see you now.

SPEARPOINT *(Charming)* Thank you, my dear.

(They go upstairs toward the balcony.)

Ms HIGHSMITH Been here before?

SPEARPOINT Oh yes. I've done the state some service, did they but know it. I worked here once. When this was the most powerful building in the world. I presume we will be selling it off to the private sector soon?

Ms HIGHSMITH I'm commercial intelligence, nobody tells me a thing. Mind the bucket. We seem to have sprung a leak.

SPEARPOINT We didn't have leaks in my day.

(ATHELSTAN PENHURST, a bluff old senior diplomat and deskman, appears at the door of his office.)

PENHURST Ah, there you are, Spearpoint. Look fit. Well, come on in.

1/8. INT. Penhurst's office, FCO. Day.

Penhurst leads Spearpoint into the panelled room. Old portraits of imperial figures. A map of the red-coloured empire on the wall behind Penhurst's desk. Ms Highsmith hovers.

PENHURST How old are we, Spearpoint?

SPEARPOINT You or me?

PENHURST You, laddie. I go on for ever.

SPEARPOINT Sixty-three, Athelstan. But I don't see what . . .

PENHURST Makes you one of the old reliables. You've carried the spear for us in some of the great trouble spots of the world, haven't you?

SPEARPOINT I fought on the beaches. That was Brussels, over sewage emissions. I fought on the seas. Iceland, height of the Cod War. I fought in the fields and hedgerows. Rome summit, that was the great Mad Cow campaign.

PENHURST Should have made ambassador, eh?

SPEARPOINT Hilda certainly thinks so.

PENHURST How is Hilda? Enjoying Tunbridge Wells?

SPEARPOINT Absolutely loving Tunbridge Wells.

PENHURST Not missing Brussels at all?

SPEARPOINT All those moules and pissing mannikins? Not a bit of it. I fancy Hilda and I are settling down into premature retirement.

PENHURST Shouldn't count on it. Know Hong Kong?

SPEARPOINT I'm a West-of-Suez man. I am aware we're about to return it to its owners.

PENHURST You realize it's the last one?

SPEARPOINT The last one of what?

PENHURST Last jewel in the crown. Last pearl of a once great empire. The institution you and I were born to serve. Best trade association the world ever had. Beats Europe into a cocked hat any day.

SPEARPOINT That wouldn't be difficult, would it?

PENHURST After that we're on our own. Little offshore island living off its wits.

SPEARPOINT A bit like Hong Kong itself.

PENHURST Except they're a golden isle. Got the world's

eighth largest economy. *And* trams. *And* a top-class racetrack. Still, shouldn't have lost the War, should we?

SPEARPOINT My memory is we won it.

PENHURST Only at the time. Been losing it ever since. Feel like a spot of lunch at all? Don't mind chopsticks, do you?

SPEARPOINT I take it this summons has a purpose?

PENHURST Ever know a diplomat even go to the loo without a purpose?

1/9. EXT. Chen Tower, Hong Kong. Day.

Sir Dexter's Rolls stops outside a high-rise bank building near the waterfront. The chauffeur opens the door, Sir Dexter steps out. Looks up at his pride and joy, enters past the sign showing this is Chen Tower, the Marco Polo Bank.

1/10. EXT. Chinese restaurant, London. Day.

Establisher. The entrance of a large London Chinese, which might be in Hong Kong – until a red bus or London taxi passes.

1/11. INT. Chinese restaurant, London. Day.

At table Spearpoint and Penhurst. A *Chinese waiter* offers to take their diplomatic briefcases from the table. Penhurst indicates not to touch. Spearpoint looks over the menu.

SPEARPOINT 17, 49 and a small portion of that delicious-looking 93.

PENHURST And I'll have fish and chips.

SPEARPOINT Shouldn't be difficult, surely? We have been doing it for half a century.

PENHURST Skipping out of our colonies before we were kicked out, you mean? But we've always done it in style. Mountbatten on an elephant with massed bands playing, that kind of thing. Different this time. The Chinese want to extract maximum humiliation. Otherwise called the piss.

SPEARPOINT I hear diplomacy can be awkward out there.

PENHURST Same as everywhere else, only ruder. Trouble is,
the thing's turned into a protocol nightmare. Worse than
the Royal Wedding. Never mind the Royal Divorce.
We've been negotiating for seventeen years. Still haven't
settled the Handover ceremony.

SPEARPOINT So what's your problem, Athelstan?

PENHURST We want a big banquet, so they want a small one.
We want it at Government House, so they want it at Bank
of China Tower. We want the pipe band of the Gurkhas,
so they want the Three Tenors. Less than a month to go,
and we still haven't agreed a bloody thing.

(The waiter faintly reacts and walks away . . .)

1/12. INT. Lift, Chen Tower. Day.

Sir Dexter with his bodyguards is in the glass lift, rising higher
and higher over his domain and the Harbour. The lift stops,
the doors open. A crowd of bank workers moves to get in. But
the bodyguards block the way. Sir Dexter's is sacred space. The
button is pressed, the lift doors close, and Sir Dexter rises ever
higher . . .

1/13. INT. Chinese restaurant, London. Day.

SPEARPOINT Lots of ceremonial, then?

PENHURST They're sending Li Peng and the whole of the
National People's Congress. We field the usual token
royal.

SPEARPOINT Mrs Thatcher?

PENHURST No. She's going, of course. Booked the whole
top-floor suite of the New Mandarin Hotel. No . . . they
wouldn't accept the Queen, since they don't have one.
Prince of Wales is . . . domestically impaired. We bat the
Princess Royal.

SPEARPOINT Dignified, uncontroversial, used to handing
things over.

PENHURST BAFTA awards and so on. But the real problem's the Governor. Apparently he said a rude word in front of Chairman Li Peng.

SPEARPOINT Rude word?

PENHURST Yes, democracy. Now they're calling him Tango Dancer, and refusing to have him anywhere near the ceremonies.

SPEARPOINT Tango Dancer?

PENHURST Oh, don't ask. The Chinese are a very poetic people. Anyway, it's a calculated snub. Thing is, the Chinese think they're the best diplomats in the world. So do we, of course. That's why they call us mandarins. So, only one thing we can do. Send out a special envoy to sort it.

SPEARPOINT Have to be a top-class man, Athelstan. We can't have the empire on a dying fall.

PENHURST Or us marching out with a boot up the arse. No, got to be someone we can count on. Someone who'll bring us out without egg foo yong on our faces. Someone who can really get under the skin of foreigners.

(Spearpoint smiles faintly.)

SPEARPOINT Quite. A smooth man. A man with a glove of silk and a fist of steel. Did you have anyone in particular in mind, Athelstan?

(Angle on the waiter at the desk. He's looking at the diplomatic briefcases. He talks to his manager, who nods and picks up a phone . . .)

1/14. INT. Taipan suite, Chen Tower. Day.

Sir Dexter comes in. His bodyguards leave him at the door. In the office sits his PA, *Jasmine Tan*, early twenties, Chinese, beautiful, smart. A couple of *other Chinese secretaries* work.

JASMINE Happy morning, Sir Dexter.

OTHER SECRETARIES Happy morning, Sir Dexter.

JASMINE Miss Jang is here to see you.

(DIANA JANG, thirties, Euro-Asian, good-looking, gets up. She's taking a tape recorder from her bag.)

DIANA Diana Jang, *South China Tribune*. I rang you yesterday about an interview.

(Sir Dexter holds out the crumpled newspaper.)

SIR DEXTER That is your newspaper, Miss Jang?

DIANA Yes it is, Sir Dexter.

SIR DEXTER Take it. And tell the owner if he prints more stories like today's, he will soon not have a newspaper. It does not create confidence in the future.

DIANA You think we should have confidence in the future?

SIR DEXTER You're fortunate to live here. If you don't like it, better go.

DIANA Couldn't there be debate about its future?

SIR DEXTER Not with you. Please put that away. There is no interview.

DIANA I wanted to ask you about the Bank's . . .

(Sir Dexter goes into his inner office. Jasmine looks up.)

JASMINE Better to leave now, Miss Jang . . .

1/15. INT. Taipan suite, Chen Tower. Day.

Sir Dexter enters his office. Someone is there, inspecting the Chinese antiques in a cabinet. This is *Dang*, twenties, an oversmart yuppie and fixer. He has American-style clothes and wears shades. Sir Dexter's angry.

SIR DEXTER Nobody comes here. This is my private suite.

DANG Your staff know I am your friend.

SIR DEXTER You are no longer my friend. You no longer work here. You are forbidden to enter this bank.

DANG Oh please . . . I just came from Shanghai. The officials

there all ask about you. And thank you for your generous
gifts.

SIR DEXTER I don't deal through you any more, Dang. Now
stay right out of my business.

*(Dang looks at the antiques. Sir Dexter meanwhile presses a button
on his desk.)*

DANG These are fine antiques. I hope when things change
the authorities don't ask for them back.

SIR DEXTER Just go, Dang.

(Jasmine comes in.)

DANG Is your son coming home soon?

SIR DEXTER Show Mr Dang out. Never let him in this office
again. Now get me Mr Li Han.

(Dang goes out with Jasmine. He looks back. A hint of his threat.)

1/16. INT. Check-in desks, Heathrow. Evening.

Club-class check-in desk of South China Air. Spearpoint is
front of line with his formidable wife *Hilda*, firm, fifties,
aristocratic, very smartly dressed – and with a great deal of
luggage. Spearpoint leans over with his tickets to the *desk girl*.

SPEARPOINT There we are, my dear. Club class, Hong Kong.
And yes, I did pack everything myself.

HILDA No, he didn't, my dear, I did. Young lady, my
husband happens to be a very important diplomat.
I presume you have room in First?

DESK GIRL I'd bump you up if I could, madam. But flights
are fully booked just now. Everyone's going to celebrate
the Handover.

HILDA Really? Well, without my husband there won't even
be a Handover.

*(MARTIN CHEN steps forward. A handsome, young, Western-
educated type, the son of Sir Dexter Chen.)*

MARTIN Excuse me, sir. It may be possible.

DESK GIRL Oh, good evening, Mr Chen.

MARTIN Good evening. These two people are very old friends of my father. Can't you move some of the others on to Cathay Pacific?

DESK GIRL I'll try, Mr Chen.

(She taps the computer.)

SPEARPOINT This is extremely kind of you . . .

MARTIN My father part-owns the airline. I am Martin Chen.

(Martin presents his card. Spearpoint inspects it. Hilda smiles at Martin.)

SPEARPOINT The Marco Polo Bank? Should I have heard of it?

MARTIN I think so. Sixth biggest in world. Twenty storeys in London. Forty storeys in New York. In Hong Kong, seventy storeys.

HILDA You certainly have a wonderful lot of stories, Mr Chen. I suppose there are lots of nightclubs in Hong Kong?

(The desk girl looks up.)

DESK GIRL Fixed it, Mr Chen.

HILDA So kind. So very kind.

MARTIN When you are there, you must meet my father. Chinese people have a saying. The more you have enemies, the more you must have good friends. Please do enjoy your flight, Mr and Mrs Spearpoint.

SPEARPOINT You know who I am?

MARTIN In China there is another saying. When fiery dragons travel, the whole world knows.

SPEARPOINT Yes. You are a very poetic people.

DESK GIRL Your tickets, Mr Spearpoint. That way to the Lotus Blossom Lounge. And enjoy the golden experience of South China Air.

HILDA Oh we will. Thank you, darling Mr Chen.

(And Hilda swans off waving her First-class tickets.)

1/17. INT. Office, *South China Tribune*, Hong Kong. Day.

Diana works at her editor's desk, going through news agency reports, etc. *Will Huskisson,* fifties, an Old China Hand, comes in.

HUSKISSON Excuse the long lunch.

DIANA Better be careful, Will. Boss back in town.

(She nods towards the next suite. Through the blinds, a glimpse of the paper's owner, ALECK BONALECK, *on the telephone in his smart office.)*

HUSKISSON Oh God. Handover fever. He's doing more cunning deals with the Chinese?

DIANA He must be bored with New York. And LA and London, Denver and Sydney.

HUSKISSON Why can't I be bored that way? What happened to our Dexter Chen story?

DIANA He refused the interview.

HUSKISSON Maybe his astrologer warned him the day was inauspicious.

DIANA Maybe his lawyer warned him to button his mouth.

HUSKISSON So no lead story for tomorrow?

DIANA Oh yes there is.

(Diana shows an agency report. British send out envoy to ease Handover, *with Spearpoint's photo.)*

1/18. INT. First-class cabin, jumbo. Morning.

There's Chinese chatter on the intercom, a *Chinese stewardess* with a champagne bottle as Spearpoint and Hilda approach their destination.

HILDA I just hope when we get there you don't expect me to be a sweet diplomatic wife.

SPEARPOINT I thought you rather liked being a diplomatic wife.

STEWARDESS More champagne, madam?

HILDA Yes, dear, fill it up. I do not like being a diplomatic wife. It's the world's most boring top job. I stand around holding out cocktails and canapés while you talk to big-bummed ambassadors about how to eradicate the African warble fly. Or go off bonking the secretaries.

STEWARDESS And for you, sir?

SPEARPOINT *(Looks appreciatively)* Please, my dear. Hilda, there comes a time in a good man's life when he craves the respect of his compatriots . . .

HILDA You mean you still want that knighthood. Well, you won't get it by bonking the bimbos. Anyway, the new government's abolishing traditional honours. The most you'd get is Comrade National Treasure.

SPEARPOINT How utterly repulsive. I just want to go out with a last big bang.

HILDA And you really don't care who it is you're banging, do you? Oh, darling Mr Chen. We're having the most lovely time.

(This to Martin Chen, passing in the aisle.)

MARTIN Good. I hope to see you in Hong Kong. So does my father.

(He goes back to his seat.)

HILDA Awfully kind of him, wasn't it?

SPEARPOINT Yes. I wonder why . . .

1/19. EXT. Downtown Hong Kong. Day.

Ground-based shot: a jumbo coming in strangely low through the high-rise apartments to land at the airport, Kai Tak. We hear over the Chinese chatter of a landing announcement, then:

1/20. INT. First-class cabin, jumbo. Day.

Hilda stares in horror out of the window.

STEWARDESS Champagne glass, Mrs Spearpoint . . .

HILDA Michael! We're not flying over these buildings. We're flying between them.

SPEARPOINT It's quite all right. The pilots are used to it.

HILDA There's a woman cooking soup. *(Another look)* Chicken soup!

1/21. EXT. Runway, Kai Tak. Day.

A jumbo touches down and straight to . . .

1/22. INT. Arrivals hall, Kai Tak. Day.

Spearpoint and Hilda come out of customs, Spearpoint pushing the heavy laden cart. Hilda is fanning herself against the heat. Spearpoint looks around. There are the usual meeters and greeters, with their signs saying Citicorp, Mitsubishi, IBM, etc.

SPEARPOINT Of course there'll be some kind of official reception committee. Probably the Governor himself. See anyone who looks British?

(Pick up on a rather seedy figure emerging from the back of the group of greeters: LEO CHESTERS, British, middle-aged, wearing a panama, and sweating. He holds a sign saying Spearpoint. It's upside down.)

CHESTERS You're Mr and Mrs Spearpoint?

HILDA Not today, thank you.

CHESTERS I'm Leo Chesters, number three, Government House. The Governor's left-hand man. You've brought a lot of luggage. Not thinking of staying on, are you?

(Chesters takes the cart, heads for the exit.)

HILDA Awfully hot, isn't it, Mr Chesters? And I really don't think much of your airport.

CHESTERS Nor do we. That's why we're building a beautiful

new one. Unfortunately with their usual cunning the Chinese have managed to delay it till after the Handover.

SPEARPOINT Mr Chesters, I expected the Governor to . . .

CHESTERS The Governor sends his apologies. He's at his summer house in Fanling, writing his speeches. He has a lot of speeches.

SPEARPOINT What about the Deputy Governor?

CHESTERS Sent her apologies. She's in Shenzen.

SPEARPOINT Writing *her* speeches?

CHESTERS She has even more speeches. She's been asked to the Handover. The Governor hasn't.

SPEARPOINT Which is precisely why I'm here.

CHESTERS We did wonder. We have been working on this for the past seventeen years. Well, well, what do you know? The great taipan.

(Sir Dexter comes in through the entrance doors, with his two bodyguards. He stops, looks round.)

HILDA Who is it?

CHESTERS Sir Dexter Chen. One of the great power-brokers of Hong Kong.

(Martin Chen passes. He stops, smiling.)

MARTIN Ah, Mr and Mrs Spearpoint. I'm glad you enjoyed your flight.

HILDA Oh, we did, my dear, very much.

MARTIN Good. Have a happy travel in Hong Kong. And you must meet my father soon.

(And Martin goes over to embrace his father.)

CHESTERS So you've met Number One Son.

HILDA Such a nice boy. He arranged for us to fly First class.

CHESTERS Oh yes? Wait till you meet Number Two.

(Diana appears before Spearpoint.)

DIANA Mr Michael Spearpoint? Diana Jang, *South China Tribune*. Could we have a photo and a brief interview?

SPEARPOINT *(Looks appreciatively)* Of course, my dear. Hilda, would you excuse me a moment?

(Spearpoint goes. Hilda turns to Chesters.)

HILDA I know these brief interviews with girls in brief skirts. They usually go on a very long time. Mr Chesters, why not take me to the Governor's limo?

1/23. EXT. Car park, Kai Tak. Day.

Rolls-Royces and Mercedes in the car park. Hilda stares in disbelief at Chesters' battered old car.

HILDA *That's* the Governor's limo?

CHESTERS Mine, really. A poor thing but mine own. The Governor's chauffeur sent his apologies.

HILDA He's writing speeches too?

CHESTERS He's left, actually. Most of them have.

(Chesters opens the door for Hilda, then begins trying to fit the luggage in the boot, which is filled with snorkelling stuff.)

HILDA I can't wait to get to Government House.

CHESTERS You're not staying at Government House. In view of the political sensitivity of the mission. Besides, most of the furniture's gone. And there's a nasty smell of burning secret files.

HILDA Well, where are we staying?

CHESTERS Hotel, actually. The Blue Moon.

(He tries stacking the luggage on the roofrack.)

1/24. INT. VIP suite, Kai Tak. Day.

Spearpoint smiles icily as the photo is taken.

SPEARPOINT I prefer the other profile, if you don't mind. Now, my dear, how can I help you?

DIANA Mr Spearpoint, I understand you've been sent out by

the British government to take charge of arrangements for the Handover?

SPEARPOINT I'm here to make quite sure things go as smoothly as they possibly can, yes.

DIANA Meaning that now they're not going smoothly? The Chinese are being difficult?

SPEARPOINT No, they're going extremely smoothly. But my job is to make sure they go even more smoothly than they are. The British have become rather expert at handing over colonies. You could say it's one of the things we do best. We'd like to think we're leaving Hong Kong with a certain . . . style.

DIANA And what's your opinion on the prospects for freedom and democracy? Once you've made your departure with a certain . . . style?

SPEARPOINT I'm sorry, Miss er . . .

DIANA Jang. Diana Jang.

SPEARPOINT You seem to misunderstand the nature of my mission. My task is simply form and protocol. My personal opinions on freedom and democracy are neither here nor there. One way or the other.

DIANA You just deal with pomp and ceremony?

SPEARPOINT I deal with the difficult business of making a great moment of history occur.

DIANA The retreat of the British from Hong Kong? But when you have retreated, people here are afraid there'll be no one to protect them.

SPEARPOINT May I recall to you the words of our Prime – former Prime Minister, when he visited Hong Kong last year? You'll never walk alone, he said.

DIANA But he didn't say who would walk with us. If the Chinese suppress democracy or imprison dissidents, will you intervene? Send in troops? Call in the United Nations?

SPEARPOINT Miss Jang. The important thing just now is that this is a time of celebration.

DIANA The British are celebrating leaving Hong Kong?

SPEARPOINT Yes. No.

1/25. EXT. Car park, Kai Tak. Day.

Hilda in the car, tidying her face. Chesters still tries desperately to accommodate the luggage.

HILDA A good hotel?

CHESTERS Oh yes, a good hotel.

HILDA A very good hotel?

CHESTERS Yes, an absolutely excellent hotel. After all, the British taxpayer's paying.

HILDA Mr Chesters, let me make one thing clear. I expect to be treated properly. I am the daughter of an earl. Now, I think we made a mistake leaving my husband with that little bimbo. Would you just go back and grab the old goat before the heat gets to him?

CHESTERS Yes, my lady.

HILDA Oh, and Mr Chesters. Leave me your hat.

(Chesters hands over his panama. Hilda puts it on. Chesters wipes his brow and heads back.)

1/26. INT. VIP suite, Kai Tak. Day.

Spearpoint, with Diana, is now looking round desperately for aid.

SPEARPOINT I'm simply saying the Handover is both a sad and a happy event.

DIANA But how can it be both, Mr Spearpoint?

SPEARPOINT One can be sad for the past that is slipping away from us. And happy for the bright new future now dawning.

DIANA Oh, you mean, the British will be happy and the people of Hong Kong will be sad . . .

(Chesters appears, wiping his brow.)

SPEARPOINT There you are, Chesters. At last.

CHESTERS No hurry, sir.

SPEARPOINT Yes there is. Now, Miss Jang, I think I should get to know this place a great deal better before I start giving you my first impressions.

DIANA Good, so you'll call me when you have some.

SPEARPOINT No, I think you'd better call me.

DIANA At Government House?

CHESTERS No, he's staying at the Blue Moon Hotel.

DIANA So your mission doesn't have the support of the Governor?

SPEARPOINT I didn't say that. Nobody said that.

DIANA Anyway, thank you, Mr Spearpoint.

(She goes. Spearpoint turns furiously to Chesters.)

SPEARPOINT Impertinent girl.

CHESTERS Hope you didn't say too much, sir. The press are being very aggressive just now. With the Handover.

SPEARPOINT Who owns this bloody paper anyway?

CHESTERS Aleck Bonaleck. The Australian media magnate. One of these pirates who want to take over the world.

SPEARPOINT Oh, well he should have some understanding of the British position.

CHESTERS Doubt it, sir. He's an Aussie republican. Very anti-pom.

SPEARPOINT You could have said, Chesters.

CHESTERS You could have asked, Mr Spearpoint. You are a very experienced diplomat.

SPEARPOINT Yes, a very experienced diplomat with a severe case of jet lag.

CHESTERS I had heard it gets particularly bad in First class . . .

1/27. EXT. Downtown Hong Kong. Day.

We pick up Chesters' old car on the freeway as it goes through downtown, postmodern Hong Kong, with its great advertising signs and posters. We hear over:

CHESTERS *(OOV)* Care for shopping at all, Mrs Spearpoint?

HILDA *(OOV)* Do horses like oats, Mr Chesters?

CHESTERS *(OOV)* Well, you're in the shopping capital of the world. More billionaires per square inch than Miami. More designer boutiques than Milan.

1/28. EXT. Blue Moon Hotel. Day.

Chesters' old car pulls up amongst the expensive Mercedes and Rolls-Royces outside the luxury hotel. Porters rush out to get the luggage. They get out of the car.

HILDA I really think I'm beginning to like Hong Kong.

CHESTERS We can always arrange someone to take you around. Show you where the shops are . . .

(They go into the hotel.)

1/29. INT. Lobby, Blue Moon Hotel. Day.

An important location for us, because it will be where a lot of business has to be done. It's big, glossy and postmodern. Lots of chairs and bar areas. Chesters comes over to the waiting Spearpoints, bearing a room key.

CHESTERS We asked for a suite overlooking Victoria Harbour, but it seems to have gone. Anyway, there we are. The shopping mall's downstairs, Mrs Spearpoint. Oh, they do like big tips. Fifty dollars should do. We do represent Britain, after all. Well, I'll leave you to get over your jet lag, and return to my snorkelling.

(Spearpoint has had quite enough.)

SPEARPOINT Sit down, Mr Chesters.

CHESTERS Sit?

SPEARPOINT Sit. *(Chesters does)* Mr Chesters, I realize my visit may not be entirely welcome. But I'm here on a diplomatic mission, not a duty-free shopping trip. And there are certain decencies I like to see observed. Like being met by the Governor. Properly briefed about hostile journalists. Fetched from the airport in a car that could at least pass an MOT inspection . . .

HILDA And put up at Government House.

SPEARPOINT I realize the East does strange things to a man. Sun, sea, drinks on the veranda . . .

CHESTERS Yes, sir, there's a lot to be said for it.

SPEARPOINT But, Mr Chesters, you and I are servants of the Crown. It's a solemn responsibility. We're firm, steadfast, strong under fire. We fly the flag. We stand up for empire. When all around us lose their heads, we keep ours.

HILDA We show these natives just what it is we're made of.

(A crowd of oriental guests has gathered curiously around.)

SPEARPOINT *(Embarrassed)* At any rate I suggest we start as we mean to go on. First I want you here with me each morning at nine . . .

CHESTERS Really? As early as that?

SPEARPOINT As early as that. Then I want you to arrange a meeting for me with the chief Chinese representative. As quickly as possible.

CHESTERS You mean Mr Li Han? He's not very well.

SPEARPOINT How long has he been ill?

CHESTERS Months. He is perfectly well for the Americans or the French. It's just the British he's not very well for.

SPEARPOINT When is he likely to be better?

CHESTERS After we've gone, I should think.

SPEARPOINT So you've made no arrangements for me to meet my Chinese opposite numbers?

CHESTERS Oh yes. We've arranged a lunchtime drinks reception at Government House tomorrow.

SPEARPOINT I'll meet some Chinese there?

CHESTERS Yes. Assuming they choose to come. We're not too popular with either side at the moment. The pro-Chinese think we side with the pro-democracy people. The pro-democracy people think we're letting them down.

SPEARPOINT Who's right?

CHESTERS Both. We do side with the pro-democracy people. And we are letting them down.

(Spearpoint stares furiously at Chesters.)

SPEARPOINT And so you intend to hold a reception for me tomorrow to which no one at all will come?

CHESTERS Oh, some of the expats will come. They wouldn't miss a G and T at Government House for anything in the world. But the Chinese don't really trust gweilos any longer.

HILDA Gweilos, what's that?

CHESTERS What the Chinese call us. It means white ghosts.

HILDA Oh, isn't that lovely?

CHESTERS Yes, it means we're the foreign devils who came and haunted their land for a bit before they got driven out. So have a good night's sleep and I'll pick you up just before noon tomorrow. And do enjoy Hong Kong . . .

(Chesters goes. Spearpoint glares after him.)

1/30. EXT. Expensive apartment block, Hong Kong. Day.

An opulent high-rise apartment block high on the hillside on the Kowloon side. An expensive sports car (Porsche?) drives up and Martin Chen, in sports clothes, gets out.

1/31. INT. Jasmine's apartment, Hong Kong. Day.

The buzzer goes and Jasmine Tan goes to the door. She opens it to Martin. Her delight.

MARTIN Jasmine!

JASMINE Martin, you came home.

MARTIN I flew in this morning. How are you?

JASMINE How long do you stay?

MARTIN Until the Handover. Don't you want me to come in?

JASMINE Of course. I missed you so much.

(She embraces him passionately.)

1/32. EXT. Hong Kong. Day.

Establisher. The morning sun coming up over noisy, busy, summery Hong Kong.

1/33. INT. Corridor, Blue Moon Hotel. Day.

A *Chinese maid* pushes a laden breakfast trolley up to the door of a suite and unlocks it.

1/34. INT. Suite, Blue Moon Hotel. Day.

The bright morning sun pours in. The Chinese maid wheels in the breakfast. Spearpoint sits writing a report on the balcony, while Hilda, in her smart dressing gown, is watching the news on local TV: about a kidnapping? Hilda takes a large piece of fruit and puts it in her mouth.

HILDA What on earth are you doing out there, Michael?

SPEARPOINT Report for Whitehall. I'm sure they'd like to know how inefficient this Government House lot really are. No wonder relations are in such a mess. If you ask me, the whole British diplomatic operation out here has been a total disaster.

HILDA That will be why they need some idiot to come out and take the blame.

SPEARPOINT *(Coming in)* They need someone to come and take a firm grip on the whole thing. Did you sleep well, Hilda?

HILDA Not really. Hong Kong is awfully noisy. You will do something about it, won't you?

SPEARPOINT What would you like me to do? Call the desk and ask them to turn it down a little?

(Spearpoint has picked up the South China Tribune *from the tray. He stares at it. The main story, with his photo, reads:* COUNTDOWN NEWS: ENVOY SAYS BRITISH ARE GLAD TO LEAVE.*)*

SPEARPOINT Oh my God. I didn't, did I?

HILDA Don't say you've put your foot in it already, darling. Here, try a peach.

1/35. INT. Lobby, Blue Moon Hotel. Day.

Spearpoint stands impatiently in the lobby, looking at his watch. Chesters, cheerful as ever, comes in, waving the newspaper.

CHESTERS Morning, sir. See you're in the paper already.

SPEARPOINT Now look, Chesters, I was misreported. I did not say that. Not exactly that.

CHESTERS The press here are so unreliable. I did try to warn you.

SPEARPOINT Yes, when it was far too bloody late. Has the Governor seen it?

CHESTERS Doubt it, he's still in Fanling.

SPEARPOINT And the Deputy Governor?

CHESTERS Still in Shenzen. They both sent their apologies, by the way.

SPEARPOINT Meaning neither of them will be at this Government House reception?

CHESTERS They thought it was best if they didn't attend.

SPEARPOINT If only to make absolutely sure that nobody at all was there?

CHESTERS No, to ensure the people who would refuse to come because they don't like the Governor would have to find a different excuse not to come. I hope Mrs Spearpoint slept well?

SPEARPOINT How thoughtful of you. You'll be glad to know Mrs Spearpoint took your advice. And is even now buying up the entire contents of the Hong Kong boutiques.

CHESTERS Don't think she could afford it. Unless the taxpayer's paying.

SPEARPOINT No, Chesters, the taxpayer isn't. As usual I'm paying.

CHESTERS Sir, I've been giving some thought to this Handover business.

SPEARPOINT Have you? You amaze me.

CHESTERS You're an eminent diplomat. You must know lots of influential people in London.

SPEARPOINT I think you could say so, yes.

CHESTERS The people who run all these quangos. OFGAS and OFTEL and OFFTAP.

SPEARPOINT OFWAT. I know some of them. Well?

CHESTERS I came out here in the Colonial fifteen years ago. But with this Handover the Chinese won't be keeping me on. Wrong age, wrong training, wrong colour, wrong side.

SPEARPOINT What about it?

CHESTERS I still want to serve my country, sir. These quangos do seem to change their top execs pretty regularly. I thought you might be able to whisper a quiet word in a useful ear.

SPEARPOINT Mr Chesters. Perhaps if you showed yourself able to whisper a word or two in an important Chinese ear, then I might just be willing to whisper a word or two in a top-level ear back home.

CHESTERS Very good, sir. I think you're beginning to see how Hong Kong works. Had a nice morning, Mrs Spearpoint?

(Hilda has appeared, laden with designer bags.)

SPEARPOINT Sure you can carry all that, my dear?

HILDA You were right, Mr Chesters. The shops are wonderful. And I should like to be the best-dressed woman at the Governor's reception.

SPEARPOINT By the sound of it, you'll probably be the only woman at the Governor's reception.

HILDA I'll go and change. No hurry, is there?

CHESTERS None at all, Mrs Spearpoint.

(Spearpoint glares at him.)

1/36. INT. Bedroom, Jasmine's apartment. Day.

Martin and Jasmine have just made love. As they talk, he lies in bed while she gets up and takes her time getting dressed. There's an erotic mood in the air.

JASMINE How was London?

MARTIN London was London. Grey. The sun wasn't real sun. The rain wasn't real rain.

JASMINE Come on, tell me, Martin. I haven't seen you for so long. Are the buildings very old? Are the gweilos very stuffy?

MARTIN No. The buildings are new. They dress like clowns. You know what we liked about them. The Queen, funny voices, roast beef. Now they aren't like it any more. They can't talk, the beef is poisoned, they don't even like the Queen any more.

JASMINE Why?

MARTIN They want to be something else. The Scots and the

Irish and the Welsh insult them, and they like it very much. Sometimes they want to be European, but the Europeans hate them. Sometimes they want to be American, but they are too dull. Really they want to be lager louts.

JASMINE What?

MARTIN Lager louts. You see them in Lan Kwai Fong.

(Jasmine laughs, comes to sit on the bed, looks at him.)

JASMINE You don't like me to come there with you.

MARTIN You know I want you to. If you want to.

JASMINE I want. But I don't have passport.

MARTIN It's easy. Everything's easy.

JASMINE Oh yes? Everyone wants a British passport. And I am secretary. I have no relatives. Do you think your father . . . ?

MARTIN Don't say anything to my father. Leave it to me, I'll make it OK. I know the right people. Just trust me, darling . . .

1/37. EXT. Government House. Day.

Establisher. The distinguished colonial building. We see Chesters' old car arriving.

1/38. EXT. Front steps, Government House. Day.

Spearpoint, Hilda (in something new and fancy) and Chesters are ascending the steps to the noble white building. *Packers* with crates squeeze past them.

HILDA Is this Government House? Daddy would have loved it. Are you sure we should be handing it back to them?

CHESTERS Apparently we have very little choice.

(SIMON PALFREY, head of security, early forties, stocky, ex-SAS, stands waiting at the top of the steps. He comes forward to shake hands.)

PALFREY Mr Spearpoint, Mrs Spearpoint. Simon Palfrey, head of security. Excuse the mess, we're shutting down. Stripping down the royal portraits, staff leaving, redundancy looms. In fact it's just like home.

CHESTERS That'll do, Simon. Anyone arrived?

PALFREY On the terrace with their drinkies. Not a bad crowd at all. They must know you're not asking for funds for the Tory Party for once. Oh, I've booked a table for lunch at Aberdeen Harbour. If you're not doing anything important.

SPEARPOINT I very much hope we will be.

HILDA We'd be quite delighted, Mr Palfrey.

(Loud explosion. Spearpoint ducks for cover.)

SPEARPOINT Good God, what was that?

CHESTERS It's all right, sir. They haven't invaded, not yet. It's just the noonday gun.

1/39. EXT. Terrace, Government House. Day.

On the terrace, the *Local Great and the Good*. British and Chinese. Formal dresses and the odd decoration. Waiters serve bits. Chesters leads out Hilda and Spearpoint.

CHESTERS Not bad at all. They've done you proud. I see at least seven billion dollars. Property billionaire. Gambling billionaire. Shipping billionaire. Oh, and come and meet Mr Bang Ho . . .

SQUIRES I say. It's not? Carrot, Carrot Spearpoint?

(Spearpoint turns. An elderly florid Brit, SIR JOHNSON SQUIRES, with a very old DJ and a large G and T, stands beside him, claps him on the shoulder.)

SPEARPOINT I beg your pardon?

SQUIRES Lancing School, 1948 to '53. You were captain of cricket, I was captain of rugby.

SPEARPOINT *(Delight)* Oh, my God. Well well. Dorothy Squires!

SQUIRES Damn me. What are you doing here?

HILDA I take it you two know each other?

SPEARPOINT Diplomatic. I'm envoy plenipotentiary.

SQUIRES Not really? Always said you'd come to nothing. And you did!

SPEARPOINT What are you doing out here, Dorothy?

SQUIRES Run the old family Hong, for my sins. My people came out here in 1842 to sell opium to the Chinese. Now we sell them TV sets. Not much difference, really.

(Hilda takes Palfrey's arm.)

HILDA Won't you take me round the gardens, Mr Palfrey?

CHESTERS Sir, Mr Bang Ho would like to show you his pink Rolls.

SQUIRES Ah, you. Go and get me another of these medicinal drinks.

(Chesters goes inside with Squires' glass.)

SPEARPOINT Can't believe it. Dorothy. How long have you been out East?

SQUIRES Came out 1955, year before Suez. Still came by liner in those days. POSH, remember? Port Out, Starboard Home. Place was beautiful then. No high-rise. No big money. Trees all the way down Nathan Road.

SPEARPOINT Will you be going home?

SQUIRES Course not. Nothing there, is there?

(Chesters comes out from the reception room with a G and T.)

CHESTERS Someone inside you should meet, sir.

SPEARPOINT Mr Li Han?

CHESTERS Not quite Mr Li Han. A Chinese cadre.

SQUIRES Careful now. Cunning beggars, you know. Here, is that my G and T?

SPEARPOINT Delighted to see you, Dorothy.

SQUIRES Bloody silly name, eh? Listen, Carrot. If I can be of
any help, any help at all, call me at the Hong Kong
Club . . .

1/40. INT. Reception room, Government House. Day.

A fine room. But contractors have been taking paintings from
the walls. Against the wall, inspecting some painting – no
doubt some atrocity committed by the British against the
Chinese – a small Chinese man in rather drab clothes. This is
Bao Lau, an official Chinese cadre. Chesters leads Spearpoint
over to him.

CHESTERS Mr Bao Lau, I'd like you to meet Mr Spearpoint.
Foreign Office, London.

(Lau doesn't turn away from the painting.)

LAU I like this painting. You don't take it away?

CHESTERS It is going home, yes.

LAU Unless we come to arrangement.

SPEARPOINT Mr Lau.

LAU Mr Bao.

SPEARPOINT We have very important things to discuss. The
arrangements for the changeover.

(Lau continues checking the decor.)

LAU The Handover. What about the chairs?

CHESTERS They go too.

LAU I think the Chairman would like the chairs. You are in
charge of protocol?

SPEARPOINT And so are you, I gather. So may we . . .

LAU Very nice. By protocol you should not be here.
Handover is a matter for Beijing and London. This is not a
three-legged stool.

SPEARPOINT What is it?

LAU A two-legged stool. Soon a one-legged stool.

SPEARPOINT The fact remains there's a month to go and none of the details have been settled.

(Lau picks up a beautiful silver table decoration.)

LAU Beautiful silver. What details not settled?

SPEARPOINT The final ceremonies. We're proposing a state banquet here at Government House.

LAU We think two banquet. Little one for you at Government House. Big one for us at Bank of China Tower on Freedom Day.

SPEARPOINT Surely one should be enough.

LAU No. Because you are leaving and we are coming. What important people do you bring?

SPEARPOINT The Princess Royal. The Prime Minister.

LAU We have much more important people. David Copperfield, the Three Tenors. Do you bring ships? I like these very pretty candlestick. Do they stay?

CHESTERS No, they go.

SPEARPOINT Yes, we bring ships. The Royal Yacht *Britannia* to take off the Governor. And frigates to take off the garrison.

LAU We bring whole People's navy. Also flying mechanical dragons.

SPEARPOINT And incidentally it's a matter of honour for Britain that the Governor be there at everything.

LAU Not possible for me to discuss the question of the Governor. I am only a minor cadre.

SPEARPOINT Then let me discuss it with a major cadre.

LAU Mr Li Han does not have time to talk to a minor cadre.

SPEARPOINT I do happen to be envoy plenipotentiary.

LAU Of a very small country. Fifty million.

SPEARPOINT Fifty-seven million, if you want to be precise.

LAU One billion, two hundred million. Mr Chester, you don't take that nice table?

SPEARPOINT I hear Mr Li Han is unwell. Can you tell me when he's going to be better?

LAU Yes. He will be better after the Handover.

1/41. EXT. Gardens, Government House. Day.

Hilda walks round the tropical gardens with Palfrey.

HILDA I suppose to be a security man you have to be very strong, Mr Palfrey?

PALFREY You can say that again. It's more brawn than brains with me. Must be a boring job, yours, wife of a British diplomat.

HILDA How well you understand me, Mr Palfrey.

PALFREY They asked me if I'd show you round Hong Kong. Fine by me, if you like.

HILDA I can't think of anything better. Look, isn't that Sir Dexter Chen?

(Hilda nods toward the terrace. Sir Dexter has appeared, with bodyguards.)

PALFREY Blow me. Look, would you excuse me . . .

HILDA Of course. But do come back, Mr Palfrey . . .

1/42. EXT. Terrace, Government House. Day.

Spearpoint and Chesters come from within to rejoin the party on the terrace.

SPEARPOINT Outrageous. Shocking diplomatic manners. Almost a calculated snub.

CHESTERS It was a calculated snub. But you can see it from their point of view. For a couple of centuries they've had to kowtow to us. Now they think it's time we kowtowed to them.

SPEARPOINT I'm not used to kowtowing to anyone. Or dealing with small fry.

CHESTERS Quite right, Carr . . . Mr Spearpoint. The only problem is the small fry are the only ones who'll take you to the medium fry. Who'll arrange for you to meet the big fry.

SPEARPOINT That's ridiculous.

CHESTERS Under the celestial emperors they kept foreign ambassadors waiting for years outside the Forbidden City. Most of them died before they ever saw the Peacock Throne.

SPEARPOINT Well, don't imagine I mean to sit on my diplomatic backside till rigor mortis sets in.

CHESTERS Never mind, maybe the heavens have blessed you and your problems are going to be solved. Look, Sir Dexter Chen. Never expected to see him these days at Government House. Morning, Sir Dexter, may I get you a drink?

(Sir Dexter has arrived with his bodyguards and Palfrey.)

SIR DEXTER No, I am not here. I am on my way to the China Club. I simply wish to see a friend of my son. Mr Michael Spearpoint.

SPEARPOINT Ah, good morning, sir. I'm Spearpoint.

SIR DEXTER My son asked me to arrange a small reception in your honour. To meet some Chinese people. Tomorrow night, it's possible?

SPEARPOINT Yes indeed. I'm honoured, Sir Dexter.

(A bodyguard presents an elegant invitation.)

SIR DEXTER I know your hotel. My car will collect you and your charming wife. Don't bring your bodyguards. I will send mine.

SPEARPOINT Surely you'll have a drink?

SIR DEXTER No, I have not been here. Good day, Mr
  Spearpoint.

(He turns and goes, with his bodyguards.)

CHESTERS Here and not here. Very Chinese. Well, you've
  made an impression. Or acquired an obligation. What
  about lunch?

1/43. EXT. Floating restaurant, Aberdeen. Day.

Establisher. One of the splendid floating junk restaurants in
Aberdeen Harbour.

1/44. INT. Floating restaurant, Aberdeen. Day.

Spearpoint, Hilda, Chesters and Palfrey looking at the Chinese
menu.

CHESTERS I assume you both like Chinese?

SPEARPOINT I have eaten my way through most parts of the
  world.

CHESTERS Good, because this is authentic. I'll explain, shall I?
  That's dog, that's rat.

PALFREY Dung beetle. Bull's penis. You could find that a
  rather big dish, Mrs Spearpoint.

HILDA Yes, I can imagine. I'll have that.

SPEARPOINT *(Puts down the menu)* Look, Chesters. It's time
  we had some explanations. What's going on? Are the
  Chinese deliberately trying to be difficult?

CHESTERS Not trying, sir. I'd say succeeding.

SPEARPOINT We agreed to hand back the colony. We signed
  the Joint Agreement. We behaved like gentlemen. Even
  Mrs Thatcher.

CHESTERS They don't see it like that. They don't think the
  colony was ever ours to begin with. They call it the
  National Humiliation. And they are the Middle Kingdom.
  They had printing and gunpowder when we still ran
  around wearing woad.

PALFREY They understand power. And they know they've
got some and we haven't. They say when the fierce dragon
meets the paper tiger, the paper tiger runs away.

CHESTERS They're specialists in honour and humiliation. And
they've already decided how much honour to allow us.
Not a lot.

PALFREY They try every trick in the book.

CHESTERS They watch every time we remove a piece of
furniture. Count the chairs. Make our staff sign their oaths
of loyalty. They've got a parallel administration. As far as
they're concerned, we're just . . .

HILDA White ghosts.

PALFREY Right, Mrs Spearpoint. White ghosts.

SPEARPOINT Mr Chesters, there's an old British saying.
Where there's a will there's a way.

CHESTERS There's an old Chinese saying. He who sits high
on a mountain will suffer from the wind.

SPEARPOINT And what does that mean?

CHESTERS I don't know, sir. But they say it.

*(Dang comes into the restaurant, in his shades. A Chinese girl with
him. He looks round, sees Palfrey, comes over, taps him on the
shoulder.)*

DANG Hi, man.

PALFREY Yes, hi, Dang. What is it?

DANG On my way to Happy Valley. Like to bet?

(Palfrey gets up, takes out his wallet.)

PALFREY 'Scuse me, race day.

(Palfrey and Dang begin an extended conversation in the background.)

CHESTERS Gambling fever. Fate and chance. That's what
Hong Kong's all about.

SPEARPOINT Now look here, Chesters. We've a serious
problem, right here on our plates, and not a bloody thing

has been decided, has it? I want to you to tell me what you recommend.

CHESTERS *(Picking up menu)* Not sure, sir. Probably the dog.

1/45. EXT. Happy Valley racetrack. Day.

Establisher. Pan from the spectacular setting to the spectacular racetrack. A race in progress. Horses thunder down the course. Punters cheer and roar.

1/46. INT. Stand, Happy Valley racetrack. Day.

Closer, on Dang and his girl in the crowd, cheering on the race. Then pick up on Martin Cheng, walking down the stand. He sees Dang and sits beside him.

MARTIN Hi, Dang.

DANG How about it? Martin Chen's in town.

MARTIN You're winning?

DANG I always win, man. They run races just for me.

MARTIN I'll see you later. In the Club Room.

(He gets up and goes. Dang stares after him.)

1/47. INT. Club Room, Jockey Club, Happy Valley racetrack. Day.

A smart and expensive crowd, expat and Chinese. Martin talks to Dang over drinks at the bar.

DANG Too difficult. I get you Canadian.

MARTIN British, Dang. Full British, right of abode. Official passport, nothing stolen. I want her to have proper permanent citizenship.

DANG You really want something. Who is she?

(Martin takes out a set of passport photos of Jasmine and shows them to Dang.)

DANG I know this girl. She works in your father's office. Jasmine Tan. She's your . . . ?

MARTIN Yes, she is.

DANG Get your important father to fix it, then.

MARTIN Dang, my father mustn't know. He thinks I should marry some film star. An English aristocrat. Something good for the hong.

DANG It means big price. Very big price.

MARTIN Don't start screwing me. I know too much. You could end up in jail. Or the harbour.

DANG You've been away too long. You don't know what it's like. Everyone wants British passport now. Take a look at Immigration Tower. Think how much I have to pay . . .

MARTIN You say you can fix anything. Fix this for me. And then I'll keep my father off your back.

(A roar from outside.)

1/48. EXT. Happy Valley racetrack. Day.

End of a race. Horses thunder past the winning post.

1/49. EXT. Hong Kong. Evening.

Evening streets. We pick up Diana driving her car through a crowded Chinese market.

1/50. EXT. Blue Moon Hotel. Evening.

Diana drives up to the entrance to the hotel. The evening glitterati, expensive Chinese, getting out of cars to go to events.

1/51. INT. Lobby, Blue Moon Hotel. Evening.

Diana enters the lobby with its glitterati, looks round. Pick up on Bao Lau in a chair, reading a Chinese newspaper. Diana goes toward the bar.

1/52. INT. Bar, Blue Moon Hotel. Evening.

Diana comes in, glances round. A group plays Chinese pop music. Diana leaves. But we pick up on Hilda dancing with Palfrey – and clearly enjoying it.

HILDA What do they call the music?

PALFREY This stuff? Just Chinapop.

HILDA It's fun, isn't it?

PALFREY For the tourists. If you want the real thing, you'd
have to go to Lan Kwai Fong.

HILDA What's Lan Kwai Fong?

PALFREY Where the clubs are. Where the action is.

HILDA Right. Get your boots on, Mr Palfrey.

PALFREY Mrs Spearpoint, I'm supposed to be taking care of
you. Maybe . . .

HILDA Maybe nothing. My old goat's writing his reports for
London. What am I expected to do?

PALFREY I ought to check . . .

HILDA You're not here to nanny me, your job's to do what I
tell you. I am the daughter of an earl . . .

(Palfrey looks at her – sort of fun after all.)

1/53. INT. Suite, Blue Moon Hotel. Evening.

Spearpoint works on his papers. A knock on the door. He goes
to find Diana Jang standing there.

SPEARPOINT *(Angry)* You, Miss Jang. What do you want?

DIANA You said you would call me. You didn't.

SPEARPOINT No, I didn't, did I? Do you know why?
Yesterday I gave you an interview at the airport, in perfect
good faith. And what did you print?

DIANA I printed what you said, Mr Spearpoint.

SPEARPOINT Yes, you printed what I said. But you tricked
me into saying it.

(He's about to shut the door, but Diana comes in.)

DIANA Oh really, Mr Spearpoint. I am just a little local
journalist, you are a world diplomat.

SPEARPOINT An experienced diplomat who had just suffered

a gruelling flight from London. And if your article's an example of what the Hong Kong press is like, I'm not in the least bit surprised the Chinese object.

DIANA You've only been here two days, and already you want to censor us. You sound just like the Chinese.

SPEARPOINT I'm British, Miss Jang. And we British happen to believe in fair play.

DIANA I see. You think it wasn't cricket.

SPEARPOINT No, it wasn't cricket. But you don't play the game here, do you? What do you want? Another interview? You aren't going to get one.

DIANA No, I thought you might buy me a drink.

SPEARPOINT Why on earth would I do that?

DIANA Because you're a perfect English gentleman.

SPEARPOINT That particular operation has always had its limits, I can assure you.

DIANA Also because I have another story about you. I know who paid your air ticket to come here.

SPEARPOINT Do you really? Well, with its customary generosity, the British taxpayer paid my ticket to come here.

DIANA Not exactly.

(Diana waves a copy of a plane ticket. Stamped across it are the words: 'COMPLIMENTS OF SIR DEXTER CHEN'.)

SPEARPOINT Ah. The flight was crowded. So Sir Dexter's son kindly gave us a helping hand.

DIANA I'm sure. Sir Dexter owns half the airline. And it would be very important for him to put you under an obligation.

SPEARPOINT I'm not under an obligation. I may have my flaws, Miss Jang. Too much ambition, even a little lechery. But within my limits I happen to be an honest man.

DIANA In China there is a saying. If you have enemies, you also need good friends. Sir Dexter has many enemies. Now he has a good friend.

(Spearpoint takes Diana by the shoulder.)

SPEARPOINT Come along, Miss Jang.

DIANA What are you doing?

SPEARPOINT I'm taking you downstairs. To buy you a drink.

1/54. INT. Lobby, Blue Moon Hotel. Evening.

In a big chair sits little Bao Lau. He lowers his paper to watch as Hilda appears from the lift, in a wrap, and joins a waiting Palfrey. They head for the taxis. A moment later Spearpoint and Diana appear and head for the bar. Lau lifts his paper again.

1/55. EXT. Terrace, Blue Moon Hotel. Evening.

The waiter brings drinks to Spearpoint and Diana. The ice between them is just beginning to thaw.

DIANA You know, Mr Spearpoint, sometimes I feel sorry for you British. You spend two hundred years building a great empire. Then you spend another hundred taking it down again.

SPEARPOINT It's called history, Miss Jang. And we are rather used to it.

DIANA But you get it so wrong. In India, Africa, the people wanted you to go, and you wanted to stay. In Hong Kong the people wanted you to stay, and you wanted to go.

SPEARPOINT Not all the people wanted us to stay.

DIANA Oh, not the great taipans like Dexter Chen. They're already rich and powerful. When you go they will be even more rich and powerful. And they're in with the Chinese. Are your negotiations going well?

SPEARPOINT Not exactly. The Chinese side are stricken with a mortal illness. The British seem to have sunstroke. The Governor's fled to the mountains, the Deputy Governor's communing with her ancestors, and my wife has decided to shop till she drops. I wouldn't say they were going well.

DIANA *(Laughs)* But otherwise you're enjoying Hong Kong?

SPEARPOINT Otherwise I'm enjoying Hong Kong. And you print a word of that in your bloody paper and I'll personally come and close it down.

DIANA The trouble is, the British are honest diplomats, the Chinese are clever diplomats. I know, I'm one myself. Part-Chinese, anyway. Shall I explain about Chinese diplomacy?

SPEARPOINT Go ahead, Miss Jang.

DIANA Diana. Do you know about Golden Grease? If you want to persuade a Chinese cadre, first you give him a little present. The island of Taiwan would do very nicely. Then you must love his relatives, his ancestors, his friends. Then you find out who he can influence . . .

SPEARPOINT Unfortunately these people aren't easy to find.

DIANA Except sometimes they find you.

(She waves the air ticket.)

1/56. INT. Lobby, Blue Moon Hotel. Evening.

Bao Lau behind his Chinese newspaper. Spearpoint, with briefcase, goes to the desk. Bao Lau rises.

SPEARPOINT 2017, please. Has my wife gone upstairs?

DESK CLERK I think she's out, sir.

LAU Mr Spearpoint, you look for your wife?

SPEARPOINT Mr Lau!

LAU Mr Bao. She is out. I think she goes dancing.

SPEARPOINT Does she really?

LAU I think so. You like the hotel?

SPEARPOINT Excellent.

LAU Very Western. Very good for cocktail. Very bad for talk.

SPEARPOINT You're meeting someone, Mr Bao?

LAU I hope to meet you. Do you like Chinese food?

SPEARPOINT Oh yes. I love Chinese food.

LAU Good. Follow me.

(Lau begins to walk out of the hotel.)

SPEARPOINT Right then. I'll . . . follow you.

(With his briefcase, he follows Lau out of the hotel.)

1/57. EXT. Street, Hong Kong. Night.

Lau leads the way through a very dark Chinese area. People push carts, carry bundles, sit on steps. Lau stops to let Spearpoint catch up.

LAU Hong Kong very different at night.

SPEARPOINT It is, isn't it?

*(Suddenly a firecracker explodes along the pavement right under his
    feet. Spearpoint reacts.)*

SPEARPOINT Oh my lord.

LAU You like Chinese firecracker?

SPEARPOINT Aren't they delightful?

(Now a dragon dance weaves along the street and surrounds them.)

LAU All Hong Kong celebrates the dawn of Chinese rule.
    Many more firecracker soon. Here, we go inside. Please.

*(And he dives into an obscure and gloomy doorway. After a moment,
    Spearpoint nervously follows him in.)*

1/58. EXT. Happy Times Casino. Night.

Establisher. A nightclub casino in the Lan Kwai Fong district. Bright lights and noise.

1/59. INT. Hot Lips Disco. Night.

A busy, noisy nightclub. At a table, Hilda and Palfrey being served drinks by a waitress. Hilda inspects the elaborate concoction.

HILDA What do you call this?

PALFREY Sampan Surprise, Mrs Spearpoint.

HILDA Hilda, darling. It's very good, isn't it? Warms the
cockles of the heart, as Daddy liked to say. Tell me, Simon
. . . it is Simon, isn't it?

PALFREY That's it, Simon.

HILDA Tell me, my dear, what are you going to do when
you go home?

(Palfrey laughs.)

PALFREY Oh, I'm not going home. No jobs, are there?
There's got to be life after empire, right? I mean, that
stuff's done and finished.

HILDA So what is this . . . life after empire?

PALFREY Look around you. Sun, drink, girls. Money flows
like water. They're rich, and they need security. It's the
kidnap capital of the world. All these taipans need
bodyguards. Experienced security advisers.
Troubleshooters.

HILDA That's what you do? Shoot trouble?

PALFREY You could say that. Before this, I was SAS.
Sergeant. Been round all the world's trouble spots. Belfast,
Falklands, the Gulf. Cyprus.

HILDA Was Cyprus a trouble spot?

PALFREY It was after we got there.

(Dang appears beside the table.)

PALFREY Not now, man.

DANG I brought you your winnings. Happy Valley.

*(Palfrey rises. Dang takes out his wallet and nods toward Hilda. The
following is quiet and out of Hilda's hearing.)*

DANG A bit old for you, man.

PALFREY I thought you lot venerated your ancestors.

DANG I need to talk to you.

PALFREY Another time, call me, eh?

(Palfrey rejoins Hilda.)

1/60. INT. Chinese café. Night.

A drab café filled with eating Chinese. Spearpoint and Lau have many plates before them on the table. Also several bottles of beer, from which they have drunk well. Lau takes his chopsticks, picks up food and offers it bird-fashion to Spearpoint.

LAU Please.

(Spearpoint stares at the morsel.)

SPEARPOINT Very well. Thank you.

(He accepts the morsel.)

LAU It's good?

SPEARPOINT Very good.

LAU There is Chinese saying, to be good host you must also have good guest. But some gweilos do not know how to be good guest. See . . .

(He points up to the TV screen. A clip is showing of George Bush at a state dinner in Japan. He vomits and slips under the table.)

LAU President George Bush.

SPEARPOINT I suppose that's what's called loss of face?

(Lau giggles and nods.)

LAU Another one, see! Your dragon lady. With tiger Chairman.

(A clip of Mrs Thatcher with Deng Xiaoping. Followed by a clip of Mrs Thatcher falling down on the steps at the Great Hall of the People. Lau giggles.)

LAU You see this on your television? We see it many times on ours.

SPEARPOINT I bet you do.

LAU Protocol is so important. Very important in China.

SPEARPOINT Quite important in Britain too.

LAU That is why our work is important.

SPEARPOINT Isn't it? I quite agree.

LAU Unfortunately not always appreciated. Minor cadres, they call us. Paper men. Excuse me to be frank. I took very much beer. But if we did not work, wars would start. Bombs would fall, rockets would shoot. The world would end in fire. Then who do they blame?

SPEARPOINT Us, of course. As usual.

LAU The minor cadres. The paper men. But it is our chiefs, the party members, who are the paper men.

SPEARPOINT I couldn't agree more. Tell me. How is Mr Li Han?

(Lau looks up cunningly.)

LAU Ah-ha. Not very well.

SPEARPOINT Still not well? Not even slightly better?

LAU Not yet.

SPEARPOINT Is there something I could do, something I could send him, that might improve his health?

LAU When he tells me, I will tell you.

SPEARPOINT Because you're the paper man.

LAU I am the paper man. Please.

(Lau leans forward with another morsel.)

1/61. EXT. Hot Lips Disco. Night.

Hilda, worse for wear, assisted to a taxi by Palfrey.

HILDA I mean it, thank you. And when I say thank you, Simon, I really mean thank you.

PALFREY I thought so.

HILDA Why don't we do it again? Not tomorrow. We're dining with that boring old taipan.

PALFREY The night after? Fine by me, Mrs Spearpoint.

HILDA Hilda! Now where am I going?

PALFREY He knows.

HILDA How does he know when I don't know?

PALFREY I told him.

HILDA Clever Simon. Kiss!

(They kiss. Hilda gets into the cab, waving as it goes.)

1/62. EXT. Chinese restaurant. Night.

Lau helps Spearpoint into a rickshaw. He clings on to his briefcase as he subsides. Lau speaks to the driver.

SPEARPOINT Paper men!

LAU Minor cadres!

SPEARPOINT Anyway, excellent evening. Night.

(Spearpoint goes off in his rickshaw.)

1/63. EXT. Hong Kong. Morning.

Establisher. A shot of morning Hong Kong, busy and bustling, the sun rising into the sky.

1/64. INT. Suite, Blue Moon Hotel. Day.

The new morning sun shines through the windows. It wakes Spearpoint, who looks down at himself. He's fully dressed. He looks over at Hilda on the other bed. She's asleep . . . and also fully dressed. The phone rings. Spearpoint scrabbles for it. Hilda stirs . . .

1/65. INT. Lobby, Blue Moon Hotel. Day.

A cheery Chesters greets an enfeebled Spearpoint as he comes from the lift.

CHESTERS Morning, sir. You said nine o'clock. I hope I didn't wake you?

SPEARPOINT Mr Chesters. I happen to have been working on papers for the past two hours.

CHESTERS *(Holds up a briefcase)* In that case, sir, you probably missed this.

SPEARPOINT Ah. How did you . . . ?

CHESTERS A rickshaw driver handed it in. Unusually honest, I must say. And the Hong Kong constabulary sent it over. Very lucky, eh?

(Spearpoint inspects the contents of the briefcase.)

SPEARPOINT I appreciate that, Chesters. And everything seems to be there.

CHESTERS Of course I imagine the contents were photocopied first. And sent straight to Beijing. Lucky there wasn't much in it. Just Foreign Office briefs. And your comments on the incompetent staff at Government House. You must have had an enjoyable evening.

SPEARPOINT I didn't have an enjoyable evening. I had a hard-working dinner with Mr Bao Lau.

CHESTERS Good, sir. So everyone got something out of it. Including the rickshaw driver. Did you manage to arrange a meeting with Mr Li Han?

SPEARPOINT Not exactly. Of course these things are bound to take a little time.

CHESTERS Aren't they? Well, if you're not in meetings this morning, Mr Bang Ho offered to take you to his apartment and show you his gold taps.

SPEARPOINT I don't think so.

CHESTERS Alternatively the Governor has suggested you might like a trip round the Harbour on his launch.

SPEARPOINT Good. Then I'll meet him at last.

CHESTERS Oh, you won't meet him. You're in the launch, he'll be on his yacht. Making arrangements for Mrs Thatcher's visit. You did know she's coming out for the Handover?

SPEARPOINT That rather assumes there's going to be a
  Handover to come out for, doesn't it, Chesters?

CHESTERS I expect it will all work out. It usually does in
  Hong Kong. Is Mrs Spearpoint joining us?

SPEARPOINT Somehow I have the feeling the last thing Mrs
  Spearpoint wants this morning is a bouncy trip round the
  Harbour.

CHESTERS I heard she had a hard-working evening too.

1/66. EXT. Governor's launch, Harbour. Day.

Spearpoint stands with Chesters in the Governor's launch as it
ploughs its way through the Harbour.

CHESTERS Over there the base, HMS *Tamar*.

SPEARPOINT You have to hand it to the Royal Navy. They
  really did pick a strategic location. Presumably if any
  problems did arise, we'd be pretty well equipped?

CHESTERS Oh, definitely. We must have, what, maybe a
  hundred flutes. Two hundred trumpets. Maybe fifty heavy
  calibre big drums.

SPEARPOINT That's it?

CHESTERS We've scaled down the garrison. We've just got a
  couple of pipe bands, enough to make a noise at the
  Handover. All the equipment's been sold, or just handed
  on to the Chinese.

SPEARPOINT So they could simply walk in at any time?

CHESTERS The People's Army are just over the border.
  Can't wait to get to Sock Shop. Of course they always
  could walk in at any time. All they need do was cut off the
  water. When the bottled lager ran out we'd have had to
  surrender.

SPEARPOINT Why didn't they?

CHESTERS Maybe they were afraid of alarming the
  Taiwanese. Who would have called in the Americans.

Who would have started the Third World War. Or maybe they were afraid of losing their sunglasses.

SPEARPOINT Their sunglasses?

CHESTERS The Chinese love foreign sunglasses. They all came in through Hong Kong. Of course now they make their own foreign sunglasses. And their own foreign CDs.

(Spearpoint is scanning the banking towers.)

SPEARPOINT What are all these?

CHESTERS The bank towers. See, there's the Hong Kong and Shanghai. Next the Chen Tower. Then the tallest, the Bank of China Tower. The Chinese government in waiting. That's where you'll find Li Han.

SPEARPOINT Except I can't, can I?

CHESTERS Don't worry. Sooner or later he'll find you . . .

1/67. EXT. Shopping district. Day.

The antiques district. Shops are filled with items of pottery etc from China. Hilda looks in the window of an expensive store, which is called something very Chinese (like 'More Than Pleasant Antiques').

LAU *(OOV)* You like Chinese antiques?

(Hilda turns. And there is little Lau, bowing.)

HILDA I'm sorry? I don't think we've . . .

LAU Mrs Spearpoint, my name is Mr Bao Lau. I saw you yesterday. Government House. It was my pleasure to host your husband last night.

HILDA Really? Well, you know, the real trouble is, I don't know my Ming from my Tang.

LAU Most of these are not good. Very cheap copies.

HILDA Oh dear. Then I won't bother . . .

LAU Some are original. Smuggled over the border.

HILDA Are they really? How amusing.

(Lau holds open the shop door.)

LAU They keep the good things inside. If you like me to advise you, shall we go in? I know this man a little bit.

HILDA Oh, would you, Mr Bao Lau?

(They go inside.)

1/68. EXT. Waterfront/beach. Day.

Somewhere like Repulse Bay. Palfrey and Dang are strolling by the water. Palfrey looks at passport photos of Jasmine Tan.

PALFREY Nice face. When do I see the rest of her?

DANG Her name's Jasmine Tan. And you never see the rest of her. She wants a full British passport. Legal, proper, right of abode.

PALFREY Join the queue. So does half Hong Kong. In some special category, is she? Vital political position? Anglo blood? Relatives in Blighty?

DANG Secretary in a bank.

PALFREY *(Hands back photos)* Hard luck then. You could try and get her out illegally. Through Macau.

DANG She wants to be British lady. She has very powerful friend. He's a banker.

PALFREY Who isn't, round here?

DANG Top big money banker. One of the high towers on the waterfront. You owe me a favour, man. I'm trying to find you good job . . .

1/69. EXT. Shopping district. Day.

A little later. From the antique shop, a Chinese man comes carrying a large terracotta horse to a waiting taxi. A second man appears carrying a large terracotta soldier. Then Hilda appears, shaking hands with the owner. Lau follows her out.

HILDA Thank you so much, Mr Lau.

LAU I think you have chosen very well.

HILDA Oh yes, I expect so. But you are quite sure these are genuine?

LAU Yes, genuine. The man promises me.

HILDA Tell me again?

LAU Qin Dynasty. About 210 BC. They come from Xian in North China. From the burial mound of Emperor Shi Huang-Di.

HILDA Shi who?

LAU No, Shi Huang-Di.

HILDA They seem awfully cheap.

LAU He made you very good price. His Handover Sale.

HILDA There's hardly room in the taxi . . .

LAU I will get you another. The Blue Moon Hotel?

HILDA How did you know? Yes. And thank you, really, Mr Lau.

(One cab leaves with the terracottas, another with Hilda. Bau waves from the kerb . . .)

1/70. INT. Penhurst's office, FCO, London. Day.

Ms Highsmith comes in to Penhurst, working at his desk under the imperial map. She begins to lay documents out in front of him.

Ms HIGHSMITH Bag just in from Hong Kong. Complaint from Mr Spearpoint he's not getting enough cooperation from Government House. Complaint from Government House they're not getting enough cooperation from Mr Spearpoint.

PENHURST Well, who's right?

Ms HIGHSMITH Hard to say, sir. Spearpoint complains the Governor's incommunicado. Government House complain Mr Spearpoint left his official papers in a rickshaw.

PENHURST *What?* Did anyone read them?

Ms Highsmith Government House, presumably. The briefcase was returned to them.

Penhurst At least they didn't get to Beijing.

Ms Highsmith Government House think they did. That's apparently what usually happens to papers left in rickshaws.

Penhurst Dear Lord. Anything important?

Ms Highsmith His Foreign Office briefing. And his rude report on Government House.

Penhurst I wanted Spearpoint there to help the Governor. Not feed his critics in Beijing. Still, I suppose it could be worse.

Ms Highsmith I think it is, sir.

(Ms Highsmith puts a newspaper in front of him.)

Ms Highsmith Interview Mr Spearpoint gave the *South China Tribune*. Saying the British are delighted to be leaving Hong Kong.

Penhurst Well? We are, aren't we?

Ms Highsmith Yes, but we're not supposed to say so. Especially in Hong Kong. There's also this rather awkward question of whether Spearpoint's been taking bribes.

Penhurst Spearpoint? Bribes?

Ms Highsmith His air ticket out there.

Penhurst Nonsense. We paid for that.

Ms Highsmith Not First class. According to our informants, he was given First-class tickets by Sir Dexter Chen. Owner of the Marco Polo Bank.

Penhurst At least he's *Sir* Dexter. I presume he's one of us?

Ms Highsmith Not quite. Wants the Chinese to make him deputy governor. He's an Instant Noodle Patriot. That's the name they give rich taipans jostling for position in the new Chinese administration. Very poetic people . . .

Penhurst Look, just cable Spearpoint and tell him enough is enough. Remind him I sent him out to pour oil on troubled waters. Not upset the colony, provoke the Chinese or start a bloody world war.

Ms HIGHSMITH Pleasure, sir.

1/71. INT. Suite, Blue Moon Hotel. Day.

Spearpoint, working in his room, is on the phone.

SPEARPOINT If it says Highly Confidential, don't read it out to the hotel lobby. Bring it to my room at once.

(A knock on the door. Spearpoint goes to open it. A PORTER marches in with a terracotta soldier, ANOTHER with a horse. Hilda follows.)

SPEARPOINT You were quick. Oh, great heavens . . . For goodness' sake, Hilda. Has this something to do with you?

HILDA You mean my shopping, darling? What do you think? I thought they'd just suit the drawing room in Tunbridge Wells.

SPEARPOINT Hilda, they might suit Covent Garden, they will not suit the drawing room in Tunbridge Wells. I begin to wonder whether I was entirely wise to bring you here . . .

HILDA I think they're lovely . . .

(The porters stop in front of Spearpoint and hold out their hands. Another porter with the London cable.)

1/72. EXT. Chen Tower. Evening.

Jasmine Tan is coming out of the building after work. Dang appears from behind a pillar.

DANG Jasmine Tan.

JASMINE *(Startled)* You. What do you want?

DANG Don't get upset. I'm fixing your passport.

JASMINE He asked you?

DANG I'm Martin's friend. But I need more papers. Identity Card, certificate of birth.

JASMINE What, now?

DANG I can come to your apartment tonight.

(*Jasmine looks frightened.*)

JASMINE No. Here, my Identity Card. Isn't it enough?

(*She takes it from her bag.*)

DANG OK. If I need anything else . . .

JASMINE Never come to this building again.

DANG I'm not afraid of Sir Dexter Chen. If I talked, Chen Tower would come falling down . . .

1/73. EXT. Portico, Blue Moon Hotel. Night.

Hilda and Spearpoint, dressed to the nines for a dinner party, wait for Sir Dexter's car.

SPEARPOINT And how do you intend to get them home?

HILDA Lord Elgin got his marbles home.

SPEARPOINT Yes, well, Lord Elgin had his own ship waiting for him in the harbour.

HILDA And we have the Royal Yacht *Britannia*.

SPEARPOINT And what do you suppose the Princess Royal will say when she sees those bloody things come marching up the gangplank?

HILDA You don't like them?

SPEARPOINT Hilda. Either they're fakes and you've been been taken for a very expensive ride. Or they're genuine and you've been fobbed off with some inferior dynasty. They're not Ming, are they? Or Sung? Or Tang?

HILDA No, Qin.

SPEARPOINT Who ever heard of Qin?

HILDA They were in a Handover Sale.

SPEARPOINT Yes. And you're the one who did the handing over. Really, Hilda.

(Sir Dexter's Rolls rolls up. A bodyguard gets out and gestures them to the car . . .)

1/74. EXT. Road to Peak. Evening.

As the red sun goes down, we see Sir Dexter's Rolls driving up the precipitous road toward the top of the Peak.

1/75. EXT. Sir Dexter's house. Evening.

The Rolls arrives at the guarded gates of a splendid house right at the top of the Peak, overlooking the Harbour. It drives through the grounds to the brightly lit portico.

1/76. INT. Living room, Sir Dexter's house. Evening.

The room is large windowed. Wonderful views of the Harbour. Chinese antiques and hangings. A number of distinguished, very well-dressed Chinese men and women, the Hong Kong glitterati. Chinese robes and dresses mingle with expensive designer wear. The Spearpoints enter, to be greeted by Sir Dexter.

SIR DEXTER I'm honoured you came to my house.

HILDA It's glorious. And what a view. I remember Daddy had one of the Arc de Triomphe.

SIR DEXTER It's steep, not really a safe place to build a house. And we have very bad typhoons here in the summer. But in China when we build, we always ask a geomancer. He looks at the lines of energy, to see if the chi is right. Chinese people like to gamble with fortune and fate. But also we like to take out a little insurance.

SPEARPOINT Very wise, Sir Dexter.

SIR DEXTER Mrs Spearpoint, I hear a little rumour you collect antiques. Would you do me the kindness to let me show you my own small collection?

HILDA Oh, these are marvellous.

SIR DEXTER I specialize in Qin. A most artistic dynasty, I hope you agree.

HILDA Of course I do.

SIR DEXTER Unfortunately the best pieces are impossible to find.

HILDA Are they really?

(Hilda smiles triumphantly at Spearpoint.)

SIR DEXTER Especially pieces from the emperor's terracotta army. But those are protected antiquities. They all belong in the National Museum in Beijing.

(Reaction of Spearpoint. He's beginning to sense the set-up. Martin Chen and his decidedly less attractive brother Lee join him.)

MARTIN Welcome to Hong Kong, Mr Spearpoint. I like you to meet my brother Lee. I run the bank in London. He runs the bank in Shanghai.

SPEARPOINT Well, as your father says, it's always best to take out a little insurance.

LEE We do. My father has always been so generous to the British. He gave money to the Tory Party, then the other . . .

SPEARPOINT The Labour Party? Very wise.

LEE Chair to Oxford University.

MARTIN The Chen Chair of Equine Competition . . .

SPEARPOINT Horse racing? The undergraduates will love that.

LEE But naturally he must help China too.

MARTIN We are true Chinese. In fact he has friends everywhere. My father would like to help you. He has heard you have a problem. Why don't we go on the terrace?

(The brothers lead a suspicious Spearpoint outside.)

1/77. EXT. Terrace, Sir Dexter's house. Evening.

A spectacular if not dangerous view over the Harbour. The party is continuing within. Spearpoint with Martin and Lee.

SPEARPOINT I have a problem?

MARTIN The Chinese officials do not want to meet you. They can be difficult. Try to hold you to ransom.

LEE Yet this door could open easy. Mr Li Han is here at the party now.

SPEARPOINT Is he really? How nice to hear his health's improved.

MARTIN But my father also has problem.

SPEARPOINT Really? Another problem?

MARTIN With Marco Polo Bank. World's sixth biggest bank.

LEE The British and Hong Kong authorities are investigating our trading. We don't understand.

MARTIN In China we have a saying. Money is like a middle-aged woman. It is not polite to ask questions about where she has been.

SPEARPOINT Unfortunately in Britain we have a saying too. No smoke without fire.

LEE This investigation is not necessary.

MARTIN There was a rogue trader, but he is disposed of. In the modern market, such things happen in every bank.

LEE You are my father's friend. He wishes to do you a favour.

MARTIN He asks only one small favour in return. He knows you have great influence with your government. British Establishment all went to the same school, I think.

SPEARPOINT *(Seeing the trap)* Yes, I do have some influence. But I'm afraid it really isn't enough to . . .

(Sir Dexter comes out, followed by the distinguished, well-dressed, silver-haired figure of LI HAN.)

SIR DEXTER Mr Spearpoint. Here is someone who would like to meet you. Mr Li Han.

SPEARPOINT A pleasure. I'm so glad to see you're well.

Li Han I am always well. I met your wife, Mr Spearpoint. Such a purchaser of antiques.

Spearpoint I think we can say that shopping was invented for Hilda. And Hilda for shopping.

Li Han We were talking of her interest in the terracotta army. Perhaps you know the story. The emperor Shi Huang-Di had lifesize copies made of his soldiers and horses. So when he died, they could be put into his burial mound. Now they have been excavated, and put in the Beijing National Museum. They are priceless antiquities, national treasures. To steal them is a capital offence.

Spearpoint A capital offence?

Li Han (*Draws hand across throat*) A capital offence. Mr Spearpoint, I think we delayed our meeting too long. But now the time is right. Come to Bank of China Tower, ten tomorrow. You will find me on very top floor.

1/78. INT. Sir Dexter's Rolls. Night.

The car driving back from the Peak, with driver and body-guard. In the rear, Hilda and Spearpoint are having a quarrel in loud whispers.

Hilda I just bought a few antiques, that's all.

Spearpoint Hilda, they were not antiques.

Hilda They looked old to me.

Spearpoint They're priceless antiquities. Don't you know about the terracotta army? Qin dynasty?

Hilda An hour ago you'd never heard of the Qin dynasty.

Spearpoint Well, I have now. An amazing find. They were excavated a few years ago and taken to Beijing. The only problem is half a bloody regiment's ended up in our hotel bedroom.

Hilda All right. I'll take them back if you want.

Spearpoint Too late for that now, Hilda. It's stolen treasure. You've committed a capital offence.

HILDA How capital?

SPEARPOINT Very capital. You could end up being publicly
beheaded in Tiananmen Square.

HILDA I've always wanted to go to Tiananmen Square.

1/79. INT. Lobby, Blue Moon Hotel. Night.

(Hilda heads toward the lifts. Spearpoint follows.)

HILDA I think you're being extremely unpleasant.

SPEARPOINT Hilda. I just had a message from London
warning me about upsetting sensitive Chinese sensibilities.
Now you commit a capital crime.

HILDA That's not what the little man said. He said I was
getting a great bargain.

(Hilda gets into the lift.)

SPEARPOINT Little man? Which little man?

HILDA The little man I met on the street. The little man who
helped me buy the antiques.

(Things are dawning on Spearpoint.)

SPEARPOINT What was this little man like?

(The lift doors close. Spearpoint presses the button. They open again.)

HILDA A little Chinese man.

SPEARPOINT Most of them round here are, aren't they?

HILDA He knew you. You dined with him last night.

SPEARPOINT Ah. Was he about this little?

(He demonstrates with his hand.)

HILDA Or a bit littler.

(The doors close again, with Hilda inside.)

SPEARPOINT Of course. Of course. I should have guessed,
shouldn't I? It was Mr Bao Lau.

(Two guests come for the lift. They stare at him curiously.)

1/80. EXT. Bank of China Tower. Day.

Establisher. The notable cubical building by I.M. Pei which towers on the skyline.

1/81. INT. Li Han's suite, Bank of China Tower. Day.

(Li Han stands by the window in his eyrie on the very top floor, staring at his huge view of the Harbour. A cadre shows in Spearpoint.)

LI HAN Over here, Mr Spearpoint. You like tea? I think it is one thing Chinese have in common.

SPEARPOINT Not at the moment. I'm here to deliver a formal protest, Mr Han.

LI HAN Mr Li. See, Mr Spearpoint. Such an interesting view. This is the tallest building in Hong Kong, you see everything. Victoria Harbour. Royal Hong Kong Yacht Club. Government House. English names. All written in water. And the water will soon wash them away. You have been trying to see me, Mr Spearpoint?

SPEARPOINT I was sent out by London to set out our proposals for the Handover.

LI HAN But I know your proposals. For some reason the papers from your briefcase already appeared on my desk. In any case, we cannot discuss them.

SPEARPOINT Why not? It is only three weeks away.

LI HAN Mr Spearpoint, in 1984 Chairman Deng and Mrs Thatcher signed the Joint Agreement. We were gracious, we agreed one country, two systems. We honoured this. You did not.

SPEARPOINT I beg to differ.

LI HAN Each day your government tries to undermine the agreement. The Governor introduced the democracy question, to set our people against us. When this failed, you chose to destroy the Hong Kong economy. We understand your blatant intention. To weaken us as an economic power.

SPEARPOINT You're referring to the Marco Polo Bank? I've already cabled your views to London. But I have to warn you Her Majesty's Government does not give in to blackmail.

LI HAN You seem not to remember history. A hundred and sixty years ago your navy took these islands by force. You made us sign the Unequal Treaties. You destroyed the dreams of the Celestial Emperor and humiliated his people. You called us coolies, forced opium on us. From those Opium Wars you created your new empire and the industrial revolution.

SPEARPOINT I always thought it was things like that that brought great nations together.

LI HAN We never forgot this humiliation. Then you were strong and we were weak. Now we are strong and you are weak. You are a village, we are a city. You are a paper tiger, we are a dragon. The People's Army, three million, waits over the border. You can go with some honour, or go without it. The rice is cooked.

SPEARPOINT The rice is cooked?

LI HAN Tell London that, Mr Spearpoint. The rice is cooked. How is your wife today?

SPEARPOINT Well. And you might like to know I don't give in to blackmail either. Whatever you might try to do to my wife. She was tricked by one of your officials. I wish to register an official protest.

LI HAN If I picked up this phone the Hong Kong police would be compelled to arrest her. She is not a diplomat, she has no immunity. In all friendship, I say it is best if we both use our influence to settle this matter. Then one day we can meet to decide how to end your colonial occupation. Thank you, Mr Spearpoint. My good wishes to your wife.

1/82. INT. Penhurst's office, FCO. Day.

(Ms Highsmith comes in with a distinguished CITY GENT.)

MS HIGHSMITH Governor of the Bank of England, sir.

PENHURST *(Rising)* Come right in, my dear fellow.

GOVERNOR Look, Penhurst, this is very bad news. How did your lot ever get on to it?

PENHURST We've an excellent Man in Hong Kong.

(The Governor sits.)

GOVERNOR I take it this is entirely confidential? Man to man? Chatham House rules? For our eyes only? Nothing on paper? Between these four walls? Strictly on the qt?

PENHURST As bad as that, is it?

GOVERNOR As bad as that. This is money we're talking about. The world's most fragile and illusory commodity. Worthless bits of printed paper that depend entirely on trust. And we of the Old Lady are at the heart of that trust. I know she's not what she was. Old fashioned, ineffective, prone to caution. But when our history's written, let's have it said we were always discreet.

PENHURST I presume from all this you really are investigating the Marco Polo Bank?

GOVERNOR Do you realize the problems the new tiger economies pose to world banking? Do you know Hong Kong has 500 banks within its 300 square miles? It's the golden goose of the Pacific. Its foreign reserves are greater than Britain's. When it joins with China it will become the world's biggest economy.

PENHURST Well?

GOVERNOR Frankly the problem is these people just haven't had our experience. Their bank practices are lax. Poor regulation. Insider trading, false accounting, rogue dealing, unsecured futures, money laundering. You name it, there it is. And we don't want that here, do we?

PENHURST I thought we already had it here.

GOVERNOR Yes, but we don't want it, do we? In fact we
have to put a stop to it.

PENHURST In case we become a tiger economy too?

GOVERNOR Quite. Can't have that sort of thing in the heart
of the Square Mile. But that's what we risk with the Marco
Polo Bank. It's merged with Waterburg's, one of the oldest
banks in the City. It also acts for the Bank of China. So in
the City there's a foreign bank a hundred times bigger than
BCCI, accredited by us. If we don't make sure it's well
regulated, what happens?

PENHURST What does?

GOVERNOR Disappeared accounts, money laundering, lost
pension funds, fraudulent dealing, unsecured futures. Rat
trading.

PENHURST Rat trading?

GOVERNOR Yes, extensive rat trading. Followed by starving
pensioners, government embarrassment, year-long fraud
trials. At once followed by calls for my head on a platter.

PENHURST Yes, but trying to take the wider and less selfish
view, have you considered the effect your inquiry could
have on international relations?

GOVERNOR I know the Foreign Office will consider this total
heresy. But I think having honest money is good for
international relations.

PENHURST But why launch this at such a sensitive time?

GOVERNOR Because it is a sensitive time. If word got out,
millions could be wiped off the Hang Seng. The whole
Hong Kong economy would be in jeopardy. Just when we
are supposed to hand the colony over in good order.

PENHURST Quite. My point exactly. Your bloody inquiry
could set off an international crisis. God knows where it
would end.

(The Governor getting angry.)

GOVERNOR What are you asking us to do? Cancel it?

PENHURST You could postpone it a bit. Until after the Handover.

GOVERNOR I see. When the Chinese have taken over, our influence will be nil. When the dollar will have disappeared into the yuan and Chinese investment will be taking over the world. This is our last chance to make sure we have a clean world economy. Run on proper Bank of England lines.

PENHURST Even if that means international crisis?

GOVERNOR Even if it means world war. Let it never be said the Bank of England shirked its duty. So tell your Man in Hong Kong the Old Lady Says No. Good day, Mr Penhurst.

(The Governor sweeps out. Ms Highsmith pops in.)

MS HIGHSMITH Well, sir?

PENHURST I'm afraid the Governor of the Bank of England believes in sound money. I'd better see the Chancellor of the Exchequer.

MS HIGHSMITH I've heard a rumour he does too, sir.

PENHURST If we told him there's a major threat to British interests in the Pacific Rim?

MS HIGHSMITH He thinks the Americans should have the Pacific Rim, sir. To keep out the Aussies.

(Penhurst reaches for his umbrella.)

PENHURST I'm having lunch with the Russian delegation. You know what to do, Ms Highsmith.

MS HIGHSMITH Yes, sir. Cable Mr Spearpoint . . .

1/83. INT. French restaurant, Hong Kong. Night.

(Spearpoint and Diana are dining tête-à-tête in a high-rise French restaurant. The Hong Kong towers are lit up beyond the window.)

SPEARPOINT You know, my dear, this is wonderful.
Excellent food. Superb wine. Elegant setting. Charming
company. How did you know this is just what I wanted?

DIANA It happens to all you gweilos. First you gorge on
Chinese food. Then you start to crave for a really good
French restaurant. And you must admit this is a really good
French restaurant.

SPEARPOINT It's a strange thing between the British and the
French. Most of the time we utterly loathe each other. But
they only have to wine and dine us, and it's Entente
Cordiale and Vive la France all the way.

DIANA What about the British and Chinese?

SPEARPOINT A bit more difficult. We still believe in the
mysterious Orient. And think you're all remarkably
inscrutable.

DIANA Actually we are quite scrutable. And of course we
think you are foreign devils. White and cold and very dull.

SPEARPOINT When actually of course we're quite warm. So
does that mean never the twain shall meet, do you think?

DIANA Oh, you're so English, Michael. But of course it can
meet. Just take Hong Kong. Or us, tonight . . .

SPEARPOINT I presume this meal has a purpose?

DIANA I wanted to entertain a perfect English gentleman.
Also I heard a very interesting rumour today. Your
government is investigating the bank of Dexter Chen . . .

1/84. INT. Happy Times Casino. Night.

*(The roulette wheel spins. The ball falls in its slot. A pile of chips is
pushed over to the winner – Hilda, at the table with Palfrey.)*

HILDA I won I won I won.

PALFREY Congratulations, Mrs Spearpoint.

HILDA Hilda. What are you betting on next?

PALFREY Not me, Hilda. I'm spent out.

HILDA Don't be silly, Simon. Have some of these.

(She pushes a pile of her chips to him, makes her bet.)

PALFREY You sure?

HILDA Of course. You're giving me the most wonderful time, my dear. I haven't had so much fun in yonks.

1/85. INT. French Restaurant. Night.

(Spearpoint and Diana, tête-à-tête.)

SPEARPOINT My dear, I can't possibly comment on rumours. It's far more than my portfolio's worth.

DIANA So you're not interested in Dexter Chen? Did you know before he was a banker he was a smuggler?

SPEARPOINT Smuggler? What did he smuggle?

DIANA Anything that would ship across the border. People, money, guns, treasures, drugs. He came here with nothing after Mao's revolution. He had to find a way to survive.

SPEARPOINT Which he clearly did. How did he become so respectable?

DIANA Typical Hong Kong story. He made good friends and silenced his enemies. When Hong Kong got rich, he got richer. He went into banks and property. When the Queen came she put one of those things round his neck.

SPEARPOINT You mean a knighthood?

DIANA It's very important in Britain, yes?

SPEARPOINT There are some people would say so, yes.

DIANA Then Chairman Deng invited him to invest in China. Now he could be on both sides. More British than the British, more Chinese than the Chinese.

SPEARPOINT You seem to know a great deal about him.

DIANA I was investigating him for the paper. Now they spiked the story. I told you, he's an influential man.

SPEARPOINT And why are you telling this to me?

DIANA I think soon they'll fire me. And aren't you an influential man too?

SPEARPOINT I do have a fair clout, yes. One doesn't drink at the Athenaeum for nothing.

DIANA You must know the big newspaper owners. You see, I do you a favour. Perhaps you can do me a favour.

SPEARPOINT Ah. So you're asking me whether I'd care to whisper a very quiet word in someone's ear?

DIANA I thought we could collaborate more closely. Don't you think?

(Spearpoint smiles and raises his glass.)

1/86. INT. Taxi, Hong Kong. Night.

(Hilda and Palfrey in the back of a taxi. Hilda with a half-open handbag full of winnings.)

HILDA Wow-ee.

PALFREY Well, you're one lucky lady, I'll say that.

HILDA And my luck hasn't finished yet, has it, Simon?

(She puts up her face to be kissed. Palfrey responds. The taxi driver glances in the mirror to see them tangled together in the back . . .)

1/87. EXT. Blue Moon Hotel. Night.

(Another taxi pulls up. Spearpoint with Diana in the back. He kisses her, gets out.)

SPEARPOINT A wonderful evening. Thank you. I'll see you again tomorrow?

DIANA Of course you'll see me tomorrow. Sleep well . . .

(Spearpoint goes contentedly into the lobby.)

1/88. EXT. Banqueting House, Whitehall. Evening.

Fine cars roll up. Members of the great and good descend to enter a state banquet. Penhurst, in DJ, is there, greeting a distinguished *Russian arrival*.

PENHURST Dobri vecher, Minister. We met in St Petersburg,
if you remember, when it was still Leningrad. And you
were still KGB . . .

MS HIGHSMITH *(OOV)* Sir?

(Penhurst turns, to see Ms Highsmith under an umbrella.)

PENHURST This just happens to be a state banquet, Ms
Highsmith . . .

MS HIGHSMITH Yes, sir, but there's just been an urgent from
our ambassador in Beijing.

PENHURST *(To visitor)* Do excuse me. What?

MS HIGHSMITH The Chinese called him in to say they'll no
longer be allowing our frigates in or out of the Fragrant
Harbour.

PENHURST Don't think I know a fragrant harbour.

MS HIGHSMITH It's their name for Hong Kong, sir. It means
we won't be able to relieve the garrison after the
Handover.

PENHURST Oh, good evening, Prime Minister! Nonsense, we
sail in anyway. Those are still British waters.

MS HIGHSMITH Yes, sir. Until the Handover. Then they
become Chinese waters. So we can't get out again. Then
there's the problem of the Royal Yacht *Britannia*. We'd
hardly want to lose her, even if it is her last voyage.

PENHURST What have they done this for?

MS HIGHSMITH Retaliation for our interference in the
Chinese internal economy.

PENHURST We haven't interfered in their infernal economy.

MS HIGHSMITH They mean the Marco Polo Bank, sir.

PENHURST Ridiculous. Well, we won't budge, of course.
The Old Lady has said no.

MS HIGHSMITH And the Chinese never budge. It would
mean losing face. So it's serious.

PENHURST We can't let the Chinese spoil a state banquet for
the Russians. I should be in there with the canapés now.

MS HIGHSMITH I suppose I could notify the UN. And send
Mr Spearpoint another cable asking him to deal with it . . .

PENHURST What a good idea. Ah, bon soir, Monseigneur.
Vous avez passé des bonnes vacances?

(And Penhurst joins the entering throng.)

1/89. INT. Suite, Blue Moon Hotel. Night.

Spearpoint and Hilda, in their separate beds; each sleeps a sleep
of emotional contentment. A smile touches both their faces. A
knocking on the door. Spearpoint turns on his bedside light,
gets up, goes to the door in pyjamas. A porter hands in two
London cables. Spearpoint reads the first: 'THE OLD LADY SAYS
NO. BALL IN YOUR COURT. PENHURST.'

SPEARPOINT Oh no.

(He reads the second): 'CHINA INTENDS HONG KONG
BLOCKADE UNLESS YOU ACT FAST. BALL EVEN MORE IN
YOUR COURT. PENHURST.'

SPEARPOINT Oh no.

HILDA What is it, Michael? Anything important?

SPEARPOINT No, my dear. No need to bother your weary
little head. Just a major world crisis I have to resolve.

HILDA Nothing to do with me, is it?

SPEARPOINT Oh no, Hilda. Nothing to do with you.

HILDA Jolly good.

*(Hilda turns over. Spearpoint turns to look anxiously, gloomily, into
the camera, and . . .)*

End of Episode One.

EPISODE TWO

2/1. Titles.

With Hong Kong background, as before.

2/2. EXT. Whitehall. Day.

Establisher. A pan from Big Ben, striking four, to the facade of the Foreign Office.

2/3. INT. Penhurst's office, FCO. Day.

Penhurst stares gloomily at his imperial map as Ms Highsmith comes with papers.

Ms Highsmith Sorry, Mr Penhurst, am I interrupting?

Penhurst Just wondering how this Hong Kong business is going to end. Not with a bang but a whimper, eh?

Ms Highsmith Some of us are afraid it might be the opposite, sir. The Chinese called in our ambassador again this morning. The Hang Seng's dropping, they're threatening further retaliation.

Penhurst What does Spearpoint say?

Ms Highsmith Hasn't reported, sir. Must be too busy.

Penhurst It's serious?

Ms Highsmith Very. The Royal Yacht *Britannia*'s already on its way. Mrs Thatcher's announced the plans for her visit. Says she wants to meet the old Chinese leaders with whom she signed the Joint Agreement. Oh, Princess Diana says she wants to go. She's asked if the Chinese could bring some sick children, so she can solace them.

PENHURST Oh my Lord . . .

Ms HIGHSMITH Of course Mrs Thatcher's office have objected. They're worried Princess Di's sick children will get in the way of Mrs T's elderly leaders.

PENHURST And Princess Di in the way of Mrs Thatcher.

Ms HIGHSMITH David Copperfield's going out to do a big spectacular. The Three Tenors are a total sell-out. In fact everything's going well unless . . .

PENHURST . . . unless we end up with a bloody world war. I saw the Governor of the Bank of England. He won't budge an inch on this inquiry into the Marco Polo Bank.

Ms HIGHSMITH Sir, why not send him to Hong Kong on a fact-finding mission? First class, our expense. If he sees what's going on, it might change his mind.

PENHURST Bloody expensive.

Ms HIGHSMITH Cheaper than world war, sir.

PENHURST Who'd look after him?

Ms HIGHSMITH I'll cable Mr Spearpoint . . .

2/4. EXT. Hong Kong. Day.

Another establishing shot over Hong Kong. But, for a key change of mood, perhaps we show it in mist and cloud, its buildings floating upward out of Harbour fogs. Maybe we see Chinese doing their morning t'ai chi in the street . . .

2/5. EXT. Star Ferry Pier. Day.

Sir Dexter, with bodyguards, gets off the ferry and into his Rolls.

2/6. INT. Sir Dexter's Rolls. Day.

The chauffeur hands Sir Dexter his newspaper. The headline: COUNTDOWN NEWS, 20 DAYS TO GO. BRITISH INVESTIGATE MAJOR HK BANK. CHINA OBJECTS.

SIR DEXTER Take me to the Hang Seng. Be quick.

2/7. INT. Lobby, Blue Moon Hotel. Day.

Spearpoint picks up the London cable from his desk, turns – to find himself confronted by a grizzled, elderly police inspector in uniform. *Inspector Jock McManus.*

McMANUS Mr Michael Spearpoint . . .

SPEARPOINT That's right. Well?

McMANUS I'm Jock McManus, Chief Inspector, Royal Hong . . . that is Hong Kong constabulary. A wee word, sir?

SPEARPOINT I have to go to the airport and meet the Governor of the Bank of England. What about?

McMANUS Your wife, sir.

SPEARPOINT It's not the terracotta army.

McMANUS No, not the terracotta army, the tartan army, any army. She's being doing some odd things, sir. For the consort of a top British official.

SPEARPOINT Hilda? Odd things?

(McManus opens his notebook.)

McMANUS Three nights ago, dancing at the Hot Lips Disco. Two nights ago, gambling at the Happy Times Casino. Where she won a lot of money and went on to the Nothing Much On Nightclub. Last night—

SPEARPOINT Inspector, Hilda's an independent woman. And she does have a bodyguard.

McMANUS You mean Palfrey? She can wind him round her finger any time he likes. Sir, Hong Kong's a dangerous place. There are fifty thousand Triad gangsters out there all looking for fame and fortune. Those boys can make someone like her disappear faster than a dog at a Chinese wedding. If you'll pardon the expression . . .

SPEARPOINT Inspector, I do have an international crisis to attend to. If you're worried about my wife, speak to her yourself. She'll be in the most expensive boutique downstairs. You can't miss her, look for a wide-open cheque book.

(Spearpoint heads off for the door.)

McMANUS Sorry, sir, didn't understand what you meant about the terracotta army . . .

(But Spearpoint has gone.)

2/8. EXT. Jasmine's apartment block. Day.

Jasmine comes out and joins Martin, waiting for her by his sports car. They kiss. But she's unhappy.

MARTIN Something wrong, Jasmine?

JASMINE I don't know . . .

MARTIN You still want to go to London with me?

JASMINE You know I want. But why use him?

MARTIN You mean Dang? That guy can fix anything.

JASMINE He came to see me at Chen Tower. He wanted more papers, for my passport. I know he wants something. From your father. He's dangerous, Martin . . .

MARTIN He owes me a favour, he knows everyone. Immigration Tower, Government House. I'll talk to him.

JASMINE Just go to your father.

MARTIN I can't. He wouldn't accept you, you know that. It's the only way. Leave it to me . . .

2/9. INT. *South China Tribune* offices. Day.

Diana, in the office, searches through files. Aleck Bonaleck on the other side of the blind. Huskisson comes over.

HUSKISSON What are you looking for?

DIANA Anything on Sir Dexter Chen . . .

HUSKISSON The boss told you to spike that story.

DIANA It's the biggest story in town, Will. There's something going on in that bank.

HUSKISSON OK, but I just hope you've got decent insurance. Better still, another job to go to.

DIANA Don't worry, Will. I think I have . . .

(She grabs her tape recorder and goes.)

2/10. INT. Arrivals hall, Kai Tak. Day.

Spearpoint stands in the hall holding a sign saying 'The Governor of the Bank of England'. After a moment, the Governor appears. An atmosphere of noise and panic round about.

GOVERNOR Bank of England. Here I am.

SPEARPOINT Michael Spearpoint, the special envoy.

GOVERNOR Our Man in Hong Kong. I've heard about you. You started this trouble.

SPEARPOINT I merely told London what was going on.

GOVERNOR Don't you know it's a bad thing to gossip about money? Could cause a meltdown. Remember Wall Street in 1929? The collapse of the German mark that brought Hitler to power? If we don't keep the lid on this, we could easily end up with a panic.

(The Governor blunders on. We see the panic round him. More Chinese rushing to the desks.)

2/11. EXT. Immigration Tower. Day.

Stock shots of large numbers of Chinese crowding around the Immigration Tower for passports . . .

2/12. INT. Taipan suite, Chen Tower. Day.

Sir Dexter comes in, leaving bodyguards at the door. He stalks imperiously through the office. Pick up on Jasmine Tan at her desk, looking anxious. She watches as Sir Dexter goes into his inner suite . . .

2/13. INT. Taipan suite, Chen Tower. Day.

Sir Dexter comes into his inner office. There, sitting in his chair, is Dang.

SIR DEXTER You, Dang. Nobody comes here. Get out now.

DANG I read your horoscope, Sir Dexter. It's not your lucky day.

SIR DEXTER Get out of my chair, don't you know respect? Who let you in?

(Sir Dexter reaches for the alarm button on his desk. Dang puts his hand on it.)

SIR DEXTER You're threatening me? You're very foolish. Who are you? A cheap punk with a clever mind—

DANG I need to talk to you.

SIR DEXTER I've nothing to say to you. Go.

DANG Remember, I used to work for you once.

SIR DEXTER Yes. You cheated, you were fired.

DANG I did what you asked me. Now people are checking me out. Newspapers—

SIR DEXTER What do you want?

DANG If I had plenty of money I could leave Hong Kong.

SIR DEXTER Dang, don't you know you're nothing? I paid you well, that's all you'll get. Remember this. I am powerful, and you are not.

(Sir Dexter reaches for the desk, presses the button.)

DANG There's a journalist, Diana Jang, asking questions. What happens if I talk?

SIR DEXTER You won't keep talking very long.

(Jasmine comes in, nervous.)

SIR DEXTER Call my guards and get him out of here.

JASMINE Please just leave, Mr Dang.

(Dang looks at Sir Dexter, at Jasmine, goes.)

SIR DEXTER Oh, Miss Tan. Clear your desk. I know how he got in. And send for my son Lee . . .

2/14. EXT. Chen Tower. Day.

Diana sits in her car outside the building. Dang exits, walks toward the car. Diana takes a photo, then ducks down . . .

2/15. INT. Hang Seng. Day.

In a corridor the Governor and Spearpoint meet an elegant Chinese, *Mr Fok*, and shake hands. Hang Seng bustle around.

GOVERNOR This is Walter Fok, Head of the Commercial Crimes Commission. And this is Mr Spearpoint. They sent him here to make sure the Handover went smoothly.

FOK Oh yes, I read about you.

GOVERNOR You'd better explain the situation. Spearpoint thinks our investigations aren't necessary.

FOK You understand the Hang Seng is a very well-regulated exchange.

GOVERNOR Exactly, follows London rules—

FOK But now with the Handover there are more Chinese practices. You understand?

SPEARPOINT You mean Golden Grease?

FOK That sort of thing. In the past months many bankers, traders, even legislators have gone to prison.

GOVERNOR Happens in London too.

SPEARPOINT Except ours do seem to get out rather quickly.

GOVERNOR Our attitude remains quite clear. We prefer the people who run the world economy not to be criminals.

FOK The Marco Polo bank is huge, very hard to regulate. Banking and trading. Offices in Shanghai, London, New York. Money is going everywhere. Now we find accounts not settled, secret funds, rat trading—

SPEARPOINT Rat trading?

FOK When commissions are converted to the personal use of the banker.

SPEARPOINT It could be one rogue trader?

GOVERNOR That would be convenient, wouldn't it?

SPEARPOINT What's happening now?

FOK Come and see the floor.

(They head toward the trading floor.)

2/16. INT. Floor, Hang Seng. Day.

More signs of activity and panic as the Marco Polo price drops. Spearpoint, Fok, the Governor watch.

GOVERNOR See. Bank share price is dropping fast.

SPEARPOINT They're all dropping.

FOK Yes. Chinese actions have created a panic.

SPEARPOINT And there's nothing the British side can do about it, Governor?

GOVERNOR That's your problem, Spearpoint. Ours is to ensure banking integrity now and in the future.

FOK Even with Handover, we need to make sure the money is clean and the dollar sound.

SPEARPOINT Even if it ends up worth nothing at all?

GOVERNOR Yes, even if it ends up worth nothing at all.

2/17. INT. Dress boutique. Day.

A very smart designer store. In front of the mirror, Hilda tries on something elegant in Asian designer style. A *Chinese assistant* assists. Palfrey watches.

CHINESE ASSISTANT It make you look very beautiful, madam.

HILDA Lovely. What do you say, Simon?

PALFREY Pretty good. Expensive too, I bet.

(Hilda twirls in her dress.)

HILDA You really are a master of the fawning arts of flattery, aren't you? I think it looks superb.

PALFREY What did this inspector say to you?

HILDA Oh, he was worried about some of the places you take me too.

PALFREY You wouldn't be doing it to annoy that old bloke of yours, would you?

HILDA Certainly not. That's an added bonus. I told you, I haven't had so much fun in years.

CHINESE ASSISTANT You want, madam?

HILDA I want. So I'll have.

(Hilda reaches for her handbag – stuffed with money. In another corner of the store, pick up on little Bao Lau, incongruously half-concealed behind a lingerie model. He speaks into his mobile.)

2/18. EXT. Street, Hong Kong. Day.

Spearpoint comes out of the Hang Seng. A hooting from across the street. Angle on Diana, in her car, waving him over. He comes across the street and gets in the car.

2/19. INT. Diana's car. Day.

Spearpoint gets in the car, looks at Diana.

DIANA Well?

SPEARPOINT I don't believe it. You know me, Diana. A simple British diplomat, here to handle pomp and protocol.

DIANA I know, you told me at the airport . . .

SPEARPOINT Now we have the Royal Yacht happily steaming past Aden, the Three Tenors trying to remember

'Nessun Dorma', and Mrs T is loading up her handbag. Meantime the Chinese navy's blocked the channel, the Hang Seng's gone into meltdown and in a couple of days all Hong Kong will be on the run. So what does my government do? And the Bank of England?

DIANA What, Michael?

SPEARPOINT Look for the scapegoat. Find the fall guy. Dump it on Spearpoint.

(Diana puts a photograph of Dang in front of him.)

What's this?

DIANA He's called Dang. He worked at Marco Polo Bank. I think he's your rogue trader.

SPEARPOINT I've seen him before.

DIANA I know, all Chinese look the same to you.

SPEARPOINT Not all, Diana. Not you for instance . . .

DIANA Charmer. Come to the office. And I'll show you our file on Chen's bank.

2/20. EXT. Designer men's Shop. Day.

Another smart store. Bao Lau peers through the window. Inside Hilda is buying Palfrey something expensive – say a cashmere sweater she holds up against him.

2/21. INT. Office, *South China Tribune*. Day.

Diana and Spearpoint look at files as Huskisson works in the background.

DIANA You see? We've been tracking it for months. Trading between exchanges. Fake accounts. You've heard it before. But he's the one, our trader. One of these sharp streetwise Chinese types. Talk to him if you like, he's still around.

(Spearpoint pushes aside the file.)

SPEARPOINT The trouble is, my dear, I don't believe it. This is serious stuff. A head-to-head between London and

Beijing. Banks in meltdown, frigates in the channel. All that over one lone trader?

(Huskisson comes over with an agency story: 'Death of Deng Xiaoping rumoured'.)

HUSKISSON Could have something to do with it.

SPEARPOINT Go on, I don't understand.

HUSKISSON Whenever Deng's death is reported, Chinese exchanges go into free fall. It would release a struggle for the succession and maybe bring back the hardliners. You'll see, there'll be a retraction shortly.

SPEARPOINT So?

HUSKISSON The Chinese generally start an international incident to distract attention. Blame the problems on the West and the British.

SPEARPOINT And dump it all on Spearpoint . . .

DIANA So fierce dragon roars at paper tiger. Does paper tiger run away?

SPEARPOINT It's not a bad idea. The People's Army does have three million men and a stock of nuclear warheads. And we're down to a thousand bandsmen and a regimental dog called Pickles.

DIANA Michael, you're a famous diplomat. You can find a way.

HUSKISSON The lady believes in you.

SPEARPOINT When all around are losing their heads, I hang on to mine, you mean? When others panic, I do not? When all is smoke and confusion, I know just what to do?

DIANA Of course. You can pull something out of the hat.

SPEARPOINT Oh yes? Is there anything in your hat? Because there's nothing in mine. In fact I've already packed it.

DIANA Think of something. Think a bit Chinese.

(Spearpoint stares up at the TV screen. It's showing the clip of Mrs Thatcher stumbling.)

SPEARPOINT Just a minute. What's all this?

HUSKISSON Iron Lady worships at the shrine of the Great Helmsman Chairman Mao. They show it here all the time.

SPEARPOINT I mean this bit.

(The loop shows Mrs T's second visit, 18 December 1984. In the Great Hall of the People, she meets Deng Xiaoping. They sit down, sign the leather-bound protocol of the Joint Agreement, toast each other.)

HUSKISSON That's her second visit, December 1984. Iron Lady meets Tiger Chairman. Mrs T and Deng Xiaoping sign the Joint Agreement.

DIANA Bottoms up. Cheers all round. One Nation, Two Systems. And everyone's happy.

HUSKISSON They were, then.

(Struck by an idea, Spearpoint gets up.)

SPEARPOINT If then, why not now?

DIANA I don't understand you, Michael.

SPEARPOINT Mrs Thatcher's coming, yes? And didn't Deng say his last wish before he met his ancestors was to see Hong Kong returned to the Motherland?

DIANA He's ninety-two, Michael. Not been seen for three years. The Death Watch squad say he's either dead, or kept alive on drips by forty doctors.

SPEARPOINT But you just said they can't afford to declare him dead officially.

HUSKISSON Not now. Not with the Handover.

SPEARPOINT There's an old Chinese saying. If one big problem, find one big solution.

DIANA Where are you going, Michael?

SPEARPOINT I'm off to see Dexter Chen.

(Spearpoint goes. Diana stares after him as Huskisson pulls a message off the fax. It says: 'Rumours of Deng's death denied by Beijing'.)

2/22. INT. Taipan suite, Chen Tower. Day.

Spearpoint enters. To cross with a tearful Jasmine Tan leaving. Sir Dexter in the office.

JASMINE   He forced me to let him in there . . .

SIR DEXTER   Miss Tan, I expect complete loyalty from my office. Just don't return . . . *(He sees Spearpoint)* Mr Spearpoint, I think I should refuse to see you. You are the man who is destroying my bank. But you are an English gentleman, I am an English gentleman. Come in.

2/23. INT. Taipan suite, Chen Tower. Day.

Sir Dexter waves Spearpoint to a chair.

SIR DEXTER   Mr Spearpoint, I trusted you. Because of your friendship with my son, I invited you and your esteemed wife to my house. I introduced you to Mr Li Han. I thought I had made a friend. I asked only one small favour. To use your admirable influence with your senior friends in London. Clearly I did not offer enough. You should have said, I am always generous.

SPEARPOINT   You know yourself, British institutions can be very rigid and old-fashioned.

SIR DEXTER   You would not help me, or you could not help me. So the rice is cooked . . .

SPEARPOINT   But maybe not quite reached the boil. Sir Dexter, you want to save your bank. I want to save the Handover. Maybe there's a way. I can probably deliver the Governor of the Bank of England. You can deliver Mr Li Han . . .

SIR DEXTER   Deliver them where?

SPEARPOINT The Governor's here. If we were to arrange a small meeting in some quiet place . . .

SIR DEXTER A yacht. There is always my yacht . . .

2/24. INT. Jasmine's apartment. Day.

A tearful Jasmine opens the door to Martin Chen.

MARTIN What happened?

JASMINE Dang came to Chen Tower. He made me let him into the Taipan suite. He threatened your honourable father, asked him for money.

(Martin embraces the crying Jasmine.)

MARTIN Did my father know it was you?

JASMINE Your father knows everything. Now I have no job, no passport, no friends. You can forget I even exist.

MARTIN Dang didn't tell him about us?

JASMINE I don't think so. Why do you trust him? He's a bad man.

MARTIN We need a passport. Now we need it even more. You still want to go to London with me?

JASMINE Of course. But now I will never get a passport. Everyone wants to leave.

MARTIN I'll get it, don't cry, I'll get it . . .

2/25. EXT. Yacht, Harbour. Day.

Sir Dexter's yacht, for the private summit. A waiter serves drinks to Spearpoint, Li Han, Sir Dexter and the dour Governor as they look out over the water.

LI HAN You must admit Hong Kong is charming.

GOVERNOR I never doubted it.

LI HAN And this quarrel between us, so unnecessary. We did warn Britain not to interfere in our economic affairs on the eve of the Handover.

GOVERNOR And we warned you, if you want Chinese

money to play in the world economy, you'd have to abide by international rules.

(Sir Dexter intervenes.)

SIR DEXTER Governor, I have always revered our great British institutions.

GOVERNOR Have you really?

SIR DEXTER The Queen, who came to Hong Kong and knighted me. No small honour, eh, Mr Spearpoint? The Houses of Parliament, whose members on both sides I have generously assisted. Oxford University, which now has a chair in my name.

GOVERNOR Yes, our ancient universities have always taken a rather relaxed attitude toward benefaction.

SIR DEXTER My regard for the Bank of England is no less. I could be just as generous.

GOVERNOR I beg your pardon?

SIR DEXTER Whatever you need to settle this matter.

GOVERNOR Sir Dexter, if you're offering the Bank money, it's got some. If you're offering it to me, I'm not interested.

SIR DEXTER The Governor of the Bank of England, not interested in money?

GOVERNOR Not in the sense you mean. And I think this discussion should cease as of now.

(Spearpoint hastily intervenes.)

SPEARPOINT Gentlemen, we seem to be back at cross purposes. We're all here because we want something. You, Governor, surely want to avoid a world depression.

GOVERNOR I do prefer prosperity to disaster on the whole. But only within reason.

SPEARPOINT You, Sir Dexter, want to save your bank. You, Mr Li Han, hardly want to take over a broke Hong Kong that's emptying of people.

LI HAN What do you want, Mr Spearpoint?

SPEARPOINT All I want is a happy Handover. May I put to you a small plan, may we call it the Spearpoint Plan . . .

(The camera pulls back over the Harbour. We see the high towers again.)

2/26. INT. Lobby, Blue Moon Hotel. Evening.

Bao Lau is back, sitting behind his newspaper as he watches the evening parade. First Hilda arrives from the lifts. She meets Palfrey, takes his arm, and heads out toward the taxis.

Lau folds up his paper and is about to rise, when Diana comes in. Lau lifts the paper, watches as Spearpoint appears from the lifts, gives Diana a kiss on the cheek, then walks with her toward the taxis.

Lau folds his paper. Dang comes into the lobby and looks around, then leaves. Lau is at last able to fold his paper and go to the exit . . .

2/27. EXT. Happy Times Casino. Evening.

Establisher. The facade of the brightly lit casino. Taxis are driving up.

2/28. INT. Happy Times Casino. Evening.

We start on the spinning roulette wheel. Widen as once more a large pile of chips is pushed over to Hilda, there with Palfrey. Their intimacy with each other has clearly grown.

HILDA I've done it again. I've done it again.

PALFREY You're really one lucky lady.

(Hilda takes the chips, divides them.)

HILDA Play those, darling, while I go and turn some of this into money.

(Palfrey watches her go over to the cash desk. He turns and plays. We pick up on Dang, who has just come in and stands watching in his shades. He sees Hilda go toward the cash desk. He goes and slips into the vacant seat next to Palfrey.)

PALFREY Stay away from me, Dang.

DANG You know, you're crazy, man. Playing like this.

PALFREY Nothing to do with you.

(Palfrey loses.)

DANG That's the money I gave you for the passport?

PALFREY It's from my lucky lady. Beat it, Dang.

DANG At least get me the passport. Where is it?

PALFREY Those things take time to fix.

DANG I don't have time. I'm in trouble, man . . .

(Palfrey wins. Dang grabs a couple of his chips and goes. Palfrey turns. Hilda has now disappeared. We pick up on Bao Lau, across the club, drinking a beer. And talking on his mobile. Palfrey clocks Lau.)

2/29. EXT. Diana's apartment. Night.

Establisher. An expensive high-rise apartment block on the heights.

2/30. INT. Living room, Diana's apartment. Night.

An open-plan apartment decorated in a smart, modern Asian taste. Chinese music plays on the stereo. Diana and Spearpoint at table, eating Chinese food from a wok.

DIANA Spearpoint Plan? What is the Spearpoint Plan?

SPEARPOINT Never mind, my dear. Suffice it to say at this minute all sides are giving it due diplomatic consideration.

DIANA And if they don't agree?

SPEARPOINT I think they might. Even if they don't, we'll still have achieved one chief goal of statesmanship.

DIANA What's that?

SPEARPOINT Stopping people hitting each other. If only for the time being.

DIANA You're brilliant, Michael.

SPEARPOINT Oh, you helped too.

DIANA It's a celebration? I haven't heard you say you like my food.

SPEARPOINT I am giving that my due diplomatic consideration. But you know how hard it is for a diplomat to disclose his real feelings.

DIANA You could issue an official communiqué.

SPEARPOINT Very well. Subject to Chatham House rules, and pending confirmation from my masters, I have to say your chicken is quite superb.

DIANA *(Laughs)* You know, when I met you at the airport, I thought you were such a stuffy old gweilo.

SPEARPOINT I thought you were a vile tabloid hack. But then our positions were utterly opposed.

DIANA And now?

SPEARPOINT I can't help thinking we're moving ever closer to some kind of Joint Agreement.

DIANA An Entente Cordiale?

SPEARPOINT Even a Grand Alliance.

DIANA Your side's in favour?

SPEARPOINT Definitely. I recognize yours may need more time to consider.

DIANA I don't think so. What happens now?

SPEARPOINT Really we should dispense with official formalities and go into private conclave.

DIANA Oh why?

SPEARPOINT To make sure our respective postures really are totally compatible.

(Diana glances at the open door of her bedroom.)

DIANA Through there, perhaps?

SPEARPOINT That seems ideal.

DIANA You deceitful gweilo.

SPEARPOINT You inscrutable oriental.

(They get up and go to the bedroom, leaving the food.)

2/31. INT. Happy Times Casino. Night.

Hilda comes down a corridor and enters the door leading to the ladies'.

2/32. INT. Ladies' loo, Happy Times Casino. Night.

Two very decorated girls are in there, chattering. Hilda goes to the counter, opens her handbag, which is full of money, and takes out her lipstick and a few gaming chips, which she puts on the counter. She looks in the mirror at her face. The Chinese girls leave. Hilda smiles at herself in the mirror, and picks up the lipstick.

2/33. INT. Lobby, Blue Moon Hotel. Night.

Through the glass doors, we see Spearpoint arrive in a taxi. He comes into the hotel, a smile of sexual contentment on his face. He goes over to the desk.

SPEARPOINT 2017. Is my wife back?

McMANUS *(OOV)* Mr Spearpoint.

SPEARPOINT Inspector McManus. What can I do for you?

McMANUS You could accompany me to the police car, sir.

SPEARPOINT I beg your pardon? Now look. I'm a British diplomat, I have immunity. What have I done?

McMANUS Not you, sir. It's your wife. She's been kidnapped.

SPEARPOINT *(Stares at him)* Nonsense. Who'd want to kidnap Hilda?

McMANUS Don't know, sir, never met the lady. I just know she's disappeared from the Happy Times Casino. And you're a rich and influential man . . .

(As he follows toward the flashing blue light outside.)

SPEARPOINT Now just a minute. Influential, yes. Rich,
no . . .

2/34. EXT. Happy Times Casino. Night.

Crowd outside. Police cars. The police car with Spearpoint
and McManus draws up and they get out. Spearpoint looks
round in surprise.

SPEARPOINT What was Hilda doing in a place like this?

McMANUS I tried to warn you. She's been spending all week
in places like this, and worse. Now when we get in, expect
three-monkeys time.

SPEARPOINT What?

McMANUS Nobody saw anything, nobody heard anything,
nobody's saying anything . . .

(McManus leads the way in.)

2/35. INT. Happy Times Casino. Night.

Gambling has stopped. Staff are being unwillingly interviewed
by Chinese police. As McManus and Spearpoint enter, Palfrey
comes over.

PALFREY Really sorry, Mr Spearpoint.

(Spearpoint goes for him.)

SPEARPOINT Sorry? Good Lord, man, you were looking after
her. You were the troubleshooter. If you'd taken her to
more sensible places, there wouldn't have been any trouble
to shoot.

PALFREY Hilda's a feisty lady, sir. You don't take her
anywhere, do you? She takes you.

SPEARPOINT You're talking about Mrs Spearpoint?

(McManus comes in between.)

McMANUS All right, gentlemen. Let's just find out what
happened. Mr Palfrey?

PALFREY We got here around eight. Mrs Spearpoint wanted

to gamble. She'd been on a winning streak all week. We sat down at the tables and she was off again. She won thousands.

MCMANUS She was flush with money?

PALFREY Right. She got up to change some of the chips back into cash. That would be around eleven. Half an hour later, I sent someone to go and look for her.

SPEARPOINT You waited half an hour?

PALFREY In the ladies'. You know how long that can take. Anyway, she'd gone.

SPEARPOINT I hold you entirely responsible for this.

MCMANUS Please, gentlemen. Now, did you see anyone suspicious in the club?

SPEARPOINT Look around you, for goodness' sake. They're all suspicious.

PALFREY I think someone's been following us all day. A Chinese cadre.

SPEARPOINT Bao Lau?

MCMANUS Ah, you know this gentleman?

(A CHINESE WPC comes, says something to McManus)

MCMANUS I wonder if you'd mind just accompanying me to the ladies' toilet, Mr Spearpoint.

2/36. INT. Ladies' loo, Happy Times Casino. Night.

The toilet much as before. On the counter is Hilda's lipstick and a couple of gaming chips. On the mirror is roughly scrawled the unfinished word 'hel—'. Spearpoint and Mc-Manus come in with the Chinese WPC. Spearpoint stares at the lipstick and message.

SPEARPOINT Oh, my God.

MCMANUS Don't touch anything, Mr Spearpoint. The lipstick's hers?

SPEARPOINT I think so. And the writing.

MCMANUS Any idea why she'd write the word HELL?

SPEARPOINT I think she was writing HELP, don't you, Inspector? It seems logical, when you're being kidnapped.

MCMANUS Most people being kidnapped don't write anything at all.

SPEARPOINT Where would they take her?

MCMANUS If it's Triads, she's probably in Shenzen by now.

SPEARPOINT Shenzen? But that's in China!

MCMANUS These gangs work both sides of the border. It's only thirty miles away.

SPEARPOINT We damned well guard it, don't we?

MCMANUS They go by sea. They have the fastest speedboats in the Harbour. Not on government budgets, you see.

SPEARPOINT You've contacted the Chinese authorities?

MCMANUS 'Fraid they're no help, sir. Half of them are in with the gangsters. And if she's released it doesna mean they'll return her. They might send her to Beijing.

SPEARPOINT No! They mustn't be allowed to do that. *(McManus staring at him)* Look, you'd better come back to the hotel . . .

2/37. INT. Suite, Blue Moon Hotel. Night.

Spearpoint, McManus and the Chinese WPC. McManus is inspecting the terracotta items with interest.

SPEARPOINT Let me explain, Inspector. I'm a special envoy. Engaged in delicate negotiations with the Chinese government. They're trying all they can to raise the stakes. What's the best way to exert maximum pressure?

MCMANUS Yes, very nice, sir. I've no idea.

SPEARPOINT Behead the wife of the British negotiator.

MCMANUS Sorry, sir, I'm not used to these diplomatic niceties. You're saying they'd take her to Beijing and put her to death because she nicked these old pots?

SPEARPOINT Those are not old pots, Inspector. They're priceless antiquities. And she didn't nick them. She was tricked into acquiring them by that man Lau. The man who was in the Casino. The man you'd better arrest.

(There's a knock on the door. McManus stiffens.)

McMANUS Stay there, Mr Spearpoint. Constable?

(The policewoman goes to the door and opens it. A porter hands in a message.)

McMANUS Just leave it to me.

(He pulls on gloves and takes the envelope.)

SPEARPOINT What are you doing, Inspector?

McMANUS Fingerprints. Not that these laddies would leave any. They're probably far cleverer than we are.

SPEARPOINT It wouldn't be difficult, would it?

(McManus is reading the note.)

McMANUS 'You will soon receive our ordures . . .'

SPEARPOINT I think it means orders, don't you?

McMANUS 'If you care for your wif, do not contact the police, or say goodbye for ever.' Bit late now. Signed The Yellow Dragon.

SPEARPOINT Oh my God. Who are The Yellow Dragon?

McMANUS Not one of the usual Triads. Got a photo of the vict— of your wife, sir?

SPEARPOINT *(Goes to dressing table)* Here. There's Hilda with the Queen.

McMANUS Just the job. Now, I suggest you get a good night's sleep, Mr Spearpoint. Then tomorrow we'll go round the tattoo parlours.

SPEARPOINT Inspector. Hilda never went to tattoo parlours.

McMANUS It's where the gangs hang out. Night, sir.

(And McManus and the policewoman go. Leaving Spearpoint to bad

*dreams, the terracotta army . . . and Hilda's nightdress, lying on
the bed.)*

2/38. EXT. Hong Kong. Morning.

Establisher. Another morning view of the city, including the
Star Ferry.

2/39. EXT. Star Ferry Pier. Morning.

Sir Dexter and Martin Chen get off the Ferry and into the
waiting Rolls.

2/40. INT. Sir Dexter's Rolls. Morning.

Sir Dexter grabs the local paper from the driver. Headline is:
COUNTDOWN NEWS: 16 DAYS. HANG SENG SLIDES. MANY
LEAVE.

MARTIN Father. I want to talk to you. About Jasmine Tan.

SIR DEXTER No.

MARTIN Your personal secretary. She spoke to me. She said
you fired her. Because of a mistake.

SIR DEXTER There was no mistake. She let that punk Dang
into the Taipan suite.

MARTIN He threatened her. You should take her back.

(Sir Dexter puts down the paper.)

SIR DEXTER What is this girl to you?

MARTIN She asked for my help.

SIR DEXTER I presume she's your mistress?

(Martin doesn't answer. Sir Dexter looks at him.)

SIR DEXTER If so, get rid of her.

MARTIN No, father.

SIR DEXTER You hear what I say to you. Get rid of her.

MARTIN Yes, father.

2/41. INT. Lobby, Blue Moon Hotel. Day.

An anxious Spearpoint comes out of the lift. Diana, waiting, hurries over to him, embraces him.

DIANA Michael, I'm so sorry. You must be really upset.

SPEARPOINT How did you hear?

DIANA We had a tip-off at the paper. Don't worry, there'll be a press embargo till she's found. Is it Triad?

SPEARPOINT A gang called The Yellow Dragon.

DIANA Yellow Dragon? I don't . . .

(McManus comes over.)

MCMANUS Morning, sir. Any calls in the night?

SPEARPOINT No, there weren't. You haven't found her.

MCMANUS Don't worry, we will. One way or the other.

SPEARPOINT One way or . . . ?

DIANA *(Hurriedly)* Michael, call me if you need me.

MCMANUS Ready to walk the street, sir?

(Chesters appears, cheery as ever.)

CHESTERS Morning, sir. Have another good evening?

SPEARPOINT No, Chesters. No.

(Chesters is left staring as the others go. He wipes his brow.)

2/42. EXT. Downtown Hong Kong. Day.

Spearpoint accompanies McManus on a tour of Hong Kong's underworld. We see them come out of a couple of seedy clubs.

2/43. INT. Tattoo parlour. Day.

A sinister corner of town, a sinister atmosphere. Various Triad types hang around as *Fang*, the tattooist, a big man, works with his needle on a Chinese punter. McManus comes in, followed by the Chinese WPC and Spearpoint. Fang looks up, goes on tattooing. The gangsters gather round Spearpoint.

MCMANUS *(Inspects the tattoo)* Hello, Fang. Very pretty.

FANG You like one?

(McManus shows the photo of Hilda and the Queen.)

McMANUS Do you know this woman?

FANG Yes. Queen of England. Where do you like me to put her?

McMANUS The other one. She's gone missing, Fang. Was she taken last night?

(Fang shrugs and continues with his creative endeavours.)

McMANUS Come on. What's the word on the street?

FANG Word on the street is, no one on the street.

McMANUS Nobody was taken out through the Harbour?

FANG Cars maybe. Not people.

McMANUS Know a gang called The Yellow Dragon?

FANG Not Triad. Not part of the old tradition.

McMANUS Very well, Fang. Take care, eh, laddie?

(Fang nods. Spearpoint releases himself from the gangster crowd around him, and follows McManus.)

2/44. EXT. Street escalator. Day.

The busy street escalator through Hong Kong. Commuters go to work. Pick up Dang on the escalator. He looks round nervously. Clocks Lee Chen, coming down the escalator behind him. Dang begins to move down. Coming up in front are Dexter's two bodyguards. Dang seems cornered. But he escapes off the escalator, down a side street. Lee is joined by the bodyguards. They gaze after him.

2/45. EXT. Victoria Harbour. Day.

Muddy waters, sampans and junks. McManus and the WPC talking to a Chinese on one of the junks. Spearpoint stands on the quay beside a police car. McManus and the WPC come off the gangplank.

McMANUS Nothing there either. People leaving the colony

illegally, but that's to be expected. I think Fang's right. These aren't your common or garden gangsters.

SPEARPOINT How can you believe someone like him? He's . . . well, he's a gangster.

McMANUS These laddies have their honour, Mr Spearpoint. And this case smells different.

SPEARPOINT I told you. It's a political plot. Isn't it about time you picked up Bao Lau?

McMANUS Mr Spearpoint. On July 1st you get on the *Britannia* and sail back to Blighty. I stay and work for the Chinese. I'm not going to arrest a cadre without evidence. In any case they say he's been posted back to Beijing.

SPEARPOINT You see? They smuggled him out of the way.

McMANUS Look, sir, why don't you go back to the hotel and wait?

SPEARPOINT For what?

McMANUS The kidnappers to make contact. After all, they're going to want that ransom soon.

2/46. INT. Street phone box. Day.

A frightened Dang trying to make a connection. He taps on the phone, puts it down in a fury.

2/47. INT. Lobby, Blue Moon Hotel. Day.

Spearpoint comes to the desk. He's followed by McManus.

SPEARPOINT 2017, please.

DESK CLERK Message for you, sir.

McMANUS Hang on. Who left this?

DESK CLERK A boy from the street.

McMANUS Give me your gloves.

(*McManus takes the gloves and then opens the message. He reads.*)

McMANUS 'If you want to save your wif, fill a briefcase . . .'

SPEARPOINT Yes, a briefcase . . .

McMANUS '. . . with five million Hong Kong dollars. Be ready to deliver the money tomorrow night. Yellow Dragon.' What did I tell you?

SPEARPOINT Five million dollars? And where am I supposed to find five million dollars?

McMANUS Think you'd better pay it, sir, if you really want your wife back. It's not as bad as it sounds. You divide by twelve to get pounds.

(He slips the note in an evidence bag.)

2/48. EXT. Diana's apartment. Evening.

Diana's apartment block. And we hear over:

SPEARPOINT *(OOV)* I'm sorry, Diana. Really very sorry.

DIANA *(OOV)* It's all right, Michael, really . . .

2/49. INT. Diana's apartment. Evening.

Spearpoint and Diana in dressing gowns, having evidently just suffered disappointment. Spearpoint paces round, Diana on the bed.

DIANA I understand. She's all you can think about.

SPEARPOINT No, you don't. Five million dollars is all I can think about. Who do these people think I am?

DIANA Famous British diplomat. Staying at top hotel.

SPEARPOINT Courtesy of the British taxpayer. It doesn't mean I have money.

DIANA Your government has money.

SPEARPOINT They can't even pay the nurses properly, why would they cough up five million dollars for the daughter of an earl?

DIANA You're famous, Michael. You must have it.

SPEARPOINT Sorry to disappoint you, Diana. But what I have is a government pension, a mortgaged bungalow, a Mondeo that won't start, and a large tray of unpaid bills from Hilda's lifetime dedication to shopping. Not five million dollars.

DIANA Go to a bank. This place has four hundred.

SPEARPOINT Oh yes? What do I offer as security? Hilda's left ear?

DIANA Try Sir Dexter Chen?

SPEARPOINT I've nearly destroyed his bank. I can hardly ask him for five million dollars as well.

DIANA I thought you were getting him off the hook?

SPEARPOINT The Spearpoint Plan? I think that's done for, don't you? Now the Chinese have kidnapped Hilda. Anyway, nobody at the Foreign Office will even answer the phone.

DIANA Why not?

SPEARPOINT I expect it's Wimbledon week. Summer, Diana. World politics won't resume until the football season . . . Wait! I've got it! Dorothy Squires!

DIANA Who's she?

SPEARPOINT We played rugby at school together. Darling . . . I think we should try again . . .

(She looks, laughs, embraces him and . . .)

2/50. INT. Hong Kong Club. Day.

We're in the very English embrace of the famous Hong Kong Club at lunchtime. Panelled walls and quiet waiters. The diners are well-dressed expats and rich Chinese. Sir Johnson Squires sits at a corner table for two, sipping a large G and T. He rises and waves genially as Spearpoint comes in.

SQUIRES Over here, Carrot.

SPEARPOINT Good of you to meet me, Dorothy. I'm in a bit of bother.

SQUIRES Thought you should see this before we hand it over. The Old Hong Kong Club. Used to be expats only. Now we admit the better Chinese. Well, why not? Richer than we are. Smarter than we are. But that's us, isn't it? We were born to watch the old world die.

SPEARPOINT I suppose we were. This is very difficult . . .

SQUIRES Take it you can manage Chinese food? I've ordered dim sum. Don't have to eat it if you don't like it. Just guzzle the claret.

SPEARPOINT I find myself in some serious trouble.

SQUIRES Ah. Diplomatic trouble? Woman trouble?

SPEARPOINT Not exactly.

SQUIRES Wallet trouble, then. Finding ourselves a bit short, are we?

SPEARPOINT Quite a bit short. Rather a lot short.

(The waiter arrives with the dim sum.)

SQUIRES Never do business in front of a waiter. Typhoon weather, eh? Always could tell typhoon weather.

(The waiter goes.)

SQUIRES Right, out with it, Carrot.

SPEARPOINT My wife Hilda's been kidnapped.

SQUIRES Good God. Wish someone would take mine. Want her back? You have thought it through?

SPEARPOINT I have thought it through. Hilda has her faults. But a British diplomat doesn't leave his wife floating face down in Hong Kong Harbour. Not if he can help it.

SQUIRES No. See the point. Quite so. Enough said.

SPEARPOINT They're asking five million dollars. By tomorrow night.

SQUIRES Good Lord, pricing it a bit high, aren't they? Hong Kong or US?

SPEARPOINT Hong Kong.

SQUIRES That's better.

SPEARPOINT The truth is, Dorothy, I haven't got it. I'll never have it. Hilda spent every penny I ever earned. She shops, you see.

SQUIRES You're sure you've thought it through? Easy to get emotional at times like this.

SPEARPOINT It's my duty to get Hilda back, Dorothy. It's what one does.

SQUIRES Right, just asking. Well, consider it done. I'll send the cheque to your hotel tomorrow morning. Just pop it round to the Chen bank and you'll meet your deadline. Five mill HK, that is what you said, isn't it?

(He makes a note in his notebook.)

SPEARPOINT I don't know how to thank you, Dorothy.

SQUIRES Come on, man. Old Lancingtonians stick together, don't they? Especially in the bush. Know you'd do the same for me. Don't start blubbing, fella. Try the dim sum.

(And Spearpoint gratefully does.)

2/51. EXT. Star Ferry Pier. Day.

Sir Dexter comes off the Ferry, gets into his Rolls.

2/52. INT. Sir Dexter's Rolls. Day.

The chauffeur hands Sir Dexter the morning paper. It says: COUNTDOWN NEWS, 15 DAYS. BANK PANIC. MANY LEAVE. Sir Dexter stares at the paper.

SIR DEXTER Driver. Get me to the bank.

2/53. EXT. Chen Tower. Day.

The bank, with panicked investors. After a moment we see Spearpoint come out of the bank. He carries a new briefcase. He looks round, crosses the street to Diana's car, gets in.

2/54. INT. Diana's car, outside Chen Tower. Day.

Diana in the car as Spearpoint gets in.

DIANA You were a long time . . .

SPEARPOINT That bank was full of panicked investors.

DIANA You couldn't get the money?

SPEARPOINT Luckily all Hong Kong knows Sir Johnson
Squires. There it is, Diana.

(Diana looks at the briefcase.)

DIANA That's what five million dollars looks like.

SPEARPOINT Yes. Boring, isn't it?

(A Chinese face looks in the car. Spearpoint hugs the briefcase.)

DIANA Now, what about the handover?

SPEARPOINT I really haven't given it a thought since . . .

DIANA Not that Handover. I mean this one. Haven't they
been in touch?

SPEARPOINT Oh, yes, a letter lying there in my hotel room.
The Floating Dragon Restaurant. Nine o'clock tonight.

DIANA I know it, it's in Aberdeen.

SPEARPOINT You will come, won't you? I need your
support. And I don't speak Chinese . . .

DIANA You're not going to tell the police?

SPEARPOINT What do you think?

DIANA You want your wife back in one piece?

SPEARPOINT How else do you think I want her?

DIANA I know about these people. They aren't amateurs.
They do it for a living.

SPEARPOINT And in my opinion Inspector McManus
couldn't organize a tango in a brothel. No, Diana, I shan't
tell the police.

*(Diana checks the mirror and clocks a police car cruising down the
street.)*

DIANA They're behind us now.

SPEARPOINT Well then, what are you waiting for? Go, baby,
go . . .

2/55. EXT. Street outside Chen Tower. Day.

Diana's car takes off at speed down the street. The police car stops. Inspector McManus appears from Chen Tower, stares at the speeding car in surprise, gets into the cop car . . .

2/56. INT. Taipan suite, Chen Tower. Day.

Sir Dexter with Lee Chen.

SIR DEXTER Where is Martin?

LEE I don't know, father.

SIR DEXTER The bank's in trouble and he goes away. He's with that girl?

LEE I don't know about the girl.

SIR DEXTER And where's that little punk Dang?

LEE We're looking for him now.

SIR DEXTER Look harder. I want him brought in to me.

2/57. EXT. Floating restaurant, Aberdeen. Evening.

Establisher. The Harbour. And the floating restaurant with its bright lights and its Chinese noise. We hear over:

SPEARPOINT *(OOV)* But I've been here before . . .

2/58. INT. Floating restaurant, Aberdeen. Evening.

A nervous Spearpoint and a tense Diana at a corner table. The restaurant busy, but some empty tables. On the vacant chair beside Spearpoint, the briefcase we saw with the ransom money. He has his hand on it. He's staring round in recognition.

SPEARPOINT It's where Hilda and I ate, the day after we arrived.

DIANA I'll get you a drink from the bar.

SPEARPOINT Sit down, Diana. It's waiter service, the man's coming. How will they do this drop?

DIANA I don't know, I've never done it before.

(The waiter comes over.)

DIANA Mai tai, I think. Two mai tais. *(The waiter nods and goes.)* You've got the money safe?

SPEARPOINT *(Pats briefcase)* Right here. Five million dollars. The more I think about it, the more it seems a lot. You are sure it's the going rate?

DIANA It's more for a wife. And this is Hong Kong. We are a fast-growing tiger economy.

SPEARPOINT So I suppose we just compose ourselves and wait for the buggers to make contact.

DIANA Stiff upper lip, eh?

SPEARPOINT Quite. Stiff upper lip.

(Spearpoint drums his fingers. The waiter comes back with the drinks and a note in a saucer. Diana nods at the saucer. Spearpoint seizes it.)

DIANA What's it say?

SPEARPOINT Thirty dollars. It's the bloody bill.

(He reaches in his wallet and pays the waiter.)

DIANA Someone came in.

(Bao Lau comes into the restaurant, sits down, and opens up a Chinese newspaper.)

SPEARPOINT Well, well. Bao Lau, the Chinese cadre. They said he was in Beijing. It's what I told them all along. It's the Chinese authorities, trying to blackmail me into submission.

DIANA Michael . . .

(Palfrey comes into the restaurant, sits down at another table, waves for the waiter.)

SPEARPOINT Palfrey from Government House? What's that fool doing here?

DIANA You don't think the Governor's office . . . .

SPEARPOINT Kidnapped Hilda for a lark? No I don't.

(Dang, in his shades, comes into the restaurant. He goes over to another table. Not far from Palfrey, but totally ignoring him.)

DIANA Dang. The rogue trader I told you about.

SPEARPOINT Of course. I knew I'd seen him before. It was here. Talking to Palfrey.

DIANA They don't seem to know each other now. Why would Palfrey deal with a lowlife like that? He's a crook and a gangster.

SPEARPOINT They gamble together. I don't like it.

(A beat. Spearpoint taps his fingers on the table. Palfrey receives a beer, ignoring Dang. Dang gets up, goes to the bar, turns and glances toward Palfrey. Lau gets up, opens his mobile, and begins talking into the phone. Diana suddenly gets up.)

DIANA It could be me. I'm in the way.

SPEARPOINT No, my dear, you mustn't go.

DIANA They don't expect to find me here. I could ruin everything. It's best, Michael. I'll be at the apartment. You know where to find me . . .

(Diana gets up, pecks him on the cheek, goes. Spearpoint, alone, looks after her, then stares round. For another moment or two, nothing happens. Then everything. Palfrey gets up, goes to the bar, joins Dang. Lau puts away his phone and walks toward Spearpoint. Meantime the waiter comes to the table, and removes Diana's drink. Lee Chen appears at the entrance to the restaurant, and looks round.)

LAU Mr Spearpoint, how are you today?

SPEARPOINT Yes, the paper man. And they told me you were in Beijing.

(In the background, Lee sees Dang, heads for him. Dang, talking to Palfrey, reacts.)

LAU When tall trees whisper, it is often hard to hear what they say. May I sit down?

SPEARPOINT Yes, Mr Bao.

(Dang leaves Palfrey and makes a break for it, coming through Spearpoint's end of the restaurant and on to the deck.)

LAU I am paper man again. I have important message for you. From Mr Li Han.

SPEARPOINT Do you? What does he say?

(Lee rushes through the restaurant and follows Dang on to the deck. Spearpoint turns to see Dang jump on to an adjoining boat, followed by Lee.)

LAU He kindly consents to see you. At once, Bank of China Tower. He also says, if you have present, that would be very polite.

SPEARPOINT Oh, I do. This.

(Spearpoint reaches for the briefcase. Expression of surprise. Our angle shows the briefcase has gone.)

LAU Something wrong, Mr Spearpoint?

SPEARPOINT Yes, it's gone! My briefcase. It's bloody well gone . . .

LAU Again? Really, Mr Spearpoint . . .

(Confused, Spearpoint stares desperately round the restaurant. Palfrey has disappeared. McManus comes in, with TWO POLICEMEN, and comes straight over to Lau.)

McMANUS Come on, Mr Bao. We'll discuss it at at police headquarters.

LAU Discuss what, please? Tell them, Mr Spearpoint, I am a paper man.

McMANUS Take him away. You should have told us, Mr Spearpoint. Never mind, we had a tail on you all day. We're not fools in the Hong Kong police . . .

(The policemen are taking Lau away.)

SPEARPOINT Why him? There were three other suspects here.

McMANUS Three other . . .

SPEARPOINT Dang, Palfrey, Lee Chen. It could have been any of them. Why arrest Mr Bao?

McMANUS Because you told us to, Mr Spearpoint . . .

[Note: a very complicated scene, but here's what's happening: the person who actually takes the briefcase is Palfrey, for reasons that come clear in the ending. Dang is pursuing Palfrey, and trying to threaten him at the bar, in order to get the passport for Jasmine. Lee is after Dang, on his father's instructions, to silence him about what happened in the bank — so Dang rightly feels in danger from Sir Dexter. Bao Lau does have a message from Li Han for Spearpoint, about the Deng double. The waiter is totally innocent. We should also maintain in the viewer's mind the suspicion, not mentioned by anybody, that the person who has taken the briefcase is really Diana.]

2/59. INT. Jasmine's apartment. Evening.

The doorbell rings. And again. Jasmine goes to open it. Dang is standing there, distressed, jacket torn, blood on his face.

JASMINE You. Go away.

DANG I'm in trouble. Let me in.

JASMINE No.

(Dang gives the door a shove and pushes his way in.)

DANG You must let me stay here.

JASMINE I'll call Martin.

(Dang grabs her.)

DANG No. No Chens. You still want your passport, don't you?

(He's holding her. She looks at him in terror.)

2/60. INT. McManus' office, Police Headquarters. Evening.

Spearpoint waits anxiously in the Inspector's office, with its local crime posters. McManus comes in.

McMANUS Dead right, sir, it wasn't him. He'd been sent by

Li Han. Now the Chinese have made a formal protest. They're threatening to cut off our water.

SPEARPOINT And if they don't, I will. Have you found Hilda?

McMANUS Not a sign, sir.

SPEARPOINT And none of your men saw who took the ransom?

McMANUS I only had two, sir. And one of them had diarrhoea. But now we definitely know one thing. It wasn't Bao Lau.

SPEARPOINT I see. And now you intend to eliminate the rest of the population of Hong Kong one by one until you find who walked off with five million dollars? Which my friend Dorothy Squires gave me out of the kindness of his heart so I could have my dear wife back?

McMANUS That's how it is, sir. Win some, lose some.

SPEARPOINT So I'm not just down one wife, I'm down five million dollars?

McMANUS Looks like it, sir.

SPEARPOINT And your bloody stake-out will have scared off the kidnappers? So there's no knowing what they'll do next?

McMANUS I suppose there are two possibilities. One, the kidnappers got the money but haven't let your wife go.

SPEARPOINT And the other?

McMANUS Someone else picked up the money. In which case you'll probably get another message from the kidnappers.

SPEARPOINT Another message? What for?

McMANUS I expect they'll want another five million dollars, don't you, sir?

(Reaction Spearpoint, furious, and . . .)

2/61. EXT. St James' Park, London. Day.

Trees in bloom, the tourists out. Penhurst sits on a bench in his best panama, reading *The Times* as Big Ben chimes in the background. Ms Highsmith comes and sits beside him. He doesn't put down the paper.

Ms HIGHSMITH Beautiful June day, sir.

PENHURST Yes, it was. What, Ms Highsmith?

Ms HIGHSMITH Our Man in Hong Kong, sir. His wife's been kidnapped.

PENHURST Go on. Nothing surprises me. How much are they asking?

Ms HIGHSMITH Five million Hong Kong dollars.

PENHURST Funny. Know Lady Hilda quite well. Never have guessed she'd have fetched it. Well, tell him if he wants us to field the ransom he hasn't a hope in hell.

Ms HIGHSMITH He paid the ransom himself. Unfortunately his wife hasn't been returned.

PENHURST Found in the Harbour?

Ms HIGHSMITH Not found at all. It's caused another crisis. Beijing saw our ambassador again this morning. It seems the Hong Kong police arrested a Chinese official without evidence. They say it's deliberate provocation on our side to sabotage the Handover.

PENHURST What made them arrest this man?

Ms HIGHSMITH Mr Spearpoint. Said it was a plot to take his wife to Beijing and behead her.

PENHURST Really. Just like that.

Ms HIGHSMITH Apparently he had his reasons. His wife had stolen some priceless treasures from the Chinese National Museum.

PENHURST Seems perfectly likely, with Hilda.

Ms HIGHSMITH Of course Mr Spearpoint had it all wrong.

The Chinese don't behead you any more. They shoot you in the back of the neck.

PENHURST There's one consolation, then. *(He folds his paper)* Well, Ms Highsmith, I'm clearly going to have to go out there. And see what I can do to sort these local difficulties.

MS HIGHSMITH Yes, sir. I've already packed a briefcase with your papers.

(Penhurst gazes pensively at the London scene.)

PENHURST Just look at it, Ms Highsmith. London in June. Ascot and Wimbledon. Opera at Glyndebourne. Test match at Lord's.

MS HIGHSMITH I know, sir. But every person this day must do his or her duty. There's one piece of good news. Princess Di isn't going. She wants to solace sick children in Miami instead.

(They've got up, walk together across the sunny London park.)

2/62. INT. Room, Hong Kong. Day.

Start on a TV set. A very presentable mugshot of Hilda – replaced by a *presenter* on the street.

PRESENTER *(TV)* Now that high-profile kidnap story. We've learned that Lady Hilda Spearpoint, wife of a top British official, was kidnapped four nights ago in Lan Kwai Fong. Inspector McManus, what can you tell us?

(McManus, door-stepped, appears in shot.)

MCMANUS *(TV)* All I can say is we're conducting active enquiries.

PRESENTER *(TV)* Has a ransom been paid?

MCMANUS *(TV)* Money was paid. But the lady's still missing.

PRESENTER *(TV)* Do you think the victim's alive or dead?

MCMANUS *(TV)* All I can tell you is we're working on the presumption it's either one or the other . . .

(A hand reaches out and switches off the TV set.)

2/63. INT. Lobby, Blue Moon Hotel. Day.

Spearpoint comes into the hotel, goes up to the desk.

DESK CLERK Message for you, sir.

(He holds out an envelope.)

SPEARPOINT Oh, my Lord . . .

DESK CLERK Do you need these?

(He holds out his white gloves. Spearpoint looks at the message. Relief.)

SPEARPOINT No, all's well. It's from London.

(Spearpoint tears open the message. We see that it says:
'SITUATION VERY SERIOUS. MEET ME, FLIGHT SCA101 KAI TAK, TOMORROW A.M. PENHURST.')

LEE *(OOV)* Mr Spearpoint.

(Spearpoint looks up. Lee Chen stands beside him. He does not look friendly.)

SPEARPOINT Not now, Mr Chen. I have to go straight to the airport to meet my superior . . .

LEE My father likes to speak to you. In the lobby. I think you better come . . .

(Spearpoint looks at Lee, follows him across the lobby. Sir Dexter rises from a chair.)

SIR DEXTER Mr Spearpoint. Do you remember at all the old English five-pound note?

SPEARPOINT *(Stares at him)* The crisp white one, yes?

SIR DEXTER What did it say? Promise to pay the bearer five pounds. Signed, Governor Bank of England. Something like that. I met the Governor. I introduced him to Mr Li Han. You had a plan. Promises were made to rescue my bank . . .

SPEARPOINT And they'll be kept. On our side at least.

SIR DEXTER Mr Spearpoint, we are gentlemen. But I no longer believe your promises. Show him, Lee.

(Lee puts a cheque on the table.)

LEE Three days ago you came to Chen Bank. You drew this cheque for five million dollar. Made out to you. Signed by Sir Johnson Squires.

SPEARPOINT Yes, I did.

SIR DEXTER The cheque is drawn on his Hong. But Sir Johnson sold it, several days ago. After he sold the Hong, he spent two days at Happy Valley. He lost on every race. Sir Johnson is bankrupt. This was drawn on a nil account. You owe me five million dollars.

(Spearpoint stares at him.)

SPEARPOINT There's some mistake. I went to school with Dorothy Squires. I'm sure if we just sat down and discussed it like gentlemen . . .

SIR DEXTER He's no longer in Hong Kong. He flew out yesterday. For a very sudden holiday in Phuket.

LEE We want our money back, Mr Spearpoint.

(Spearpoint is stunned.)

SPEARPOINT I'd be glad to oblige you. Unfortunately I can't. The money was for my wife.

SIR DEXTER She's buying antiques again?

SPEARPOINT She was kidnapped. That was her ransom.

SIR DEXTER So you have your wife back. And I want my money back.

SPEARPOINT I don't have my wife back. Someone stole the ransom.

SIR DEXTER Forgive me if I do not believe you.

SPEARPOINT I am a British diplomat, Sir Dexter.

SIR DEXTER Exactly. Mr Spearpoint, your government has accused me of fraud. Now you have committed a fraud yourself. In Hong Kong we are very honourable people. Those who do not pay debts always pay in other ways.

(Spearpoint tries to pull a rabbit from the hat.)

SPEARPOINT I do have something. I happen to have some priceless Chinese treasures in my suite . . .

SIR DEXTER Figures from the terracotta army? Qin?

SPEARPOINT *(Getting it)* Of course. Your collection! You used them to frame my wife.

SIR DEXTER We are both diplomats, Mr Spearpoint. And I had to act in the interests of my bank.

SPEARPOINT Then maybe it would be in the interests of the bank if you took them back instead of the money. At least we'd be quits.

LEE We want the money . . .

SIR DEXTER Wait a minute, Lee. What is quits?

SPEARPOINT You'd know if you'd been to an English school. I was part of a fraud, you were part of a theft. That's quits. When I lose my wife, and you lose five million dollars . . .

SIR DEXTER . . . that's quits!

LEE Father. He owes us five million.

SIR DEXTER No, he is right. English gentlemen understand these things. Give me back the figures, and we will be quits . . .

(He holds out his hand to Spearpoint. They shake – to Spearpoint's clear relief . . .)

2/64. INT. Suite, Blue Moon Hotel. Day.

Spearpoint opens the door and proudly stands back to let the Chens into the suite. They look around.

SPEARPOINT You'll find them over there, Sir Dexter.

SIR DEXTER Yes, Mr Spearpoint. But where?

(Spearpoint stares at the room. The figures are no longer there.)

SPEARPOINT No, you won't. They've gone.

LEE Father. Now I deal with this.

(He seizes Spearpoint by the shirtfront.)

SPEARPOINT Please. We're English gentlemen . . .

LEE I am not.

SPEARPOINT Sir Dexter, let's discuss it. There must be an explanation. We'd better call the manager and find out who's been . . .

SIR DEXTER I don't think so. Those figures were smuggled into Hong Kong. I have no wish to be arrested. Have you no better suggestion?

SPEARPOINT If I could stop the enquiry into the bank . . .

SIR DEXTER Let him go, Lee. Mr Spearpoint, you have three days to rescue my bank or pay me back five million dollars. Or I shall make sure we really are quits, in the Chinese way. And don't try to leave Hong Kong. It would not be wise. Come along, Lee . . .

(Lee releases Spearpoint. The Chens go. Spearpoint smooths his shirtfront and tries to recover his diplomatic dignity.

2/65. INT. Jasmine's apartment. Day.

Jasmine answers the doorbell. Diana is there.

DIANA Jasmine Tan? Diana Jang, do you remember me?

JASMINE The journalist. You came to the bank.

DIANA They tell me you don't work there any more.

JASMINE I lost my job. Why . . .?

DIANA I'm trying to find someone. The person who lost you your job. His name's Dang.

JASMINE He's not here now.

DIANA But he was? I need to ask him some questions. Can I come in?

(Jasmine unwillingly holds open the door.)

2/66. EXT. Kai Tak. Day.

A jumbo jet touching down on the runway.

2/67. INT. Arrivals hall, Kai Tak. Day.

Penhurst comes from the customs area, pushing his cart – with golf clubs. A Chinese official politely directs him toward the VIP suite.

2/68. INT. VIP suite, Kai Tak. Day.

A nervous Spearpoint holds his hand out to Penhurst, his diplomatic master.

SPEARPOINT I thought we'd better meet in here, Athelstan. A lot of people are trying to leave Hong Kong at the moment.

PENHURST Quite. Something to do with you, isn't it? Spearpoint, I sent you here to get under the skin of the foreigners. Well, you bloody well have, haven't you?

SPEARPOINT You know diplomacy's very different here.

PENHURST That explains your remarkable record?

SPEARPOINT Is it remarkable?

PENHURST Oh, yes. First you outrage the locals with a press interview saying we're pleased to be shot of them. Then you lose your briefcase, so Beijing knows our positions. Then you're accused of taking bribes from a taipan we're about to lock up for fraud. You fall out with Government House. And the Chinese authorities. The blessed Hilda robs the National Museum. Then you let her get kidnapped, now you've lost her altogether . . .

SPEARPOINT Hardly my—

PENHURST Not content with all that, you have a Chinese cadre arrested, and get our ambassador in Beijing threatened with expulsion. I sent you here to arrange a banquet. Not a hard task for an experienced diplomat who thinks he should have been ambassador. Yet in two short weeks you've taken the situation from near tranquillity to the brink of world war.

SPEARPOINT It's true there is a little local tension, but—

PENHURST A little local tension? The Chinese navy's on full
alert. Taiwan's on war footing. The American Seventh
Fleet is sailing here at full knots. And there's a typhoon
blowing up in the South China Sea.

SPEARPOINT You're not going to blame me for that?

PENHURST At the moment I'd blame you for anything. You
couldn't have done much more if you'd tried. Now, is
there anywhere I can get a decent bath? And an even
better gin and tonic?

2/69. INT. Back of tattoo parlour. Day.

Dang is playing pool (or mah-jong?) in the back room with
other gangsters. Fang comes in through the bead curtain, directs
his attention to what's going on in the main room. Diana is
there, asking questions of other gangsters. But she turns and
goes away. Dang, relieved, goes back to his game.

2/70. EXT. Terrace, Blue Moon Hotel. Day.

Penhurst comfortable in a lounger. Sunblock on his nose, a big
drink in front of him.

PENHURST Heavens, man, we are British diplomats. Artists in
bridging opposed positions and soothing ruffled feathers.
We may have no empire, but it's still what we do best.

SPEARPOINT You know I've always deferred to your
excellent judgement, Athelstan.

PENHURST Let's take the problems in order. Number one,
Hilda. Always liked Hilda, feisty lady. Not the sort to get
herself into trouble.

SPEARPOINT Athelstan, she is in trouble. She's been
kidnapped. She's tied up in a cellar somewhere. Or
chopped into sausages. Or sold into white slavery in
Macau.

PENHURST Nonsense. These people asked five million dollars.
Must think a lot of her. Won't kill the goose that lays the

golden egg. Anyway Hilda's the sort to make the most of an experience like that. Even enjoy it.

SPEARPOINT Enjoy being kidnapped?

PENHURST Bit of white slavery in Macau would probably set her up a treat. Look, if Hilda wants to return to you, she will.

SPEARPOINT So we do nothing?

PENHURST Golden rule of diplomacy. Always let them come to you. Leaving you free to concentrate on problem number two. Stand-off with Beijing, know what's causing it, don't you?

SPEARPOINT Yes, Athelstan, the Marco Polo Bank.

PENHURST You're in cahoots with the taipan. Took his air tickets, didn't you? All you do is get him off the hook, smooth the Chinese and settle the Handover.

SPEARPOINT I've been saying that to London for days.

PENHURST We do expect a little local initiative. You are Our Man in Hong Kong. What happened to the Spearpoint Plan?

SPEARPOINT It was fine. Until Hilda got kidnapped. And I ended up owing Chen five million dollars.

PENHURST Well, that's what banks are for. Give you money when you don't have any. Wouldn't be any point in them otherwise, would there? There really is fraud in the bank?

SPEARPOINT Oh, definitely.

PENHURST Right. Find a sacrificial lamb. Someone who'll take it right where it hurts, on the chin. Put someone in the slammer and everyone's happy. That's it, then. My goodness, I'm feeling peckish.

SPEARPOINT There's a fine restaurant here, if you care to . . .

PENHURST Don't worry. All taken care of. There you are, Chesters. How's our Governor?

(Chesters stands there.)

CHESTERS Very well, sir. Looks forward to giving you dinner. So does the Deputy Governor.

PENHURST Well, Spearpoint, see you in the bar after. Oh, everyone tells me I should see Chinese opera. See if you can get tickets.

CHESTERS I suppose you haven't heard anything from . . .

SPEARPOINT No, I haven't, Chesters . . .

(And Penhurst goes merrily off with Chesters.)

2/71. INT. Auditorium, Chinese theatre. Night.

The famous stylized yowl of Chinese opera. The performance is under way. In the audience Spearpoint sits between Penhurst and Diana. Penhurst is getting bored and conversational.

PENHURST Who's the pretty girl, then?

SPEARPOINT It's in Cantonese. Miss Jang has kindly agreed to be our translator.

(Diana is whispering into Spearpoint's other ear.)

PENHURST What's she babbling about, Spearpoint?

SPEARPOINT She explains the young man is a student who has to go to Beijing to take his examinations to be a mandarin. But his father has forbidden him to go.

PENHURST He's dressed as a girl.

SPEARPOINT It is an opera, Athelstan.

PENHURST Girl's dressed as a boy.

(By now the audience round about is getting restive. Hissing, etc. Diana whispers in Spearpoint's ear.)

SPEARPOINT The girl's father wants her to go to the city and become a concubine. But the girl doesn't want to go. Because she loves the boy.

PENHURST What now?

SPEARPOINT The boy dressed as a girl thinks the girl dressed as a boy is a boy.

PENHURST And the girl dressed as a boy thinks the boy dressed as a girl is a girl? And this sort of thing is going to keep on all bloody night?

(Hisses and catcalls. Spearpoint stares across the auditorium. Somewhere on the other side of the theatre, or in a box, is Hilda. Spearpoint rises. Boos, hisses, catcalls.)

SPEARPOINT Athelstan. Over there. Isn't that Hilda?

PENHURST Course it isn't Hilda. Hilda's busy white-slaving in Macau.

DIANA Sit down please, Michael. Just wait till the interval.

PENHURST For heaven's sake, man. Are you trying to get us lynched?

2/72. INT. Huskisson's car, street outside tattoo parlour. Night.

Angle from car on the night scene, with Huskisson observing from the driver's seat. Dang comes down the street, carrying food. He looks round anxiously, goes into the tattoo parlour. After a moment, Huskisson picks up his mobile phone and presses the buttons . . .

2/73. INT. Foyer, Chinese theatre. Night.

Spearpoint in the foyer at the interval, watching the audience come out, looking for Hilda. Diana with Penhurst.

PENHURST Hallucinations, of course. Happens to people when they come out East. I'm Athelstan Penhurst. Spearpoint's chief.

DIANA Diana Jang. I'm a journalist here.

PENHURST Really? Known old Spearpoint long?

DIANA Only since he arrived. Excuse me . . .

(Her mobile phone ringing. She answers, listens. Then goes over to Spearpoint. The interval bell goes. Penhurst turns to re-enter. Then clocks Spearpoint and Diana leaving the theatre.)

PENHURST Well! Beggar me!

2/74. EXT. Tattoo parlour. Night.

Spearpoint, Diana and Huskisson, beside Huskisson's car, survey the seedy night scene.

SPEARPOINT In there?

HUSKISSON I saw him go in about ten minutes ago.

SPEARPOINT Is this wise? That's a gangster place.

DIANA You want to find out what happened?

SPEARPOINT All right, let's find out what happened . . .

(As Spearpoint summons his courage to the sticking point, they cross the street and enter . . .)

2/75. INT. Tattoo parlour. Night.

Fang with his needle, working, looks up as the three come in. He points the needle at Spearpoint. It takes Diana to say something in Chinese and calm him down. Fang leads the way to the inner room . . .

2/76. INT. Inner room, tattoo parlour. Night.

. . . where Dang, playing mah-jong, with gangsters, jumps to his feet.

DANG Who are you? You come from Chen?

(Fang says something in Chinese.)

SPEARPOINT No, we're not from Chen, Mr Dang. We did meet once, very briefly. In the floating restaurant at Aberdeen.

(Dang does not look charmed. Fang says, in Chinese, 'This is the gweilo whose wife was kidnapped.')

DANG Don't try and set me up for a kidnap. I'm a money man, not a gangster.

FANG He not gangster. Not Triad.

DANG OK, I was at the casino. But kidnap, it's not my style.

FANG Not his style.

SPEARPOINT But you were in the casino that night.

DANG I went to see Palfrey. He was fixing me something.

HUSKISSON What happened then?

DANG The rich woman went to change money. Lot of money. Maybe I took a few chips from the table. Then Palfrey got up and went to his car. There was a cadre there.

DIANA Who did the kidnap?

DANG I don't know.

SPEARPOINT You were at the Floating Dragon the other night.

DANG To see Palfrey. A commercial thing. He was fixing a passport. He still owes me.

SPEARPOINT Did you steal my briefcase?

DANG You crazy, man. I was running for my life. Lee Chen was after me. Those Chens want to kill me.

FANG That why he hides here.

DIANA Because you're the rogue trader?

DANG I did some deals for Dexter. OK, some for myself too. Now they want to see me floating in Victoria Harbour.

(Spearpoint leans forward.)

SPEARPOINT Mr Dang, let's do some trading ourselves. I do have some influence, not least with the Police Commissioner.

DIANA And remember you're lucky we got here first. Chen's looking for you everywhere . . .

(Dang looks at them. The gangsters gather round.)

2/77. INT. Room, Police Headquarters. Day.

A large windowless room filling with journalists, photographers, sensing a big story breaking. On a raised platform, McManus with other officers. He taps a small gong to call for order.

McMANUS Some of you may find this a familiar scene.

Remember Singapore a few years back. Happily I can say we've been a little more efficient in picking up our rogue trader . . .

(During this we see Spearpoint standing beside Dang.)

SPEARPOINT It's all right. You have my word . . .

(Dang, bowed head, moves to go and sit by McManus.)

McMANUS This young man has come voluntarily into custody and made a full confession of irregular dealing when he worked for the Marco Polo Bank. He says he was acting alone, and when he's paid his debt to society he'll move to Canada to manage a casino. His name's Dang and he'll answer any questions his lawyer allows . . .

DIANA *(From the floor)* A triumph for you, Inspector.

McMANUS Aye, I think you could say that . . .

(Spearpoint smiles and turns to go . . .)

2/78. EXT. Police Headquarters. Day.

Spearpoint steps into the street. He's joined by the Governor of the Bank of England. The two men fan to relieve the humidity. Distant thunder rolls.

SPEARPOINT I didn't see you in there.

GOVERNOR Oh I wasn't. Not officially.

SPEARPOINT You're becoming quite Chinese. Satisfied?

GOVERNOR You can hardly expect me to say that. But I think you will find the market picks up in a day or so. That reminds me, I must change a traveller's cheque. Rather good shopping in Hong Kong, had you noticed . . .?

2/79. EXT. Sir Dexter's house. Day.

Establisher. The house on the mountainside. Sir Dexter's Rolls drives up. Spearpoint gets out.

2/80. INT. Sir Dexter's house. Day.

Sir Dexter, Martin and Lee wait to welcome Spearpoint.

SIR DEXTER Welcome again to my humble house, Mr Spearpoint. Good to see an old friend.

SPEARPOINT Good to see you, Sir Dexter. A happy moment. Honour restored.

SIR DEXTER Honour is very important to me. And the bank too. Your esteemed wife, has she been restored?

SPEARPOINT I'm afraid not. Nor has my briefcase.

SIR DEXTER So forget a little matter of five million dollars.

SPEARPOINT Thank you, Sir Dexter. I hoped you'd say that.

SIR DEXTER But we must not forget your Spearpoint Plan. I have called Mr Li Han. He too is very happy.

MARTIN Mr Spearpoint, a drink on the balcony?

(Martin leads Spearpoint on to the balcony.)

2/81. EXT. Balcony, Sir Dexter's house. Day.

Spearpoint and Martin, looking out over the view. Martin pours from the bottles on the table.

MARTIN My father had a problem, you had a problem. Now you are both satisfied.

SPEARPOINT Yes, I think we are.

MARTIN Now only I have a problem. You know the Chinese saying, a friend likes to help a friend.

SPEARPOINT I have heard it often lately.

MARTIN I have a friend. A very good friend.

(He shows Spearpoint the photo of Jasmine Tan.)

SPEARPOINT She doesn't look much of a problem to me.

MARTIN I wish to take her to London. My father mustn't know. She wants so much to be a citizen of the Queen. Dang was fixing me a British passport. Now if he goes to jail . . .

SPEARPOINT Well?

MARTIN More than ever I see you are a man of the very
greatest influence. I expect you know many top people in
the Home Office?

SPEARPOINT You thought I might have a quiet word in a
useful ear?

(Martin smiles very warmly.)

MARTIN Mr Spearpoint, what a good thing I helped to bring
you to Hong Kong. I see you understand us all so well . . .

2/82. EXT. Bank of China Tower. Day.

Establisher.

2/83. INT. Anteroom, Li Han's suite, Bank of China Tower. Day.

The door of Li Han's office opens. An elderly Chinese gentleman, Deng lookalike 1, emerges, followed by Li Han and Bao
Lau. Li Han shakes hands with Deng 1.

LAU (In Chinese) Next.

(We now see four other Chinese gentlemen, Deng lookalikes, sitting
on chairs in the room. Deng 2 rises to enter the office.)

2/84. INT. Departures hall, Kai Tak. Day.

Spearpoint escorts the Governor of the Bank of England toward
Departures. The Governor seems in great good humour.

GOVERNOR That should settle it, then. The Hang Seng's
climbing by the hour. Chen's bank's looking nice too.
Panic should soon be over.

SPEARPOINT Delighted to hear the Old Lady's been satisfied.

GOVERNOR Well, I suppose if Richard Nixon could change
his mind about China, so can I.

SPEARPOINT He was impeached shortly after. But I really
wouldn't worry about that. Oh, excuse me. I see *she's*
arrived . . .

(A swinging handbag. And we see Mrs T in the middle of a crowd of press.)

Mrs T Delighted. Absolutely delighted. I know nothing more exciting than to come back to Hong Kong.

Chinese Journalist Are you confident about democracy here?

Mrs T Am I confident? He asks me am I confident? Of course I'm confident. My dear man, Deng and I signed an agreement in 1984. The British are an honourable people, the Chinese are an honourable people. We said One Country, Two Systems. That's how it will be.

Chinese Journalist But recent tensions—

Mrs T We all have tensions, but we learn to overcome them, don't we? Thank you very much, ladies and gentlemen. Now there is work to be done . . .

(Mrs T goes on her way.)

2/85. INT. Anteroom, Bank of China Tower. Day.

Spearpoint and Bao Lau stand waiting.

Spearpoint She's at the New Mandarin. Dennis at the Hyatt.

Lau I thought they knew each other? You realize if we let Our Man attend the British banquet, there must be perfect security. Medical facilities. And he must not be asked to speak.

Spearpoint But he will declare his support for the Joint Agreement somehow? Since we're affirming he is still alive?

(The door to Li Han's office opens. Li Han appears.)

Li Han Mr Spearpoint, come in . . .

2/86. INT. Li Han's suite, Bank of China Tower. Day.

In the office, an old Chinese gentleman, one of the Dengs, sits in a sofa chair, drinking a mug of tea.

LI HAN I would like to present you to the Chairman of the Central Committee of the People's Republic. Mr Deng Xiaoping.

(Spearpoint stares. Deng looks up and waves a hand.)

SPEARPOINT I'm truly honoured to meet you, Chairman. I hope you had a good journey from Beijing.

(Li Han translates this into Chinese. Spearpoint turns to Bao Lau. Deng says something to Li Han.)

SPEARPOINT I thought he spoke some English.

LAU Once. He was much younger then.

(Li Han comes to translate.)

LI HAN Chairman Deng says how delighted he is to attend the Handover ceremony and meet Mrs Thatcher again. He would like to shake hands with you. Please.

(Spearpoint goes over. Deng rises with difficulty. The mug falls from his hand, he sinks back in the chair.)

LAU You leave now. At once.

(Spearpoint glances at the groaning Deng before he is hustled from the room.)

2/87. INT. Anteroom, Bank of China Tower. Day.

Bao Lau hustles out a mystified Spearpoint.

SPEARPOINT He's all right?

LAU You saw nothing. You tell no one.

SPEARPOINT Of course not. Especially if your side accept our Governor at the banquet.

LAU Very well. Your Governor is present. We agree. Now leave, Mr Spearpoint . . .

2/88. EXT. Square, Hong Kong. Day.

A pro-democracy protest or vigil, taken from stock.

2/89. EXT. Harbour. Day.

The Royal Yacht *Britannia* coming into dock. Stock shots (from recent documentary on the *Britannia*?).

2/90. EXT. Government House. Evening.

The evening of 30 June. Establisher. Grounds and House ready for the Handover dinner. Marquees, etc. The Union Jack flies on its flagpole.

2/91. INT. Reception room, Government House. Evening.

The great banquet table laid. Servants polish glasses, put out the plates for the final banquet. Chesters pops in. He picks up a large silver table decoration with interest.

2/92. EXT. Streets, Hong Kong. Evening.

Revelry in the streets (material shot for the Chinese New Year?). Dragon dances, fireworks, etc. A dance in which a Union Jacked paper tiger is being teased by a Chinese dragon.

2/93. INT. Lobby, Blue Moon Hotel. Evening.

Chesters, in an untidy DJ, waits in the lobby. Spearpoint and Penhurst appear from the lift.

CHESTERS Good evening, gentlemen. Your carriage awaits. You did bring a brolly, by the way? Typhoon weather.

PENHURST English, old boy. Never without.

SPEARPOINT I take it tonight I will at last meet the Governor? I have been expecting to see him for weeks.

CHESTERS You should have said, Mr Spearpoint.

SPEARPOINT You should have asked, Mr Chesters.

CHESTERS Anyway, he's very grateful to you. And the Deputy Governor. He sent his warmest thanks. And the Rolls . . .

2/94. EXT. Government House. Night.

Crowds of special guests enter the brightly lit building. A military band plays outside.

2/95. INT. Main room, Government House. Night.

The banquet. On the top table, the Princess Royal, the Governor and his lady, 'Deng', Mrs Thatcher.

Spearpoint sits at the furthest end of the long table. His neighbour is Bao Lau. The meal, in British style, is coming to its end. Lau turns to Spearpoint with a morsel on the end of his fork.

SPEARPOINT I don't think so, Mr Bao. Tonight we're playing under English rules.

LAU You know none of this could happen without us? I make you small toast. The paper men.

(Spearpoint raises his glass.)

SPEARPOINT Cheers. I do apologize about your arrest.

LAU It was bad for my face. But I am sorry too. About the Qin antiquities.

SPEARPOINT You know, I never did understand why you took so much interest in my wife.

LAU A Chinese saying. The best way into a great city is through the woman's gate. How is your wife? I saw her the other day.

SPEARPOINT You saw her the other day?

(A Toastmaster (or the Governor) gavels. Mrs T rises.)

MRS T Your Royal Highness, your excellencies, eminences, honoured Chinese guests, ladies, gentlemen, comrades. *(Laughter.)* After a hundred and fifty-six years we British are about to leave Hong Kong. We leave with regret, but in hope. And I know every one of us will feel we're leaving something or someone behind . . .

(Applause. Reaction Spearpoint.)

Thirteen years ago our distinguished guest, Chairman Deng, and I met in the Great Hall of the People. We signed a Joint Agreement, an historic document covering Hong Kong's destiny for the next fifty years . . .

(Applause. Mrs T turns toward the elderly Chinese gentleman beside her.)

Chairman, if you recall that occasion as well as I, you'll remember we raised our glasses to toast the future of the emerald city of Hong Kong. You said your greatest wish was to live to see the Handover. You have. May we repeat the toast? And reaffirm the Joint Agreement?

(Applause. 'Deng' rises healthily to his feet.)

DENG 2 Iron Lady, I agree. To One Nation, Two Systems. And the friendship of our great peoples . . .

SPEARPOINT It's not the same Deng!

LAU Mr Spearpoint, please. Don't ask. Remember, we are only minor cadres. Paper men.

2/96. EXT. Government House. Night.

A truly solemn occasion. The Union Jack on the flagpole being lowered for the last time. The guests on the lawn stand to attention as the National Anthem plays, followed by beating the retreat. But the sound of another anthem sounds across the Harbour . . .

2/97. EXT. Bank of China Tower. Night.

The Chinese flag rises on the flagpole. Another band, trying to drown out the British band, plays the Chinese National Anthem, 'The East is Red'. The Chinese bandsman waves to raise the volume . . .

2/98. EXT. Government House. Night.

The British bandsman waves his baton to raise the volume. Suddenly another megawatt sound rises over both. It's the unmistakable sound of the Three Tenors.

2/99. EXT. Harbour. Night.

Fireworks from junks on the Harbour (take from celebrations of Chinese New Year). The three kinds of music, British, Chinese, and Tenors, waft across the Harbour. A downpour of torrential rain.

2/100. EXT. *Britannia*, Harbour. Day.

The Royal Yacht with the ship's band marching and playing in pouring rain. (Clip from documentary about *Britannia* has this scene.)

2/101. EXT. Gangplank, *Britannia*. Day.

Close in on the gangplank. The British great and good are going aboard, a select number. It includes Penhurst and Spearpoint. Chesters is there to see them off. The rain torrents down.

CHESTERS Must say goodbye, Mr Spearpoint.

SPEARPOINT You're not travelling with us, then?

CHESTERS I'm stand-by economy on South China Air.

SPEARPOINT Well, at least we did get the Governor's feet under the table.

CHESTERS Yes, sir. Hope you had a good evening. I thought it went surprisingly well, considering. By the way, I suppose you never heard anything from those quangos?

SPEARPOINT 'Fraid I didn't, Chesters. I'll keep my ear open. But I'm not sure I'll pick up a great deal of gossip in my next posting.

CHESTERS Where's that, sir?

SPEARPOINT Uzbekistan.

CHESTERS Ah well. Better get on board, then. Before we all drown.

(Spearpoint follows Penhurst up the gangplank.)

2/102. EXT. Harbour. Day.

British frigates leaving. From them comes a plaintive sound. It's the Dudley Moore song 'Goodbyeeee'. It begins to merge with another sound. The Three Tenors are singing 'Nessun Dorma'.

2/103. EXT. Hong Kong. Day.

Is it possible to show the famous Chinese mechanical dragons flapping their way through the air?

2/104. INT. Check-in hall, Kai Tak airport. Day.

Chinese soldiers from the People's Republic on the line as people check in for their flights. Chesters there. On his trolley, bags and a rather large box. A Chinese soldier comes along and asks him to open the box. Chesters rather shame-facedly pulls it open. Inside is the silver table decoration from Government House. The soldier stares, takes Chesters by the arm.

But Martin Chen steps from the next line, First class. He speaks to the Chinese soldier in Cantonese. He hands him money. The soldier goes.

CHESTERS Thank you very much, Mr Chen. Just a small souvenir to take home.

(Martin looks at the large silver decoration.)

MARTIN I know. There's a Chinese saying. When the sun goes down, it's wise to keep warm.

(Martin goes back into the First-class line. Waiting for him is Jasmine Tan. She holds a British passport in her hand as she approaches the desk.)

2/105. EXT. Expensive shopping street, Hong Kong. Day.

A pan along the rich row of shops. One of them is called 'Hilda's'. Expensive dresses in the windows.

2/106. INT. 'Hilda's'. Day.

A middle-aged *American woman* goes to the counter with a pile of clothes. Behind the counter is a very elegant Hilda Spearpoint.

AMERICAN WOMAN Really great clothes. I congratulate you, my dear, really great clothes.

HILDA I'm glad you think so. They are the best in town.

AMERICAN WOMAN I'll tell all the girls at the hotel. They'll all come shop-shop-shopping. It must be really great, keeping a boutique like this. How did you do it?

HILDA Simple, my dear. I just arranged to come into a great deal of money.

AMERICAN WOMAN That's what I'm hoping for with my divorce. Anyway, stay happy.

HILDA Oh, I will. Won't I, Simon?

(Palfrey, very hunky and smartly dressed, comes into the store. The American woman looks him over.)

AMERICAN WOMAN Well. Some people have all the luck.

(With her designer bags – Hilda's – the American woman heads for the door. She passes a splendid piece of store decor. Two Chinese terracotta figures hung about with blouses, scarves, etc.)

2/107. EXT. *Britannia*. Day.

Bright sunshine. Using stock shot, we see the *Britannia* sailing in calm seas, in the Arabian Gulf.

2/108. EXT. Deck, *Britannia*. Day.

Mock-up, deck of the *Britannia*. She sails in calm seas. A few deckchairs, a naval waiter. Spearpoint lounges in one of the chairs, looking out to sea. Penhurst joins him, in his panama. The sun sets.

PENHURST End of a long day.

SPEARPOINT We didn't do so badly, did we?

PENHURST No. Could have been better, could have been worse. Still, something to tell the children about, eh?

SPEARPOINT Didn't know you had children, Athelstan.

PENHURST I don't, none that I know about. My inclinations always pointed in the left-hand direction. It's a metaphor. You know us, very poetic people. What about you?

SPEARPOINT No. There was all that diplomacy to do. And with my work and her temperament, we never seemed to acquire either the time or the taste for it.

PENHURST Good woman, Hilda. Not everyone's cup of tea, but she kept you on the straight and narrow. Funny she never turned up, isn't it? One way or the other.

SPEARPOINT Yes, isn't it?

(Penhurst eyes him, with a touch of doubt.)

PENHURST You said you thought you saw her.

SPEARPOINT Must have been mistaken. In any case I was much too busy at the end to think about it. With the Handover, I mean. No, it's a complete mystery.

PENHURST Shouldn't have mentioned it, eh? But that's us, isn't it. Stiff upper lip. Don't show our feelings. Cards close to the chest.

(Just then Diana comes along the deck in a swimsuit.)

DIANA Old China Hands take tiffin as the evening sun goes down?

(Diana strokes Spearpoint's back, then sits down.)

PENHURST Perfect timing, my dear. Sun just over the yardarm. Where is that waiter?

SPEARPOINT Busy with the royals, I expect.

(Penhurst stretches out and looks at the blue sea, with the Royal Yacht's ensign flapping in the breeze.)

PENHURST Look at that. Last time you'll see that flag over these waters.

319

SPEARPOINT Still, it never was the winning, was it? Just the playing of the game.

PENHURST Remember what they used to say, Spearpoint? POSH?

SPEARPOINT *(Wistful)* Ah, POSH. Port outward, starboard home.

PENHURST Now it's just starboard home. Back to little offshore England, whatever its fate may be. End of us, of course. Still, I suppose we should be glad we got out with our heads in the air and the skin on our backs.

DIANA I'm really looking forward to your little England. I hear the shopping in London is really the best . . .

(Spearpoint doesn't know how to take it. For an instant he appears to frown, then he elects to smile.)

End Credits.

SHE'S GOT TO HAVE IT:
THE FIRST GREAT SHOPAHOLIC

In October 1993, I took a Russian ferry across the Baltic and sailed to a great and beautiful city that had just got its old name back: St Petersburg. As it happened, I had chosen a bad week. But it is often a bad week to go to Russia. As I arrived, Boris Yeltsin began shelling the Moscow White House, where the Duma was holed up, trying to defeat an attempted palace coup, and the country was in chaos.

Russia was in confusion. Communism was being dismantled, the age of the Free Market had arrived. Only it wasn't free. Despite the new Prada and Gucci stores on Nevsky Prospekt, the chief spectacle was desperate poverty. Outside the Petersburg Public Library, children were selling ancient books grabbed from the great collections inside to passing tourists.

Alas, the books they were selling were just the ones I had come to see: a remarkable eighteenth-century library, the Library of the Enlightenment. For 1993 was not the first time Russia had a consumer society. 250 years earlier Russia produced one of the world's great shopaholics: Catherine II, Catherine the Great.

Following an earlier palace coup, Catherine ruled Russia from 1762 to her death on the imperial toilet in 1796. She was German, a little princess from one of the Prussian principalities, who at the age of fourteen married her cousin Karl. Renamed Peter III, he became Tzar of all the Russias – despite the fact that he spoke German and hated Russia.

Unsurprisingly, he had a very short shelf life, but Russian rulers often do. The marriage was almost certainly unconsummated; nobody told him what to do. Lusty enough by nature, Catherine was instructed to produce an heir. Helped by one of her several lovers, the one-eyed Grigor Orlov, she had her husband dethroned in a coup d'état, and he died soon afterwards in prison.

The world was told he had a severe attack of the haemorrhoids, and he was undoubtedly assailed from the rear. Catherine had a good deal to do with it, but she understood the value of public relations. First condemned as a killer, she was soon celebrated across Europe as the wise and beautiful Minerva of the North.

The thing that made her name was that Catherine shopped. She shopped as only a great Empress with generous Dutch bankers could. She shopped till everyone in Europe dropped. Catherine bought anything and everything. Shoes and shawls, gems and geegaws, gold and amethyst and silver. Paintings and sculptures, porcelain and pewter, buttons and bows. No matter what, she bought it. In this she followed the basic rule of shopping. What creates value isn't what's sold: it's who buys.

Catherine created taste, added value. She turned dreck into collectable, dross into gold. But she was wise enough to choose good advisers. She bought art on the most massive scale, in London, Paris, Amsterdam, Potsdam. In London the great collection of the impoverished Lord Walpole, intended for the British Museum, was knocked down to the monarch by the excellent Mr Christie.

In Paris she bought so much great collectors retired wounded from the fray. Leonardos and Van Dycks, Raphaels and Rembrandts, Veroneses and Dürers, were crated up and shipped off north. One famous collection, the Brankampf, went down in the Baltic while the ship's captain was carelessly praying. It didn't matter, there was plenty more. 'It's not love of art,' Catherine explained, 'it's pure and unvarnished greed. I'm more of a glutton than a taster.'

Soon she had a problem. Not only her palace, the Hermitage, but the fine imperial city of Petersburg itself became too small for the stuff she had bought. Now she had to buy architects to build great new galleries, academicians to open museums, sculptors to decorate the squares, philosophers to tell her what to think about it all.

'How things have changed,' said one philosopher, Denis Diderot, novelist, pornographer and creator of the French *Encyclopedia*, the great book of the Enlightenment itself, 'we sell our paintings and sculptures in peacetime, Catherine buys them in the midst of war. Now the sciences, arts, taste and philosophy have all departed for the North, and barbarism retreats to the South.'

These kind words came from one of the great free spirits of the eighteenth century. Yet in truth she happened to have bought him too. With great cunning, she made him the librarian of his own wonderful library (the Library of the Enlightenment), paying him a vast salary to keep his own books on his own shelves till he died. Then they, and his papers, would go from Paris to the Hermitage.

Diderot was an excellent acquisition. One of the great philosophers of an age of philosophy (the other was Voltaire, and Catherine sewed him up too), he knew everything. He scoured Paris for her, buying pictures, finding architects and sculptors. He sent musicians, milliners, ballet dancers and chefs north to Petersburg. When she wanted to raise a statue to her predecessor, Peter the Great (to one great from an even greater), he selected the French sculptor Falconet, and for good measure designed the statue – the *Bronze Horseman* – as well.

Then one day Catherine found herself between lovers (she had twenty or more over her reign, many carefully picked from the palace guard), so there was a window in her day. The lover's hours, between three and six in the afternoon, were free. She decided to spend the time on philosophy, and promptly summoned Diderot to the Hermitage.

He was now sixty, and had scarcely ever left Paris. The journey was grim, the Russian winter cold, he got the famous Neva colic. Still, each day, he taught the Empress. He was an enthusiastic teacher; she complained when he left each day her thighs were black and blue.

Yet they got on perfectly (and may have been lovers) and together they devised a perfect Enlightenment Russia, a Utopian society. It was a society dedicated to human rights: life, liberty, the pursuit of happiness. The serfs were freed, the parliament was independent. There were open schools, an independent police force, hundreds of universities.

When, after six months, Diderot went home, they parted very fondly. 'You have taught me everything,' wrote Catherine. 'How to be a great monarch, how to create an ideal Russia.' However she did add as an afterthought: 'There is just one difference between us. You write on paper. I write on human skin.'

True. While they talked, the Chechens of the day were executed on torture wheels rolled into villages; imperial claimants were often put to death in the Peter and Paul Fortress, visible from the Hermitage. Ideas were one thing, power another. But Catherine gained perfect publicity. She was hailed as the most enlightened ruler in the world.

Diderot died in 1784, six years after Voltaire. The books of both men went to the Hermitage. Catherine devised the most beautiful library to hold them, overlooking the Neva. It held one of the world's great collections of books and papers, as fine as the paintings (many chosen by Diderot) that hung in surrounding galleries, mile after mile.

In 1776 the American colonies rebelled against Britain. When First New Nation was formed, its Constitution followed the principles of Diderot's paper Utopia. In 1789 a similar revolution came to France as well. After all, French Men of Reason and Enlightenment had invented it. Alas, it was followed by the Terror.

When Louis XVI was guillotined, fear rang through the monarchies of Europe. Catherine at once kicked out the French, locked her library, and sent its centrepiece, a statue of Voltaire by Houdon, to the Hermitage attics. She died still afraid of revolution. By then it was said there wasn't a peasant left in Russia; all had become serfs. Soon Napoleon marched on Moscow. After that adventure, no Tzar cared to open the room again.

It became a mysterious place. From early on, the books and unpublished papers were raided and stolen. Diderot published little of his work in his lifetime. Now it began appearing in the strangest places – Germany, Russia, Italy, Britain. The Voltaire statue itself had many adventures. After the Russian Revolution it was put on a train and sent to the Kremlin. Returned to Leningrad, it left again on the last train out before the Germans besieged the city in the Second World War.

It was these papers and books, now housed in the Petersburg Public Library, that I went to see, following the shopaholic trail. I was to discover the plunder still continued, the books and papers being sold on the street.

Suppose, I thought, amongst this disintegrating library there was a great unpublished novel by Diderot, and it fell into my hands? I started a novel about it, Petersburg then and now, and called it *To the Hermitage*. Five years into the book, I returned to Petersburg. The library was now well protected, and the Hermitage had become a user-friendly place: surely the greatest art museum in the world.

Thanks to Catherine Russia acquired many more artistic shopaholics. In every generation the treasures of Europe were purchased, many by private collectors. Most lost their collections to the state when the bloodbath arrived at last in 1917, and the Tzars were no more. Now everybody should go to the Hermitage.

And if you do go, remember the first great shopaholic. She may not after all have created the perfect Russia. But she probably invented the consumer society, the designer-and-celebrity marketplace we all enjoy today. Which is why a lot of us should be grateful to Sophie von Anhalt-Zerbst. Otherwise Catherine the Great.

A MODEST PROPOSAL

LIKE MANY WRITERS, I seem to have spent a lot of my life not merely writing – that lonely inert activity that breeds back pains and strange fantasies – but coming up with various devices and notions intended to bring help to others trapped in my own situation. It so happened that I started to write, an innocent schoolboy, at a strange time, when writing was not what it is now. It was the austere period shortly after the end of the Second World War, when, for a juvenile Proust, the basic necessities of writing were hard to come by, and hard to afford.

It took years before I had saved enough to acquire the first essential of writerly existence: an old second-hand Remington Portable. The typewriter cost, as I recall it, a hefty £5, and was amazingly slow-working, needing oiling as often as a steam locomotive. Many of its keys were out of alignment, giving my work just that sort of incriminating character that had Alger Hiss in trouble not long after.

Even paper, recently rationed in wartime, was a problem: so expensive and scarce that most of my early work was done on the tattered backsides of other people's previous writing. Carbon paper, which in those days had a sticky-toffee surface and a smell that clung after work, was more expensive still, but indispensable; the only other way of making a copy was hiring a scribe or Dickensian clerk. The ball pen would soon be invented, but writing was in the age of the steel nib, and the new technology was still to come.

So writing was an underfunded, arduous, sometimes back-breaking form of secretarial work. It meant long days at the keys on a hard chair at an uncomfortable, half-lit desk. It was grim, done in a spirit of parsimony (always reuse old paper-clips), a climate of bohemian indigence and rejection. I can't remember how long it took to recoup the cost of that clanking typewriter, but it was several months of hard-written articles.

A Bob Cratchit of writing, I dreamed of better things. But it was only in the mid-fifties, when I moved for a while to the USA, that I discovered writers' paradise. Here, amid all the joys of American affluence, was everything the author needed; no wonder American novels were so good. There were glorious portable typewriters, light as a bird's feather, with flowing silver lines, fingertip touch, easyfit ribbons. There were great stores filled with writers' materials: every kind of paper, glorious yellow legal notepads, binders and folders, staplers and fixers, brilliant desk lamps, joyous filing cabinets, gunmetal desks on wheels that tracked round the room.

A natural philanthropist, I had always longed to help my fellow writers, especially at home. Now I dreamed of yet greater inventions, every kind of fantastic authorial possibility. Suppose typewriters could be driven not by thumping fingers but electricity, diesel, steam? Suppose they could become an intelligent machine, holding a dictionary so that every literal could be noted and corrected? Suppose they could format, design, publish, copy?

I was not, of course, alone in these immodest proposals. In the following years the act of writing changed faster than it had since Gutenberg. I was a natural customer for every new step. I stood first in line for the electric typewriter, when, big and purring, it was presented to the admiring community of writers and scholars. I was there when it yielded to the smaller, cleverer electronic typewriter, with self-correction and compact ribbons.

When the heritage of Babbage and Turing began bearing fruit, and the word processor came to market, I was there again. My own first example was a cumbersome screen affixed to a typewriter, which then churned out in an afternoon the work done in a morning. But wonder soon followed wonder. Soon the machine, in a glorious boldness, had become all-thinking. It had become author and dreamer, imaginer and conceiver, creator and genius, book and printer, editor and publisher, critic and reader. All my immodest proposals were satisfied, and some more.

Yet it overreached. It was instructive, intrusive, insistent, demanding. It found friends of its own, leasing its contents to someone else's machinery. It displayed messages I had not put there, yielded up facts I did not wish to know. It communicated, interrupted, asserted, complained. It became part of the world of redundancy, noise, superfluity, of excess communication and transmission.

Today my modest proposal is this. We now need to create a fresh instrument of writing, which needs no power supply and is not interactive. It writes what the mind tells it and not what it pleases. It requires no printers, toners, software, backup. It does not urge, pressure, warn, insist, or cry for help. It is not subject to the millennium bug.

It is made of simple materials: wood from the forest, lead from the soil. It is cheap to construct, just a core and a shell. It loves and licks the paper it works on. With it novels, poems, plays, histories, geographies, biographies, love letters, constitutions and legal documents can be perfectly well created. It will restore the writer to writing, the imagination to its proper role. I shall simply call it the pencil.

JOHN BLACKWELL

23 October 1937 to 5 November 1997

JOHN BLACKWELL, who died suddenly on Wednesday at the age of sixty, was one of the great publishing editors, indeed almost the last of the glorious pre-corporate breed. At the end of the sixties he joined Secker & Warburg, where Frederic Warburg and David Farrer were formidable presences, and Tom Rosenthal would become one. All were outstanding editors and impassioned supporters of their serious authors. Blackwell sustained, more than sustained, the spirit that made this the house so many authors wanted to or were proud to belong to. He worked with Angus Wilson, sometimes guiding the final shape and structure of his ever more complex and Dickensian texts. His stable of writers came to include André Brink, J. M. Coetzee, Saul Bellow at times, Michael Moorcock, George V. Higgins, Tom McGuane, Tom Sharpe, David Lodge, Louis de Bernières, Maurice Leitch, Guy Bellamy, many more. He sustained and promoted that remarkable list of modern European authors, Thomas Mann to Günter Grass and Italo Calvino, that made Secker a key publisher of international and modernist writing. He was a wonderful editor of fiction, and no less of works of scholarship: an ideal editor for writers whose work embraced both fiction and scholarly research.

If you happened to be one of his favoured authors (in more recent years he concentrated, finally as a freelance, on his own selected list), it was a form of fearful pleasure to deliver a manuscript to him. The text was meticulously read and studied, its structure analysed and considered, its errors and infelicities eradicated, its foreign quotations examined to destruction, its scholarship tested, often in the most arcane ways. Telephone calls exploring strange byways of the subject could come at any time of day or night. His letters were wonderful, indeed publishable. Sudden visits would occur, a once pristine manuscript reappearing, now extensively marked with yellow strips. Queries of such complexity would arise that days or weeks had to be assigned to explore points raised by his learning, scepticism, linguistic knowledge, exuberant curiosity, amazing memory. Because he was the most genial and convivial of editors, this happened in a mood of great delight. Rumour said that authors whose manuscripts failed Blackwell standards would receive odd night-time visits: wads of critical queries deposited through the letter box, their bearer meantime mysteriously disappearing into the London gloom.

Mystery shrouded, suited John Blackwell. It is a matter of fact he was born in Coventry, went to its King Henry VIII Grammar School, then entered naval intelligence for his National Service in 1955. He intensively learned Russian on a Scottish pig farm, trained as an intelligence spy, and acquired various arts of secrecy, strange knowledge and self-disguise which never quite left him. From here on, one cannot be quite precise. In a time of Cold War tension and the Gary Powers crisis, he audited Russian radio air traffic: some say in a hut in Turkey, others in a submarine off Cyprus, others in the Baltic, probably all three. He went to Jesus College, Cambridge, from 1958 to 1961, read English, and here met his wife Pamela, whom he married in 1966. After a spell as hospital orderly, schoolteacher, kitchen porter, he edited the journal of the Iron and Steel Institute, which explains that intimate knowledge of Paxton and the Bessemer process with which he sometimes confronted authors. He was a deeply convivial man and an instinctive bohemian, yet one whose personal life stayed interestingly shaded and obscure.

What is certain is that he took writing and publishing with an intense seriousness now foreign to the age of communications conglomerates, accountant management, open-plan offices, corporate bottom lines. The task was simple: the publication of good books, studied books, complicated books, thoughtful books, books that took a long time to write, digest, win proper recognition. For each he would spend days considering typefaces, testing layouts, writing perfect jacket copy, refining proofs. As Secker & Warburg moved from Georgianized houses in Bloomsbury and Soho to Michelin House and the Vauxhall Bridge Road, his way of working – long hours, night-time stints, pub conferences, a sceptic's view of clock time – grew more displaced, and he increasingly worked from home. For him, publishing did not belong to suits, conference rooms, corporate networkers, but to authors and books; books were not generic objects or commodities, but the strange workings of mind their authors tracked. He was the kind of editor one wrote for, the first ideal reader whose judgement counted most. He was a carver of wood and, in later years, a great skier and lover of mountains. He leaves a widow, Pamela, and a group of writers whose work would not be as it is without him.

MORTAL FICTIONS

LET US RETURN a moment to the Booker Prize for Fiction in 1828, the year no prizes at all were awarded. It will be recalled that Sir Walter Scott was chosen to chair the judges. In his Guildhall speech, he remarked on the truly lamentable state of British fiction, observing that there was now only one great novelist and it was improper for him to say who it was.

Yet Russian writing prospered: the excellent Mr Pushkin was fantasizing about Peter the Great yet again. France had the splendid M. Hugo, a proponent of that most important of contemporary forms, the historical novel. Philosophically and romantically, German literature flourished like some exotic blue flower, as Mr Carlyle had just shown in his brilliant new book on the matter.

Consider our American cousins, who a few years ago were despised for having no literature whatsoever. Now Mr Irving (on your Chairman's own advice) had lately been to Germany and shut himself up in Spain's Alhambra in order to invent, or perhaps one should say borrow, the new American folk tale. Mr Cooper's excellent Indians (some said they were Scots dressed in warpaint) were now the greatest Parisian vogue (why did the Parisians love Indians so much?). The problem was the British novel. If he might say so (and who better to say so?), the novel in Britain was dead.

True: but a very poor prophecy. Just at that moment, the young Mr Dickens was starting to get a few scraps into print. Mr Disraeli the lawyer was already writing pseudonymous novels with his left hand. Mr Thackeray would soon be hounded out of Cambridge with a living to earn. Before the

Reform Bill was over and done, things would start looking much better in this matter of modern fiction.

By the time the new little Queen ascended, they were growing tumultuous. No one will forget the remarkable Bookers of the 1840s, when shortlists sometimes had to run to ten or twelve. For, fed by the great historical transformations that came from Puffing Billies, steaming milltowns, massings of population into cities old and new, the general impress of the moving age, the Victorian novel, the novel of novels, was born.

And not just in Britain, with Dickens, Thackeray, Trollope, the strange, endless tribe of Yorkshire Bells. It was an international explosion, a positive carnival of fiction. In France M. Hugo led on to MM. Balzac, Stendhal and Sand. Pushkin showed us the way to Gogol, who then pointed to Dostoevsky. Cooper turned into Hawthorne, Melville, and Poe.

If the Victorian age was anything, it was an age of the novel, one of the best there has been. Yet before it was done and the Queen had left us, the novel was dead again – at roughly ten-year intervals (Dickens' death in 1870, George Eliot's in 1880, Thomas Hardy's *Jude* burned by a bishop in 1895). Luckily, no sooner did it die than it rose again, if in somewhat different clothing.

So it went on. It fell again in the Great War, to return in experimental dress in the twenties (Woolf, Joyce, Kafka, Faulkner). It again took mortal wounds in World War Two, to come back in the fifties, when papers like this one celebrated a 'new movement' in fiction and poetry. When the Booker Prize was founded in 1970, that was chiefly because the serious novel in Britain was dead again – as everyone complained, especially the many British novelists.

Thus the dirge over fiction is common – and usually quite unnecessary. Yet it takes a millennium to put these matters of literary life and death into their true perspective. For the lifespan of the novel has hardly been more than a glorious episode, a stage in a larger history: the long humanistic story of books and literature.

Just before his death in 1985, the Italian novelist Italo Calvino gave Harvard's distinguished Charles Eliot Norton lectures. His vigorous observations, a celebration of the high arts of fiction, were published posthumously in 1992, nicely entitled *Six Memos for the Next Millennium*. For these lectures show not just the maverick energies of his rich and experimental mind; they also give his thoughts on the future.

The millennium, this one, that would shortly end was, he remarked, remarkable for being the millennium of the book. It had seen the development of the modern languages of the West, and the literature that carried and explored its ideas, possibilities and fantasies. It was a clear sign of its ending that we now spent so much time wondering apocalyptically what, in the post-industrial, high-tech millennium to come, would happen to the book.

Typically Calvino, always the futurist, gave a joyous answer. He summoned up the great canon of literature, through Ovid, Dante, Boccaccio, Swift, Sterne, Musil, Joyce, Kafka, Borges, Kundera, to argue that the state of mind and human being it represented, the dreams and promises it stored, were indispensable. He said his confidence in literature's future lay in the fact that it had certain permanent things to give: 'Among the values I would like passed on to the next millennium, there is this above all: a literature that has absorbed the taste for mental orderliness and exactitude, the intelligence of poetry, but at the same time science and philosophy.'

So would I. But how confident can we feel today, as the countdown rolls, about his confidence? He offered his engaging memos in 1985: fifteen (or on my count sixteen) years before the arrival of the Four Horsemen, and four before the Berlin Wall came down. Shortly after his sudden death, the great ideological map of the century changed; the statues tumbled, defaced and deconstructed, all over Eastern Europe.

Soon came the End of History, shortly followed by the dawn of the present, all-singing, all-dancing postmodern Age of Shopping. As we get ever closer to what we are now being taught to call the People's Millennium (we'll all go together when we go), a good many more statues seem to be tumbling, and not just in Eastern Europe. The book isn't dead; isn't everyone buying *Bridget Jones's Diary*? What, though, about literature? And the novel – not just the novel, but The Novel?

The splendid humanistic canon that Calvino instinctively inhabited with such lightness of being (Ovid to Kundera) and handed on like a torch to the future is not looking comfortable. After all, it is primarily a list of (mostly) Dead White European Males – busily being theorized out of existence by its own supposed guardians and custodians, the literary scholars and critics, who are themselves the prophets of 'decanonization'.

Calvino knew all about the Death of the Author, which is supposed to bring the Birth of the Reader. He wrote one of the most brilliant (postmodern) novels on the matter, *If on a winter's night a traveller*, where two modern readers attempt to compose a novel from a set of confusing and uncompleted fragments. But he didn't know about the new reader of the postmodern age, who is instinctively not white, European or male (even when he is).

The new reader – empowered (his own favourite word) by the critics – is Miss Whiplash, contemporary, post-colonial, multicultural. She is no devotee of canons or traditions. She's a people's reader, no humanist. Indeed the humanism of the Enlightenment, which gave its spirit to much of modern literature, is also being theorized out of existence by our excellent philosophical custodians.

This impulse of decanonization and deconstruction is familiar enough: End of the World news that goes with a turnover decade, a fin de siècle. In the same chiliastic way, the Romantics inaugurated a new literary calendar, the Moderns ransacked the museums, upturned the tradition. Neither, however, dispensed with it totally. T. S. Eliot reminded us we needed tradition to teach us our own contemporaneity: 'Someone said: "The dead writers are remote from us because we know so much more than they did." Precisely, and they are that which we know.'

He was reflecting on what Harold Bloom called 'the anxiety

of influence' – the power the books of the past exert over the anxious, necessary innovation of the present. Yet we, in our postmodern way, seem to perceive ourselves as curiously historyless, in a world where history and tradition present themselves as comic icons, guilty secrets, theme-park nostalgia. Eliot perceived a past with too much power over the present. We perceive an all-embracing present with little past to it at all.

Many McLuhanite anxieties have been produced about the closing of the Gutenberg Galaxy, the fading away of the book in the new global village, the Information Superhighway, Intel Inside. I have little doubt that the book will survive. It is one of the great and truly ingenious technologies, and it merges easily with the new technologies and media. Half of our films are based on books; word processing is a form of creative writing and publishing.

My worry is not about what happens to books, but about what happens to what is inside them. Calvino trusted it would be literature, especially in the form of one of its most triumphant, original creations, the novel. And by literature he meant that work of orderliness, intelligence, poetry, science and philosophy that was his futuristic extension of humanism.

Oh, there will be novels. But will they be great novels, storehouses of enquiring human values, or just fictive publications? Unlike Calvino, I am no longer sure. Miss Whiplash – with her degree in holistic media studies and windsurfing, and her post-cultural world-reforming agenda – may not like them. Of course I could be wrong in my chiliastic thoughts; most people have been. Better ask me again when the apocalypse is over. Shall we say the Booker in 2028?

LIAR'S LANDSCAPE

Notion for a New Novel

The story of the American writer, romantic and diplomat François-René de Chateaubriand and his visit to the new United States of America during the course of the French Revolution. He travelled (and lied about where he travelled); he began a book about the experience, *Atala*, which has claim to be the first American novel ever. It was written, strangely, in Bungay, in the Waveney Valley (in a house now lived in by Elizabeth Jane Howard), where he became an indigent tutor (and the father of a child). It won Chateaubriand his fame back in France, from which he had fled. He returned, became a supporter of Napoleon, and went with him to Egypt, writing now of the great romance of the Pharaohs and the Nile. His fame grew; he was the French Byron or Pushkin. He told and retold his personal story in book after book. He became French Ambassador to Britain, and while based in London met again the girl from Bungay he seduced. His memoirs grew lusher and lusher; in final form they were published as *Memoirs From the Other Side of the Tomb*.

The present version of the story is told from the further side of the tomb: today, in the language of today, and with knowledge of all the events that have happened in history since. It's a continuation of *To the Hermitage* (Chateaubriand was a disciple of Diderot) into the next age: of revolution, romanticism and the haunted self. And much of it is about the fantastic America that Chateaubriand created and has lasted in time: the world of romantic Indians, lost tribes, great rivers and forests, that fed every imagination from James Fenimore Cooper to Walt Disney. Chateaubriand's fantasy was based on the fact that from a French point of view America was the 'lost lands', the great American empire first taken off the French by the British and then (what was left of it) sold by Napoleon to Jefferson in the Louisiana purchase of 1803, which happened just as Chateaubriand's book appeared.

'Man, you are but a hasty dream, a vision of sorrow; you exist only as misery; you are something only by the sadness of your soul and the eternal melancholy of your thought.'

François-René de Chateaubriand, *Atala* (1801)

'*Bien sur!* He invented America; a very great man.'

Mademoiselle de Nioche on Columbus
Henry James, *The American* (1877)

'What you have to do is enter the fiction of America – enter America as fiction.'

Jean Baudrillard, *Amérique* (1986)

'The unendurable oppression of the lungs – the stifling fumes of the damp earth – the clinging of the death garments – the rigid embrace of the narrow house – the blackness of the absolute Night – the silence like a sea that overwhelms – the unseen but palpable presence of the Conqueror Worm – these things, with the thoughts of the air and grass above, with memory of dear friends who would fly to save us if but informed of our fate, and with consciousness of this fate they can never be informed – that our hopeless portion is that of the really dead – these considerations, I say, carry into the heart, which still palpitates, a degree of appalling and intolerable horror from which the most daring imagination must recoil.'

Edgar Allan Poe, 'The Premature Burial' (1850)

REMARKABLE RAIN AT DETROIT

THE YEAR 1763 proved a very busy one. That was the year James Boswell first bumped into Dr Samuel Johnson. In the American colonies, two obscure British land surveyors, Charles Mason and Jeremiah Dixon, drew a dividing line along the Ohio River between Pennsylvania and Maryland that would one day separate the Northern states from the Southern, the free from the slave, so mapping the ground for a civil war. It was the time when modern philosophers, the men of the Enlightenment, plainly triumphed. That year the French sage Voltaire published his *Treatise on Tolerance* (he was mostly for it), Denis Diderot wrote his strange wonderful novella *Rameau's Nephew*, while every person of feeling was reading the romances and considering the new social contracts of Jean-Jacques Rousseau. The French sculptor Etienne-Maurice Falconet completed his rococo masterwork *Pygmalion and Galathea*, prior to setting out for St Petersburg to construct the great *Bronze Horseman*, a statue of Peter the Great, for the Russian Empress Catherine II, who had ascended the imperial throne the year before, and was on her way to becoming quite Great herself. Hargreaves invented the spinning jenny, so a whole new age of technologies, mills, looms, factories, clock-work and timekeeping was about to begin.

And that year too, at the great court of Versailles, the Treaty of Paris was signed, concluding the Seven Years War, which had brought so many of the great powers of Europe into conflict, in so many places: not just on their own troubled continent, but in India, the Caribbean and North America too. Thanks to Clive in India, and Wolfe in Canada, the peace was a triumph for Great Britain, and gave her fresh wealth, new imperial dreams, a command of land and sea. Under the Treaty the most serene and most potent George III, just lately become the round new King, had a vastly grown empire to rule and be ruled by, taking control of French Canada and Cape Breton Island, and former French lands right across to the Mississippi, as well as Tobago, Dominica, Calcutta, Madras, Pondicherry – so the British Empire now contained huge numbers of indigenous peoples the British knew nothing about at all.

And that in turn meant it was a bad year for the French, who lost two empires in their two Indies: the Indian empire, and the rich American lands of Canada and Louisiana, so important for trade – though they did retain fishing banks off Newfoundland and recover the sugar islands of Guadaloupe and Martinique. It was not a good year for the elder Pitt, who wished fighting to continue, and thought what had been won by war had been lost by the peace. But the peace made it an excellent year for British traders and the British gentlemen whose taxes paid for war. In fact, the historians tell us, 1763 could be called the first year of modernity itself: the year when the balance of powers and the map of European empires changed profoundly, when the philosophies of reform and enlightenment spread, new notions of monarchy, republicanism, freedom and liberty began to develop, and new technologies began a period of rapid change. In fact, with a New Europe, a New America, a New India, new technologies, new political ideals, you could well say that the world was turning upside down, that the Age of Reason was losing its reason, and an Age of Revolutions was about to begin.

IN THAT YEAR, when a great peace began to fall over the lands of North America, a man named Jonathan Carver, a middle-aged army captain born in Weymouth, Massachusetts, quite suddenly found himself with nothing at all to do. For the last seven years he had served in the King's armies, fighting in the French and Indian Wars that spread through the deep woods and virgin forests of the continent: across Canada and down the St Lawrence; around the Finger Lakes and down the Hudson River; along the Ohio, into the Appalachians; down the Missouri River and the Mississippi, even taking in the great torrents and steaming falls of the continent's greatest wonder, the Falls of Niagara themselves. It was a war of tricks and traps, sudden silent ambushes and howling massacres, stealthy pursuits, devious alliances, wooden forts, tented camps and dank stockades. It was a world where British redcoats, German hessians, Indian redmen, coon-skinned trappers and angry planters fought side by side. It was waged in a near-virgin world of half-settlement, where in the course of exploration vast regions had been labelled New France, New Spain, New Holland, and where Indian place names (Ticonderoga, Susquehanna) mixed with the most elegant and classical of titles: Athens, Palmyra, Syracuse, Arcadia. And now his most serene and most potent Majesty had proclaimed four new regions for himself (Quebec, East Florida, West Florida, Grenada) the name would change yet again.

Carver had been a fine colonial soldier. He'd portaged the rivers, trekked through the forests of maple and sumac, explored huge and amazing inland waterways, holed up with frightened armies in damp stockades, witnessed and nearly died in the sudden Indian massacres where the scalp was the valued trophy, penetrated lands settled only by Indian traders. He'd seen the vast inland lakes of Canada, come to the great Falls of Niagara − which, a century before, the great French traveller Father Hennepin had described as a place of such thunder that all human noise fell silent, and animals and birds fluttered away in fear. He'd learned an Indian language, Chippewa, discovered how to trick and treat with the satchems, gathered fair knowledge of the customs of the devious, dangerous yet often glowingly friendly tribes.

Yet now, a whole world away, a war that had gone on too long had suddenly come to an end. The sounds of battle ceased, the American woods felt empty. A great empire faded away into misty forests, as the French withdrew, returning to their homeland or hiding in distant corners, anticipating return. The

Indian leagues were forced into new alliances, or began new hostilities, fighting on their own account now the French had gone. Forts burned in the forests, riverbank settlements were rottting on their piles. Meanwhile a new pioneering age began as, with the power of the French receding, the Anglo-colonists began to push into the opening world. A vast mysterious universe was beginning to open, though against the King's advice. 'Let the savages enjoy their deserts in quiet,' advised the British General Gage. For, as his serene Majesty saw, now the borders of his colonies had broken, his colonists might now run free.

The truth was that for several centuries there had been, across the Atlantic, not just one New World but many. Spanish America, made of gold and silver, great ancient cities shimmering high in the Andes or on the Mexican marshes. Portuguese America, a land of pampa, plantation, slaves. French America, which spread from the cod-heavy Grand Banks through Lawrentian ice caps to the inner lakes of Canada, then on down the spinal river, 'the Great River called the Savages' Mississippi', that led to swamps, savannahs and the tropic sea of the Mexican gulf. Knickerbocker America, on the Hudson River: tribal, cautious, mercantile, made of Dutch-burgher households with names like Gansevoort, Roosevelt and Van Winkle. German America: religious, Lutheran, orderly, strict. Each had a landscape, an architecture, a culture, a faith. And then there was British America, coastal, costive, hugging and holding the long Eastern shore.

Here were fertile lands where turkeys cackled, sweetcorn and cranberries grew. Cod leapt from the sea into the net, cotton prospered, sotweed flowered. Fine bays, harbours and estuaries served a triangular trade that brought goods and plenty, wealth and prospects, migrants and slaves. Villages grew into towns and towns into cities in the European fashion. Where there had been virgin forest, colleges and universities rose. High churches stood on corners, statues appeared in squares. On fine plantations great houses rose in long prospects. Elms lined the drives, as they might in England, though boled with Spanish moss. Black slaves and not indentured labourers worked the fields; guinea fowl honked instead of peacocks; hunts chased raccoon or bear rather than the fox. Post-roads were being cut. Newspapers were printed, academies and hospitals raised. In an age of new science electricity was discovered here by coon-hatted Mr Benjamin Franklin, the wisest man in the world. It was all as Bishop Berkeley, kicking the stones in his Oxford quad, had prophesied: 'Westward the course of Empire takes its way. / The first four acts already past. / A fifth shall close the drama with the day, / Time's noblest offspring is the last.' This fifth Western empire was now growing. But how deep into the continent sat its frontiers and termini? How far did it reach? Could it be that it would spread onward and westward till the great circle was completed, Atlantic linked with Pacific, the West joined up with the East?

Who could know? It was the departing French who had touched the real heartlands while the British hugged the Europe-facing shore. Long before Pilgrim Fathers landed at Plymouth Plantation, the Jesuit Fathers had gone everywhere, mastered the forests and lakelands, prairies, tundra, ice cap, savannah, swamp. They were the ones who risked darkness, howling wilderness. They found lands far stranger than any of the British possessions: more mysterious, savage, ancient, obscure, undefined. The King wanted these lands left alone, and banned westward migration. But there were so many rumoured wonders: lost cities, old civilizations, unusual tribes, gold, silver and new minerals, unknown beasts and birds. Great mountains, twisting rivers, huge sublimities: wandered by Indians and trappers, friars and penitents, Spanish hidalgos, mysterious shamans, Siberian tribes. Somewhere in this, they had claimed (yet could any of these things be true?), were the vastest of rivers, the highest of mountains, the most spectacular of deserts, where sands glowed with each colour of the spectrum as the sun went down. Here were animals, birds and vermin of species still unrecorded; trees, herbs, vegetables with special medicinal powers not yet tapped. Turkeys weighed seventy pounds or more, skeins of geese flew in flights over seven miles long. The land rolled westward, beyond French lands to Spanish ones, past the mountains of the moon to the western sea. By lakes, passages, portages there must be a way through – the Passage to India, Carver called it. From Columbus on, travellers had gone west to find the East. Now the French were no longer in the way. As Carver saw, it was time to pursue the arts of peace with just the same energy he had pursued the arts of war. He had fine skills, an ambitious spirit, an adventurer's instincts, a lively pen. He saw his chance. He decided to put down the sword and become an explorer.

'No sooner was the late war with France concluded, and a peace established by the Treaty of Versailles in the year 1763, than I began to consider (having rendered my country some services during the war) how I might continue still serviceable, and contribute, as much as lay in my power, to make that vast acquisition of territory, gained by Great-Britain in North America, advantageous to it,' he wrote in the story of what happened to him next. 'It appeared to be indispensably needful, that government be acquainted, in the first place, with the true state of the dominions they were now become possessed of. To this purpose I determined, as the next proof of my zeal, to explore the most unknown parts of them, and to spare no trouble or experience in acquiring a knowledge that promised to be useful to my countrymen.' So in the month of May 1766 Jonathan Carver set off from the pleasant American city of Boston, searching for the Northwest Passage to the far Pacific.

YET THERE WAS, as he noted in his record, one small problem – and rather a curious one. The departing French had bequeathed their successors a huge and seemingly vacant hinterland, but also an odd difficulty. For decades now, while the British had founded their cities and villages, cut canals, invented the pot-bellied stove, the French, with their priests, trappers, soldiers, Indian allies, displaced second sons of Parisian gentlemen, had been wandering everywhere. They sailed all the waterways, set up their trading posts, converted, won over or quite often slaughtered the noble savages, trafficked in herbs, gums, pelts, fish and tobaccos. By 1682 the explorer La Salle, going south from Canada, had come to the estuary of the Mississippi: 'Now the waters grew bitter to the taste; now the trampling of the surf was heard; and their goal was won.' With a firing of muskets and shouts of *Vive le roi*, La Salle took Louisiana, in the name of Louis the Great, King of France and Navarre. It took years to settle, decades to secure key positions in between. Meanwhile the British were advancing, 'forests crashing in the dark, dark spires of smoke ascending from autumnal fires . . . The hour of collision was at hand.'*

Everywhere the French had gone they had kept annals, written the record, sent it home to France. They mapped the great interior, named the districts, settlements, townships, peaks and bluffs, currents and shallows, dedicated churches and shrines to Gallic saints. They attached their own names to the tribes, planted words everywhere. Nothing lacked a description: Terre Haute and Prairie Le Chien, Frontenac and Plaisance, Porte des Mortes and Vincennes, Des Moines and Argentia. They named the strange creatures everywhere to be seen: buffalo on the plains (*buffle*), moose in the woods (*élan*), parakeets in the trees (*perruche*), raccoons in the bushes (*raton*), alligators in the swamps (*alligator*). They converted the tribes to versions of Parisian religions, itemized Indian customs and beliefs. They even shipped sample Indians back home to Paris, so they could be studied (along with the *buffles* and *perruches*) as perfect examples of New World nature by philosophers like Buffon and Raynal, Rousseau and Diderot. They considered the New World as philosophical dilemma: was it the Earthly Paradise, pure and unsullied, the ideal form of the social contract; or was it a place of hellish decadence, corrupt, debased and depraved? In the France of the day the gallant Indians turned up everywhere: the dramas of Voltaire, the operas of

---

* Francis Parkman, *The Conspiracy of Pontiac and the Indian War After the Conquest of Canada* (2 vols., New York, 1851).

Rameau. The Noble Savage became ideal to a whole new school of philosophy.

So when the French lost their two Indies, they went not just into political but philosophical mourning – for they had lost mental territory, a realm of knowledge. Even so, the entire mid-continent was mapped and written in French: the language of Catholicism, reason, oratory, hyperbole, exoticism. But that wasn't all. With typical Gallic cunning the French cheated. As Carver explains, 'while they retained their power in North-America', the French had taken 'every artful method to keep other nations, especially the English, in ignorance of the interior parts of it; and to accomplish this design with greater certainty, they had published inaccurate maps and false accounts: calling the Indians by nicknames they had given them, and not those really pertaining to them.' Not a single thing they had said could be called reliable. For instance, they had even quite deliberately overestimated the height of Niagara Falls. 'The sources of the Mississippi, I can attest from my own experience, are greatly misplaced,' complained Carver. In fact nothing was as it was, where it was, called what it should be. The whole American interior was a Gallic fiction: a liar's landscape. Yet if these lands could be re-explored, renamed, remapped, using not the flourish of Gallic exoticism but good British empiricism, 'this I am convinced would greatly facilitate the discovery of a northwest passage, or a communication between Hudson's Bay and the Pacific Ocean.'

Which, of course, was what the great American game was about. As Adam Smith would say in another momentous year, 1776, in his great economic work *The Wealth of Nations*: 'The discovery of America, and that of a passage to the East Indies . . . are the two greatest and most important events in the history of mankind.' How splendid then, Carver proposed, if it were possible to put them together, so that the first would lead directly to the second, by way of a Passage to India, the *buffles* and *perruches* of the Americas directing the way to the elephants, apes and peacocks of the East. And it was with these useful thoughts in mind that Carver set off from Boston on three years of explorations through the wonderful lush lands of America – where every single thing you encountered was called by the wrong name.

HE GOES FROM Boston to Albany, gateway on the fringe of the frontier, then to Oswego, on Lake Ontario, not so very far from where you'll find the Baseball Museum and James Fenimore Cooper's childhood home at Cooperstown in upper New York State. He passes by the great torrent of Niagara, scene of a famous Indian massacre, the Massacre of the Black Hole in Pontiac's all too recent Rebellion. On through the huge inland waters: Lake Erie, Lake Huron, on to Lake Michigan. Passing by False Presqu-Isle, by West Duck, by Great Duck, he comes to a key destination, once founded by the Jesuits as a mission station. This is the fur-traders' centre of Michilimackinac, or 'Great Turtle' in the Indian tongue. Here the stockades still show the signs of the memorable massacre of 1763, and local Indians still follow the unnerving custom of firing their muskets just over the heads of their guests to bid them welcome.* Carver knows he has entered the most dangerous of regions. Here the local tribes long in alliance with the French or Spanish have been encouraged by the conspiracies of the Ottawas, told by prophecy that the great French king is not dead but sleeping and will soon return. They are

---

* 'Mackinac Island (pop. 942). Originally called Michilimackinac, or "Great Turtle", by the Indians, time and usage shortened Mackinac Island's name. It became a frontier outpost when the English moved the old French garrison on the mainland to the more strategic island in 1780. Transportation on the island is by carriage, bicycle or horse; no automobiles are permitted. **Mackinaw City** (pop. 934, alt. 591). On the straits of Mackinac, Mackinaw City was first settled by French traders who built a fort here. In 1761, after the French and Indian war, it was taken over by the English. Two years later the fort was burned by the Indians and the garrison massacred. Mackinac Straits Bridge connects the mainland to the Upper Peninsula at St Ignace. Built at a cost of $1,000,000,000, the five-mile bridge is one of the longest suspension bridges in the world.' (*Guide Book*)

deceptive and unreliable allies who continue to slaughter British regiments come to the former zones of New France.*

Boldly looking to a glorious future, he presses on by canoe and portage. Into Lake Michigan, across to Green Bay, over to Lake Winnebago. Here, beside the Fox and the Ousconsin Rivers, two great systems of contradictory flows of water meet and cross. One passage flows off backwards, two thousand miles east, through a network of lakes into the St Lawrence river, till it finds the sea in the chill North Atlantic. The other flows another three thousand miles southward, through swamps and floodplains, rolling and building till the great river La Salle once traced, the Mississippi, races through the savannahs and into the Mexican gulf. 'I could have stepped from the one to the other,' Carver says. He goes on and arrives at the Indian town of Saukies, 'the largest and best built Indian town I ever saw', he says. In a pleasant air of contentment, Indian braves smoke pipes on little porches, and consult tame rattlesnakes they worship as spirits. Further on is Prairie Le Chien (Dogtown), another Indian town built by the waters of the Mississippi, where in time John Jacob Astor will set up a branch of his fur-trading company Astoria.

---

* 'Michilimackinac, 12 June, 1773. Sir: Notwithstanding what I wrote you in my last, that all the savages were arrived, and that everything seemed in perfect tranquillity, yet on the 4th inst. the Chippeways, who live on a plain near this fort, assembled to play ball, as they have done every day since their arrival. They played from morning to noon; then throwing the ball close to the gate, and observing Lieut. Lesley and me a few paces out of it, they came behind us, seized us and carried us into the woods.

In the meantime the rest rushed into the Fort, where they found their squaws, whom they had previously planted there, with their hatchets under their blankets, which they took, and in an instant killed Lieut. Jamet and fifteen rank and file, and a trader named Tracy. They wounded two, and took the rest of the Garrison prisoners, five of whom they have since killed.'

The tale grows worse, with scalpings and cannibalism, until new British troops at last return. It is told at length in Francis Parkman, *The Conspiracy of Pontiac* – a narrative by the great American historian intended, he said, to 'portray the American forest and the American Indian at the period when both received their final doom.'

'I bought a canoe and with two servants, one a French
Canadian, the other a Mohawk of Canada,' Carver explains.*
The Mississippi flows south before his eyes, less a vast river
than a flood plain, its waters bearing logs and corpses, dying
animals and tumbling rocks as Ole Man River rolls on, drawing
in tributary after tributary as he sails down to the mighty sea.
Carver goes not downriver but north, to Lake Pepin, then the
Falls of St Anthony – a place recorded, he thinks, by only two
white men: a generation ago by the Jesuit Father Hennepin,
now by himself. Writing it down, it occurs to him that he sits
at the heart of all. He has reached the point where not only are
all pastures verdant but four, not two, of the great rivers of the
continent – the St Lawrence and the Mississippi, the Bourbon
and the river he calls the Oregon – seem to find common
source. This is the pumping heart, the four-valved aorta, of the
American body: four rivers discharge in opposite directions to
four great seas – 'to the bay of St Lawrence, east; to the bay of
Mexico, south; to Hudson's Bay, north; and to the bay at the
Straits of Annian [the Pacific], west.' Oh, glory. It seems to
Carver he has found the heart and soul of America, the seat of
all journeys.

Through the cold winter of 1766 Jonathan Carver stays
with the local tribe, the Naudowessies, intending to head west
to the Pacific in spring of the new year. The Naudowessies are
friendly and hospitable. He enjoys their begging dances, boasting dances, scalp dances, takes part in their feasts. By the time
the snows have melted he is one of the guys. The Naudowessies
insist he attends their great Algonquin intertribal powwow,
held at a famous venue, the Grand Cave on the Mississippi,
where the chiefs 'settle their operations for the ensuing year.

---

* **'Prairie du Chien** (pop. 5,649, alt. 635). Second oldest city in the state of
Wisconsin, Prairie du Chien is situated below high, wooded bluffs near the
confluence of the Mississippi and Wisconsin Rivers . . . In the backwaters of
the Mississippi are beds of colorful Egyptian lotus which bloom about the
first of August. *Prairie Gal*, a replica of the old paddlewheel steamer, offers
river cruises from the Villa Louis Landing.' (*Guide Book*)

At the same time they carry with them their dead, for inter-
ment.' Carver is the toast of the occasion, the belle or the beau
of the Naudowessie ball: 'I had the honour to be installed or
adopted a chief of their bands.' Asked to give a short speech at
the close of proceedings, he rises magnificently to the occasion,
speaking in a style of discourse that will resound through
generations, whenever white man speaks to red, or red to
white.

'My brothers, chiefs of the numerous and powerful Naudowessies!' he says. 'I rejoice that through my long abode with
you, I can now speak to you (though after an imperfect
manner) in your own tongue . . . I rejoice also that I have an
opportunity so frequently to inform you of the glory and
power of the Great King that reigns over the English and other
nations; who is descended from a very ancient race of sover-
eigns, as old as the earth and the waters, whose feet stand on
two great islands, larger than any of you have ever seen, amidst
the greatest waters of the world; whose head reaches to the
sun, and whose arms encircle the whole earth; the number of
whose warriors is equal to the trees in the valleys, the stalks
of rice in yonder marshes, or the blades of grass on your great
plains; who has hundreds of canoes of his own, of such amazing
bigness, that all the waters of your country would not suffice
for one of them to swim in . . .' Naturally this gets a standing
ovation and several pipes of peace.

With the sound of loud applause ringing in his ears, Carver
makes his way to the settlement of Detroit by Lake Michigan,
intending to stock up and set off on the search for the
Northwest Passage that lies somewhere, he knows, just ahead.*

---

* 'Detroit, Michigan (pop. 1,670,144, alt. 635). Greatest automobile
manufacturing city in the world, Detroit is the oldest city of any size west
of the original seaboard colonies and is today the fifth city of population in the
United States. The French settled Detroit in 1701 and gave the city its name
from their words meaning 'strait', referring to the twenty-seven-mile-long
Detroit River which connects Lake Erie and Lake St Clair. Greenfield
Village. See the laboratory where Edison created the electric light, visit the

His adventures continue, wonders never cease. He learns, for instance, about the remarkable rain in Detroit, which had fallen just a few years earlier, as the French days ended in disorder and a time of treacheries and massacres. 'In the year 1762, in the month of July, it rains on this town and the parts adjacent, a sulphorous water the colour and consistence of ink; some of which being collected into bottles, and wrote with, appeared perfectly intelligible on the paper, and answered every purpose of that useful liquid. Soon after, the Indian war already spoken of, broke out in these parts. I mean not to say this incident was ominous of them, notwithstanding it is well known that innumerable well-attested instances of extraordinary phenomena happening before extraordinary events, have been recorded in almost every age by historians of veracity.' The Indian war was the great conspiratorial rebellion of Pontiac, chief of the Ottawas, who still paid homage to the kings of France and refused to accept the British. So came one of the most famous of all the Indian massacres; the town of Detroit was besieged and savaged for five months.

Was the strange story of black rain at Detroit true or not (it is still often retold)? Some people, Carver says, have gone so far as to accuse him of lying. Unfair. Unlike the French, he would never try to win fame by giving his adventures an excess of the exotic or the marvellous. It's just Indian lands really are mysterious, the people amazing and strange, wondrous things happen all the time in the forests of America. Hence the liberal and ingenious will surely not doubt 'the truth of a story so well authenticated, because the circumstances appear extraordinary in a country where the subject of it is scarcely known.' The country where these strange things are scarcely known is England. For that is where Carver sails in 1769, hoping for some royal payment for his endeavours, funds for his expedition. For in Detroit his cash ran out, his supplies began

courthouse where Abraham Lincoln practised law, or pause in the shop where the Wright Brothers built the first airplane.' (*Guide Book*) to fail. 'This day arrived at Michilimackinac,' his diary records sadly. 'Here ends this attempt to find out a Northwest Passage.'

JONATHAN CARVER never did find his Northwest Passage. For history is, as we all know, a great master of irony, always turning success into failure, hope to despair, peace into war, this into that. And Carver could never know what we without difficulty know perfectly well (since, coming along later, we can access the subsequent pages in the Great Book of Destiny above): that he made his three explorations in a strange and elusive moment, an odd little window of history indeed, when a hope dawned and died: the hope of a great British Empire in the West.

For there would be not just one Treaty of Paris but two, twenty years apart. And what the first generously gave – a Western Empire – the second took away again. The Treaty of 1763 gave Canada and the great Louisiana lands to the British, opened the Mississippi Valley and Ohio River for exploration, changed the entire spirit of the colonies. The Peace of Paris of 1783, following the American War of Independence, took these things back, granting most of them to the American colonists themselves – no longer colonists but citizens of the world's First New Nation – and other parts of them back to the French, who had taken the chance to ally themselves with the American revolutionaries and claimed their reward. So, as far as his American possessions were concerned, the Great King whose feet stood on two islands and possessed many canoes had his head in the clouds. His American taxes had gone unpaid, his colonials declared their independence; his military campaigns failed as he fought four enemies (Americans, French, Spanish and Dutch). In the treaty he decided to forgive and forget all misunderstandings and differences that had divided him from his American colleagues, to relinquish his claim to the government, propriety and territorial rights of the thirteen colonies, and declare them free and independent states. The twenty-year project of the greater British Empire would have to start over again elsewhere, and so it did.

Meantime the former colonists became citizens of what became the First New Nation, demanding their own constitution, devoted to enlightened and republican virtues such as life, liberty, the pursuit of happiness, virtues supplied to them, along with ships, generals and vast supplies of weaponry, by the solicitous French. So what was this new nation, and who were its new citizens? It was all just a fanciful and enlightened eighteenth-century fiction that had suddenly turned into wondrous fact. 'The American is a new man, who acts on new principles,' explained Hector St John de Crevecœur in his *Letters from an American Farmer* (1782), 'he must therefore entertain new ideas, and form new opinions.' Hector Crevecœur (Farmer James, Mr Heartbreak) was a wondrous fiction himself. He was no traditional American farmer. Born in Caen, he was an ambiguous Frenchman, an ambiguous British colonist, an ambiguous revolutionary, an ambiguous Loyalist, and an ambiguous American, who fictionally pretended he was a second-generation British immigrant to write the story of his New World life for the romantic pleasure of the people of England and Europe. The new man, he explains, is the modern farmer-philosopher, who lives in an ideal and fertile land without princes and aristocrats, and cultivates his own garden. His acres are extensive, his husbandry splendid, his bees friendly, his future peaceful, his prospects sublime. Alas, by the time this highly idyllic account was published Crevecœur's American farm had been torched by Indians and he had returned to Paris. Here Rousseau's lover Mme de Houdetout introduced him to the leading thinkers: sleepless d'Alembert, squat powdered Melchior Grimm, the Abbé Reynal and the philosopher Denis Diderot; to these two the French version of his book is dedicated.

Later, when the New Men had their New Nation, the French would reward him by sending him back to New York as consul. For, thanks to their support for the American Revolutionary War (and poisoned chalice it would prove too, as one republican revolution quickly led on to another), the French had retrieved prestige, influence and possessions in old

Louisiana, the Caribbean, and their Spanish allies had taken Florida and lower Mississippi, while, according to the Treaty, the river itself was retained as British navigation. The New Nation would need mapping all over again. Britain still held Canada and much of the Great Lakes, but nearly all of what lay below the 45th parallel and to the Mississippi fell to the new Americans, and they still had to discover the limits of their own country and continent. The world Carver had begun to map for British minds was becoming rapidly something different. Even the people quickly pushing westward were different: energetic, anarchic, lawless, republican. And yet, as Carver wrote in his record of three years of American exploration, *Travels Through the Interior Parts of North America*, what remarkable wonders had been in store for the British, and what an amazing future had been dawning, 'when the present troubles in America began, which put a stop to the enterprise that promised to be of inconceivable advantage to the British dominions.'

Carver's book did not appear in London till 1778, three years after the American Revolution began.[*] On his travels, he had prepared everything, thought of everything. He had drawn the likely route of the Northwest Passage, on from the Mississippi, up the line of the river he called the Oregon. He marked the landscape, divided the land in eleven new provinces – Winnebago Land, the Land of the Western Sea, Oregon and so on – with British names for British folk. What a dream, he said, had been there for the taking! Somewhere near Lake Winnipeg, by the Mountain of Shining Stone, the route to the West lay open and easy. 'Should peace once more be restored, I doubt not that the countries [his new 'cantons' of America] will prove a more abundant source of riches to this nation [Britain], than either its East or West Indian settlements; and I shall not only pride myself, but sincerely rejoice in being the means of pointing out to it so valuable an acquisition.' No

---

[*] Jonathan Carver, *Travels Through the Interior Parts of North America, in the years 1766, 1767 and 1768* (London, for the author, sold by James Walter, 1778).

doubt before long, he added, the journey will succeed. Perhaps, when those who make it ponder their success, 'they may bestow some commendations and blessings on the person who first pointed out to them the way.'

Yet who these successful explorers will be is hard to imagine, and what they find he will probably never know (as he never did). 'But as the seat of Empire from time immemorial has been gradually progressive towards the West, there is no doubt that at some future period, mighty kingdoms will emerge from these wildernesses, and stately palaces and solemn temples, with gilded spires reaching to the skies, supplant the Indian huts, whose only decorations are the barbarous trophies of their vanquished enemies.' In short, with great prescience he predicts Meriwether Lewis and William Clark, who try to find the North-west Passage by way of the Missouri River, discover the prairie dog, and reach the Pacific early in 1805, twenty-five years after Carver's death, only to find the passage too difficult, the story of their travels too hard to write. (Lewis died disappointed by his own hand; Clark became governor of Missouri Territory, waving wagon trains onward to the West; others completed the journals of their discoveries.) But Carver also predicts much else: Las Vegas, Palm Springs, Los Angeles, even the Westin Bonaventure Hotel, postmodern spires reaching to the skies to supplant the begging dances and the boasting dances, the tepees and Indian camps. But sadly, now, the American Revolution meant his own voyages through the wonders were over and done with. All that was left was his book.

YET IN THE END it was Carver's book, not his journey, that became the wonder. Eventually over thirty editions of his *Travels* appeared, making it perhaps the most popular American travel tale there has ever been. Like many books, not least the French travels that had gone before, it became the text of a half-named, a nearly imaginary America, the tale of one more lost empire. It was a glimpse of a world that might have been, a world many wanted there to be. In it Carver did what he intended; he remapped, redesigned, renamed the inner continent. Nameless things once named in French now had names in Indian, Greek, or English. Fresh landscapes were given to the fresh continent. The regions were mapped from 'New Britain' on the eastern coast, through 'Louisiana' in the middle, to 'New Albion' in the still unpeopled West. The book was no longer a surveyor's guide, or an appeal for millennial funding for research and exploration. It was not even the story of a strange voyage into the unknown, like the reports of Captain Cook or Captain Bougainville. It was a great fiction, a possible America made in words.

Carver praised the Indians, in all their mixture of ferocity and gentleness. He lists their languages, he records their customs, explains their love rituals, marriage practices, burial customs, techniques of massacre with tomahawk, their arts of scalping. He reports on the charming songs the Naudowessies sing to each other: 'I will arise before the sun, and ascend yonder hill, to see the new light chase away the vapours, and disperse the clouds,' runs one typical after-dinner ditty. 'Great spirit, give me success. And when the sun is gone lend me, oh moon, light sufficient to guide me with safety back to my tente, loaden with deere.' He describes, in splendid detail, American nature. The beasts ('THE SKUNK: This is the most extraordinary animal the American woods produce'); the birds ('THE WHIPPERWILL, or, as it is termed by the Indians, the Muckawiss: . . . The Indians, and some of the inhabitants of the back settlements, think if this bird perches upon any house, that it betokens some mishap to the inhabitants'); the serpents ('THE TWO-HEADED SNAKE: The only snake of this kind that was ever seen in America, was found about the year 1762, near Lake Champlain'); the insects ('THE BEES in America principally lodge their honey in the earth, to secure it from the ravages of the bears'); the trees, plants, vegetables ('THE SQUASH . . . THE PECAN NUT . . . THE CRANBERRY BUSH').

The book – said publishers' publicity, as publicity should – was the literary event of the age. This was a time when travel tales were king; even the popular novels people now read were stories of wandering, picaresque tales of an opening world.

Here was the first record in English of that widening westering empire, as rich, said the press release for the 1838 American edition, as a romance, as fascinating and credible as the voyages of Marco Polo (a rather suspect recommendation, it has to be said). Jonathan Carver, alas, did not live to enjoy the fame of his bestseller. Two years after publication, in 1780, he died in London, apparently of starvation, as writers do. That year the book was translated into German and began to win its wider reputation. In 1782 Crevecœur's *Letters from an American Farmer* appeared, and everyone began to think anew about the new man in the new world. In 1784 – this was the year when Diderot died, and when Beaumarchais, who used his theatrical fortune to provide ships and men for the American Revolution, staged his revolutionary drama *The Marriage of Figaro* – Carver's book was translated into French and widely read.

Now the new American republic was a year old, the French Revolution five years ahead. The minister in Paris was Thomas Jefferson, soon to be third American President. He did not fail to see the book's significance, and made secret plans for the opening up of the Northwest Passage, which he drew to the attention of his secretary, Captain Meriwether Lewis, who in due time recruited Captain William Clark to join the quest. At this time the lands Carver pointed to and Jefferson wanted to see explored had been restored to the French and Spanish, who refused to allow a new exploration (to be made, Jefferson claimed falsely, 'as a literary pursuit'). Only as a result of the Louisiana Purchase of 1803 did the great journey dreamt by Carver begin. By then others had seen the fascination of the book. Not least was a strange young Frenchman, a self-romanticizing viscount from Brittany, child of a rake-hell seafaring family that specialized in fishing the Grand Banks, pirating, slaving, privateering, plundering British ships. He too read Carver and Crevecœur, the travels of William Bartram and the American tales, and felt the magical claim of the Northwest Passage. His name was François-René de Chateaubriand. His trademark, the trademark of a romantic of the coming age of change and revolution, was cosmic gloom. More than all of us, he was a lover of stories. Now, in Carver, he found the story he needed.

'I HAD SCARCE LEFT my mother's womb when I suffered my first exile,' René notes in the mysterious memoir he wrote of his life, called *Memoirs From the Other Side of the Tomb*. Here we need a surgeon-general's health warning; of all unreliable books this is the most unreliable. It's a pleasure to say what one writer delights to say about another: as we read it we can never know which or what is true. 'I always imagined I was writing these memoirs in my coffin,' René explains thoughtfully. And they certainly were written for posterity, or whatever followed it, and did not appear in full until 1920, when Chateaubriand's days (1768–1848) on this side of the tomb, where I write this and you sit and read it, were well over and done. The memoirs are gloomy, romantic, tragic, yearning, Byronic: constantly revised, retraced, retracted: written over a time of chaotic history that changed everything, including the unreliable values and loyalties of their author. Chateaubriand spent his lifetime as we may suppose he will spend eternity, if there is one: explaining why his existence was useless in the first place, why it was a cosmic idiocy to allow him on this planet at all.

For Chateaubriand was a man of rank in an age of revolutions, an elitist in a time of populists, a sensitive reed in a universe of brutes, a maker of one history in a time that had something else in mind: out of it, yet at the middle of all. That he was a true aristocrat in a time that dispensed with them explained what was most precious about him, his love of liberty, 'the special characteristic of an aristocracy whose last hour has struck.' He belonged with ruins, lost spaces, tumbling empires, grand corpses. Like most Romantics, his life felt one wearisome last hour. But for all his anguish he did not waste it: 'I have explored the seas of the Old World and the New . . . After sleeping in the cabins of the Iroquois and the tents of Arabs, the wigwams of the Huron and the remains of Athens . . . after enduring poverty, thirst and exile, I have taken my place as minister and ambassador, trimmed with gold lace and plastered with ribbons, at the table of kings, the festivities of princes and princesses, only to fall back into poverty and taste prison life . . .'

René picked up his soul-searching Romanticism on the stormy Breton coast, and in the collapsing libraries of his relatives, where he read work after work about lost French empires. For him as for a generation of Frenchmen (one reason why so many aided the American Revolution, which in turn brought their own), the lost lands of Louisiana were painfully real. He came from Brittany, from St Malo, itself burned by the British in the Seven Years War a decade before his birth. British ships destroyed the Brest fleet at the Battle of Quiberon Bay, and took Belle Île, off the Breton coast, battles his family had fought in as they defended their nation and pirated the seas. Now it was paper and memory, an old romantic past. He read the books of those who remembered and recorded, like the great accounts of the Two Indies by Reynal and Diderot, where the whole social history and economic promise of these regions was set down. He watched Diderot's plays, he read tales of the American savages, he followed Carver and the story of the Northwest Passage. He saw the lure of those old Louisiana spaces. He imagined, again and again, Les Deux Indes, the old French empires, now filled with glorious mist. He thought of the slopes of the Himalayas, the banks of the Ganges; the tepees of the Canada Iroquois, the tents of the Natchez in the Louisiana swamps.

The books he read bred the idea of writing: 'I was still young when I conceived the idea of writing the epic of the man of nature, and describing the manners of savages by linking them to some great event.' And great events were about to happen; no sooner had he reached the age of reason than madness struck in the form of the French Revolution. His patron, the great minister Malesherbes, and his brother went to the guillotine. Writing, as he says, from the far side of the grave (though he survived to live into his eighties), he summed it up in a famous sentence: 'Now proceed, reader, cross the river of blood which separates forever the old world in which you have been born from the new world on whose frontier you will die.' It was his own fate to survive, to go from monarch to republic and then to directorate, from the clarity of the Age of Reason to the bloodlust of the Age of Terror and then the new potency of the Age of Napoleonic domination. 'The severed heads changed my political disposition,' he explains, 'these cannibal feasts filled me with horror, and the idea of leaving France for some distant land took root in my mind.'

The distant land was not hard to find. Through Malesherbes he met Jefferson in Paris, and following the spirit of Carver he offered to go and find for him the Northwest Passage. 'In the event of success I should have the honour of bestowing French names on unknown regions, and endowing my country with a colony in the Pacific,' he remarks. In 1791 he sailed for America: 'I'm emigrating from the world! Either I die on the way, or come back bigger than when I left.' He decided to become 'a backwoodsman, before becoming the Christopher Columbus of North America.' America did all it could to entertain him. But when he got there the place proved larger than and quite unlike what he expected, while the Northwest Passage was far from easy to reach. He wandered through the backwoods, in the wake of Carver. In the meantime he adjusted his ambitions, from bold western exploration to the writing of books. 'I promised to poetry what might be lost to science; and if I did not find in America what I was looking for I found a new muse.'

THE NEW MUSE appeared in the form of a maiden, a sylph, a fair-skinned Indian princess. She bred a Louisiana narrative, a fanciful memoir, a feather-hatted, loinclothed dream of a novel. For what he had found in America, and the French lands of Louisiana, was a fictional utopia – hardly spoiled by the thing that spoils everything, reality. His imagination was romantic, exotic; he was a dreamer over dying things, ruins that crumbled in the sand, cabins that tumbled into the swamp, ways of life that were dying or over, those who would live without heirs. Not too much troubled by fact, he conjures the most lost of all the French landscapes: 'that delightfully beautiful country, called by the people of the United States the New Eden, and named by the French, musically, Louisiana.' This is the most splendid and quite the lushest of worlds: 'caribou bathe in the lake; black squirrels caper in the thick foliage; mockingbirds, Virginia doves bigger than the sparrow, alight on the grass red with strawberries.' Huge vines 'jump from the maple to the tulip tree, forming a thousand grottos, a thousand arches and a thousand porticos.' At the heart of it all is the sylph, the beautiful self-sacrificing Indian princess from the tribe of the Natchez, Atala, who has acquired nun-like Christian values. Her sacrificial death symbolizes all: the end of things, the dying of a way of life and a race, the elimination of the Indian noble savages who were so beloved of the French philosophers, and whose members were slaughtered, naturally, by the French themselves.

The tale he wrote was called *Atala*, and it appeared secretly in Napoleonic Paris in 1801. It was the Harry Potter of its age, an amazing success. With its American theme, dying heroine and tragic Indian philosopher, the chief Chactas, it became one of the first great works of Romanticism. Doré illustrated it, Delacroix painted the famous last scene by Niagara Falls, Verdi did the opera, Sèvres did the plates. Its popularity in France was predictable, for 1801 was the year Napoleon revived French imperial fancies by secretly reacquiring Louisiana back from the Spanish. The revival lasted only a moment, for two years later he would sell it off to the American president, Thomas Jefferson, for sixty million francs, or in other words the price of a cheap B-movie. But thinking himself ever cunning in statecraft, Napoleon had the British to spite. Besides, his dreams now acquired a different and sphinx-like face; he was heading for Egypt and the wonders of older empires. Meantime on the other side of the Atlantic, Jefferson enjoyed his bargain, the United States tripled in size at a stroke, and

America had the chance to become a transcontinental nation, which it quickly seized.*

Atala, though not quite meant to be a fiction, has fair claim to be considered the first American novel. It presented the first grand literary myth of the glorious savage, the dying Indian, the romantic West, the wonderful open spaces where the greatest of feelings dwelt. It was only the beginning, for with the opening of the West tale bred tale, fiction fiction, book book. The lands began to unfold, the stories immediately followed – like the swarms of bees that, according to frontier legend, preceded the advance of white settlement. The stories were rich and never seemed quite true, about a strange and paradisal eternity, populated by tale-tellers, leading through the backwoods to the lands of the Mississippi and then the prairie – 'the biggest clearing on the Almighty's footstool' – that lay beyond. When the first great American novelist, James Fenimore Cooper, invented the first American hero, Leatherstocking, he owed everything to Chateaubriand. His early novel about the French and Indian Wars, *The Spy*, ended up – where else? – at Niagara Falls. By the time he'd done Leatherstocking and his Indian friends, philosophers of the wilderness had stalked each region of the moving frontier in book after book.

It's Leatherstocking who is the very first to discover the Northwest Passage, in *The Prairie*, reaching the West Coast by 1803. This means he arrives well in advance of the real-life explorers, Meriwether Lewis and William Clark, who do not complete their perilous trip over the unexpected terrible Teton mountains (which Carver fails to mention) until 1805. 'I have seen the waters of two seas!' Leatherstocking says. 'America has

---

* As Napoleon said to Talleyrand: 'I renounce Louisiana. It is not only New Orleans that I cede: it is the whole colony, without reserve; I know the price of that which I abandon. I have proved the importance I attach to this province, since my first diplomatic act with Spain had the object of recovering it. I renounce it with the greatest regret; to attempt obstinately to retain it would be folly . . . This accession of territory strengthens for ever the power of the United States and I have just given to England a maritime rival that sooner or later will humble her pride.'

grown, my men, since the days of my youth, to be a country larger than I once had thought the world to be.' 'I went in search of quiet,' he adds, 'it was a grievous journey that I made.'* For already the books brought the travellers, travellers the spirit of the age. For a moment there was a glowing relation between the red man and the white man. Americans went west to live with Indians in their tepees. But grievous enough it turned out to be; and the path that Carver opened, Chateaubriand dreamt of, Leatherstocking followed led inexorably on. As the Indian grew more romantic, he also grew more dead. So to the Indian Removal Bill, slaughter, genocide, modernizing history; Las Vegas, Palm Springs, Hollywood, Sunset Boulevard, Grauman's Chinese, Happy Hour in the postmodern lobby of the Westin Bonaventura Hotel.

IF RENÉ WROTE the first American novel (soon followed by an autobiographical second, called unsurprisingly *René*), just where did he write it? As with everything in his life, he told and retold the story, giving this account and then that. But we may be fairly sure he didn't write much on his extensive, exhausting, confused American travels, which covered much ground and lasted just five months. Nor, surely, did he write it back in France, for he returned as a soldier, fighting for Royalist

---

* Cooper's *The Prairie* (1827) is the third of the five Leatherstocking novels, but the last in time; it tells of the Louisiana Purchase, Leatherstocking's old age and death, and his Indian burial. Leatherstocking (Natty Bumppo) heads west, to and beyond the prairies that now open out beyond the Mississippi, where civilization, meaning America, now casts its shadows before. His journey is grievous because he knows he is moving just ahead of a future tribe who will occupy the continent, destroy its customs and flatten its wilderness: 'What will the Yankee Choppers [the pioneers who are now cutting down the forest for farms and settlements] say, when they have cut their path from the eastern to the western waters, and find that a hand, which can lay the "arth bare at a blow, has been here and swept the country?" What the world of America is coming to and where the machinations and inventions of its people are to have an end, the Lord only knows,' Leatherstocking adds. And as far as we know the Lord still doesn't.

armies, and was firmly on the losing side. Not at the Battle of Thionville, where he was wounded. Probably not on the island of Jersey, where he fled to escape and recover. According to one account, he devised the tale in Kensington Gardens in London, but he was not in London for long. Britain was too full of émigrés, so, short of money, the gloomy vicomte had to offer his services as tutor and translator. Calling himself M. de Combourg, he made his way to East Anglia and the swan-filled, coot-haunted, reed-bedded valley of the River Waveney, which forms the border between Norfolk and Suffolk, and meanders in ways even Ole Man River Mississippi cannot imagine until by way of old peatbogs, lush broads, reedbeds, old cuts, windmill-pumped dykes, alder swamps and cattle meadows, staithes and flint-churched settlements, inlets and estuaries it spills out slowly and cunningly into the salt of the cold German Northern sea.

Yes, M. de Combourg found his way to the bluffs of the Waveney at Beccles, where the Society of Antiquaries employed him as a translator. Once in Beccles there is nowhere better to go than to Bungay; here he fell off his horse and was picked up by a vicar's daughter. Beccles is quite grand and spacious, with big houses and private marinas; Bungay has swans and swamps, a touch of gloom to it, having been built round the strongest fort in East Anglia.* Remains still stand of the old Bigod castle; in the fine parish church, once the heart of a lost priory, a mad black dog is said to howl and pick off the odd careless worshipper, even to this present postmodern

---

* 'Bungay, Suffolk (pop. 4,100). Finest town in the Waveney Valley; centre for the printing of books; possibly once an island, and then the head of navigation. Ruined castle; fine buttercross; parish church of St Mary, formerly church of the Benedictine nunnery. It was here, on a terrible Sunday in August 1557, that the Black Dog of Bungay appeared amid a thunderstorm ("All down the Church in midst of fire / The hellish monster flew; / And passing onwards to the Quire / He many people slew"). Another local poem celebrates a different matter: "Beccles for a puritan, / Bungay for the poor. / Halesworth for a drunkard, / And Blythborough for a whore."' (*Guide Book*)

day. In a fine Georgian house in Bridge Street by mill and river lived the vicar from a nearby parish in the country, Iketshall St Mary. Here, recovering from his fall, René lodges, teaching and amusing the rector's young daughter, Charlotte Ives. He is splendid, engaging, gloomy. She is fifteen, quiet, naive, charming. She becomes the inspiration to the book he is now writing: the story of Atala. By simple transposition the Indian maiden, the sylph, becomes a vicar's daughter: and vice versa. So the first true American novel is written beside the English River Waveney, about five miles away from where I write this: its frogspawn, progeny, successor.

Miss Ives, Miss Ives: now should he marry Miss Ives? He thinks yes. So does her mother. Alas, there's a small problem he's somehow failed to mention. 'Stop, I am a married man,' M. de Combourg cries, quite truthfully, when mother suggests it, and leaps on the mailcoach to London, leaving his Bungay sylph behind. Naturally, this being René, it happens with a great outburst of romantic pain – the kind of pain that in a good man never stops. 'The memory of Charlotte penetrated and warmed my work, and, if that were not enough, the first longing for fame inflamed my exalted imagination.' Charlotte has not just made him write a great novel; she's taught him to become a famous man. Twenty-five years on, when he writes these words, he has turned into one of the best-known, most vivid figures of his age: writer, soldier, traveller, statesman. In the year 1800, starting life again with the new century, he returns secretly to France with a false Swiss passport: M. Lassagna. He publishes his book, the story of the Indian princess from Bungay. Fame comes, Indian princesses sweep Europe. He lives on, splendidly, wonderfully, agonizingly, under the different eras of post-Revolutionary France. He sees a grand and despotic new emperor crowned, Bourbon kings return, history tack this way and that.

In 1803 – now he's over thirty – he begins his memoirs, from the far side of the grave. He writes a chapter, another, one here, the other there: one in his villa in the Valley of the Wolves, another in Potsdam at the great imperial palace of

Sans Souci, where Voltaire once served Frederick of Prussia. He himself has served Napoleon, been to Egypt, toured the Orient, celebrated the revival of Christianity and faith. Now he's M. Romanticism, Vicomte Gloom, the French Byron, the Parisian Pushkin, author of many books. Later he's made French Ambassador to Britain. His fame is great, his loves and lusts are many, the steaks of his famous chef are the talk of the town. One day a black-dressed lady, Lady Sutton, recent widow of an admiral, calls at the embassy seeking assistance; she wants some help and preferment for her two sons. She asks if he happens to remember her. 'Yes, I remembered Miss Ives! I took her by the hand, made her sit down, sat down by her side.'

They talk, and they find they have the very fondest memories of each other. At last through the embassy window he watches his early muse, his Suffolk Atala, walk away back toward quiet and Bungay. Could the son for whom she asks preferment (he'll do what he can) be his child? At any rate, he knows that, for all his fame, he's a dead man. He can see the length of the road he's travelled; he's the most famous man in France, she's off to Bungay. 'First love of my life, away you go with all your charms!' he thinks. Should he have married her? I could have been what I am, a great man and a universal hero, he considers; or I could have lived in Bungay. In which case, 'I should have become a sporting gentleman. I should have forgotten my native tongue, for I wrote in English and my ideas were taking shape in English in my head. The Empire, the Restoration, the divisions and quarrels of France, what would all that have mattered to me? Is it certain I possess genuine talent, and that talent is worth the sacrifice I have made of my whole life? Shall I outlast my tomb?'

Oh, isn't it wonderful, isn't it parfait, the way these romantic adventures, these dreams of young bliss, first love, great reputation flavour his life? Off the pretty widow goes on her silent way back to Suffolk; off he goes, onward, upward, back to the London ladies, the Paris mistresses, René the enchanter, haunted by youth, death, memory, Indians; forward to more greatness, more amours, more ribbons, more fame, more travels, more adventures, more books, all of which might be forgotten, unless he outlasts his tomb. Meanwhile, of course, the tomb insistently beckons; on the far side is posterity. What's the hurry? René lives vigorously on till the age of eighty, and dies at last in a house in the Rue du Bac in Paris on 4 July 1848.

As it happens, 1848 too will prove a very busy year, and yet another year of Revolutions. 'Let the ruling classes tremble,' MM. Marx and Engels cry yet again in their *Communist Manifesto*, published the day he dies. In Paris streets history boils; ten thousand Parisians die in the June days just before his own demise as Cavaignac tries to crush the workers' revolution. Another monarch is toppled, another Napoleon comes to rule a new republic – only again to proclaim himself emperor. New republics seem to be emerging everywhere: Rome and Venice, Sardinia and Naples, Prague, Frankfurt, Cracow. Poets of the next generation turn ministers, like Lamartine, or die on barricades in Poland and Hungary, like Petofi. As Marx and Engels say, first came the bourgeois revolution, which 'has accomplished wonders far surpassing Egyptian pyramids, Roman aqueducts and Gothic cathedrals; it has conducted expeditions that put in the shade all former Exoduses of nations and crusades.' But by the laws of historical inevitability, this must lead to yet another, the revolution of the proletariat – when the nothings of the earth claim to be somethings, and 'All that is solid melts into air, all that is holy is profaned, and man is at last compelled to face with sober senses his real conditions of life, and his relations with his kind.'

On liberty day, amid the fervour and frenzy, the bloodied hopes and failures, René himself stops dancing, faces with his sober senses the real conditions of life, and promptly melts into air. Another republic may be coming, but it is earth, sea and air that wait to receive him. This is a man who understands history and its illusions, revolution and its fantasies, the great game of beginnings and endings; a man who in regime after regime has balanced old with new, past with future, knowing that what France wants is always the same: plenty of the former plus a dose of the latter. Now he has had more than his fill of history, that careless, tireless, tedious taskmaster, always promising so much when it has so little to offer, always doing this when it has claimed to do that. Seven years before his death he writes the last page of his story, ends the posthumous memoir, concludes the prequel to the sequel. 'The scenes of tomorrow do not concern me, they call for other painters; it is your turn . . .' he announces, teeing the ball for the writers and history men of the future, bequeathing the age of modernity, mechanization, secularity, speculation, proletarianization, powered flight, psychic depression, relativity, European suicide, atomic lunacy, genetic meddling and everything else to those who must interpret and transform it and understand it even less than he does, 'I behold the light of a dawn whose sunrise I shall never see. It only remains for me to sit down at the edge of my grave; then I shall descend boldly, crucifix in hand, into eternity.'

Despite the sudden unnecessary intrusions of history – bodies in the gutter, muskets firing in the streets – the last touches are quite wonderfully planned. As with everything in our man's operatic existence, the scenery has long been painted, the stage set, the scenes and lines rehearsed, the band hired, caterers booked and even the Atlantic waves have been trained. There's a respectful service of obsequy for a famous man in Paris. But the true journey is homeward to St Malo, where his corpse is placed in the cathedral. The tomb already lies open and waiting, off to sea on the islet of Grand Be. Two regiments from the garrison stand guard, the citizens watch from the ramparts, as the coffin is carried on to the rocky shore. On huge poles the titles of all his books are hanging. Two hundred Breton priests follow the catafalque over the tideway. A great storm is blowing, or maybe the day is clear and the sun shining brilliantly: either version of the tale will do. Carved from granite, the tomb has only date and cross. Only a modest or very vain man would choose such a monument; the vicomte was not modest. 'A great French writer wished to repose here,' says the inscription, 'to listen to nothing but the sea and the wind.' Now cross-Channel ferries ply back and forth to St Malo, holidaymakers with their four-wheel drives roll ashore. But the great man is still remembered. The cafés and restaurants of St Malo serve their steaks and seafoods Chateaubriand. The islet can be reached by causeway at low tide. The plain stone grave is constantly visited. There is nothing the world loves better than the tomb of a writer safely dead.

Less often visited is the Georgian house on Bridge Street, in the bend of the river Waveney in Bungay. Yet it would surely please the gloomy vicomte – who really was quite the vainest of men – to know it stands still, its atmosphere calm and pleasant, its spirit untroubled. Its gardens are charmingly woven into the old priory ruins, so religion is not far distant; the mill at the back is still pounding, so nature is not far away. A small blue plaque over the entrance says that a big man lived in this little place, and wrote a book here. It might please him even more to know this is still a house of fictions: still written in, lived in by a writer, Elizabeth Jane Howard, and visited by many others.

I was there for dinner only last night. And when I sat down to dine in the green candlelit conservatory, I was touched by a thought that often came to René's mind as he made his slow agonized way from his stormbound cradle to his seashore tomb. As he said, one day he was offered a wonderful choice. He could live out his days in the grand revolutionary world of history, amid destiny, adventure, risk, grandeur, fame, the spectacle of bloodied and severed heads, pitting himself against grand events. On the other hand, he could live in Bungay, speaking English, chasing a pheasant or two, forgetting history and political obligations. And as, over a bottle of wine or two, I reflect on this, I realize I too and many of my friends have quite often chosen history, when they might perfectly well have chosen Bungay. And the more I think about it, the more I think that I, they, and maybe even he, probably made quite the wrong choice.

CHAPTER ONE

TALES FROM BEYOND THE TOMB

1. Welcome to rene.com

Now that I am really and quite definitely dead – and this time not pretending, not simply using the strange camera angle from the bottom of a leaden coffin as the ideal means for imposing my romantic, gothic, mournful, cosmic, deeply gloomy viewpoint on the world – some serious reflections can begin at last. My story, my history, the tale of my remarkable upbringing, my young loves, my desires, my lusts, my desires, my woes and misfortunes, my formidable wanderings and quite remarkable travels, my profound and illuminating thoughts on this world-shaking topic or that one: all these things have been recorded by me many times before. They are widely known and universally remembered, which is why hundreds of thousands of people visit my solitary tomb each year to pay their homage. But my genuinely posthumous thoughts – my freshest observations and amendments, my millennial sentiments, my corrections, reconstructions, reappraisals and deconstructions, my twenty-first-century reflections on time, space, power, sex, the body, pleasure, pain, past, present and future, my views on things now ruined and forgotten and things that are yet to come, as well as some deeply experienced advice on writing, living, imagining, dreaming: this is what's needed now. The truth is I now have the time and the space for it: all the time in the world. I even have the technology: welcome to rene.com.

In the world that now sails onward into the unknown future, everything may be different: time, space, God, the

Devil, sex, gender, politics, technology, desire itself. But for
me nothing truly changes. There may be children now who
are told they have no need of history; nonsense, that is where
they live. Flesh fails and the body rots; it betrays its incum-
bent. But the word is bigger than flesh. From childhood on
I constantly sat down to write. Almost every day of my life,
though I lived it to the full, I wrote something. I have no
intention of stopping merely because of my death. Such is the
nature of writing. It's a priestly calling, a demanding and
everlasting vocation, and the soul that has been summoned
never ceases to perform. And what is written lives far longer
than we do – or so we would like to think. Words persist:
revised, recycled, reprinted, rewritten, they go on for ever.
And as they do so, we go on too. In the end, writing is our
story, the one thing we each of us have. As for me, I have
always made the most of myself, and I may as well continue to
do so. I have made my story glorious. Consequently it has been
told, revised, retold, corrected quite frequently, most often
though not always by me. But why let it pass to others? It is
my story, and I shall keep on telling it. After all, I always
claimed that it could only be properly written from a station in
eternity, a mouldering residential hotel on the further side of
the tomb.

Why my story? Because I am a man, a person, a sensibility,
an expression, a flamboyance. But I am a great deal more than
that. I am an age, an epoch, a spirit. I am an attitude, a
beatitude, a spirit, an esprit. I lived long, went everywhere, did
everything. I felt more than most, created much, observed a
whole universe, put it into words. What is more I became an
unending and an undying narrative. I not only started to tell
my story; I never ceased recounting it – reshaping it, recreating
it, recomposing it; adjusting it, revising it, transforming it,
making it modern and topical, bringing it up to date. When
history changed, as it did so often in my presence, so did my
story. After all the future always rewrites the past; that is why
we have it. Every story of things leads on to many others.
An old testament requires a new one. A Bible demands an

apocrypha. One gospel requires another, a third, a fourth. The authorized version insists on a revised version. Every story needs a supplement: a prequel, a sequel. Creation is never complete. Every account needs a correction. Every construction requires a deconstruction (or so they say in Paris, where I spend a good deal of time these days, sitting amid the falling stones of the Panthéon, as the dust settles on Mirabeau and the finials fall on Voltaire). So it is with me. As I have been able to construct myself, so I insist on deconstructing myself. What I have already started, nothing can induce me to stop.

In other words, story is exactly like history itself: indeed in French the two words are one. And it is of history that I have been both the great proponent and the eternal victim. Throughout my life, history was in constant revision of itself, going in this direction and then that one, starting one revolution only to turn it into another. Violence prevailed, nonsense flourished, the young of one generation bore no resemblance to the young of the next. The calendar itself restarted; I was there on Day One, the beginning of the world, which lasted for a few years, until it was abolished; millennia are like that, here today and gone tomorrow. I witnessed all, I believed in little. Simple wisdom: who was it says that she who marries the spirit of the age is bound to become a widow in the next? I knew that from the start; even so I often joined my soul to causes, my words to power, attached my devious, tricky imagination to the no less devious and tricky deeds of history itself. I sought excitement in the heart of battle, marched with soldiers through forest and ancient desert. I risked high seas and rocky shores; I wandered the dangerous solitudes of the deepest and most remote forests, where painted savages roamed. I flirted with bloodstained revolutionaries. I dallied with emperors, kings, dictators. I rode beside generals and whispered in the ear of popes. Indeed I have been quite unlike any writer in the whole history, or story, of the world.

For, as we know, Homer told great and epic tales of the Greek and Trojan heroes, of malicious interfering gods, charioted kings, helmeted chieftains, glowing princes, great battles, cunning strategies, glorious deaths. But who was Homer? Christopher Marlowe wrote vaunting lines for Tamburlaine, prince of tyrants, the man who knew it was passing brave to be a king and ride in triumph through Persepolis. But the man himself was a spy and pub-brawler, soon dead in a tavern. Shakespeare wrote gloriously of great kings and tragic heroes, Tudors and Plantagenets, pretenders and impostors, assumers and ascenders, those who aspired to the haunted throne and put on their heads the hollow crown. But who was Shakespeare? A petty bourgeois, up from the provinces. None of these great writers were themselves the heroes. None took the trouble to become ministers, princes, ambassadors and kings. Writers mostly tell of history, and generally a long time after it has happened. But I . . . I have known history, known it at the most intimate quarters, felt it, smelt it, been stabbed in the back by it. I have made history; I have been history.

And that is why I have written as no one else before or after me has ever written, however hard they have tried to achieve what I achieved before me, or tried to imitate me ever since. Little wonder that, knowing so much, feeling so much, doing so much, being so much, bearing so much, I do write so remarkably well.

2. The View from Tombland

In recent years, reconsidering my history, rethinking my passions, researching my website, I have made a point of visiting, or more often revisiting, some of the great tombs of the world. Like many in my lifetime, tombs and mausoleums have always interested me: the crypt, the casket and the catacomb were always my concern. I was always a great traveller; some people would claim I am the true inventor of romantic tourism, the tourism of feeling rather than discovery. And nowadays, as a kind of necrological Michelin, a Rough Guide to the Boneyard, I still make a point of going to such places, which I still consider the most important sites on the globe. Right now – whatever that might happen to be – I am in a place called Tombland. I have to admit it is something of a deception, since the name does not mean what it says. 'The name of Tombland is supposed to derive from the fact that this was a Saxon market place: not a grave but a "toom", or open land,' I read in the guidebook I have just bought. Never mind: riot, slaughter and hangings have happened here, and there are graveyards on every side. I who have visited the tombs of the Pharaohs and the sarcophagus of Our Lord am entirely content. For to me the world itself is a Tombland, and the name is entirely natural.

In truth Tomblands lie all around us – mournful islets of calm that seem to exist outside time, life, history. As I say this one is in fact a famous old scene of riots, rebellions, murders, hangings, of men flayed in public, gentlemen hacked to death by the raging mob. All these past survive into the reasonably quiet present, which is itself merely the prequel to a disordered future. And everything will end up in the greater Tombland: a place of memories, ruins, hauntings, tracings, ghostly land-scapes, dark revisitings; a scene of broken statues, memorials, ivy-grown monuments, crumbled gravestones, dripping cata-combs; a scene of desolations, collapses, ruins; a site of recan-tations, weepings, loss, eternal regrets. With the tomb, statue and pyramid, as with art itself, we attempt to defeat flesh and vanquish nature, enter the resounding tomb of meaning. But the tomb is silent. Death, decline, the slippage of meaning: all these things are exactly the same. Tombland is the place where one epoch mixes with another. Here the living accuse the dead, and the dead rise to blame the living. One generation tries to improve what others have done before; thus they create the absurdities of their own present. What at least we can see from the other side of the tomb is that nothing is eternal, nothing fixed; life is always a traffic with death. Here grand-children lie with their grandparents, brothers with sisters, and nothing has the order, nothing reveals the progress, that in life we feel so entitled to expect.

In Tombland it is as, in my lifetime, I always assumed. Our

existence is pointless. Nothing is the better for our intervention or interference. None of us ever made the world any better, and most of us made it worse. Following the same rules, decency should never be expected to triumph, or civilization advance. History has the shape of a circle. All that rises falls into ruin. The wise do not displace the foolish. Sense does not dislodge barbarism, nor kindness and goodness control evil. The Europe of my age was foolish, brutal and senseless, even though dreamers thought the age of liberty had arrived and men like the Little Corporal tried to command events and turn history into meaning. The Europe of your age has been even more foolish, brutal and senseless, as more revolutions came (they come all the time), and more Little Corporals tried to shape destiny. The world is a civil war, without civility; those who attempt to command it make it worse. Tombland exists to remind us that utopia and dystopia are all one. Here everything is possible, and everything is pointless. Nothing can truly be done about anything at all. The one difference between this and so-called meaningful and purposeful existence is that here one knows the truth: we are all powerless to change, correct or improve anything, and might as well not try.

Apart from these natural limitations, Tombland is a truly pleasant place. This particular one happens to be in a favourite place of mine – in Norfolk in East Anglia, a fertile, pleasing and quiet district of England where my young life restarted once. One should never return; but the odd fact is that nothing here has changed all that greatly. The city of Norwich, where I am, is in various ways smart and designer-conscious, like all wealthy cities these days; yet it still has, like any good city, a faintly ruinous touch to it. In the Middle Ages its Tombland was, as I say, a scene of riots, rebellions, protests, drunken revels and witches' sabbaths so severe that the Cathedral was fired, the clergy maimed and the Pope put the city to excommunication. Nowadays, in the hooliganized England of today, the district is still a scene for crowds of the nose-ringed, fornication-obsessed and besotted hooligan young in which John Bull specializes to gather and savage themselves on the weekend nights. But here there are high trees and tall cathedral walls; large lawns, statues to heroes, flint and plaster houses, medieval or Georgian, once built for rich bishops, fat priors, ambitious deans, unctuous prebends, servile deacons, but now possessed by the new clergy: lawyers and solicitors, doctors and consultants, architects, interior designers and dot-com million-aires – all of them classic sources of disorder and bourgeois revolution, as I found out to my own cost.

Still, for the moment peace reigns. The lawns are neatly cut, school choristers sing, a flint road leads through playfields to the reedy riverside, where swans, geese and moorhens battle for edible handouts from the tourists, the schoolboys, the summer sailors moored at a cruiser marina on the far bank. Elderly people from retirement homes nearby sit on benches to stare at the water; the noise of traffic booms. Excellent spot. Good pubs are within easy walking distance, most serving the splendid regional ales. There are drinkspots of another kind, with names like Ha Ha, the Bum and Bottle. An Internet café, several restaurants, Spanish, Chinese, Thai. There are some that serve local fish and game at acceptable prices; I would particu-larly mention Tatler's, and recommend the jugged hare. There are bookshops, one the fine Tombland Bookshop, which I use a good deal (one reads a lot in Tombland). The Tombland News Agency, which keeps me abreast of daily events, mostly irrelevant. Solicitors' offices for the new sport of litigation. Hairdressers called Hiz, for the vainer kind of man (I am one myself). Various leading estate and property agencies, adver-tising fine rural properties, from castles and medieval manors to architect-designed bungalows in a third of an acre, far too little, surely, for any man to live. A Quaker meeting house. A Huguenot church, filled to this day with the descendants of those European Strangers who, rather like myself, became exiles here and helped make a fine city finer.

The noisy nightclub, guarded by crophead bouncers, pulsing with the body-pierced and the besotted – yet founded, I hear, by the fine European dancing masters who in past times made these provincial cities elegant with their classes in the waltz and the gavotte. A gentleman's club with discreet casino. An ancient hotel, the Maid's Head, taking all credit cards, and ideal for meeting other Tomblanders in the pleasant smoke-stained back bar in the coaching yard. A tourist office, advertising various watery pleasures of the region. There are even buses to Beccles and Bungay, though just now I am in no hurry. I am entirely content where I am. The shadow of the great Cathedral spire, built of Caen stone, brought over the Channel and up the reedy river, hovers over me. I prefer to look at the monuments in the chapels, the stone tombs in the nave, always remembering that it is through the solemn realms of death that one enters the presence of God, eternity and writing. Planes taking holidaymakers to Tenerife or Madeira fly over. The traffic buzz of a bypass sounds in the air, sirens of police cars and ambulances wail at night. Yet here in the cloister, apart from the mobile phones of tourists, traffic seems distant, hints of disaster irrelevant, the nights calm. And the people of this fine city seem much as they always were: reserved, polite, respectful, cautious, but kind to strangers, especially from afar. Yes, I always feel in Tombland I shall be treated as I expect to be treated: with attention, respect, homage, admiration – all that befits a very remarkable and famous man indeed.

3. I Was Born . . .

'I was born . . .' oh yes, how often have we read openings of that kind, how many stories start in that drably familiar way, 'I was born, in the year 17—, in the town of St Malo, my father being a famous soldier, or cobbler, or priest, or butcher . . .' And so began almost all of the novels, written in one country or another, that I read so keenly as an untidy boy when, exiled from my parents, my older brothers and sisters, even from myself, solitary, dirty, neglected, dreaming, seemingly idle, I wandered, a fictional hero myself, through the darkened libraries, smoke-ravaged towers, untidy salons of the worn-out Breton ramparts and castles that belonged to my ancestral forebears, and to which I knew I was entitled by every right. In these days the novel, the fictional history, was the latest thing, and it was easy to predict the episodes that would follow: the familiar childhood misfortunes, the learning about life and love, the endless travels by land and sea, encounters with wars and brigands, beautiful foreign temptresses and mysterious nuns or countesses, the first meeting with the pure one, the endless diversions with maids and whores. The hero would encounter great events and suffer uncountable misfortunes and tortures. He would be persecuted by emperors and archbishops, warlords and popes. Perhaps he would be held by brigands in Sicily, perhaps sold into slavery to the Turks. No matter. He would finally return home, discover his childhood loved one, now rich, make his peace with his father, take up a happy and virtuous life. It was after reading too many such books I made a serious promise. If I ever chose, for whatever reason, to undertake to tell the story of my own quite worthless existence, I would never begin it in that way. And as you can see, I have faithfully kept my promise. In any case, I have always believed things start where they finish. So my tale begins at the other end.

I died then, in my eightieth year, on the rez-de-chaussée of an apartment in the Rue du Bac in Paris, on a day of loud fusillades: a bloody day for my riotous city, a day of joy and freedom for the rebellious Americans, who perhaps will never know how much they are indebted to me. My wife – to whom I had been throughout my life steadfastly loyal, even if never for a moment faithful – died just a year earlier. I was not uncheered by the event. For I still had the support of my mistress and my muse, the famed Mme Juliette Recamier, of whose talents everyone knows. Though by now in her life she was blind as a bat, and I was feeble, gouty, rheumatic, loud-creaking, we adored each other to the last. The moment I became a widower I made my divine Juliette an impassioned proposal of matrimony; given our geriatric circumstances, she thought it something of a redundancy. I finally agreed. We spent our time together, as Victor Hugo described: 'The woman who could no longer see groped for the man who could no longer feel.' In the end we scarcely outlived each other, though I did contrive, as I intended, to go first. I had been expecting this moment the whole of my life, and all possible arrangements had been settled. To the last history tried to cheat me, arranging great events to upstage my own memorial. By now I cared nothing for it, and it was not to succeed. Though Paris attempted to neglect me, the sea did not. A fortnight after I died my corpse reached St Malo. Next day, according to my precise instructions, I was buried on the seaward tip of the Grand Be, in a tomb that I had acquired from the city and had long been awaiting me. The tiny islet (to which I recommend a respectful visit) lies in the Atlantic breakers, just off the town, to which it is joined by tidal causeway; now you see it, now you don't. In Old Breton, I had discovered, the word 'be' actually means a grave. I had not known that at the time I planned my future there, but you see how sound my romantic instincts are. So the tomb is in a place of perfect name, an ideal location, and an exact position – for, in death as in life, I stare out to sea and far-distant prospects, while at the same time lying in full view of the very room in which I was born.

And now you ask, where then was I born? I was born in the year 1768, in a small house in the ramparted port of St Malo, my father coming from one of the great aristocratic families of Brittany, though he struggled through hard times. In those days St Malo was a republic to itself, a fortress protected on every side: on three by the sea, and on the fourth by a great wall. A fingerland grasped from the raging ocean, a natural haven for seafarers, it had been made chief stronghold for generations of the bravest and most daring of Breton sailors, those who ventured furthest and risked most. The very name of the region is Amorica, and though there are those who claim the lands of the New World were named for Amerigo Vespucci, we know better. For the lands and shores of North America were always Amorican regions, and we made it our hunting grounds, taking the cod off the Grand Banks, later on pirating from our rivals the British. And why, far to the icy south, are those islands the British called Falklands truly called Malvinas? They are named after us, the citizens of Malo. As for Britain itself, it is named after Brittany; unless, as is just as possible, the people of Brittany are the true Britons, driven out by the Norman invader. Alas, history, our courage and our ramparts never stopped the British from attacking us, much as we never stopped robbing from them. In fact they invaded and set fire to St Malo during the Seven Years War, less than ten years before my gloomy and inauspicious birth.

It was my birth you were asking about, and I shall tell you everything. I was born in the small upstairs room of a house in the Rue des Juifs, long since departed by the Chateaubriands and long since turned into an inn. And I entered the world at the time of the September equinox, the time when wild storms rage and the tide runs highest; and never more so than in that remarkable year of 1768. I was a late child, and by now of childbearing my mother had had, as it were, far more than her fill. But my sombre and terrifying father, who had girls aplenty but one son only, felt grimly that if his aristocratic titles and privileges were to be truly handed on he needed further male heirs; little did he understand the futility of his dreams. The contest between my father and mother proved unequal; however grudgingly she went about it, my mother was compelled to bear me and shove me out into the world. But she plainly took care to find the worst opportunity; beyond the windows a violent storm still remembered in the region surged so fiercely the roar of the wind and the crashing of the waves entirely stifled the sound of my infant cries. Most of those present (the room was crowded) thought they were attending not a birth but a death.

And so they might as well have done. Eighty years on, and the whole feeble thing was over. Just beyond the windows lay, for all to see, the grim and rocky coast, where the storm blasted and the high waves crashed. Plain in view could be seen the town calvary, the Breton pardon, where a carved Christ and his stone saints hang in line beside the town gibbet, which at the time was as usual occupied by the usual rotting flesh. Beyond the wind-flapped corpse lay the islets; it is on the promontory of one of these that my pleasant resting place is to be found. In fact, like the world itself, I was always a circular ruin. In the moment of my beginnings you could already read word of my end. In the pulse into life you could witness the silence of death. In the creak of the cradle you could register the sedimentation of the tomb. My birth was prophecy, portrait, promise and warning. Those who thought I was a dead-letter delivery were nearly right. I might just as well have been, placed in the tomb at once. For that is where, after the eighty years of living and breathing servitude I had to endure after my mother so grudgingly and indifferently inflicted life on me, I have ended up.

Stand today on the shoreline and try to survey and imagine me now. Now turn in another direction and stare if you can at an even more impressive promontory, the Mont-Saint-Michel, another islet, another causeway, another great graveyard, created like my own little island when more ancient storms brought great seas to scour our coasts, leaving these strange, solemn, granite remnants in the very midst of the ways. At Mont-Saint-Michel there live and die those who choose to retreat from the world to go to a higher one, who live in a world of confessions and pledges, pilgrimages and penitences, orisons and vespers, effigies, coffins, tombs and graves. These are the places of monks and abbesses; such was the fate intended for me, and such was the destiny to which my own sister came. Look out to sea even further and you might glimpse the island of Jersey, fertile and abundant, castled and abbeyed; here more of my people lived, and there my strange destiny would eventually take me. Further on still lie the islands of Britain, which I long considered the enemy until one day it became my unexpected friend; and I went there too. And then, beyond, to the west, the great savage lands of America, where my father found his first piratical fortune, and where in time I found mine.

So, then, I was born, as I said, in the year 1768 in the town of St Malo, the scarce-wanted late child of a pirate Breton aristocrat who scarcely had time to notice I was there. Thus I started life amid an ancient, picturesque and scarce-disturbed town and seascape, of oilskinned sailors, rocking fisherboats, black-dressed and lace-bonneted women, the gossips of the town. In the shallower waters of that coast, beyond the view of the calvary and the gibbet, set into the waters, stand many wooden fishing towers: strange retreats where my fellow Amoricans, seafarers by nature every single one of them, even if they venture out no further, spend their nights alone in a gloomy and cosmic solitude, gazing at the stars, holding bright flares to the water, to lure fish into their nets and so into our superb gastronomy and our capacious Breton stomachs. I too was born a solitary, a stranger, a wanderer, an exile, a spiritual pirate. That is how I started here; that is why I return.

But I was also born a gentleman. And if, today, in your age of egalitarianism, you wish to understand me, please me, even speak to me, this is one fact about me you must not forget. For, above all else I was born – in that ill-chosen year of 1768, as I think I already mentioned – into a world that was already coming to its end, so that all I saw was an illusion. I was born into a time where any who believed in high ideals would be crushed by the lowest of realities. I was made for bravery and heroism and condemned to idleness and misery. I was made for splendour and condemned to filth. I was a philosopher of the time when they betrayed philosophy, a man of reason when reason was the first thing they abused and rejected. It was as much as a Chateaubriand could have expected; we had always known we were made for disaster. No sooner were we restored to wealth than we were made penniless, no sooner did we succeed than we failed, and no sooner were we born to hope than we died. All we had for certain was our honour, which we never lost. Across Europe mine was a grim age of dispossession, such as has afflicted this continent from time to time, and still does; but none were dispossessed as thoroughly or as ruthlessly as the French, for only in that country was modern history taken to the full.

And so in me you find a man of two worlds. In the world before the Terror I was high and puissant, the Chevalier de Chateaubriand, aristocrat, adventurer, hero, descendant of the Breton knights. In the world after it I was, well, François-René Chateaubriand, citizen, a people's cockade in my hat. In the world beyond the tomb I can be whoever and whatever I like, and that is precisely what I am. Well, I am content to have been the unrepentant dupe of two or three noble ideas: liberty and fidelity and honour. And in truth I always preferred my name to my title. But it is my title that reminds me how futile our liberties are, how rarely we experience fidelity, how unusual a thing is honour. And how, for all the chattering cant of equality, fraternity and justice, a new and improved history can stink quite as horribly as the old.

4. Being a Gentleman

Yes, I was born a gentleman. And the truth is that all the important figures of my age – by that I mean not generals, conquerors, politicos, lawyers or hangmen, but poets, prophets, thinkers, dreamers – were gentlemen too. Seedy provincial law-hacks may have overthrown kings, rewritten national constitutions, even changed the calendar ordained by God. Upstart Corsican corporals may have created some of the greatest victories, as well as some of the most shameful defeats. But in the end they do not construct the real world: which is not real at all, but shaped only by ideas and the imagination. In old French there is a very beautiful word, *élite*. It means elect, the chosen, the finest flower, primus inter pares, the pick of the crop. In English its meaning somehow declines or fades: it signifies something petty and snobbish, or a printers' type that has twelve letters to the inch. To me, it means that higher is always better than lower, as better is better than worse, gold is finer than dross, wheat better than chaff, truffles better than ordure, quality better than trash. In the same way little is smaller than big, and nothing inferior to something.

Yet these simple and quite obvious principles – the rules of taste – were not to outlast my lifetime; more than half my life was spent in an era when the opposite was mistakenly thought true. Thus my age was the time of the gentleman as exile. It would be these exiled gentlemen who made our modern consciousness, shaped our deepest feelings, took us from the arid wastes of reason and materialism to the deeper and duskier world of passion, sentiment, wisdom. Consider if you like a particular hero of mine: George Gordon, Milord Byron. In the portraits you will at once spot the likeness between us. As I have always admired him, so he even more admired me. Since he was a decade younger, it was his work that owed everything to mine. As for his brooding 'Byronic' heroes, they were simply versions of my 'René' – as he once freely acknowledged in a letter of homage he wrote to me (now lost, alas).

He was of course a most noble, titled, well-educated gentleman, a scion of Harrow, lionized by British society till he became lover to his own half-sister, Augusta, an act of moral courage for which he was most heartily despised. Man of sentiments, lover of liberty, he was soon rejected everywhere, called diabolic, satanic or vampiric, confronted by countless insults and the gossip of jealous and abusive women, expelled by his class, many of whom shared the same tastes and instincts, indulged the same desires and had the same manners. 'You recollect that with the exception of a few friends I was detested and blackened by all ... nothing can ever atone for the atrocious caprice – the unsupported – almost unasserted – the kind of hinted persecution – and shrugging Conspiracy – of which I was attempted to be made the victim ...' he reasonably complained.

So he was forced to see the truth of his own self: 'He stood a stranger in this breathing world / An erring spirit from another hurl'd'. Unwanted, victimized, conspired against, blackened by all. Yet at the same time deeply needed, an elegant Satan and Faustus who became one of the living wonders of the Romantic world. Exile was all that was left; so he travelled, travelled the rest of his life away among those who appreciated what his richly satanic spirit meant to the world. Ever a gentleman, he toured with a milord's retinue: manservant, maidservant, mistress and monkey. He wandered like an adventurer, carried a revolver, shot where and what he liked. Wherever he went he demanded what he needed, was always obliged with whatever he wanted, no matter how splendid, extravagant, amazing or outrageous it was. The whores and courtesans of Venice shivered with delight at the thought of his arrival in the watery republic. The purses of every pander and pimp swelled at the thought of profit. The canals filled with the rocking gondolas of caped libertines and dominoes as they sat beneath torches on the foetid water and watched a great man take his ripe vampiric pleasures. He lived like a voluptuary, cultivated darkness like fallen Satan, felt himself to be a suffering saint, dreamt fancies and fantasies like a woman. He died like a hero in wartime, fighting for Greek liberty, freedom from foreign tyranny – not liberty for himself but someone else.

Or take the grand explosive dreamer, Percy Shelley, who complained 'I am born darkly, fearfully afar.' He was a lesser class of gentlemen (father but a mere Member of Parliament) but another outcast, ejected from Oxford and society for his rebellious passions, hatred of monarchs, carnivores, matrimony, God. Adored and pursued by women all his days, he too offended sexual rule and custom, and fled into exile, leaving a ghost behind: his first wife Harriet drowned herself in the Serpentine. He travelled through Europe with a no less varied, seductive retinue: a clever new wife, Mary; her stepsister Claire, probably also his mistress; three children, one of them Claire's by Lord Byron; not to say a manservant and a maidservant, who were doubtless lovers; then a retinue of tempting, loving friends. From the Alps down to the Apennines they travelled; the great cities unrolled, Florence and Pisa and Venice and Rome and Naples and then Lucca and back to the shores of the Gulf of Spezia again. Though not as high in the social empyrion as Byron, he could still travel like a milord, summoning a thousand a year from the estates of the family that despised him; afford to rent good apartments, buy books, print

elegant volumes, hire carriages and horses, build sea-going
boats – boats not quite as grand as Byron's, perhaps, but enough
to challenge the elements to the last. And he too was always
despised by those who envied him, for his ethereal visions,
his grand dismays, his sexual dreams, his libertarian ideals, his
incestuous instincts, his hopes of progress and poetry, his sense
of life beyond the tomb. He died afloat, in a romantic tempest,
the ghosts of love and liberty all around him, his body floating
home from the storm-racked bay and on to the shoreline,
where in a strange and pagan ceremony it was burned amid the
sea and the raging waves, consigned to a destiny that, when I
think of it, seems much like my own.

Look at Aleksandr Pushkin, born to the Russian landed
gentry, a family going back six centuries, to a mother duskily
descended from the great Abyssinian princes called to the great
Russian court. A man educated at the finest of schools, the
academy at Tzarskoye Selo, where the best courtiers were
trained. A gentleman, a bored flâneur, a man who, like his
own Eugene Onegin, had tired of all and tasted everything:
attended all the possible balls, concerts and operas, pursued and
bedded all the possible women, risked fortunes and fought
duels, gambled and drunk nightly, tried to secure the state of
his soul: 'Once more an idler, now he smothers / The
emptiness that plagues his soul . . . The old was dated, through
and through, / And nothing new lay in the new.' Naturally
his fate was exile too; the poet was far too free and honest in
his views on tyranny and, driven from court, only just escaping
execution, he went to waste his days in Bessarabia and Odessa,
until the court felt the need to have him, or his charming wife,
back again. Sexual intrigue surrounded him, slander and satire,
the fate of the cuckolder who was cuckolded himself. A
gentleman's duel finally disposed of him, before he was even
forty; he died, his work half-written, of the wounds of love
and boredom and dishonour.

Each of them – the great men of my Romantic age – was
gentleman, discard, outcast, dreamer, redeemer, exile. All had
prospects of power and grandeur; all discarded them for some-

thing finer. All wandered agonized out of an old world that was no longer worthy of them into a new one they somehow could not make happen. Each dreamt of some innocent Utopia: a settlement amongst Indians on the banks of the Susquehanna; an innocent naked paradise in the Pacific seas; a tomb by the water; an eternity where dreams of freedom could wander, and their poetry sing its message to the future. And I, in France, was much the same, the dreamer in the age of ruins and exile. Or almost the same. For, if you consider Byron, Keats and Shelley, Pushkin, then think of Chateaubriand, you will find one great difference. They were born after me, but died before, suddenly and young: Keats in papal Rome in his twenties, Shelley self-immersed in a storm off Lerici by thirty, Pushkin by a pistol in Petersburg, Byron caught by fever and treachery at Missolonghi by forty. All managed no more than half a life or less.

Which means they never saw the age of sober senses, huge smoke-cities, wage-labourers and the puffing railroad engine; the drab office and tiresome shopping arcade; the new respectability, ancient male sexual longings silenced and crushed in the chaster virtues of the feminine, the frockcoats and the toppers, the Bessemer process, the time when factory whistle and cash box ruled – not to say the aspirin, the electric light bulb, the underground railway, powered flight, the contraceptive pill. They remained forever romantic heroes. I danced on and on, and learned a much longer story. At the end Juliette Recamier and I, in our eighties, were dancing still; she blind as a bat in a belfry, I a feeble widower, doing my dance of death on groaning pins. They were romantic exiles, dreaming poets, who before they died could see nothing ahead but the most glorious evolutionary prospects: Greek and Italian liberty, sexual paradise everywhere, fraternity and equality, the open promise of the future. I lived through the outcome; I saw what really happened. By the time you are eighty, one revolution is like another. Equality is boredom. Sex is phantom pleasure, the barricades a mad illusion, a useless bloodletting caused by those who fail to remember the world belongs not to those who die young but those who trouble to get old. I saw what happened; that is why I am different.

This is the point. Unlike the others, I survived. I started out before; I shaped and guided them; I long outlasted them. And since I outlived them by decades and generations, and told my story to era after era, I was able to outrun and excel every one of them, and so become what above all I aspired to be: the most famous, the most interesting, the most romantic, the most lovable man in the world. It was my public display of what I became — Mr Misunderstood, Monsieur Romanticism, the tragical, dark and gloomy genius, far more lovelorn than Byron, much more victimized, abused and admired than the adorable roguish Pushkin, a good deal more agonized and angelic than the ethereal Shelley, feebler in body and more sensitive in features than the breathless white-faced Keats — which made my reputation. So I turned into what I am. I became famous, over and over again. I was forgotten, over and over again. So it has gone on. Yet my life has never been entirely overlooked, my tale never been silenced and never completed. I have gone on telling it; and I have never ceased to go on changing my story, my memories, my image or my mind.

5. Telling My Story

It was in the year 1811, the year Napoleon started on his madman's plan to throw his armies on Moscow, one of the greatest follies of history, that I first began to tell my story, from the other side — which of course is now *this* side — of the grave. I was still myself extremely alive, only at the midpoint of my days. I had come to a quiet if not dangerous point in my fortunes. I started to write in my Hermitage, my now long-gone house in La Vallée des Loups, Wolf Valley, close to Sceaux, now a banlieu, a destination on the Paris regional Métro line, but in those days a remote and distant land of beauty and pleasure where a man of soul could hide. Very close to here, at Chatenay, a great grinning genius, Voltaire, author of *Candide*, and man of wisdom, was born a mere century before. And now a second genius, the author of *The Genius of Christianity*, a man of not just thought but of passion and feeling too (in other words, *moi*, myself), had chosen this site for his retreat and his reflections, financing the purchase with grateful thanks to a certain world-famous Indian princess. Yes, it was my darling muse from the Natchez, my mournful Atala, who raised the roof there, the profits from her imaginary existence turning into chateau and garden, lake and pond, bamboo grove and tree. Here I sat in solitude, loving every tree and bush, worshipping every insect, hugging every bush. I was in great disgrace at the time, having fallen out with the little Corsican madman who, having once rescued France, now chose to trample her underfoot, and who made crazily sure that my world would change yet again, from elegy through hope, then back to elegy. I mean Napoleon Bonaparte, of course. It is on that single man that not only my nation's terrible misfortunes but even this present book can be blamed.

I began to write my tale one day in October, on my birthday (though it was not; I was born, as I said, at the September equinox but had confused the date, so unreliable is memory, I find). At first it was meant simply as a memoir, a recollection of my life as lived so far. But such was my history, such my part in history, that memories no longer served. For as history changes, so do memories, and what we think we recollect, what we believe we value, is reconstructed. Could I believe what I said? Was I anything like what I said I was? And since then, as I've said, the story has been told and retold, in many versions, as befits a man whose life has taken on many shapes, suffered many fortunes and reverses, and gone on far too long. Over time and circumstance, the story continued and constantly changed. Revising and improving, I was determined that no one would ever see it in my lifetime, and that the world should wait fifty years after my death, or far better a hundred, before it was read. Even that selfless thought was a vain one; that was not how it was to be. It was not vanity but the poverty that descends with old age (and it can happen to any, even the greatest, finest and most famous) that made me sign contracts with a publisher, one of those venal souls who plant their bottomless bottoms only on the bottom line, and by whose honour and promises I was, as usual, shamefully deceived. By then my house in Wolf Valley was long lost.

My house was lost, yes. But my tale was not. It was likewise not personal vanity but the endless solicitation of admiring friends that encouraged me to give regular readings, gathering huge crowds around me in Madame Recamier's much sought-after salon. So in some strange fashion my unknown work suddenly became known everywhere. Without any intervention at all by me, episodes slipped out and appeared in the most widely read magazines, further confusing the story I had already confused so carefully myself. Though I repudiated everything and wearily explained I had written nothing, I was constantly asked for more of the same. However much I shuddered with shame and embarrassment as the tale spread, I was helplessly famous. Naturally I denied everything, insisted that the stories I told were not mine, or were totally fictional; many still chose to take them for the truth. But this, I fear, is the unhappy fate of the writer who simply wishes that his work never be read.

Now I have ended where I always had the fantasy of beginning, from the moment my womb-encrusted eyes opened on to the sight of my sea-girt tomb. In much the same way, the end of my story returns to its own beginning, having now acquired a greater backwards and forwards, a splendid backlog and a very confusing future. From where I stand, or rather lie, now, the story I told is of itself without any importance, since everything that matters to us in our lives is of little moment to us once we are dead, apart from the right to eternity itself. The story of our story is that there is no story. What matters is not our story, but what is *made* of our story: how it is managed, manipulated, rewritten, deconstructed by other hands than our own. The same is true of history – as Bonaparte, for whom cunning plans and calculations were everything and in the end nothing, found at last to his cost.

So like the enigmatic Sphinx I now sit in the desert, amid

great desolation, at the heart of Tombland. The sands roll away in all directions; the doors of open graves and the lids of empty sarcophagi lie around me. The truth is that this is a perfect literary site. From here I can see backward and forward, to the past, someone's present present, and the future, all of which are exactly the same to me. I stare at the sun; I blink cat-like with a vast and hidden knowledge. I can be wise and certain, without any risk of contradiction. I can explain everything, I can reflect on everything: emperors and kings, citizens and serfs, eternity and futility. The statues of everything, from gods and men to beasts and birds, lie tumbled in the sand; ruin is the universal condition, as it was when I was alive. I wander from one Tombland to the next, over fallen palaces, broken temples to an infinity of lost gods, smashed pantheons to forgotten heroes, battered crypts and bone-stacked catacombs, entombment chambers, mummified and blackened corpses.

Strange: how the world of ruins automatically became ours. This truth was observed by my friend, or quite possibly my enemy, the Comte Constantine de Volney, another visitor to Niagara, who said in his book *The Ruins of Empires* that it is in the nature of great nations to fall into decline or revolution, and leave tragic ruins behind; while those ruins come to represent both our past and our future, showing the futility of the present. And, since we generally end up mourning what we suppose to be progress or improvement, it is indeed the ruins, and not the revolutions, that most concern the human race. Which is why, from my sea-splashed tomb on the island, or any of the other scenes of ruin, tomb and monument that form my present habitation (a position which is also called posterity) I can observe everything. Even the dawn of a new millennium, which some innocent people may think to be the dawn of an apocalyptic new dispensation, does not amaze me; the world is returning to its time-weary ordinariness as I write. And so, from the world of tombs and ruins, I can once again tell, but this time in much better order, my story. Of which, let me warn you, not one word should be accepted as honest. Or reliable. Or true.

6. The Art of Fiction

For I am a liar – and, I hope, a very good one. All life-stories are lies, all storytellers are liars, each one doing his or her job with various degrees of skill, intention, cunning, intricacy, conviction, deceit and grandeur. But I am a true and complete professional, and I've learned the hard way. In fact on several occasions I have served as ambassador for my country. My aim, in general at least, is never exactly to deceive, or be in any way dishonest; that is the lowest and cheapest level of lying. Mine is the poet's or the fiction-maker's aim, which is to improve, enlarge, create through the power of imagination the improvement of the unimprovable world. For the world is nothing until we think about it, and begin to name and dream it. It is a bare nullity until words, ideas, dreams and imaginings have been added. The world is made up of millions of lies, added together. And it is all the better for the great ones, not least the versions and variations and falsifications, I have, over time, in story after story, book after book, decade after decade and era after era, laid over it.

On this matter I am shameless. Deception is without question the poet's duty. Like all writers, I lie for my own purposes, good and bad. My personal gratification and advancement, I will not deny it; who is going to look after us, if we do not look after ourselves? My life, like my death, is a valuable commodity I have never neglected to develop. The advancement of my fickle foolish nation, France: so sadly humiliated, just before my birth, by the loss of her two great empires in the two Indies; so tragically divided, in the years of my early manhood, by the tide of blood and cannibalism; so strangely left, in the time of Empire, amid its ruins and trophies; so haunted by the gains and losses which are the true breeding grounds of imagination. The advancement of history, the miserable process my sad life has coincided with, in its hideous passage from reason to terror to feeling. The protection of justice and liberty, the growth of religion and spiritual wisdom.

The advancement, quite naturally, of bodily pleasure: of food and drink and love and music and dance and women. It is fiction's task to keep the world alive, and the things we love in it: since everything I love is debris, and all the important places and people in my life have been destroyed in their turn, it is the only way to keep the world alive . . .

Just a few days back, as I browsed over the shelves of the pleasant and quiet second-hand bookshop that lies just across the street from the cathedral gardens where I pass my days here in Tombland, I came across a fascinating volume of literary essays. They were entitled *Inventory*, and written by a fellow countryman of mine, a M. Michel Butor. He resides in the later twentieth century, and calls himself an 'anti-novelist', which I understand to mean that he does not hate and despise novels, as some do, but thinks they have never been written correctly until he came along. The novels he writes himself he calls, I gather, 'experiments', as writers generally do: works made of confusion and senselessness, randomness and strange codes, multiple layers of time and mystifications of space, and telling stories that are set in imaginary cities which bewilderingly change as they are observed. His world is at the furthest extreme from mine, his ideas at odds with all I think and feel. His stories are a welter of facts and objects that cannot be mastered by the imagination – whereas mine, by contrast, is a world of the imagination casting its glorious powers over all, seizing feelings and sensations from every single object. No wonder I expected nothing from his book. And how could I have been so wrong?

For M. Butor is an inventive wonder, a postmodern miracle: a pussy cat. Far from proving my adversary, he turns out to be my admirer, my acolyte, I might even say my sycophant. Like me, Butor has had his imagination taken over by the remarkable wonder of America, though, as a writer of five generations later, it proves a place one can scarcely believe exists. Yet even so he walks in my footsteps, even to the booming banks, the crumbling rim, the tumbling torrent, the exhilarating drop of the Falls of Niagara themselves. One of his books (he calls it an

'American mobile' and a 'stereophonic novel', and it is certainly full of a million sounds and voices, noise, boom, woof and tweet) is called *6,810,000 Litres of Water A Second*: the speed, of course, that the great watery torrent surges over Niagara's twin Falls, nowadays with the chief purpose of keeping Eastern America in street lamps and computer electrics. Turn to this Moebius strip of a postmodern tale – which Butor also describes as 'a liquid monument in perpetual motion', the form of the book cleverly aping the torrents themselves – and you will even hear a voice (not mine, for I am no longer here) reading from the pages of my own American novel, *Atala* – in other words from the first great literary representation of the great Falls themselves.

For *Atala* was indeed the book that unlocked the literary and metaphysical magic of America and the raging torrent at its heart. (It also, by the way, provided me with that fine now lost house in the Valley of the Wolves.) I was the first; since then the whole story has fallen into a confusion, a medley, for since my work an immense number of voices have created innumerable Niagaras which, in ever declining and more disgusting order, tumble to mist and spray over the great falls. How could I have known that I would be the one who had to catch them at their one true moment of sublimity: the last moment not simply for my Indian tribe, the Natchez, who died a hundred years before me, but for myself as well? How could I know that the sublime tumult I witnessed from my horse as I sat there was actually the beginning of the end? But so it has always been for me. Ruins follow me everywhere: even nature's ruins, the ruins of mountains, cataracts, waterfalls. After me it's downriver all the way.

Generously M. Butor reminds us of all the other voices that sounded since I wrote, and their defamed Niagaras: the voices of surprised explorers, awed visitors, bored tourists, Sunday painters, weekend poets; the murmurs of newly-weds and tightrope walkers, barrel riders and padlocked escapologists; the groans and shouts of suicidal depressives, daredevil leaptakers, the whispers of gigolos and the lovelorn, mourning widows or discarded lovers, the yells of ice cream and hamburger merchants, waxwork makers, souvenir sellers, tat-vendors, trash vulgarians, commercial entrepreneurs who have turned the spectator into the condom-clad tourist and Niagara itself from sublimity into bathos. Perhaps the only consolation is that the Falls they see and those I once saw are in no real way the same. For by the laws of geological recession the great rim has receded, making its way along the Niagara River on a long journey from east to west. Thus the Falls the descendants of Atala saw before my own birth are not the Falls that I stared into; the Falls that engrossed me are not those that Tocqueville or Lyell saw; which are not the same Falls that the Canadian army saw in 1837 when, faced with an incursion from America, they sent the American vessel *Caroline* over the Falls and on fire; which are not the same Falls that Oscar Wilde saw ('Every American bride is taken there, and the sight of the stupendous waterfall must be one of the earliest if not the keenest disappointments in American married life'), which are not the same as those visited by M. Butor in the age of postmodern hyper-tourism, and which led him to write his own fiction.

And I should add that writing respectfully in my own footsteps is not the only homage M. Butor pays me. In the pages of his book *Inventory* he justly hails me as a founder of the modern novel, then goes on to write about me with that special form of blinkered modern cunning that belongs to the twentieth century, an epoch imprisoned by the psycho-thumb of Herr Doktor Sigmund Freud. 'There are two men in Chateaubriand,' he observes, 'M. le Vicomte, the "ambassador", the politician who converted to Christianity at the right moment, without bothering to decorate that moment with mystical trappings . . . stubborn defender of a throne and an altar he knew to be increasingly rickety [did I?]; and an "other", whose indiscretions were a terrible embarrassment to him, who was always being contrasted with him, who never ceased to haunt him and who alone interests us today.' Clearly it is as well there were two of me, since one would never do. And, in the eyes of M. Butor, I must be very glad of my 'other', my

'demon', since it is he who has made me 'one of the greatest
poets of our language, whose inventions have had an influence
on the transformation of taste, on our present taste . . .'

So what is he saying? That in this doubled self of mine there
is the man of history and politics, an opportunist who knows
when it is smart to be revolutionary and when a conservative
Christian. And there is also a demon, a noble savage, driven
by strange passions, sublime, pagan, erotic, a creature of vast
dreams and formidable indiscretions. Between us *moi* and *lui*
turned religion from ancient faith into modern indulgence,
convent chastity into sublime eroticism, death itself into the
most voluptuous pleasure. Because one of us is always yielding
to the other, everything I write is actually its own opposite,
falling on its face or disguising its origins. As we say in Paris
these days, *il s'abyme*; it deconstructs itself. Which means that
my gift, which some thought classical and others romantic, is
truly a modern one, since everything slips over itself, everything
descends into its own void, every plot and narrative is sucked
up by the quicksands beneath its feet, words cannot mean what
they say, forms cannot be what they mean, and everything slips
down into the tomb.

But why must I reject my own life, upturn my own tale,
murder my history, decapitate my sentiments, destroy all my
trophies, send my loved ones off to the guillotine, put all on
the far side of the tomb? The answer lies in my hidden secret;
he unlocks it. 'It is incest that troubles our René above all.' Is
that it then? My entire life and philosophy thus explained,
based on an unspeakable union, the forbidden link that twins
brother and sister as lover and lover, and makes all love into
two shared portions of one dish, the bond that says two souls
who must one day lie under the same gravestone might as well
lie in the same bed? Yet who hid the secret? Did I ever deny
it? Wasn't it I, who in my novel *René*, forged in the passion of
René and his divine sister Amelia the highest form of love,
without which neither the history of Egypt nor the spirit of
modern feeling could ever have existed? And having said so,

didn't I pass it to others, in the age of overripe imaginations and too many revolutions?

'Incest is, like many other incorrect things, a very poetical circumstance,' Shelley said in an unsolicited testimonial. Byron practised it; Shelley himself claimed that the family that played together stayed together, and favoured the most intricate connubials that linked relative with relative, the living and the dead, in intricate spirals of relationship the biographers still enjoy unravelling, as a visit to the Tombland Bookshop testifies. 'Great is their love who love in sin and fear'; this is the motto of Manfred and The Revolt of Islam, The Cenci and Annabel Lee. 'Sympathies of a scarcely intelligible nature had always existed between them': so Edgar Allan Poe wrote of the young Usher twins, Roderick and Madeleine, who held together across the doorway of the tomb itself. Who is the most perfect loved one; surely the one who most resembles and mirrors ourselves? So Poe himself married his child-cousin Clemmie, saw her die, and searched for her too on the other side of the tomb. Thus our love for the things that bind lives to deaths, deaths to lives. Mesmer and Galvani, the mechanical man, the werewolf and the vampire: what would we do without them?

And what better than a twin bed for eternity can we hope for, preferably with en suite bathroom and minibar, as we head for our winter bargain-break on the further side of the tomb?

7. Sisters

Still, enough of these thoughts. It's the story of my own life and death we are all waiting here for, and I fear in my usual fashion I'm delaying things a little too long. Now you have me born then, a piratic young aristocrat, come to life in a grim and curfewed town, a battlemented island that was not quite an island, rather a bold savage finger stuck into the arse of the violent Atlantic Ocean – which, displeased, never ceased taking its revenge. In this ramparted old town, smelling of brine and tar, the ancient ways still served. Old women in heavy black dresses and high lace headcaps oversaw everything and gossiped about all. They soon had me down with a bad reputation. Even as a tot I was sharp, clever, sly and rebellious, a tattered little chevalier destined for bad things. I spent my time with drunks and brawlers, played by the calvary and the gibbet, teased the hangman, wandered the shoreline, became regular companion with the wind and the waves. I stared out to sea, in fear and expectation, fought the storms, risked my life on the sea wall, nearly drowned many times in the huge swamping tides, watched the mists come in over the Grand Be. Boats sank at sea in front of me; the waves presented me regularly with the corpses of foreign sailors and the strange flotsam of battered ships; I went to sleep to the sound of the beating waves. I was neglected, my education entrusted to priests and providence. Death was at hand, danger frequent, religion never very far away. When I was eight I was taken to the nearby Abbey of Notre-Dame, my clothes changed from white to purple, given over by way of the tomb to the Lord. Monks chanted in the cloisters as the Abbé pronounced that I would one day take my vows, travel to the Holy Land, become a pilgrim and an exile. All these predictions came true, though none of them in the ways he meant.

My mother Apolline was a little social woman, and really interested only in my older brother, Jean-Baptiste, who was elegant, promising, and already near-adult, already determined to make his way in Paris and at court. Of my four living sisters, three were near-adult also, and dreaming of marrying the comtes, the chevaliers, the seigneurs who would become their ambiguous and eventually very dangerous fate. My mother, flitting the streets in her best dresses, loved St Malo; my father, old rogue of a shipmaster, slave trader and corsair, grim and bald and cruel and sharp, had higher ambitions. He wished to restore our aristocratic fortunes, and, paying far too much, he purchased the battered old chateau of Combourg, deep in the old Amorican woods and forests, away from the sea and off

the road that leads to Rennes. He took it along with its titles
– Count and Seigneur de Granges and heaven knows which –
and here he retreated, so we scarcely saw him at all.

I had, of family still living, my brother, who as I say was
ambitious and distinguished, and undoubtedly destined for
preferment in Paris, and my four sisters, most of them near-
adult and longing for marriage. These had only small meaning
for me; the only person close to me was the youngest sister,
Lucile. She was two years older than I, but just as ragged,
neglected and overlooked as I was. Clothed in her sister's
cast-offs, wearing overlong dresses and a metal collar, she was
ungainly and pitiful. She went to the same nurses as I, the same
small schools, and was left in my care like a toy. I could have
misused her in any way, discarded her. In fact she came to
see me as her protector, and I came to see her as my friend.
We were two exiles, and a bond of common melancholy, of
temperament and taste, increasingly drew us together. When
the family retired to Combourg, we wandered the fields and
forests together, often not speaking for hours, and then, even
as children, we talked together about the feelings, poetic and
religious, that the sensations of nature inspired.

As time passed by, she acquired a deep and severe beauty,
and the face of someone inspired by gloomy thoughts. Now
there were only four of us together, in a great chateau that
could have housed hundreds: my ever more distant and gloomy
father, my mother, religious, and longing for the company of
St Malo, my sister and myself. In a house that felt full of ghosts,
my father became a kind of ghost himself. We scarcely saw
him, and only at night did he appear to wander his own ruins,
flitting in his oldest robes between the flaring torches, then
disappearing into the disguising mists of night-time again.

By day we walked and talked of our gloomy solitude; when
my words seemed profound to her she said, 'You must write it
down.' In the dark towers of the castle she went to bed each
night in fear and dreamt prophetic dreams. Sleepless, she often
sat before the great clock on the staircase and waited till
midnight struck: the hour of crimes and terrors. Melancholy,

which drew us together, also began to drive us apart. For she moved toward the consolations of religion and the convent, while I, drawn to adventure, manhood and poetry, looked upon women as power, flesh and muse.

For words now affected me; by now I had become a great reader of books. From the ruined shelves that surrounded me I picked up the records of Father Hennepin, the great Jesuit father who travelled with the La Salle expedition through the French lands of Canada, and travelling from Lake Frontenac and following the Niagara River, they came upon great falls: 'an incredible Cataract or Waterfall, which has no equal. The Niagara River near this place is only an eighth of a league wide, but is very deep in places, and so rapid above the great Fall, that it hurries down all the animals which try to cross it, without a single one being able to withstand its currents.' A vast quantity of water, which is discharged, he says, from 'four fresh Seas, stops or centers here, and so falls about six hundred feet down a Gulph, which one cannot look upon without Horror . . . The rebounding of these waters is so great, they plunge down a height of more than five hundred feet.'

So wonderful was this account, so great its magic, that I knew I would visit it. Indeed who, reading such words in childhood, would not want to turn such words into sights, such sights into sensations, such sensations back again into even greater words? Such are the arts of writing, the powers of story, the draw of facts and fictions, especially for a dreaming ragged boy who has a sense of a destiny that is still unnamed and can only be strangely fulfilled.

I decided to go to Paris, enjoy my rank, and become a philosopher . . .

HONOURED

THE FIRST APPROACH came unexpectedly and rather like a secret. The letter, in an official windowed envelope of no apparent distinction, had been sent on by my literary agent almost accidentally. Seventy-five years ago, when he received something similar, Joseph Conrad mistook it for an income-tax demand, and nearly threw it away. And it was a secret: an official letter from the Prime Minister's office, kindly murmuring of his mindedness to recommend me for an honour.

The form attached presented me with two boxes: one to be ticked if you agreed to let your name go forward, the other to be marked if you wanted to hear no more of this product. Anyone who has ever at any time read the *Guardian* will understand the surge of anxiety, guilt even, that wells up at this moment. We all know the moral dangers of the baubles of office, the trappings of rank, the odours of power. On the other hand any sensible person will immediately realize that first sensations are of excitement and pure delight. In a liberal mind like mine, the result is utter confusion. Ten minutes after I had posted back the form, I could no longer remember which of the boxes I had ticked.

The event itself approaches like a secret too. You might suppose, as I did, that the New Year Honours list (double-sized this year) would be announced on New Year's Day. In fact it's not; it appears on New Year's Eve, and the news is released to a select band of journalists the day before that, at twelve noon. So the first real knowledge that an honour really was dawning came when Anglia TV's newsroom rang to advise me a crew would be appearing on my doorstep very shortly, forelocks at the ready.

So to the following night, and the great moment itself – the moment of what used once to be called the Apotheosis. This was no secret; in fact I have to say it was very splendidly done. Fireworks rose over every major city on the globe. The Eiffel Tower erupted and the Washington Monument glowed. The River Thames caught fire, or almost. Thousands of distinguished people celebrated in long unmoving lines at Stratford tube station. A thousand years of past history was immediately discarded, and a new thousand ushered in.

Myself, I spent my magic moment of transformation not up a tower, on a wheel, in a tube station or inside a riverside dome. As I have for the last twenty-five years, I spent the turn of the year with a small group of fellow academics and writers at a house with bubbly in a Norwich suburb. As midnight neared, we stepped outside to watch a dozen or more rockets rise high over the Earlham housing estate, and then stepped back in again to see the millennium come. My academic host naturally disapproves of television, but he did have a set 'for the kids'. It was possible, by placing a magnifying glass in front of it, to discern Greenwich, the Queen and the Prime Minister, singing the statutory 'Auld Lang Syne'.

So the whole world and myself went from one condition to another; and both of us seemed equally confused. Everyone expected planes to drop from the sky, and all computing to grind to a halt. The sheer ordinariness took us all by surprise. The year 2000 seemed just like old-fashioned 1999. What had been and what was coming appeared identical. And it was exactly the same with me (except that I could now look at my titled wife with an entirely new respect).

I reflect that honours and life-changes are curious things, and perhaps not always for the best. Some time back, when *Punch* was still *Punch*, the great magazine offered to help me celebrate my birthday, by lending me a Rolls-Royce for a few days. All I had to do in return was write an article describing the difference it made to my life. I knew it would make none; I was completely wrong.

The car would not enter between our gateposts, so we had to spend hours parking it with very unenthusiastic friends. My children, instead of sitting in the back screaming for refreshments as usual, covered themselves with thick rugs and lay down embarrassed in the back. Restaurants found better tables; there was generally a free brandy after the meal. On the other hand, I was asked to join a society for Successful Builders, and whole districts of the city became No-Go Areas. To be honest, I was not sorry when the car went away.

Will it be that way now? I'm hardly sure, since the illnesses of the season mean that over the past couple of weeks I've scarcely gone beyond my front door. I have yet to go to the pub and get the saloon-bar reaction. The post has been splendid: a wonderful pile of kind associations, remembered events, old friendships. Former student protesters, devout anti-monarchists have been kind enough to join in. They were nice to me at the doctors' surgery, and even some fellow writers have been amazingly kind.

But the truth is that honours – the baubles of office, the trappings of rank, the odours of power – have always made writers anxious. Independent and critical spirits, they live in another world. Joseph Conrad refused that offered knighthood, though he did confess that, if only on behalf of Poland, he longed for the Nobel Prize. Thomas Hardy rejected one too, reputedly because he did not want his first wife to get a title, and preferred the OM.

Rudyard Kipling refused one, and so did John Galsworthy, neither of them famously alienated figures. But these were in times when honours were highly political, and had everything to do with class and influence. Peerages were purchased, and many of them went to aspiring, influential nouveaux riches. Lloyd George famously dispensed nearly 300 knighthoods in eighteen months, often in the form of reward for services rendered or yet to come.

In today's deeply different society, the issue of honours is still confused. We live in an age of democracy which is also an age of celebrity. More than ever before, writers exist in a world of prizes, recognitions, awards. Public honours are reflections of public values. Honours given to writers are honours given to literature, an affirmation of its cultural place and significance, in times when there are anxious fears it has fallen into neglect.

Nowadays writing, literature, takes its place in a world of a massive explosion of style, media and communications activity. It is swamped by the modern technologies, caught amid a welter of every kind of creative expression. Works of literary imagination are still a fundamental part of modern culture, especially our own, but it is important they should be affirmed.

My own feelings on the matter are deeply shaped by the experience of Angus Wilson, one of our great recent writers. He was my academic colleague, and together we founded the creative-writing MA at the University of East Anglia in 1970. In 1970 he was offered and accepted a knighthood. He found it a difficult decision, since he was a radical, a critic of British society, a campaigner for gay rights, and the prime minister was Margaret Thatcher.

Angus Wilson, rightly, took the honour as being not simply for his own work but his passionate efforts on behalf of literature and for his belief in its centrality. He had travelled the world lecturing on British fiction; he had worked with innumerable young writers, had fought for literary freedom and the interests of writers and writing.

The outcome, it should be said, was both happy and sad. His own work grew even more experimental, and he campaigned for literature, gay rights, social reform. Finally the corporate materialism of the British eighties grew too much for him. He believed the climate was destroying serious writing; he moved with his partner Tony Garrett to France. Then he fell ill and was unable to write.

He returned to Britain not too long before his death in 1991. Happily, his feeling that the eighties had destroyed literature in Britain was wrong. In fact the decade was a flourishing, vital, transforming one for the British novel. Some of the leading writers were his own former friends and students, including Ian McEwan, Rose Tremain and Kazuo Ishiguro.

The new freshness that came into writing then is still very much alive as the new millennium comes in. Writing – literature – is a central expression of our culture, and London is as never before an international, multicultural publishing centre, and a forcing ground of creativity in the arts. A sense of creativity has surged through the culture. We have enjoyed a vital period in the novel; we have seen London become what he wanted it to be, a cosmopolitan literary capital. Which is why, among all the letters and cards that have come, the most pleasing comes from Tony Garrett, Angus's partner. And, he adds, also from Angus Wilson.

AFTERWORD

by David Lodge

Malcolm Bradbury was my first real 'writer-friend' and also the closest, although after the first few years of our relationship we were physically separated, most of the time, by the distance between Birmingham and Norwich, which until the construction of the A14 was one of the most tedious journeys in England. In 1961, aged twenty-six, I was in my second year as Assistant Lecturer in English Literature at Birmingham University when the Head of Department, Professor Terence Spencer, decided that we ought to have a specialist in American Literature, and accordingly advertised for one. I remember being in his office one day when he showed me an application for this post from a man just a few years older than me, called Bradbury, currently an extra-mural studies tutor at Hull. He had an impressive CV, and a number of interestingly varied publications to his name, including a novel, *Eating People Is Wrong*, which I had heard of though not read. 'I don't think we need bother interviewing anybody else, do you?' Spencer said nonchalantly (heads of departments enjoyed the power of feudal barons in those days) and I readily agreed. I was the only teacher in the department under forty; I looked forward to having a colleague of the same generation, and one who seemed to have the same ambition as myself, of combining an academic career with creative writing. I had published my first novel in 1960, and Malcolm his in 1959. Naturally I read *Eating People Is Wrong* before he arrived in Birmingham, and naturally he read *The Picturegoers*.

We quickly became friends, as did our wives. We found we had a lot in common, in educational background and in literary taste; but there were also marked differences between us which showed in our respective novels. I was a Catholic, in those days a fairly orthodox one, and a Londoner; Malcolm's roots, in spite of some early years in Metroland, were essentially provincial, and his values were those of secular liberal humanism. These differences can be traced through our respective literary oeuvres, but are more obvious in some books than in others. If our 'campus novels' were sometimes confused in the minds of readers (a phenomenon Malcolm amusingly alludes to in his 'Wissenschaft File'), and we were both on occasion congratulated on writing each other's books, that was partly because we had the same kind of experience to draw on, and found that we perceived the academic world with a similar sense of humour.

Edith Wharton, writing in her memoirs of her friendship with Henry James, says, 'the real marriage of true minds is for any two people to possess a sense of humour or irony pitched in exactly the same key, so that their joint glances at any subject cross like interarching searchlights.' I often had that experience with Malcolm, long after he left Birmingham, when our eyes would meet after a remark or anecdote overheard in some conference bar or senior common room, as if silently to say, 'Toss you for it?' But it was his influence and example that first encouraged me to develop a vein of comedy in my work, which in my first two novels was restrained by a soberly realistic technique. The third one, *The British Museum is Falling Down*, was dedicated in part to 'Malcolm Bradbury, whose fault it mostly is that I have tried to write a comic novel.' A crucial part of that influence was collaborating with him, and a Birmingham undergraduate called Jim Duckett whose talent Malcolm quickly spotted, on a satirical revue in the *Beyond the Fringe* mode, commissioned (again through Malcolm's initiative) and performed by the Birmingham Rep in 1963. I have written elsewhere about how much I learned from that experience, and what fun it was – indeed I am not sure that writing was ever such fun again.

Malcolm was a great collaborator, and a somewhat fantastic account of his early enthusiasm for that form of literary composition is included in this volume. I do not know whether it was literally true that he and his friend Barry Spacks would bash away simultaneously at their typewriters until one called out 'Stuck!' and then change places and continue each other's stories, but it is a wonderful image, both sublime and ridiculous, of collaboration overcoming the frustrations and anxieties of the creative process. Malcolm responded to the stimulus of other people's ideas and could often see in them possibilities of which their originators were unaware. I remember an instance of this that happened shortly after he came to Birmingham. I had found in a local second-hand bookshop a copy of a light romantic novel, by a completely forgotten novelist, published in 1915, called *Nymphet*. That is the familiar name given by the hero of the story to an eleven-year-old girl who facilitates his eventual union with his beloved. It is also of course the generic name bestowed by Humbert Humbert on the eponymous heroine of Vladimir Nabokov's celebrated novel *Lolita*, published forty years later, which was generally thought to be the only application of this archaic word in modern literature. It was possible, by close reading and interpretative ingenuity, to see beneath the innocent sentimental surface of *Nymphet* the unconscious representation of an adult man's erotic attraction to a pre-pubescent girl, and to regard it therefore as some kind of precursor of Nabokov's masterpiece. It seemed to be an idea worth writing up, and I accordingly did so, and sent my essay to a few magazines – without success. I showed it to Malcolm and he offered to rewrite it and split the fee if he placed it. Being hard up at the time, I agreed. Malcolm transformed my straightforward essay into a personal anecdotal piece in a humorous self-mocking style which he had honed in contributions to *Punch*, and sold it under the title of 'Nympholepsy' to the American magazine *Mademoiselle*, which paid a great deal more than *Punch*. Pocketing my share, I was impressed – and perhaps a little piqued by his achievement. I began to write humorous anecdotal pieces on my own account, and managed to publish them here and there.

Malcolm had a pragmatic, professional commitment to writing which was contagious, and I suspect that my literary output might have been significantly different, and narrower in focus, if I had not met him at a formative stage of my career. It was this basic, inexhaustible appetite for the craft and business of writing which, among other qualities, made him in due course such an inspiring teacher of younger writers. When I first met him he already seemed to cover the whole waterfront of possible authorship, from the most austere literary criticism to popular journalism, adjusting his style effortlessly to the medium and the moment. And he was always thrifty with ideas, aware that they do not grow on trees. (In 1988 I encountered 'Nympholepsy' once again, much elaborated, revised and updated, in a chapter of *Unsent Letters*.)

When Malcolm was lured away from Birmingham to the University of East Anglia, in 1965, I was in America on a fellowship. Had I been at home I should certainly have tried to dissuade him from moving, though in retrospect it was probably essential for our individual development as writers that we should separate. The confusion of our names and identities in the public mind would have increased exponentially if we had remained colleagues for much longer. More importantly, it was necessary that we should have different experiences to write about. *Changing Places* and *The History Man* both appeared in the same year, 1975, and both were about the same basic phenomenon – the global radicalization of universities in the late sixties/early seventies – but observed in quite different places and fictionalized in quite different ways. *Changing Places*, incidentally, was turned down by three publishers before Malcolm suggested I should send it to his own publisher, Tom Rosenthal at Secker & Warburg, who accepted it, after which my fortunes as a novelist improved steadily. My editor at Secker was the inimitable and irreplaceable John Blackwell, who soon took over Malcolm too, and to whom Malcolm paid eloquent tribute in an obituary essay reprinted here. Writers who are in the same field are inevitably rivals to some extent even when they are friends, and many authors would hesitate to invite such a friend to join their own publisher's list, but Malcolm's gesture was typically unselfish. Of course, it gave a further excuse for people to merge our identities in the conceptual compound novelist, Blodge . . .

Malcolm himself agonized about leaving Birmingham, where he was very happy. He told me that on the day when he finally, definitively, irrevocably had to make up his mind, he went out with two letters in his pocket addressed to the University of East Anglia, one saying yes, and the other saying no. Just in time to catch the last post, he mailed the one that said 'No'. The next day UEA rang him up and said, 'You don't really mean it, do you?' And he agreed that he didn't, and so he went to Norwich. I was reminded of this anecdote when reading 'Honoured', in this volume, about his hesitation over accepting the offer of a knighthood, and how he couldn't remember, ten minutes after posting the reply form, whether he had ticked 'Yes' or 'No'. In fact Malcolm hated to say no to anybody, as many people discovered to their advantage – publishers, newspaper editors, TV producers, British Council officers, conference convenors, and secretaries of literary societies. This trait partly accounted for the extraordinary variety and range of his literary output, which is reflected in the contents of this book.

I am particularly interested in the fragments of autobiography it contains, especially of his childhood, which was uncannily like my own in many respects. We were both children of the War and the Blitz, traumatically separated for a time from home and parents, dimly aware of a vast historical drama being played out in which our little lives had been caught up with unpredictable consequences. It made both of us, I think, temperamentally somewhat prone to anxiety, cautious in the conduct of our adult lives, and grateful for the opportunities which opened up in peacetime for the first beneficiaries of the 1944 Education Act. Like Malcolm, I went to a grammar school (a state-aided Catholic one), funded by passing the 11-plus, and my parents, like his, had to be convinced by the headmaster that it was a good idea for me to apply to university, rather than to leave school at sixteen and start earning my living. A few years later I think both of us would have been encouraged to apply for Oxbridge, but because his father would not countenance a third year in the sixth form, he went to the University College of Leicester, while I didn't even consider an alternative to my local university, and went to University College London, commuting from home. As Leicester took the London University exams in those days, we pursued essentially the same syllabus, and later both of us obtained London MAs – then a two-year research degree.

It is interesting to speculate what difference it would have made to our subsequent careers if we had gone to Oxbridge. I suspect he would have adapted to it better than I, and he might have stayed on to become a don. In later life he enjoyed the occasional sojourn as a visiting fellow at Oxford, and for many summers chaired an annual seminar for foreign academics and writers run by the British Council in a Cambridge college. He always seemed very happy and at home in these settings – the smooth lawns, gravelled paths and ancient buildings soothed his spirit, and the ritual of hall and high table appealed to him – but the redbrick University College Leicester, housed in a converted lunatic asylum, provided more useable copy for a first novel in the fifties. (After all, a brief visit there had inspired Kingsley Amis to write *Lucky Jim*.)

Though politically he was slightly left of centre (and a staunch SDP supporter during its brief life), Malcolm was at heart a kind of liberal Tory, or Tory liberal, rather like E. M. Forster, one of his favourite novelists, valuing tradition and pastoral life, tolerance and civility, distrusting modernity and the revolutionary desire for change. These preferences became more overt in his later work. In the essays collected here, especially those on East Anglia, the North Yorkshire coast, and Scotland, the past, as inscribed in landscape and architecture, is always treated with respect and nostalgia, while the impish satirical asides are directed at everything that is modern, trendy, and commercial. In one of the funniest pieces a fictional character from the past, Robinson Crusoe, is brought back to suffer the indignities of celebrity in our media-dominated culture.

Another English novelist whom Malcolm particularly admired was Evelyn Waugh, a kind of Tory anarchist, and like Waugh he revelled as an artist in features of the modern world which he deplored as a human being, because they provided such rich material for satire. 'Convergence' is a gem of this kind, evoking the babel, or bedlam, of a multicultural conference taking place in the commercialized paradise of Hawaii, by simply (though it is not at all simple to achieve) letting us hear the different voices of the hosts and participants using and abusing the English language in their various ways.

> Most peoples from everywhere come through here these days, because we're a great stopover, and so our population has every kind of ethnic source . . . In my poem, we have the pear blossom passing across the face of a fixed star. Then, in despair, the girl spreads the hair in her armpits, and the wind carries her away . . . Excuse me, sir, I should like to point to a falsie in your argument . . . It seems so weird, says the girl, being here without John. He's had to stay on in New York City. He teaches a course on the enjoyment of death.

The way this last speaker's isolated remarks and questions unfold a little plot, threaded through the polyphonic babble, is typically deft.

Bathos, broken English, the comedic clash of cultures – this piece is recognizably the work of the author of *Rates of Exchange* and *Dr Criminale*, but there are other examples of Malcolm's fiction in this book, two very early and one very late, that are quite different in style. 'A Week Or So In Rome' and 'The Waiting Game' are interestingly dark stories, apparently set, and probably written, in the fifties, in both of which a relationship (marriage in one, an affair in the other) seems to fail because of some chronic inadequacy in the male partner. The ways in which being 'abroad', on holiday, ostensibly to enjoy oneself, can actually exacerbate the tensions and resentments between a couple are well portrayed. There is some comedy in 'The Waiting Game', especially at the beginning, but none at all in 'A Week Or So In Rome', which is especially hard on the male character. In one of his essays Malcolm records that he conducted a WEA course on French existentialism in Nottingham as a young man, and there is a kind of bleak fatalism, a pervasive *nausée*, in these stories, and a tendency to gnomic generalization in the narrative discourse ('love is partly disgust, I would swear') that suggests Malcolm did for a while genuinely feel the appeal of the fashionable Parisian philosophy of the day. One wonders whether he tried to publish these stories, and if so, when; and if not, why.

Questions also hover around the fragment of the novel he was working on at the time of his death, which gives its name to this volume. *Liar's Landscape* is, tantalizingly, just a little too short for us to be able to project how it would have developed if Malcolm had lived to complete it. There is a long historical prologue, about the exploration and appropriation of North America by Europeans in the eighteenth century, which is interesting and informative, but makes us impatient for the story to begin; and even when the hero, Chateaubriand, finally makes his entrance, it still doesn't really begin, or more accurately it keeps beginning over and over, sometimes at the end. Clearly the author is playing a game with his readers' expectations of what constitutes a novel, and there is a continuity in that respect, and in others, with his last completed work, *To the Hermitage*, published in 2000, just six months before he died. That novel was about the Enlightenment *philosophe*, novelist and encyclopaedist, Denis Diderot, focusing on his residence at the court of Catherine the Great of Russia, but their story was spliced with another one, about the author himself, in modern times, embarked on a cruise which is a kind of conference on Diderot, a tale full of farcical incident, caricatured pedantry and humorous digression, like Sterne's *Tristram Shandy* (to which Diderot paid the compliment of imitation in his *Jacques le Fataliste*). In *Liar's Landscape* there is the same combination of a historical central character and a modern authorial perspective, but these elements are more closely interwoven. The voice of the authorial narrator, situated in a bit of old Norwich quaintly called Tombland, blends in counterpoint with the voice of the author of *Memoirs From the Other Side of the Tomb*, quoted or impersonated. Chateaubriand had an extraordinary life, full of adventure, narrow escapes, love affairs, political intrigue, and literary fame – enough material for half a dozen novels – and we get some sense of the rich possibilities of his story in the flowing, allusive, doubly-voiced discourse of *Liar's Landscape*:

> He . . . has served Napoleon, been to Egypt, toured the Orient, celebrated the revival of Christianity and faith. Now he's Monsieur Romanticism, Vicomte Gloom, the French Byron, the Parisian Pushkin, author of many books. Later he's made French ambassador to Britain. His fame is great, his loves and lusts are many, the steaks of his famous chefs are the talk of the town. One day a black-dressed lady, Lady Sutton, recent widow of an admiral, calls at the Embassy seeking assistance: she wants some help and preferment for her two sons. She asks if he happens to remember her. 'Yes I remembered Miss Ives! I took her by the hand, made her sit down, sat down by her side.'

This is the daughter of the vicar of Bungay in Suffolk, whom Chateaubriand met when he was a penurious refugee from the revolutionary Terror, passing under the name of Monsieur Coburg, and she was only fifteen; whom he tutored and admired and might have married, if he hadn't inconveniently been married already. It's a charming, poignant tale, and it may well have been what first attracted Malcolm's attention to Chateaubriand as the possible subject for a novel, because it began in a place, and a house, now owned by the novelist Elizabeth Jane Howard, which he knew well ('I was there for dinner only last night'). The experiences of Chateaubriand in England alone would have made an enjoyable historical novel of a familiar type, filling out the known facts with imagined emotional and psychological detail, but if Malcolm had intended to make this story the centrepiece of his *Liar's Landscape*, he would surely not have dealt with it so summarily at the outset, squandering much of its narrative interest in a few vivid paragraphs. The historical prologue suggests that the core of the novel would have been Chateaubriand's adventures in America as a young man, but it is impossible to be sure. The whole fragment is in effect an extended, teasing, discursive prologue to an absent story. There is a particular poignancy in the hero's admission, near where it breaks off: 'It's the story of my own life and death we are all waiting for, and I fear in my usual fashion I'm delaying things a little too long.'

In the case of *Furling the Flag*, the other unfinished work of fiction in this volume, at least we can discover how the story was going to develop, and end, by referring to the television script on which it is based, which was never produced but is printed in its entirety here. Television drama was an important part of Malcolm's professional life as a writer, and it is appropriate that it should be represented in this collection. He was one of the first English literary novelists to embrace the medium enthusiastically, and he kept faith with it throughout his career, in spite of many frustrations and disappointments. In the late sixties and seventies the Drama Department at BBC Pebble Mill in Birmingham was something of a powerhouse of innovative production; Malcolm made contact with the people there while he was in Birmingham, and maintained it after he left. The first fruit of this association was a 'Play for Today' in 1975 called *The After Dinner Game* which he wrote – typically – in collaboration with a colleague and friend at the University of East Anglia, Christopher Bigsby. It was a studio play, as most TV drama was in those days, rehearsed like a stage play and then recorded on video by a multi-camera method in twenty-minute 'takes', which had to be aborted and done again from the beginning if anyone fluffed their lines. I went along to

Pebble Mill at Malcolm's invitation to watch this tense, complicated, collaborative operation, impressed by, and a little envious of, his involvement in it. The experience kindled in me a desire to get involved myself one day, though it was many years before that came to pass. The technology of video-recording evolved rapidly in the meantime, allowing for a movie-like flexibility in shooting and editing which was more compatible with novelistic narrative than the inherently theatrical studio play. An early example of Malcolm's grasp of the medium's possibilities was his adaptation of John Fowles' story, 'The Enigma', which I greatly admired (it was enhanced by a brilliant cameo performance by Nigel Hawthorne). He went on to make many successful adaptations of other writers' work (e.g. Tom Sharpe's *Porterhouse Blue* and *Blott on the Landscape*, Kingsley Amis' *The Green Man*, Stella Gibbons' *Cold Comfort Farm*), but not his own outstanding novel, *The History Man*, transmitted by the BBC in 1980. Instead it was very ably, and faithfully, adapted by Christopher Hampton as a four-part mini-series, and it turned out to be one of the seminal television dramas of the eighties, making Anthony Sher into a star, and giving the novel a kind of second life, with a much bigger readership. When the novel was first published, in 1975, it was a daringly subversive take on the radical orthodoxies that then held sway on university campuses, but by 1980 Mrs Thatcher was in power, the Left was in ideological retreat, and right-wing pundits greeted the televised *History Man* with glee as a vindication of their views. This was something of an embarrassment to Malcolm, as one may infer between the lines of his essay 'Welcome Back to the History Man', though he enjoyed the new level of fame it brought him.

His next novel, *Rates of Exchange*, set in the imaginary East European state of Slaka, was published (and shortlisted for the Booker Prize) in 1983, and in due course Malcolm was commissioned to adapt it himself as a serial for the BBC. Two weeks before principal photography was due to start (in Hungary), the project was cancelled, due to a dispute, or crisis, over budgeting in the BBC's Drama Department. Only someone who has been involved in television production, and knows how difficult it is to get a major TV serial 'green-lighted', and has some idea of the countless rewrites demanded of the screenplay-writer even after that point has been reached, can begin to imagine the depth of Malcolm's disappointment. Many writers would have given up the medium in disgust, but characteristically he soldiered on – pausing, however, to relieve his feelings in a satirical novella called *Cuts*. And, again characteristically, he found a way to use some of the apparently wasted work much later.

In the years that followed this setback, Malcolm wrote several original and ambitious serial 'tele-novels' about subjects of topical significance. *Anything More Would Be Greedy* addressed the enterprise culture of Britain under Thatcherism. *The Gravy Train* was a carnivalesque satire on political intrigue and corruption in the bureaucracy of the European Economic Community (as it was known in those days), and had the novelty of being funded by a consortium of TV companies in several European countries, with a multinational cast. It won a 'Golden Nymph' award for Best Mini-Series at the Monte Carlo Film and TV Festival. A few years later Malcolm wrote (and I suspect proposed) a sequel in which some of the same characters were sent to an East European country to experience the political and economic upheaval that followed the collapse of communism. This was *The Gravy Train Goes East*, and the country was, of course, Slaka.

A pivot of both these mini-series was the character of Spearpoint, the British diplomat (played by the accomplished Ian Richardson, who specialized in such roles), his impeccable manners and dignified professional persona contrasting comically with the mayhem and mischief in which he becomes embroiled. Spearpoint is also the central character of *Furling the Flag*, which would have completed a trilogy. This was a risky television venture because (to adapt Karl Marx's well-known epigram) it attempted to anticipate as farce what was about to occur as history: the handover of Hong Kong by Britain to the Republic of China in 1997. Perhaps time ran out; at any rate, like so many scripts 'in development' it was never produced. Some while later Malcolm began to turn it into a novella, somewhat in the style of *Cuts*, and to my mind it reads very well and entertainingly. But by now it was tied to an historical event whose outcome was known, and onto which it would have been difficult to graft the original comic plot; so perhaps the script is not, after all, a reliable guide to how the novella would have developed and ended.

All these television scripts, and many others (both produced and not produced) which I have not mentioned, took up a great deal of Malcolm's writing life; and some of his literary friends regretted the displacement of so much time and energy from the novels he might have written instead. The income the screenplays brought in was, of course, an incentive to continue writing them – Malcolm always got a pragmatic Johnsonian satisfaction out of making money by his pen – but I do not believe that was the real reason. There was also the satisfaction of reaching a large audience through television – with one episode of *Inspector Morse* or *Dalziel and Pascoe*, he might reach more people than the readership of his entire output of novels – but he knew as well as anyone that most popular television drama is perceived by the audience as the product of its stars rather than its writers, and the specificity of each episode is quickly forgotten. That was not the real reason either. Essentially I think he just found the fun and busyness of being involved in this medium irresistible: the stimulus of collaboration, the challenge of problem-solving, the thrill of visiting a set or location and realizing that all this expensive, complex activity had been brought into being by one's own words. He wrote expressively about this in the introduction to a little book in which the scripts of his first three television plays were published:

> Where novels are fictions that exist between two imagin-
> ations, that of the writer and the reader, the television play
> activates an enormous actuality. Directors say goodbye to
> their children and block out months in their diaries. Actors

. . . commit themselves to roles and impersonations that
will keep them standing cold on street corners or huddled
in bleak church halls for extended periods of their lives . . .
Planes are chartered, houses hired and then totally refurn-
ished to make them into something quite different, streets
in the centres of great cities are blocked off, caterers with
steaks assemble, men with booms chat up girls with make-
up . . . writing television plays is really a very long way
from writing novels, where none of these things happens
at all, and the invented world stays within the reasonable
comfort of one's own head; and they are actually a strange
way of stepping out from the imagined into what some
people might mistakenly call the real world. Television
plays are an activation of many types of onscreen and
offscreen behaviour, generating a complex pattern of
enacted images, shaped by both the social and the ever
increasing technical sophistication of those images. Writing
a television screenplay is an act of profound self-instruction
in the grammar of inventive writing itself, a process in
which one is simultaneously trying to guide and shape the
massive fleshing out of the imaginative drives that set
writers to work in the first place, and testing out the
possibilities of narrative sequence and development, the
growth of image and sign, in a collective situation with
developing collective laws. [*The After Dinner Game: Three
Plays for Television*. Arrow, 1982, pp. 11–13.]

This book belongs to a genre that used to be called, rather
lugubriously, 'literary remains', though being by Malcolm Bradbury it is not at all lugubrious in effect. It is a book for readers
who already know and love his work, and cherish every bit of
it; who will be grateful that a substantial amount of his fugitive
journalism has been preserved, engaged by the autobiographical
memoirs, and fascinated by the unpublished stories and fragments of unfinished work-in-progress. His son Dominic's Foreword explains movingly how the book evolved, 'to explore the
art, craft and life of the writer and commemorate the work and
passions of someone who lived a storyteller's life to the full.'

In February 2001, some two months after Malcolm's death, a memorial service was held in Norwich Cathedral which drew a huge crowd of people from the many different walks of life which he had shared during his career – writers, academics, actors, directors, producers, publishers, journalists – as well as family and friends from far and near. I was invited to speak on that occasion, and I have incorporated some of the things I said in this Afterword. Let me end with the conclusion of my address on that occasion:

> Another writer-friend gave me a desk-diary at the beginning of last year, with a handwritten passage or sketch by a writer or artist on every page. The text for the day of Malcolm's funeral, which I attended, Monday 4th December, had in one sense an uncanny appropriateness. It was contributed by the Irish novelist Brian Moore, who must have submitted it not long before his own death, and it was a quotation from Roland Barthes's essay on Chateaubriand. As many of you will know, Malcolm was working on a novel about Chateaubriand when he died. The quotation is: 'Memory is the beginning of writing, and writing is, in its turn, the beginning of death.' But if I understand that statement correctly – and Barthes is an elusive writer – I don't really agree with it. It has always seemed to me that writing is a kind of *defiance* of death, because books live on after their authors have gone. Certainly the greatest consolation we have for Malcolm's passing is that we can re-experience his company, his character, and his life-enhancing sense of fun, through his books. But that is not the same, of course, as a living, breathing, laughing friend.